Praise for *The Nesting*

"A taut, scary thriller that winds the suspense so tightly you can barely breathe. I was rooting for the heroine all the way to the terrifying conclusion. This one will definitely keep you up at night."

—Simone St. James, *New York Times* bestselling author of *The Book of Cold Cases*

"[A] hypnotic psychological thriller. . . . Readers will keep guessing what's really going on right up to the surprise ending. *Rebecca* fans won't want to miss this one." —*Publishers Weekly* (starred review)

"An original and haunting thriller, filled with secrets, ghosts, and Norse folktales. *The Nesting* is an evocative and chilling tale that will keep you guessing and is best read with the lights on."

—Alice Feeney, *New York Times* bestselling author of *Daisy Darker*

"Dive into *The Nesting* for some creepy full-body chills." —Shondaland

"An atmospheric thriller." —*New York Post*

"[A] nail-biting Gothic suspense novel." —*OK!*

"[A] fast-paced, gripping plot." —Chicago Review of Books

"A thrilling blend of lore and suspense, *The Nesting* is a gripping, deliciously tense page-turner that will give you chills."

—Rachel Harrison, national bestselling author of *Black Sheep*

"Chilling, totally engrossing, and full of intrigue. The pages just whizzed by."

—Katherine May, *New York Times* bestselling author of *Enchantment*

"Norwegian fjords and folktales are beautifully evoked in this vivid and compelling novel."

—Rosamund Lupton, *New York Times* bestselling author of *Three Hours*

"*The Nesting* is at once a taut psychological thriller, an eerie Nordic fable, and a thoughtful meditation on stewardship. . . . Ms. Cooke tells her story with a spare, elegant prose that betrays a poet's ear and also a poet's discipline. . . . The characters are heartbreakingly three-dimensional. . . . A quick read with a long echo."

—Christopher Buehlman, author of *The Blacktongue Thief*

Praise for *The Lighthouse Witches*

"Right from the start, I was hooked on this eerie, cryptic novel. I don't know how C. J. Cooke does it, but every time I pick up one of her books, I can't stop reading until the last page."

—Samantha Downing, *USA Today* bestselling author of *A Twisted Love Story*

"If you like your thrillers chilling and Gothic, *The Lighthouse Witches* is a creepy and atmospheric read."

—Book Riot

"This chilling tale weaves a web of superstition and truth that fans of Gothic horror won't want to miss."

—Library Journal

"In her deeply atmospheric new novel, Cooke weaves together multiple genres into an intriguing story about longing, lost love, and family. . . . Cooke does an excellent job of bringing together three time periods and multiple storylines. Readers of Audrey Niffenegger's *The Time Traveler's Wife* and students of Scottish history and myth will love this read."

—Booklist

"The story is executed like a dream. A frightening, suspenseful, and otherworldly dream. It was very difficult to put this book down and go to bed at a reasonable time."

—Culturess

"*The Lighthouse Witches* captures the essence of how fear can bring out the worst in people, and rumors can carry on for generations."

—*San Francisco Book Review*

"All the best elements of a Gothic thriller are balanced in this story—grim terror and death, awe and [a] pinch of romance, amazing architectural features, and a peek into past and present witch hunts and the island public's perceptions about these. If you're looking for a chillingly good read and new favorite novel, don't delay in picking up C. J. Cooke's *The Lighthouse Witches* today!"

—Fresh Fiction

"*The Lighthouse Witches* is a dark and moody book, perfect for the spooky season. It contains some genuine scares and truly horrific moments, but it's also a really interesting story about family dynamics."

—Game Vortex

Also by C. J. Cooke

I Know My Name
The Nesting
The Lighthouse Witches

A Haunting in the Arctic

C. J. COOKE

BERKLEY
NEW YORK

BERKLEY
An imprint of Penguin Random House LLC
penguinrandomhouse.com

Library of Congress Cataloging-in-Publication Data

Names: Jess-Cooke, Carolyn, 1978- author.
Title: A haunting in the arctic / C. J. Cooke.
Description: First edition. | New York : Berkley, 2024.
Identifiers: LCCN 2023032407 (print) | LCCN 2023032408 (ebook) |
ISBN 9780593550205 (trade paperback) | ISBN 9780593550212 (ebook)
Subjects: LCGFT: Novels. | Novels. | Horror fiction.
Classification: LCC PR6110.E78 H38 2024 (print) | LCC PR6110.E78 (ebook) |
DDC 823/.92—dc23/eng/20230731
LC record available at https://lccn.loc.gov/2023032407
LC ebook record available at https://lccn.loc.gov/2023032408

First Edition: February 2024

Printed in the United States of America
1st Printing

Book design by Nancy Resnick

for all who live with
the many hauntings
of trauma

July 1973
Barents Sea, 100 nautical miles north of Murmansk, Russia

The man was covered in seaweed, gnarled fronds covering him like garlands. He was fully clothed and curled up by his bed, but his face had been gnawed to the bone, and the bloodied scratches on the wood of the door matched his missing fingernails.

The two coast guard officers shared a long look.

They circled the body slowly before crouching to inspect what had become of his legs. Beneath the torn fabric of his trousers they could see that the flesh had swollen and blackened. The mottled bare feet had split in two, no sign of the toenails, his toes lengthened to flaps of meat that had fused strangely together in a clean bisection. Like grotesque fish tails.

Dental records would confirm that he was Dr. Diego Almeyda, a twenty-eight-year-old postdoc from Argentina. He had spent his last months collecting ice samples with fifteen colleagues on board the *Ormen*, a barque-rigged steam whaling ship from the late 1800s repurposed as a research ship. Contact from the research team ceased a week ago, and the *Ormen* had drifted almost a thousand kilometers from its base in Svalbard until the Russian coast guard pulled up alongside it. Cups of coffee paused on a table in the cabin, slices of burned bread in the toaster. Bloodstains on the floor. Bullet holes puncturing the sails.

Pirates, perhaps.

But the man's death was harder to explain. The door was locked from the inside. His face and feet were mutilated. He was the sole occupant of the ghost ship, the bodies of the other researchers unrecovered.

These were the only facts.

They found pictures under the mattress, penned by Almeyda—presumably—in a frenzy.

All depicted the same scene: a figure on the upper deck of the ship.

They were a series of images, as though for a flipbook, and when organized they seemed to form a coherent spool of movement: each hastily drawn sketch portrayed a figure of a woman who grew gradually closer to the wreck, her face always turned away, until the last image. That sketch filled the page, a macabre spectacle of a woman with seaweed for hair and white, sightless eyes.

And the chilling words on that last image, devoured now by flame:

She is on board

PART ONE

The Selkie Wife

Nicky

I

May 1901
Dundee, Scotland

Nicky woke to gold morning light effervescing in the eaves of her parents' house. It was May, but in this small room winter lingered, the old fireplace unused on account of the coal stains that had ruined the stair carpet.

She pressed her feet on the floorboards, heat from the downstairs fire held in the wood, slowly creeping into her bones. The mirrored door of the Georgian wardrobe threw back the white fangs of her nightdress collar, two dark curtains of her unpinned hair framing her face. Recently, her temples had begun to shimmer with strands of gray. She was only twenty-seven, and at forty-nine her mother Mhairi still had a vivid red crown, even when she removed her hairpieces. But they said gray hair was the flower of worry, and she had spent the last twenty months in two halves—her body here in Dundee, installed in her parents' house like a child, and her mind with Allan in the Transvaal, fighting the Boers.

She frightened herself by struggling to recall the exact line of his jaw, the texture of his palms, his smell. Her own husband. So far, marriage had not been as she expected.

But then, she had not expected a war.

She washed quickly by the sink, fastened her corset, slipped her petticoat and dress over her head. Then she pinned up her hair, clipping two long ringlets that had come from her sister's head just above her ears. Her own hair was poker-straight; not even the hottest iron produced a lasting curl.

It was Monday—the day Allan's letters arrived at their house on Faulkner Street. The postman came at nine, which was yet two hours away, but on Mondays she took the chance to spend the day there, beating the rugs and airing the rooms. It had been her mother's idea for her to move back into her parents' home while Allan was dispatched—a woman living alone was *indecent*, whether wedded or not—but she had surprised herself by how indignant she felt at this requirement. Wasn't war indecent? And yet. There was certainly nothing wrong with her childhood home—Larkbrae was one of the finest homes in Dundee, sitting proud above the Tay—but she felt she had moved backward in time into her old life.

The main reason she went, aside from collecting mail, was to feel the embrace of her marital home, and all its promise: a future with Allan.

From the floors below, a voice sailed through the shadowy hall. "Wheesht, now. I've got you!"

She rushed downstairs to find her father, stooped over, his shirt and waistcoat unbuttoned, revealing his vest. Something was clasped between his palms, his strong arms held at right angles as he addressed whatever he held. His hands were covered in soot. Then, sensing her there, he looked up and tilted his chin. "Open the door."

She turned and unlocked the storm doors, watching as he

inched past, two small wings poking through the gaps in his hands. He had caught a bird, and from the soot marks on his forearms and vest she gathered it had fallen down the chimney.

"Steady, now," he said, stepping out onto the porch with his arms outstretched. He lifted his top hand away to reveal a sparrow crouching in his palm. A second later, it shot off toward the trees.

Her father clapped his hands together as he looked after it, and she watched him carefully, unnerved. George Abney wasn't a man to care about small things, and never a man inclined to save a creature that had fallen into the grate. He looked like he'd not slept all night, still in yesterday's shirt and waistcoat, his eyes shadowy and the gray hair at the sides of his head ruffled.

"Are you well, Father?" she asked.

He kept his pale eyes on the garden ahead, searching after the bird. "Yes," he said. "I think I am. I think I am." He turned to her. "Have you time for a word?"

She raised her eyebrows, certain now that something was amiss. Her father never sought her out, never asked to speak to her. They were too similar, her mother always said. Each as headstrong as the other, long grudges held.

"Is something the matter?" she asked, following him slowly along the hall to his office at the other end. He didn't answer, but she noticed he walked as though carrying an unseen stone on his back, weary from wrestling all night with the cares of his mind. Except her father never worried, never struggled. George ran one of the oldest and most successful whaling companies in Scotland, and he did so by being bullish and fierce, and sometimes cruel. Whaling was as perilous as it was necessary, for without blubber the streets and the factories would lie dark. A venture of blood and bone to sequester light.

Though George never ventured out on the ships, he had his own tempests to weather, such as the loss of three ships in as many years, and all his profits with them. The newspapers had taken pleasure in printing their speculations about the finances of Abney & Sons Whale Fishing Company, with hints that the crew of George's only remaining ship, the *Ormen*, were set to down tools in protest at their conditions.

Inside George's office, the heavy curtains were still drawn from the night before, walnut paneling and bookcases cocooning them. A lamp on his desk set an amber glow across his face, and when he closed the door she saw he was troubled, a crease deepening in his forehead.

"I want to apologize," he said, moving to his desk.

"For what?"

"I did something a few days ago that I deeply regret," he said, looking down at something. A letter. "But today, I shall put it right."

She frowned, wondering if she had missed a conversation. "Put *what* right?"

He pulled out the desk chair and sank into it as though the metal inside him had splintered. Should she call her mother, or her sister, Cat? Was he having a heart attack? There was a glass of water on the table next to the sofa; she passed it to him, watching nervously as he raised it to his mouth with a trembling hand. Then she pulled up another chair and sat close.

"Papa?"

She didn't know what else to say. She couldn't bring herself to touch him. They'd not touched in years. She knew he loved her in that deeply unacknowledged way that their family seemed to love one another, and she was suddenly moved by the thought that he might die.

"The company is folding," he said, dabbing his mouth with a handkerchief. "I've not told your mother. You're not to say a word."

The words landed like stones. *The company?* He couldn't mean the family business.

"I won't tell a soul," she said, staggered now by the realization that she was the first to receive this terrible news. He hadn't told her mother. Of course not. It would devastate her if it was true.

"We may need to sell this house," he said, nudging papers across the desktop with his fingertips, a general tabling his battle strategy. "I've written to Uncle Jim."

"For what reason?"

"To see if he would help us move to Toronto."

"Toronto?"

She'd suspected things with the company were tricky, especially after the last ship sank in the Arctic. Many said that Dundee was going the way of Aberdeen, whaling no longer profitable. The lost ships weren't being replaced.

But this was something else. Her father wasn't one to panic. He was never *afraid*.

"You need to be careful," he said, coughing hoarsely into his fist. "I'm going to put things right. But I need you to keep out of sight for a while."

She reeled. Out of *whose* sight, exactly? How would the collapse of the company put her in danger?

"Papa," she said again, touching his arm. "What things? Why do I need to keep out of sight?"

He held her in a long look, his eyes softening. "You used to sing as a child. You had such a beautiful voice. My little songbird. Why did you stop?"

She searched his face, her thoughts cartwheeling.

"You had such a lovely voice," he said, his voice a whisper, and she felt his hand against her cheek. He hadn't touched her when Morag died. Not even at the graveside, when she fell to her knees.

He turned away and waved a hand, his voice hard again. "Go on, now. We'll talk more later."

She felt panicked, the strangeness of the situation forming a hard knot in her throat. "What is it you're going to put right?" she asked as he made for the window, throwing open the curtains. A spear of light thrusted through the room.

"Go on," he said again, and she knew he would say no more.

Outside, she saw a bird in the branches of the old willow tree that poured down to the path. A sparrow, she thought, its wings still clotted with soot.

II

Nicky's marital home on Faulkner Street was a brisk twenty-minute walk followed by a five-mile tram ride from her parents' house on Douglas Terrace. She took the road that ran alongside the River Tay to hear the slap of the waves against the shoreline buffer and the call of the gulls. This part of the city was quiet, without the sound of traffic or industry, and without the cacophony of accents that swirled in the heart of Dundee. Russian, American, Indian, Polish—Dundee was a global city, now, nicknamed "Juteopolis" for the boom in the jute trade. It was good for many—sixty jute mills providing jobs for fifty thousand. The poverty that had beaten down generations beginning to ease.

She turned the strange encounter with her father over in her mind, unstitching his words from the fabric of memory as though she might find a hidden chamber inside their echo, a secret meaning.

I need you to keep out of sight.

None of it made sense. Even if the company was going to fold—a catastrophic event—she could find no reason that it should put her at risk. And for her father to share this news with her first, before her mother, or her brother . . . perhaps there was something more insidious at work. Her father's mind unraveling. Yes, that was it. George Abney never said sorry. He refuted, recompensed, or sought revenge. But, as a rule, he did not apologize.

She cut through Dawson Park to the tram stop just beyond the entrance. Ten minutes later, she was sitting on the top deck, admiring the elevated view of the water as they moved along Dalgleish Road. She thought of the Saturdays she and Allan would take the tram into town, always sitting on the top deck like this, high above the traffic. Often it was too busy to find a seat together. The seat now in front of her was empty, and she imagined Allan sitting there, reaching a hand behind him to clasp hers.

Letting her know he was there.

The city was thick with smoke and loud as cannon fire, the earthy smell of jute filling her nostrils. Her mother hated it, refused to go into town when the whale ships set sail for Greenland. There were always crowds at the quayside, waving and throwing oranges on the deck for good luck. Everyone knew most of the sailors were roaring drunk for the departure, and not because they were happy to be leaving—some of them wouldn't return, and they knew it. Disease, drownings, and starvation characterized many a whaling voyage. Even now, when the ships were double-hulled and steam-powered, the journey was no less perilous.

But often, there was excitement.

She had been with her father the day one of his ships, the *Ormen*, returned from Greenland. It was usual for them to return with a haul of walruses, penguins, and Arctic foxes, but this time they came home with polar bears—and they were still alive. One of the bears managed to break free and roamed the docks, roaring like thunder. She had never seen such chaos. The crowd dispersed like a blown dandelion clock. Some of the shipowners jumped into the Tay, tuxedos and all, black hats dotting the surface of the water. Her father had pulled her onto a side street, but at the last moment she turned back—and locked eyes with the bear.

It was so much larger than she could have imagined, bigger than the lions she'd seen at the circus. Fur the color of whipped butter, eyes like lumps of coal. It was the paws that startled her—plate-sized, with curled black claws that could spill her guts with a single swipe. For the first time, she faced the reality of her own death. It chilled her, the nothingness she saw spiraling ahead. An instinct that superseded every Sunday school lesson and Bible reading she'd ever heard.

That night, and for many after, she had lain in bed, digging her nails into her arm, reassuring herself that she was still alive.

Faulkner Street was a row of narrow terraced houses—like sardines, her mother sniffed—on the east side of the city, close enough for Allan to walk to work. He was a clerk at Camperdown Mill, a job he hated but did out of duty. He had set his sights on becoming a professional footballer, having earned a cabinet full of trophies in his youth, but an accident with an ambulance had left him lame and put paid to his ambitions.

She reached the house at lunchtime, pausing in the narrow hallway to close her eyes and take in the smell that clutched so many memories. Arriving here on the eve of their wedding day, heavy snow on the rooftops, the whole house freezing cold. Making love in the bed upstairs beneath the blankets, the wooden bed frame banging against the wall and Mrs. McGregor on the other side banging back, telling them to shut up. Listening to Allan, naked and drunk, as he played Chopin on the old upright piano by the fire.

Nicky scooped up the pile of letters on the doormat and sifted quickly through, then again to be sure. Bills, a greeting card from her friend Milly, who was working as a governess in London. Nothing from Allan.

She pressed a fist against her mouth, determined not to cry. It didn't mean anything bad, it didn't. Many Mondays passed without a new letter to pore over, to scrape away the worry that congealed over her heart afresh each day. Allan's squadron had probably been reassigned, or the Transvaal postal service had been held up. It didn't mean he was dead.

It was just past one o'clock, dust motes dancing in the morning light. She looked over the red velvet armchairs in the bay window, the bronze Axminster rug that weighed more than a man, and which she had to hoist up in the yard outside, using a winch to clean. The warm, dry day was perfect for it, she knew that, but her heart felt like a weight was pressing down on it.

She headed upstairs to the silent bedroom at the front of the house, the windows there looking onto the row of terraces opposite. She straightened the made bed, then gave in to the urge to fling open the oak armoire. There, Allan's shirts hung in a row, the sleeves flat. And a single blue dress, half the length of the shirt.

Dominique

I

December 2023
Skúmaskot, Iceland

I'm lost.

I take out my torchlight and shine it on the spiky basalt pinnacle thrusting out of the ground, about thirty feet tall. Is it the same one I passed by before? I'm not sure. The thing is, there are lots of spiky pinnacles around here, because Iceland is made almost entirely of volcanic rock. I lost internet connection miles back, so I'm having to rely on the map I drew to direct me.

I turn all the way around, my torchlight bouncing off the heavy mist that's rolling in from the sea. It's like I'm wrapped in mist, the landscape around me blotted out entirely. My watch says it's two minutes after midnight. I should probably set up camp, regain my strength. A sob lodges in my throat. I'm completely disoriented. I have no phone signal, no internet signal out here. I'm hours from civilization. Nothing but lava fields and crags, towering cliffs looming over me, shadowed against the night sky.

I press on, stumbling forward into the mist. I'm fighting the urge to sink to my knees and fall asleep. Maybe I should stop being so stubborn and just call it a night.

No, I'll keep going. Just another half hour and then I'll stop.

I'm headed to Skúmaskot, an old shark fishing village on the northern tip of Iceland, twenty-five miles away from the Arctic Circle. No one has lived in Skúmaskot for over forty years, the old school, a small church, and all the old fishing huts and turf houses lying empty. The reason I'm going is to explore the *Ormen*, a shipwreck that has been beached there since 1973. If I wake up in the morning and find I was right next to the ship all along, I'll be livid.

It's definitely the wrong time of year to be this far north, and definitely not smart to be trekking somewhere so remote. The weather is ferocious, winds that rip my coat from my shoulders and ice that seals the rocks and encases the cliffs. But the timing is crucial—the Icelandic government have decided that the ship is a hazard to wildlife, and in four weeks' time they are going to drag the *Ormen* out to sea and let her sink. Something about wanting to create an artificial reef and protect local wildlife from the chemicals that might seep out of the structure.

The *Ormen* isn't your typical shipwreck—she's partly grounded, partly in the tide. And she has quite a history, stretching all the way back to the nineteenth century. First, she was a whaling ship, built in Dundee and sent out to Greenland every summer to be filled with blubber; then she was refitted as a research ship for scientists collecting sea ice off Svalbard.

There should be scores of explorers heading to see her before she drowns, but the *Ormen* isn't typical in that aspect, either. She's ridiculously remote, hanging off the very tip of Iceland, touching the Arctic Circle. Nothing but snow, volcanoes, and the occasional polar bear that has crossed the sea ice from Greenland.

I'm out here in the middle of nowhere because I want to document the wreck before they destroy her. I want to phoenix that bitch, give her a chance to roar into a second life before they smash her into matchsticks.

First, I have to find her. And that is proving harder than expected.

Iceland is like the set of a science fiction movie: sawtooth mountains crowned with clouds, glaciers clotting the valleys, snarls of smoke rising here and there from hot springs like the breath of a slumbering monster. Now that darkness has set in and the weather has turned savage, it feels a little as though the monster is wakening, the ground shifting beneath my feet and the coastline disappearing behind fog. There are no roads this far north, no trails, just lava fields, which are treacherously uneven, especially now that I can't see where I'm going. I thought if I kept the ocean in my sight, I would eventually arrive at Skúmaskot.

The hail dies down, a gibbous moon bright as a new coin. I'm in a deep valley, snow-capped mountains rearing up at either side. A few minutes later, a gorge to my right reveals a glimpse of ocean, the moon transforming it to hammered metal. I head in the direction of the gorge, stepping gingerly across ice-encrusted rock and beneath a thundering waterfall, toward the coastline.

Icy mist peels off the waterfall in billowing sheets, but I keep to the course and hit sand for the first time since I started walking. It's an exciting moment, and when I turn to the left I can make out an inlet. A bay.

Skúmaskot.

I start running, squinting into the gloom. I can make out the outline of a roof, then another. A row of buildings, no lights. My heart is racing. I don't want to be wrong. I've passed loads of abandoned buildings, strange houses in the middle of nowhere. Always empty. If it *is* Skúmaskot, the *Ormen* should be just past the rocky outcrop next to the mouth of the inlet.

My legs are burning from the walk, but I clamber up the rocks that jut out into the tide, and it's then that I see her.

Oh my God. She's right there. The *Ormen*.

I throw off my backpack and stagger toward her, down the side of the rocks onto the beach. I start to cry, huge, gulping sobs of relief that I'm finally here. She is so much bigger and more majestic than I could have imagined. Most abandoned structures are woefully forlorn and sad, but the *Ormen* is still intact, still partially floating, craggy volcanic rock clutching the bow as though the human-made and natural entities are fusing together. The *Ormen* was barque-rigged, meaning that she went to sea with a full sail plan across three masts, but these have long since been broken. The remains of the rig are visible, three tall prongs marking where the masts used to be. Holy shit, she is a *goddess*.

The tide is in, and I dodge away as it pounds the beach in mountainous squalls. Iceland is famous for "sneaker" waves, which can suddenly spring from the relative safety of the tide, pouncing on unsuspecting walkers and dragging them far out to sea, where strong currents prevent them from swimming to shore. One of the first things I'll do is map the times of the tide and mark a boundary line with stones.

There's a ladder still in situ, probably placed by other explorers to allow easy access to the deck. I run my torchlight up the metal strakes. I scan the ladder carefully for any sign of barbed wire or anti-trespass paint. I've been bitten by that before.

At the top of the ladder, I grip on to the bolts holding it against the hull and throw a leg over the side. The deck is slippery with ice and debris, so I slide my feet forward, pausing to stare up at the main mast ahead. It would have been one hundred ten feet tall back in the day, a crow's nest at the top. Even at around forty feet it towers above, bowline and topmast hooks glinting in the moonlight like instruments of torture.

The sensation of stepping on deck is unreal, like entering another realm. I've made it. I am *here*.

II

I pause on the deck. The *Ormen* feels alive, as though she's been waiting for me. The wind whips my hair into my face, and suddenly all the time I've spent looking for her doesn't matter. I was exhausted just moments before, but now I'm energized, my heart clanging with excitement.

I take a deep breath and look around, taking in every detail of the ship. The *Ormen* seems to have a life of her own, her wooden planks creaking and groaning as they shift with the tide. The wind howls through the rigging, creating a haunting melody that echoes across the desolate landscape. For the longest time, I've felt a strange pull toward her, as though she's been calling out to me, inviting me to explore her secrets. And now that I'm here, the restlessness has ceased. I can't wait to start documenting her history.

I pull out my camera and start clicking away, capturing every inch of the ship. The darkness is thick as treacle and the deck is covered in snow, but I find gnarly bits of plastic and fishing tackle poking through, adjusting my flash to capture it. I snap shots of an old oil can, a coil of rusted chains, and a rickety crow's nest hanging precariously from the damaged mainsail. I wonder how many men risked their lives climbing to that crow's nest. The *Ormen* must have seen it all.

Opposite the top of the ladder propped against the hull is a long cabin, clearly not part of the original ship. It's an addition from the 1960s for the research team. It looks as if a caravan has been dropped on the top deck. I use my knife to prize off the board that has been nailed to the cabin door.

Inside the cabin, a wild stench hits me—vegetal, with a definite undertone of public toilet. I draw my headlight across an upturned Formica table, smashed-up chairs, hardback books splayed on the floor like dead moths.

I step carefully through the mess, tracking my torchlight slowly across the ground to check for rotten flooring and snares. Traps are everywhere in places like this—sprung jaws to take a grown man's leg off, wooden planks embedded with vertical nails, a thin-bladed wire fixed neck-high. Poison and asbestos are the most insidious, and the rifest.

The floor seems okay, and no sign of any snares, thank God—usually finding one means there are a lot more hidden in places you'd never suspect, and it takes ages to root them out.

Most of the cabin windows have been broken, but I have a solution for that. Perspex is a great insulator and keeps flies and scavengers out, so I have sheets of it in my backpack. The cabin is about four meters by three, and I'm amazed it's structurally sound. Clearly it has been visited by many explorers before. There are a couple of rugs on the floor, a dining table, and a sofa made up of old crates tied together with rope, pillows laid across them as seat pads.

My torchlight settles on a hatch in the floor, roughly in the center of the room. I slip my fingers through the metal loop of a handle, pulling gently to test it. The hatch is stiff, but I feel it give a little each time I pull. I get down on my knees to get a better grip, and to shine my torchlight down into the crack. I don't want to open it to a blast of toxic gas. Easy does it.

Gradually, it lifts. I shine my torch into the darkness below, noticing the rush of cold air and the stale mineral smell on the back of it, and the black stairs that lead down onto another deck.

The stairs are mossy, so I descend backward, gripping the edges of the steps. The lower deck is long, with doors leading off to cabins. Most of this level would have been used to store whale blubber when the ship was first built, which blows my mind. The deck looks extremely sturdy—muscular, even—but I have to be careful: the floor could give way at any second.

I hug the walls, moving past old metal electrical boxes and toppled furniture, keen to see what lies behind the doors.

I count eleven rooms and six cupboards, though most are clogged with debris. Five small cabins contain metal bunk beds, and my torchlight picks up some personal effects. Among these are—presumably from the 1970s, preserved in time—an Adidas trainer, a hardback book swollen with mold. These were the researchers' bedrooms, I'm guessing. There are traces of other explorers, too. The fifth cabin is the only cabin with a porthole window, though for some reason it's covered up with strips of plyboard taped to the wall. Perhaps the window was broken, and someone was trying to insulate it.

Back in the pitch-black corridor of the lower deck, I turn in a slow circle to draw my torchlight across the ceiling, then the walls. All seemingly intact, though cobwebbed and grimy, which is to be expected. I'm surprised at how level the floor is, though the ship moves slightly, the waves at the back nudging it every so often. The *Ormen* has sat here for five decades, I remind myself, so it's unlikely to come loose now. Possible, but unlikely.

At the other end of the lower deck is another door, my torchlight bouncing off a rusty doorknob.

As I move toward it my torchlight finds the detail in the wood, the ornate molding, and the grooves in the handle. I place my hand on it, twisting, but the door doesn't budge. It's locked tight. The door is probably swollen from damp—not uncommon.

I try the next door, a small door down a step in a corner that must lead to a cupboard. But as soon as I put my hand on the handle, everything goes silent. It's like a switch has flipped—the roaring of the sea outside and the howl of the wind stops dead, completely *gone*, until all I can hear is my breath.

I let go with a start. And then I wrap my hand around it again and the same thing happens, all the sound around me vanishing, like I'm in a vacuum. My heart is thudding like a gavel. Suddenly, a terrible urge sweeps over me to press a knife against my flesh.

I let go and take a step back, then another, my eyes fixed on the door handle, panting. What the hell *was* that?

My torchlight flicks off, plunging me into darkness. Outside, the sea is lashing the back end of the ship, wind screaming through the broken windows of the cabin. I'm jittery, my nerves getting the better of me. I should get out of here and set up camp. I'll return in the morning when it's light.

III

I'm exhausted from walking, but I struggle to get to sleep. Something is scratching at the back of my mind, like a cat clawing at the front door, begging to come in. I think of the way I felt when I put my hand on the doorknob, how everything went silent. How I had a sudden urge to lift a knife and cut myself.

A voice in my head starts up. *You're a bad person, Dom. You've done terrible things. You need to be punished.*

I press my hands against my ears until it hurts, banging them until the voice stops.

I'm finally beginning to drift off when I hear a noise outside—someone is singing. A woman. No words, just a humming sound.

The same five notes on repeat.

Not loud, but clear, as though the wind is carrying it directly to my ear.

I lie very still, listening, certain I'm dreaming. The singing grows louder, and so I reach out and unzip my tent, crawling outside into the frosty heath. The wind is savage, trying to claw off my hat. I hold on to it with both hands as I scan the beach, then the cliffs behind. No woman, and the singing has stopped.

I creep back inside the tent, tugging the zip down. As I'm locking it in place, another sound pulses through the walls of my tent. Not singing this time—a drumming sound. It grows louder, like feet pounding the sand. A crowd of people or animals are running toward me, getting closer.

My heart pounds in my throat.

The sound is thunderous. Just as I'm about to climb out of my tent and run, I hear a whinny.

Horses.

By the time I manage to emerge a second time, the horses have galloped into the distance, night swallowing them up.

Nicky

I

May 1901
Dundee, Scotland

Nicky closed the door of the house behind her and headed for the mill where Allan had worked before setting sail for the Transvaal. Last year she'd done the exact same thing as she had this morning—arrived home to collect the mail, only to find that no letter from Allan had arrived. Later, she'd learned that he had sent a letter to the mill for Mr. Campbell, his boss and an old family friend, and his letter for Nicky had been delivered along with it in error. Perhaps the same had happened this time, Nicky thought, optimistically. Even if it had not, the noise and bustle of the mill served as a welcome distraction. Since Allan had left, she often spent the afternoon there, helping Mr. Campbell with the accounts, and sometimes assisting the children with the vats.

She headed off on foot, glad of the sunlight that was swelling along the pavement, bright sheets of laundry flapping along the back lane. Along the way, she penned her own letter to Allan in her mind—she would tell him about her father, ask him for his opinion on the matter. At the beginning of the war Allan's letters had started with characteristic honesty, as he'd sworn to when he signed up—*Brutal heat out here, my love. Very lonely. Thinking of you in that pink corset . . .*

But last November, General Kitchener introduced his scorched-earth policy, instructing British and Scottish troops to burn down homes and sometimes whole towns, the inhabitants moved into concentration camps, in a bid to flush out Boer rebels.

Allan was caught up in a terrible moral dilemma. He had written to Nicky in anguish about the conditions of the camps, the horrific burning of family homes. It had echoes of the Highland clearances fifty years before. Allan's father was just a boy when his family croft was burned to the ground; he still suffered nightmares, a lifelong dependency on alcohol. And now Allan was forced to do the same to the Afrikaners, the descendants of Dutch settlers who were fighting to keep their land, just as his own ancestors had done in Scotland.

She cut through Ellis Park toward the outskirts of the tenement blocks, passing through the heavy gates alongside workers who were commencing the afternoon shift. A few glanced at her, and she lowered her hat over her eyes—she knew she stood out here in her fine clothes.

Gradually, Allan's letters had fallen silent on the Kitchener matter, and she understood from his tone that the troops had been ordered not to talk about what was happening, to keep it silent.

Until then, her fear had lingered over the possibility of Allan being wounded in battle. What if he was shot, lost a limb, returned home with half his face missing? And of course, she had considered the terror of widowhood. The grief at losing Morag was a darkness she had never imagined possible. Losing Allan would be a step deeper into that nightmare.

That he was now pitted between robbing innocent wives and

children of their homes, placing them in ill-equipped camps wherein half the children died, or doing the duty he had sworn to his country was a tragedy she had not anticipated.

II

In the jute mill, the children's voices were a salve. They were called half-timers, because they worked half the day and went to school for the other half, thirty hours a week for three shillings and ninepence. She knew that one boy, Angus, had been scalded across his chest and neck, the skin there raised up and lurid in color a year later. Another girl, Cora, had lost a finger in the carding machine, though she was lucky not to have died. Not one of the children complained.

"Hey, Nicky," a voice called as she entered the jute mill. It was Lewis, the nine-year-old Allan had asked her to keep an eye on, having lost both parents in a matter of weeks.

"Hello, Lewis," she called, pressing a kerchief to her mouth as she walked across the floor. The grease of the jute hung densely in the air, cloying in the throat.

"I've got a new joke for you," Lewis said, sweeping dust from beneath a machine.

"Go on, then," she said, crouching down to his level.

He cocked his head and swung the jute brush under an arm. "Why was six afraid of seven?"

"I don't know."

"Because seven eight nine!"

She grinned and shook off her coat. "Very clever."

He beamed. "Here's another one. What kind of streets do ghosts haunt?"

"Dark ones?"

"Nah, they haunt *dead ends*!"

She watched him laugh and nudge the younger child who had joined him, keen to hear the joke. "Come on, now, that's funny."

"Have we a new half-timer today?" she asked, studying the face of the boy beside Lewis. She didn't recognize him. He couldn't be more than five.

"This is John," Lewis said. "Say hello, John."

John looked at her warily, too shy to say hello. She leaned closer to him, noticing the tatty jute sack he wore, and the shoes that were clearly too big for him. Adult shoes.

"Hello, John. I'm Nicky. Do you know what you're supposed to be doing?"

"I'm showing him the ropes," Lewis said. "He's living wi' us now. His ma died last month an' his da's gone to work in Glasgow."

Nicky took that in. "Do you have any brothers or sisters, John?"

"A sister," the boy said uneasily. "She's called Nancy. She's eight weeks old."

"We're looking after her as well," Lewis piped up.

The other women were busy with the machines, so she took John to the oil room.

"These are the oil vats," she said, pointing at the row of barrels at the back of the room. "You have to take the rough jute and soak it, like this."

She used the tongs to gather up a bundle of jute and lowered it into the briny, amber-colored oil, showing the boy how it gradually softened into a kind of loose rope.

"The whale oil makes it pliable, you see? That's how we can make sacks and cloth."

John's eyes were like puddles, taking it all in. A year ago, she had been as mesmerized, having never stepped foot inside a mill before. Allan had shown her the process, which he had learned from the women who worked under him. Now, John bent down and copied her, his tiny face lighting up when the jute became supple and limp as cooked spaghetti. She didn't ask how he felt about losing his mother, or how things were at his new home. It might stir up sadness, and he needed to be strong to survive in a place like this.

She headed upstairs to Allan's old office, shared with Mr. Campbell.

"How's your eyesight?" Mr. Campbell asked when she closed the door to his office.

"Good, I think. Why?"

He removed his glasses and rubbed them on his shirt. "These aren't strong enough for me."

She took them from him and glanced through, the pen on the table swelling beneath the lenses to three times its size. "Jings, they're like binoculars."

"I've been here since four this morning. I've checked these figures three times now and we're still six pounds short."

On his desk sat a wooden file drawer of payment cards, a yard long. Fourteen thousand workers. She pulled up a chair and looked over the notebook where the names of their workers were written with wages owed.

"Is that a five or a three?" she asked, noticing a number in one of the columns.

He squinted. "I'm not sure. It's Ginny's handwriting. She wasn't well yesterday."

Nicky scanned the rest of the columns until her vision doubled, circling the digits that were vaguely written.

"Has the postman delivered the mail today?" she asked.

"It's over there," Mr. Campbell said, nodding at a pile on the table next to her. She sifted through the letters, her heart swelling with hope.

But nothing from Allan.

III

She spent the afternoon there, writing a letter to Allan that Mr. Campbell promised to send with the next day's post. She told him about her father, about Lewis and how she had helped Mr. Campbell. She told him about her sister, Cat, who had celebrated her fifteenth birthday last month and was learning to ride the bicycle her father had bought her.

And as always, she finished the letter with a joke, keen to ensure that she brought some levity into his day.

Why is Satan riding a mouse like one and the same thing? Because it is synonymous!

It was still light when she set off for home.

She left several minutes before the end of the evening shift to avoid the rush of workers pouring through the front doors. But despite the crowds chatting and thronging around her, she spotted a man glancing at her, fifty yards to her right, standing in a doorway. He didn't carry a jute sack with his lunch and flask like the others, and whereas the other workers headed quickly for the gates, he had hung back, a look of recognition skidding across his face when she glanced at him.

She quickened her pace, blending into a larger group of women who she knew took the same route as she did until the tram stop.

"Hullo, hen," one of the women called to her. Mrs. Manning, a woman in her sixties whose great-grandchildren worked alongside her in the mill.

"Evening," Nicky said. Then, leaning closer, "Did you have a visit from the inspector today?"

"Inspector?" Mrs. Manning said, glancing up. "No, I don't think so. At least, I hope not. Fourteen carding machines are on their last legs. I'm bringing Hamish in tomorrow to see if he can fix them."

The man wasn't an inspector, then. He was short and stockily built, his eyes hidden by a brown cap pulled down over his forehead. She was troubled by the way he'd lifted his chin to search her out, the lift of his shoulders when he saw her.

Her father's words rang in her ears.

Stay out of sight.

When she looked again, he was lost among the crowd.

The top deck of the tram was full, the bottom standing room only. Two American men were sitting side by side opposite her, chatting, one of them with a lemur perched on his shoulder eating a banana. Farther down the bus, someone was singing "The Bonnie Banks of Loch Lomond." She noticed a woman looking at her and glanced away, pulling her own hat farther down over her eyes. Heat traveled up her cheeks, and her heart fluttered. For the first time since Allan left, she felt vulnerable, exposed. She scanned the metallic flick of the River Tay, searching out her parents' house. Not long now.

She got off at Dawson Park and took the path that led by the pond and the water fountains. In the distance, she could see the docks, the tall masts of the *Ormen* combing the sky, men moving back and forth along the pier with supplies. It looked as though this year's voyage to the Arctic was happening as planned. She breathed easier—if the *Ormen* was setting sail, surely everything was fine with the company? Her father was losing his mind.

She would take her mother aside and discreetly speak to her about the matter, tell her what he'd said.

As she passed by the tall sycamore tree she'd climbed as a child, something flickered in the corner of her vision. Footsteps sounded behind, and when she glanced back she caught sight of a man striding quickly behind her, swinging his arms, his brown cap pulled low over his eyes.

She quickened her pace, spying the gates just ahead that led to the main road. Her palms were clammy, and her heart raced. Who was he?

The footsteps grew louder. She turned to confront the man, but he was already upon her, a scowl on his face as his eyes locked on her. She opened her mouth to scream, but just then he slammed his fist into the side of her skull, knocking her wordlessly to the ground.

Dominique

I

December 2023
Skúmaskot, Iceland

I'm sitting on a rock on the beach, singing. I don't sing words, but the song I sing means revenge. I don't know how or why. I can feel the vibrations of the melody in my throat, the knowledge that each note unleashes retribution filling me with joy.

I look down at my body. I'm naked to the waist, but I don't feel the cold. And instead of legs, I have a long, black tail, like a seal, fading at my waist to pasty human skin.

When I wake, I feel pummeled. What the hell does all of that *mean*? Subconscious body dysmorphia? A hidden desire to sing?

It'll be the door handle I touched last night, the horrible feelings that were stirred up. The voice in my head hisses, but I put on my coat and go outside before the words get too loud.

My mood lifts when I set eyes on the scene outside. The *Ormen* is lit up by sharp morning sunlight, her long bow buried deep in an outcrop of pitch-black rock, white tide lashing the stern. If you can imagine those big oil paintings by the Romantics you find in the

National Gallery—the *Ormen* looks just like that. Like something coming into harbor instead of a wreck.

A word drifts into my head and comes to roost: *Lovecraftian.* That's what the shipwreck looks like, the precise adjective I'd use to describe its macabre, strange, and slightly monstrous grandeur, sitting on the black sand like something conjured from the depths of the ocean. I don't think I've ever read anything by H. P. Lovecraft, but that word has unfurled in my mind without my bidding.

The rocky outcrop at the mouth of a horseshoe-shaped bay is Skúmaskot, and I can see a row of rooftops on the other side of the water, mushroomed by thick snow. The bay is dotted with small islands—or skerries—of lava rock, all thickened with snow. The stretch of beach runs as far as the eye can see, and behind me rises a dormant volcano silkened by snow, the bend of a phoenix's head rising from white ashes. To my right, three razor-sharp rocks needle up out of the sand, several headlands running along the coast.

Lovecraftian indeed.

There are no trees, which is strange. I heard the Vikings had pretty much used up all of Iceland's forests, but it lends this place a breathtaking sterility—a black-and-white desert. My wanderings have taught me that "dead space" is a misnomer—nothing is ever really dead. If anything, abandoned places are strikingly fertile, blooming with mold and vermin. The ruins I have visited are all saturated with the typical signs of neglect—rot, shit, asbestos, hanging cables, collapsing walls, dead things all but consumed by the riot of new life that tends to explode into derelict spaces. Wildlife, weeds.

Go to any museum and you'll find fragments presented in glass boxes, cleaned up and pristine, as though it's the actual past, distilled in its purest form. Ruins and abandoned places—they make you work to find their secrets.

The ecosystem of decay is rarely aesthetically pleasing, but barren? Never.

It's still bright, but the air is bracingly cold, sunlight sending the virgin snow alive with gold sparkles.

I scan the cliffs at the back of the bay and the fields beyond. The rock formations are impressive—hundreds of basalt columns, some of them four stories tall and occasionally running horizontal. There are caves here, too, but I only step inside to shield myself from the wind when it grows fierce.

I find a pathway that leads all the way to the top of the cliff, and there, right on the side of the volcano, I see movement. A white flash of fur, the flick of a bushy tail against the rocks drawing my eye. Two pointed ears. It's an Arctic fox.

Holding my breath, I stay absolutely still, elated to have seen it. I'm about thirty feet away, close enough to see the gold of its eyes. I remember hearing that regions like this were teeming with such creatures, but if you spot them it means they are probably struggling to survive. The flicker of joy I feel at spotting the fox quickly turns to worry. If Arctic foxes are struggling, there's not much hope for humans. Still, it seems healthy enough, poking its nose in the snow, and when it plucks up the small body of a rodent in its jaws I can't resist taking my camera out of my pocket for a photograph.

As I do, I slip on a rock, disturbing the silence with a loud crunch. The fox snaps its head up, its eyes meeting mine. But it doesn't dart off. I lift my camera and begin filming, crouching down and moving slowly, very slowly, toward it.

I'm curious how close I can get. Maybe it has never seen a human before. I manage to get within touching distance before it jerks its head up and zips off across the heath, vanishing into the snow.

Something flicks in the corner of my eye, at the place where the fox has just looked up at me.

A figure, facing the ocean. A woman.

I step back in shock, then look again, focusing on the spot. This time the beach is empty. I blink. I saw someone, right by the ship, standing on the sand.

But I can't have. There's no one there.

I scan the beach and squint at the tide in case the figure appears again. It's strange—I can't recall why or how I thought it was a woman standing there. Perhaps a feminine outline, but I can't envisage the figure. I must be tired, or paranoid. My excitement at finding the *Ormen* last night is already wearing thin, all the shit that spirals around my brain starting to kick up again.

And there's no movement now, other than the crashing waves and the wind ruffling the heath.

II

I head toward the spot where I saw the woman, a little nervous. How odd that I thought I saw someone. Maybe it's an effect of the light against the water, or a shadow. A lacy tide nudges at a patch of fresh snow, and long fronds of seaweed streak the black sand like strands of hair. No footprints.

I'm completely alone out here, thank God. I don't like being around other people. No phone signal, no data—just the sea exhaling up the sand, and the birds calling in the sky above. True wilderness.

In the daylight, the extent of the *Ormen*'s damage becomes apparent. At the mouth of the bay, I find parts of her scattered in the icy water: sections of the mainsail roll against rocks like tree logs, and lumps of metal and several wooden tubs lie strewn about. Rusted hooks, striking in their size.

At the starboard side I notice that the black rocks holding her in place have pierced the hull, a gash about four feet wide visible from the ground. It's too high up for the tide to get in, and it's facing away from the sea, but even so—I'll need to check it out to see if she's at risk of sinking, or splitting off from the bow. The metal girders running vertically up the sides have warped, strakes of wood splitting at the chine. Waves beat heavily against the stern, and I can see that the whole bow section sways a little, as though the rocks and waves are creating pressure on the midsection. One day, maybe even while I'm here, her whole frontage will break off.

That would be so epic, but also sad. And very, very dangerous.

Using the cracks in the hull as footholds, I climb up the side of the *Ormen* to take a closer look at the hole in the bow. Long icicles skewer down like fangs, the splintered wood slimy with seaweed. Through the gap, I see crates and barrels strewn everywhere, their contents long since spilled out and lost to the sea.

It's a thrill to climb up the ladder to the upper deck. Mercifully, it hasn't succumbed to rot. Much of the old ship remains—the masts are broken, yes, but they're enormous, thrusting up high above. Remnants of sails and rope hang down.

I explore the upper deck, filming everything. Later, I'll upload the footage for my followers. I created a social media account for this place, named The Whale Ship. It's got a few hundred followers so far. I'm not tech-savvy, but I noticed that other explorers were filming their explorations and garnering quite a number of views for people who want an armchair adventure of abandoned places. So I've done the same, and I've even brought an internet satellite terminal and solar batteries.

I find the ship's wheel under a sheet of old tarp. It's about four feet wide and all the spokes and handles are still intact, and I can't help but yell, "Arrgh, me hearties!" I take a selfie of my best pirate grin, too—it'll make a good reel. Then I stand at the stern looking down at the waves and the beach below. It's foggy now, the morning sun already retreating behind dramatic white clouds, but I can see all along the coastline from here, a long run of black rock punctuated by caves. The land above is spring heathland, like the bay, coated with snow.

The heathland must be where the horses came from last night, but there's no sign of them, no movement at all. Just me and the fox, out of sight. Watching me.

In the daylight, the cabin appears at once larger and more disappointing than last night. By disappointing, I mean that the amount of work it's going to take me to clean it up is considerable. There are a ton of books scattered about the place, a toppled bookcase indicating the source. Mounds of seaweed among fishing tackle. I pull a sheet of tarp from a corner and find a kitchenette, a fairly new kettle there. So there have been others visiting this place. Good—it's likely they'll have left their gear behind, stuff they didn't want to carry on the journey back. I see other newish items—a throw blanket, cushions. Home comforts. Not too moldy, either. A desalination tank. My heart leaps at that. Fresh drinking water. Better than my little water purifier. If I can get that tank working, I'll be made.

As I move the junk that has piled up in the cabin I notice stains on the floor, dark spatters, like oil. Definitely not water. Underneath the toppled bookcase I find a big stain, about three feet wide. It has a rusty hue at the edges.

I start searching them out, using my torchlight to help, even though it's still light. The garish brightness of the torch pulls stains out from every corner, which isn't unusual for an abandoned structure. But I take note of the ones that are rust-colored—they appear up the sides of the wooden posts in the cabin, and on the stairs through the hatch.

I think they're bloodstains. The pattern of dots around some of the larger ones is familiar. Bile rises up my throat, but the voice jumps into my head: *Every surface touched by humans is a crime scene. Every. Surface.*

The *Ormen* was a whaling ship for decades, and the mariners would have butchered their catch on board before storing it in barrels inside the hold. Still, it became a research ship in the mid-twentieth century, and I can't imagine they'd leave stains everywhere . . . Maybe they were hard to get out of the wood, so they just covered them up.

I decide to do the same, arranging the furniture and rugs to cover up the bigger marks.

I'll be warmer if I stay in the cabin, so I make myself a quick tub of noodles before pulling on my gloves and getting to work. I decide to store rubbish in one of the cabins on the lower deck, staying well clear of the one at the end with the weird handle. I'll check it out eventually, but for now I need to stay focused on making the wreck a little more comfortable. I set up my phone to film myself cleaning. It gives me a sense of purpose. It helps to distract me from the voice.

As I clear the cabin of debris, I notice signs of previous visits. There are marks on the floor, odd stains here and there. I find more books, some published in the last ten years, and some from the 1970s. I find a long row of nicks in a wooden post by the cabin door, made by a knife. Dozens of them, about a centimeter apart.

Some of the nicks are fresh, the wood beneath the cut quite pale and new. I finger them, wondering what they mean. Maybe someone was counting off the days. Two hundred eleven of them. That's quite a long time to spend on a shipwreck. I'm impressed.

And suddenly the sun disappears. It doesn't so much set as *flee*, a thin light withdrawn abruptly just after two o'clock. I've forgotten to set out my solar batteries to soak up the light. I have standard batteries in my torch, but I'll need to be more organized from tomorrow. I can't rely on these forever.

I move my tent to the springy heathland beyond the beach, intent on sleeping out here until I see if I can clean up the wreck and make it a livable space, but the wind grows fierce, whipping the groundsheet from my hands and scattering the poles. I don't have much choice after that—the combination of impenetrable darkness and ferocious gales make it impossible to gather the dispersed components of my kit, so I jog to the wreck and clamber back up the ladder, heading inside.

The upper cabin has too many broken windows to be habitable; I head down through the hatch to the lower deck, where the howling wind doesn't reach. The air is dry, not as cold. I avoid the room at the end of the corridor, the one with the creepy handle, and find a cabin that doesn't smell too bad.

I clear the rubbish out and set up my tent, minus a few poles. It's still cold, but I light a candle and make myself a coffee, the double insulation of the wooden cabin and the tent warming me up pretty quickly.

It's quite cozy in here; I sit for a few hours just listening to the ship, thinking about the voices that have passed through here, now silenced. The feet that have walked these floors. The waves pound the stern, causing the room to sway a little. But it's soothing to me now.

I've been lulled into a false sense of security. At first, I think the creaking sound is just the ship offering up her complaints, but something on the back of my neck prickles and I freeze, listening hard. A rhythmic sound. Footsteps sounding across the floor above me.

Someone is crossing the floor of the cabin.

Quickly I blow out my candle, as if I can really expect to hide from intruders. They'll definitely have torches. They may even have knives.

Creak. Creak.

I hold my breath until I feel I might pass out, listening hard and trying to work out what to do. Oh God. I can't lock the door, and there isn't anything in the room I can use to block the doorway. Carefully, I unzip my tent and crawl out, feeling around the room for my knife. My fingers touch it and I clutch it to me with trembling hands.

A beam of light shines down the stairs, brightening the corridor. My heart hurls itself against my rib cage, again and again.

"Where is she?" a voice says.

Nicky

I

May 1901
10 miles off the coast of Orkney, Scotland

Nicky woke to bloodcurdling screams, the sound so horrifying it set her teeth on edge. A second later, she realized the screams were coming from her.

Pain burned in her foot, excruciating, blinding agony. She opened her eyes and saw that she was in thick darkness, a strange room permeated with the earthy tang of dung. Whimpering, she reached down and realized that a barrel had tipped over onto her ankle, crushing it and pinning her down, a thick metal shard penetrating the skin just beneath the ankle knuckle to the sole of her shoe.

She assumed she had started to hallucinate, for in the darkness came the cluck of hens, a shuffle of hooves. Briny water slapped against her face and filled her mouth, her dress soaked through. Beyond that, the noxious stench of fish. A lamb's bleat.

Where *was* she?

A sharp stinging started up in the side of her face. Her mind tipped with memories: Allan's shirts in the wardrobe. The dress hanging next to them, haunting her. The man on the grounds of the mill. He'd been watching her. The footsteps in the park, and the man's face close to hers. An explosion of pain.

That was the last thing she remembered.

The floor tilted sharply, the barrel shifting just enough to one side for her to wiggle her foot from beneath its weight. The nail tore deeper through muscle, and with a shriek she gave one last pull, freeing herself from it.

She lay back, gasping from the hot, shocking pain of it, until she could gather the strength to reach down and touch the wound. With trembling fingers, she felt the warm pulse of blood, a sharp ridge of bone making her cry out. Her right foot had been crushed, a long, thick nail gouging the inside curve open to the ankle.

How on earth had she got here? The animals and the seawater suggested she was in the hold of a ship, where they kept the livestock for long journeys. The man in the park must have put her here. Her mind raced to fit the pieces together. Was he here, somewhere in the dark?

A sudden bolt of fear set her in motion. Pressing the palms of her hands into the wet floor, she shuffled painfully backward in the direction of the sounds that trickled into her ear amid the slap of water against the barrels and the guttural groan of the hull.

By the time she reached where she thought the door must be, she was beginning to black out from the pain, the edges of her vision flickering. She could make out shouting, and a bar of gold light seeping from a gap in the wood. A door. She lifted a hand over her head and grasped for the handle. A metal bolt met her fingers, but it was locked from the outside. She tried to knock, pounding weakly against the wood.

Finally, it creaked open, and she fell back, amber light from an oil lamp flashing in her eyes.

"Good Christ! What we got here, then?"

"Royle! Anderson! Fetch the captain!"

A set of hands lifted her, but as they attempted to set her upright her foot touched the ground, shooting a clean bolt of pain up through her body. She howled in pain and the dark corridor around her liquefied to vapor.

II

A small cabin lit by an oil lamp.

A man tying a surgeon's apron about his waist, watching her carefully.

On a table, a neat row of sharp tools, brown medicine bottles, a folded white handkerchief.

"Do you know your name?"

The man was Scottish, but his accent was Doric.

"Nicky." Her voice was a rasp. "My name is Nicky Duthie."

"Do you know where you are?"

"I . . . I think I'm on a ship."

"I'm Dr. O'Regan," he said. He stood over her, the lower half of his face carpeted with a brown beard, the top of his head bald and shining in the oil lamp. "How did you come to be on board, Nicky?"

"I don't know," she groaned, shocked by the intensity of the pain that radiated up her leg. "Someone attacked me. A man. He followed me and attacked me in Dawson Park. I woke up in the hold."

He studied her face, reaching with his fingertips to touch the left temple. It felt like he'd burned her, a white-hot blaze of pain streaking up to her skull.

"Your nose is not broken," he said. "But you've taken quite a blow to the face."

The room tilted, the door flinging open.

"Are we at sea?" she said, her stomach lurching.

"Can you see out of your left eye?"

"I . . . I think so. Have you a looking glass?"

He handed her one, and she gasped when she saw the state of her face—her eyelid swollen mostly shut, livid blue and purple, the eye bloodshot and her nose swollen to twice its size.

It was difficult to organize her words, her foot pulsing with what felt like molten iron through her veins. She was drenched, strands of her hair stuck to her cheek with sweat. The faint scent of something industrial rose from her lips. Chloroform. Not only had the man slugged her, but he had seen to it that she remained unconscious, likely so he could dump her in the hold of the ship. Her stomach turned over and she felt the urge to vomit, leaning toward the bucket on the floor.

"You need to rest," the surgeon said, his voice far away. "I'll have one of the hands set up a bed. And I'll inform Captain Willingham that we have a stowaway."

A stowaway? Something in his tone made her skin turn to ice. Still, she recognized the name of the ship's captain.

"Am I aboard the *Ormen*?" she asked. Her father's ship.

Dr. O'Regan studied her, his mouth in a straight line. "You recognize it?"

"I recognize the captain's name. May I speak with him?"

"Not until I've finished attending to your foot," Dr. O'Regan said. She watched as he soaked a clean linen in alcohol, then lifted it with tweezers and dabbed the open wound. She jackknifed forward. The pain was electric, monstrous.

"A barrel did this?" Dr. O'Regan asked.

"Yes," she gasped. "I woke up in the hold. It must have fallen over."

"It will need to be stitched. You said you were attacked?"

"I was w-walking through a park . . . A man p-punched me. He might be yet on board . . ."

"And you were unconscious when we set sail?"

"I'm . . . must have been. I don't know. I don't remember anything."

"I'll give you something for the pain," he said, lifting a small black bottle from a shelf. "You take one of these with a glass of water every three to four hours."

The label read *TABLOID: Lead with Opium.* A familiar bottle. When Morag died, Nicky's mother produced several such bottles from the bathroom cupboard and told her to take the contents as often as she needed.

The black pill tasted like rust. A moment later she felt something sweep across her like a fine mist, the room tilting again.

"I don't have any ether," Dr. O'Regan said, lifting a needle and thread. "So I'll need you to be brave. Do you want some whisky?"

She gave a weak nod. The pills had made her feel nauseated but had done little to stanch the pain that shot up her leg, fierce and incessant, as though a tiger were mauling her.

Dr. O'Regan unstoppered a tall bottle and poured her a glass, pressing a hand to her back to help her upright. Just then the door opened and a man stepped inside, nodding at the surgeon. Nicky recognized him, though their only encounter had been a decade before—he was Captain Willingham. He wore a white shirt and a tatty waistcoat, a rust-colored quiff and a silver beard whiskering a haggard face. He was thinner since she saw him last, his hands wormy with veins. He regarded her with a liquid, uncertain gaze.

"Captain Willingham," the surgeon said. Then, nodding at her: "We have ourselves a stowaway."

"So it would seem," the captain said, and it struck her that he didn't seem very surprised to see her. "You have acquired an injury."

"Pronged her foot on one of the barrels," Dr. O'Regan said. "Said she doesn't know how she came to be on board. Says her father owns this ship."

"Is that so?"

"We met once before," Nicky told him weakly. "At the docks."

"Nicky Duthie," he said, nodding. "George Abney's daughter."

It wasn't a question. He had recognized her as soon as he laid eyes on her. And he knew her married name. And her nickname.

"What day is it?"

"Tuesday, madam."

"How far are we from Dundee?"

"We departed yesterday."

"Can you turn back?"

"We're on course for the Davis Strait," he said. "We'll not be headed back to Dundee until October."

She sat upright, the shock of this news overriding the terrible pain in her foot. "Sir, you must turn back! I'm not a stowaway, I was brought here against my will . . ."

"You must be still," Dr. O'Regan protested, his hands on her shoulders. All at once, the room lurched, several bottles dropping from their place in the cabinet and rolling along the floor. The ship listed, the sound of a wave thrashing the deck overhead.

"We're in the middle of a storm," the captain said. "We must maintain our course if we're to keep to schedule."

"There's a whaling station in Iceland," she said, her mind racing. "Skúmaskot. I've heard my father mention it. Ten days from Dundee. We could arrange a transfer. I could wait however long it might take for a ship to take me home. Please. *Please.*"

She started to cry, hot, bitter tears pouring down her face. The two men shared a look.

"Let me see what I can do," Captain Willingham said at last.

Dominique

I

December 2023
Skúmaskot, Iceland

The intruders make their way down the stairs to the lower deck. Three of them, two men and a woman, dreadlocks threaded with purple velvet hanging to her waist. A voice in my head shouts at me to *run, RUN!* But my body doesn't respond. My limbs defy my instincts, locked in a crouching position, gripping the knife.

I couldn't scream even if I wanted to. My throat is wrenching itself into a tight knot. I feel doomed. Why did I risk it? Why was I so certain I'd be alone?

Images flood my mind, the sound of gunshots.

You're a terrible person, Dom.

It isn't long before a torchlight comes to rest on me like a white sword.

"Oh," a man says. "Hello, there."

He sounds faintly Scottish.

"No," I manage to say, which is an odd response, even to my ears, but I'm so terrified that I seem incapable of anything more sophisticated. One by one, they line up in front of me, the two men and the woman, their torchlights fixed on me. I am shaking so badly that the knife tumbles from my hands, useless, and I start to cry. I fold inward, my arms reaching over my head, awaiting the blows.

But they don't come.

"Hey," another voice says. An American accent. The other man. "Stand up, for God's sake."

"Leo," the woman says. "Take it easy. Remember the plan, okay?"

I can only tremble on the ground like a newborn lamb. They discuss me for a moment as if I'm not there, and I catch snippets of what sounds like the plan to kill me.

Are you sure about this?

I think she's faking it. Seriously.

We have to.

"She's breathing super fast," the woman says then, turning back to me. She's also American, or maybe Canadian, I can't tell the difference. My mind is cartwheeling, folding inward, the fear of what they're going to do to me like a white-hot iron plunging into my brain.

Someone sets a solar lantern on the ground, flooding the room with diffuse light. Their faces press through the gloom. The woman is Black, early thirties, her eyes filled with wariness. The man next to her is Asian American, the one she calls Leo. Leo chews gum and looks at me like I'm something he picked off his shoe. The other man is white, Scottish, somewhere in his fifties, his ears sticking out from beneath a pink beanie. He has a tuft of silver hair protruding from both of them. He tells Leo not to touch me.

"Samara," he says to the woman. This is her name. I make myself remember it in case this knowledge comes in useful. In case it might save me.

He crouches down in front of me. I hear the *click* of his knees, and for some reason it makes me feel safe enough to look up.

"No one is going to hurt you," he says. I catch myself noting the kindness in his eyes. *No,* I tell myself. *Don't be deceived.* He holds out his left hand. "Please."

I stare at him. Then, despite the voices in my head urging me not to, I put my hand in his. Do I really have a choice?

"Come with me," he says.

II

Somehow I've ended up in the main cabin on the upper deck, sitting on a chair while the intruders set about trying to block up the windows. I try to remind myself that they're technically not intruders—I don't own this place, even though I was here first—but this very much feels like an intrusion, and they know it. If I could, I'd run out of here and not stop until I reach a town.

I'm holding a cup of tea. I can't remember anyone giving this to me, but it feels hot in my hands. I sip it, realizing a moment too late that it could contain drugs. If it does, I don't taste anything other than sugar and a splash of milk.

Leo is wiry and super strong, hefting two-by-fours across the cabin and fixing them in place with a hammer and nails. He gives off an angry air, and I try not to make eye contact. Every time he lifts the hammer I expect him to stride across the room and bludgeon me with it. Samara finds an old oil can, about the size of a bucket, and slices the top off with a sharp blade. I flinch. Are they going to douse me with it, set me on fire?

I eye the door of the cabin leading to the deck of the ship, and the ladder. Maybe I can try to escape. I remind myself that they aren't exactly holding me hostage, but my fear is aflame with questions. And besides, my legs still won't work, everything disconnected from my brain. I just want to hide, to fold myself back into the darkness.

When they all finish bustling around, setting a row of old chairs around the oil can, I find I'm angry. It's a startling kind of anger. I hate them, all three of them. I wanted to be here, to witness the sinking of the shipwreck. Alone. And now that dream is over.

Leo puts some of the old books inside the oil can, then strikes a match and sets it alight. The man in the pink beanie hangs a solar lantern from a hook in the ceiling, and the darkness lifts.

I keep my eyes on the ground as they sit down, forming a semicircle around me and the oil-can fire. I'm still shaking, the tea spilling out of the plastic cup onto my lap.

"What's your name?" Pink Beanie Man asks.

I keep my eyes down. "Why?"

"That's an unusual name," he says with a grin. "Why." He waits for me to correct him. "My name is Jens."

I shrug. "I don't care."

"And this is Leo, and Samara," he continues. "Your tea is cold. Would you like a fresh one?"

I don't answer.

After a few moments he gets up, and I hear him in the corner of the room, boiling a kettle and stirring. He returns with two cups this time, handing one to me and one to Samara, and it's only when I see her look of surprise that I realize he has handed us actual porcelain teacups.

"God, Jens," Samara says with a laugh. "Where the hell did you get these?"

He looks pleased with himself. "Trade secret."

I allow myself to sip the tea. It tastes warm and sweet, the steam curling up from my cup an undeniable comfort in a place as cold as this. It gives me courage to speak up.

"Look," I say, to no one in particular. "I was here first."

I make eye contact with Jens.

"Okay," he says, before glancing at the other two. "Can you tell us what your plan is? I mean, why you're here?"

"I imagine I'm here for the same reason you are," I mumble. "The wreck is being sunk at the end of the month. I want to document her."

"Really?" Leo says, leaning forward. "Document the wreck?"

Samara catches my eye.

"Can you tell us more about that?" she says. "As in, *how* you plan to document the *Ormen*?"

I feel my throat tighten again.

"I've brought some cameras," I say, pushing the words past my teeth. They seem interested. Flames lick the kindling in the oil can, pulling warmth into the room. "I thought I could get some followers, maybe some paying subscribers. I felt it was a shame that they'll just, you know, destroy this whole ship after all she's seen."

"Cool," Samara says, though I have a feeling she doesn't believe me.

"I've got some followers already," I say. "A few hundred on the project TikTok account."

"TikTok?" Leo says, lifting his eyebrows.

I shrug. "Yeah?"

He shares a look with the others. What's wrong with TikTok?

"You know the *Ormen* was a whaling ship, right?" Jens asks after a few moments.

I nod. "Yes?"

"Late eighteen hundreds," Jens adds. "Then a research ship."

"Do you know why they killed whales?" Leo asks me, lifting another piece of wood and placing it in the fire can. "Why they built an entire industry out of it?"

"Not exactly past tense, is it?" Samara interjects, folding her legs up beneath her. "They still kill whales, right?"

"Yeah, but for different reasons," Leo says. "And they're starting to ban it now."

"About time," Samara says dryly.

"For their blubber," Jens says, answering Leo's question. "Whale oil was used for light. Streets, houses, trains."

"Also for whalebone," Leo says, his sharp eyes lit up by the flames. "The nineteenth-century version of plastic. Everything that is now made of plastic was probably once made from whalebone—brushes, chopping boards, fishing nets."

"I knew they made corsets from it," I say, drinking more of my tea. I feel myself relax a little, though the voice in my head tells me this is all part of the game. They want me to lower my guard. It could be ritualistic, the killing. The tea laced with drugs so they can take me apart slowly.

"They made *everything* from it," Leo tells me. "They used every single part of the whale. Zero waste. A gruesome industry, yes. But you know, much more eco-friendly than plastic."

The room falls silent again. I'm not sure why he's telling me all this.

"We'd like to make you an offer," Jens says.

I look up, puzzled. "What offer?"

"We get that you were on board the *Ormen* first," Samara says. "But we'd like to document the ship, too. We can team up, if you like. This doesn't have to be . . . you know, awkward."

I feel my shoulders lower. She seems nice. I look down at my tea, and as though reading my mind, Jens says, "It's not poisoned, I promise."

I give a nervous laugh.

"You think you can tell us your name?" Jens says.

Against my better judgment, I say, "Dominique."

He glances at the others, and I look down at my hand, thinking of the way he took it before.

How, for a moment, the feeling of another person's skin against mine was the most beautiful thing in the world.

III

I wake the next morning in my tent in the cabin on the lower deck, though it takes me a few seconds to remember where the hell I am. It all comes back in a startling rush—the wreck, the torchlight pouring down into the darkness, the three strangers. For a moment I wonder if I actually dreamed it all, and when I climb out of my tent and pull on my coat I peer into the corridor, half expecting to find that I'm alone after all.

But then I see a green glow along the wet floor, and when I step into the corridor I see a lime-green tent in the cabin next to mine.

They're here. And despite all the fireside chat last night, I feel anxious.

I head up to the main cabin, eager to get outside and feel wind on my face. My thoughts are scrambled. Sure, the *Ormen* doesn't get a lot of visitors, on account of how remote she is. But this is a big moment for her, the end of an era. She's probably one of the last whaling ships on the planet.

Will more people come? What will I do if there's a crowd of us?

Maybe teaming up with these strangers isn't such a bad idea. A considerable percentage of explorers are heavily into drugs. I don't suspect this trio are junkies, however, given the level of fitness, organization, and clearheadedness required to explore a place like this. There's also a nerd factor that I fall into, and most explorers of that ilk are anti-drugs, hard-core activists of one kind or another, too dedicated to their cause for drugs. Environmentalists, vegans, anti-establishment, anarchists, religious fanatics. A small percentile of athletes who combine exploration with long-distance running and parkour.

Outside, the sun is low but strong, a scrim of silvery light illuminating the cliffs and the bay behind us. The snow is still thick, and I can imagine it'll only get thicker as we plunge to the bottom of the year. I look at the masts thrusting up from the deck and remember again why I came. I felt a pull to her, to tell her story. This abandoned place is special. People are afraid to come here, and I can understand why. But the other side of the tracks, the margins of transgression—I feel at home, here.

Not exactly at home, perhaps. But I feel safe. It has become familiar, this life. A routine.

I watch the mists swirl across the bay of Skúmaskot, thickening and thinning, a kind of dance. It's astonishing how they change the landscape, revealing and obscuring, like an eraser. The row of derelict buildings along the bay—that's where I'll head today.

"Good morning," a voice says behind me. I turn sharply, spotting the pink beanie, the kind blue eyes in a haggard face.

"Hello," I say. "Jens."

He pushes his hands deep in his pockets and looks out at the view. The gradients of the hills press through the mist in shadowy arcs, and a low wind whistles through the sand.

"This is quite a place," he says. "A shark fishing village."

"It used to be," I say. "It's been sat like this since the 1970s."

"I wonder why it didn't become a raving tourist hot spot," Jens says. It takes me a moment to decipher that he's joking.

"Right?" I say. "So scenic. So much to do."

"It *is* scenic," he says. "Though maybe not for anyone who likes vitamin D. Do you explore a lot?"

"A little," I say. "What about you?"

He shrugs. "A little."

I watch him from the corner of my eye, reading him. There's something familiar about him, the shape of his nose, a little hooked, and the deep lines of his long face. His skin is weathered and pocked—the face of an explorer. We don't tend to look after ourselves very well. No time for SPF and moisturizer. Sometimes it'll leave you with broken bones that never heal right.

It's as I'm thinking this that I notice he only has one hand. His right sleeve is rolled up a little, revealing a muscular forearm with a small anchor tattoo, the skin gnarled at the stump where his wrist should be.

"Is there a problem?" he says, catching me staring, and I flinch, embarrassed.

"Sorry. I didn't mean to be rude."

"Lost it in a fight," he says, holding it up.

"God."

"Just kidding. Osteosarcoma. Had it removed when I was eight."

I'm not sure which story to believe. "Is that a type of cancer?"

"I barely remember it. And it was so long ago I just got used to it."

He nods in the direction of the cabin. "Come inside," he says, "I'll make us all some breakfast."

"Jens?" He turns to face me, and I hesitate.

"I was just wondering . . ." I say, worried I'll sound stupid. "Did you see anyone else down on the beach yesterday?"

His eyebrows knit together, and he glances toward the beach. "No. There's no one around for miles."

"Well, except for us," I say. He stands closer to me, scanning the coastline. The waves are thunderous and brilliant, thumping down on the sand, a fizzing sound like fireworks when they roll back.

"What did they look like?"

"I'm sure it was a woman. I think she was only wearing a dress."

"A dress?"

"I think so."

His eyes settle on me. "Maybe you saw a ghost?"

"I don't believe in ghosts."

He's amused at this. "Perhaps you saw a mermaid, then."

"A mermaid?" I think back to my dream. The long tail stretching out in front. The sound of a woman's voice, singing.

"You'll have heard Iceland's folktales about mermaids?" he says.

I haven't. Like, not at all. "Not really."

He takes a step back toward the side of the hull that overlooks Skúmaskot. The bay is bustling this morning, the sea pushing in so fast that the ice hasn't solidified all the way across. The water is deep navy, boiling around the skerries in the middle of the bay. Jens points at one of them, a tessellated formation of basalt rock, like those hexagonal structures at the Giant's Causeway in Northern Ireland.

"That's a mermaid stone," he says. "Can you see the shape?"

I squint at it. "It looks like a chair, or a throne. Is that what you mean?"

"The curve around the front of the stone is said to be created by the mermaid's long tail when she sits on the throne. It means a mermaid has lived here."

"Nice," I say, though I give a shiver, my mind turning to the way the wind sounded like singing last night.

"No," he says. "Not nice."

"Why isn't it nice?"

He turns his eyes to me. "Icelandic mermaids are not the sort you see in the movies. They want to punish both the living and the dead."

I raise my eyebrows. It seems fitting that a place like this would subvert the nicer mythical tropes into something macabre. Or Lovecraftian.

Inside the main cabin, Leo is up and stacking old bits of cardboard and wood into the oil can to build a fire. The flame grows quickly, and I stand next to it, rubbing my hands against the warmth.

Leo doesn't acknowledge me. That's fine. As long as he builds fires like this every morning, I think I can handle it.

At the kitchenette, Jens sets up a gas cooker and makes a fry-up, replete with mushrooms. The smell almost makes me cry. The whole breakfast comes from dehydrated packs much more sophisticated and expensive than mine—Jens is clearly an experienced explorer, not cutting out too many home comforts. His pink beanie tells me he's not a macho kind of guy either. He's likable, but still—I feel cautious.

Samara joins us soon after, smiling when she sees me at the fire with my plate of food.

"God, that looks good," she says. Then, to Jens: "We have eggs this time?"

"We have eggs," he replies with a proud smile.

"Score!" she says, high-fiving him.

I want to ask how long they've been exploring together. It seems they have a bit of a routine going, with Leo stacking the fire and Jens cooking meals and making tea with his delicate porcelain cups.

I listen more than I talk, gauging all the while how much I can trust these folk. My instinct tells me they're fine, but I force myself to keep my guard up. I'm the outlier here, and I remember the whispers I heard last night, when they were coming down the hatch into the lower deck. *Where is she?*

They knew I was here.

How, though? With a shiver, I think about the feeling I had

yesterday, when I saw the fox. That I was being watched. Maybe they saw me on the deck and decided to work out what to do before coming on board. Yes, that was it. They'd seen me before the sun went down. It must have been disappointing, hiking for countless miles to stake out the wreck, only to find that someone else had got there first. Maybe that's why Leo radiates such angry vibes. He doesn't like me at all.

I'm working up the courage to ask them what their dynamic is. Are they a throuple? It seems naive to ask—of course they are. As far as I can see, they all slept in separate cabins last night, but that doesn't necessarily mean anything. Sometimes explorers team up for bigger, more dangerous explorations, which is possibly the case here.

Samara is a sound engineer, which makes sense—she strikes me as someone who works remotely and sporadically, on her own terms. A professional, not the type drawn to sites that are easier to get to: inner-city urbex sites you can reach by bus. Old schoolyards, crumbling mansions. As we eat, I ask her about her favorite exploration, the one that's stayed with her, and she tells me about a place in France, an abandoned farmhouse in a medieval town. All the rooms were still furnished, probably a hundred years after the owners left. A bar of soap sitting on the bathroom sink. A pot on the stove, houseplants withering in their pots. A little girl's bedroom, dolls and handmade teddies on the bed. And a low whispering that she couldn't trace to anything.

"Weren't you scared?" I ask. We're sitting in the messy cabin, ignoring the junk around us. The fire is burning high in the oil can. It's all very wholesome.

Samara sips her cup of tea and sighs wistfully. "No. I hear it a lot, actually. A kind of whispering. Sometimes I've heard voices."

I watch her carefully. Does she believe in the afterlife? "But . . . not ghosts?"

She takes a pause, choosing her words carefully. "It's a revenant," she says finally. "Not a ghost, not the way we think of ghosts. More like breath on a windowpane or lip marks on a cup. Sound leaves a trace. The human ear usually can't hear it. Like, if you sit completely still you might pick up the odd floorboard moaning, or the wind, maybe the birds nearby. But the mic picks up traces. There's a spectral ambiance I always manage to find, even just for a moment. Like an echo."

"Wow," I say. "That sounds . . . spiritual."

"It's scientifically proven," she says. "Traces of the past hang in the air around us. Millions of them, still suspended. Like time is a glass and we kind of smear it a bit as we pass through it."

She tells me that Leo is part Korean, born in Chicago. He's a parkour expert, incredibly strong. His talent will enable him to get some cool footage out here, she says. He's not visibly ripped, his arms covered up by a long-sleeved jersey shirt, and he's quite short, about five foot five. He is sharp, his keen black eyes seeming to look right through me, and I can tell he doesn't suffer fools.

"Is that a bloodstain?" Samara says, pausing halfway across the cabin to survey a mark on the floor.

It is—the rug has shifted. "There are a lot of those marks," I say. "Gross, right?"

"It does look like old blood," Jens says, crouching down to touch it. "Or shit."

"Shit doesn't stain wood like that," Leo says.

Jens raises his eyebrows at him, amused. "Do we want to know how you've acquired this insight, Leo?"

"No," Leo deadpans. "Here's another one." He points at a splodge on the wall by the cabin door, an icky hand-sized splash surrounded by tear-shaped droplets.

"Places like this always have a history," Jens observes, trying to steady the mood. "That's why we're here, right?"

Samara looks stricken.

"Could be worse," Jens tells her. "Could be dead bodies lying around."

IV

We spend our daylight hours hefting the rest of the junk from the cabin into the hold, making it homely.

"What's behind this door?" Leo calls from the far end of the deck.

"I think it's the captain's cabin," I tell him. "I've not been able to open it."

Leo tries the handle, pushing against the wood of the door with his shoulder. "Man, it really is jammed."

"Maybe it's jammed for a reason," Samara says, and Leo frowns at her.

I tell them about the hole I found in the hull, that maybe it is causing a vacuum to seal the door tight. Samara tries the door next to it instead, the one that freaked me out when I first touched it. I haven't tried again since. I don't mention the weird thing that happened with the handle when my fingers came in contact with it. Instead, I watch her, waiting for her to remark on the sound fading or something similarly strange.

"Huh," she says.

"Something wrong?" I ask.

"Locked," she says, trying the door next to it, which opens.

"What's in there?" I ask, cautious.

"About a foot of dust," she says. "A storeroom, by the look of it."

I glance in after her—just as she says, it's a storeroom with some old boxes. Nothing sinister. Even so, I won't risk touching the door handle. Not yet.

Samara finds tins of food down in the bowels of the ship. The last explorer who stayed here must have traveled to Skúmaskot in a four-wheel-drive packed with luxuries. There's a bin and a toaster, for God's sake. The real find is the old desalination tank, providing fresh water. Often explorers leave behind things they brought to make their stay more comfortable, but we really struck gold here.

I wonder if the nicks in the wooden post are to do with food rations.

Leo finds an old generator in the cabin he's claimed as his bedroom, which brings a moment of excitement. Sadly, it's broken.

When I checked the solar battery packs this morning, I discovered they aren't charging enough for all my gear. It's minus five at night and one or two degrees during the day. Yes, we have four hours of daylight, but the quality of light changes all the time: sometimes it's bright and brilliant, the sun like a torch behind a brocade of cloud. But a moment later a mist will rise, hemming in the bay like we're on a desert island. And then it'll burn away, leaving the sky crisp and clear as a bright coin, the ocean like liquid mercury.

But it's not enough for the solar chargers that provide my—or should I say *our*—electricity: they're the only way we can charge the cameras and internet terminal, which the others are keen to use, too. The batteries *are* soaking up enough sunlight to power the kettle, the electric hob, the laptops, and our cameras, but the internet satellite terminal requires much more battery than I'd calculated, especially for uploads. We'll have to be judicious about how we use the charge, is what I'm saying.

On our walk around the deck today, we also find that the lower deck of the shipwreck has been blocked up by a thick sheet of metal that was soldered to the hatch opening, maybe to stop tourists from climbing down there and getting trapped inside. But Samara manages to prize some of the metal off the sides, creating a hole about the width of a football to shine her torch through.

"I think I see a wine cellar," she says. "And there are barrels down here. Do you think they're left over from the whaling era?"

"Let me see," Leo says, and before any of us can blink, Leo has squirreled down the hole in the floor and dropped to the deck below.

"Leo," Samara calls after him. "How're you going to get back up?"

"Are you serious?" he asks, and she doesn't respond.

We attach my camera to an extendable grip and lower it down into the hole to film him. It's flooded, so Leo wades up to his knees in filthy black water that seems much deeper at the stern, odd bits of rubbish floating on the surface—pieces of wood and metal from where the ship had hit the rocks, dead fish, old fishing nets, and endless coils of rope. We can make out a row of old barrels at the shallow end, too.

"How piratey is that?" Samara says, flashing her torch over the barrels. "Do you think they have gunpowder inside?"

"Hardly," Jens says. "The *Ormen* was never used as a battleship."

There's a sudden knocking sound as Leo tries to hack one of them open with an ax. He manages to get the lid off, and we all hold our breath as he looks inside.

"Oh my God!" he screams.

"What is it?" Jens yells back.

"There's a dead body in here!"

"Shit, get out of there, Leo!" Samara shrieks, and he starts laughing. Samara's face changes as she realizes he's pulling her leg.

"You bastard," she says.

"It's empty," he says. "God, what a stench."

"What's over there?" Samara asks, poking her head through the hatch and shining her torch into a corner. A large object sits covered up, ominous in its shape—a head and shoulders, I think. Leo sloshes through the filthy water toward it and pulls off the sheet of tarpaulin. It's a metal storage unit with cans of food dated until next year, which proves my point that recent explorers have stayed here.

"We got wine, folks!" Leo shouts, holding up two black bottles.

Leo stuffs some of the wine and food cans down his sweater and climbs back up through the hatch. Samara takes out a can opener on a key chain and sets about opening a can.

"I wouldn't risk it," I say, watching Samara dip her finger into the juice of one without a label.

"I'll be the poison tester," she says, sucking her finger. We all watch in silent trepidation as she tastes, gasping when her body goes into violent spasms.

"Jesus," Leo shouts.

"Ha!" Samara says, pointing at him, and he rolls his eyes.

"Definitely poisonous," she says, sitting cross-legged on the floor of the lower deck.

"What is it?" I ask.

"Peach slices. I'll make peach cake, I think."

I figure she's kidding, but she bakes an actual peach cake on the fire bucket using ingredients we find inside cans and old sacks—flour, peaches, flax seeds, sugar, and oil. It smells incredible. We dust down an old bottle of red wine and drink it out of our aluminum cups huddled around the fire. Jens puts candles all around the cabin to create ambiance.

In the main cabin, I sit on the makeshift sofa by the fire, looking over the work we've done, and these new faces that were strangers just a day ago. You would *never* think that this place is the same grimy shithole I walked into on my first night here. No, it's not spotless—there are still blooms of black mold on the walls and bloodstains on the floor—but with my Perspex windows nailed in place, all the rubbish cleared out, and candles glittering along the window frames, it feels almost homely.

Just before midnight I head downstairs into the lower deck, where Leo has left a few more bottles of wine from the hold. I bring one up to the main cabin, and as I'm making my way back to the hatch, I hear Samara, Leo, and Jens talking to each other in low voices. An instinct makes me pause on the stair and listen for a moment.

"How can you be so sure it'll work this time?"

It's Leo's voice. He sounds urgent, frustrated. I freeze, wondering what he means.

Jens says something I can't fully hear, but the second part I hear clear as a bell.

I'll work on her.

"Not like we have much of a choice," Samara says, with a sigh of resignation.

It sounds like they're making a plan, and so I make my way through the hatch, curious if they'll fill me in.

"More red, anyone?" I say, holding up the bottle. Leo glances at me before turning back to Samara.

"Great!" Jens says.

I wait for someone to loop me into their conversation, but they don't. Leo suddenly won't make eye contact, and Samara shifts the conversation to music. I try to read the mood. Something hangs in the air, heavy as a sword.

Jens holds my gaze for a few seconds, and there's a message there—a warning. But I can't read it.

I'll work on her. That's what he said.

Did he mean he would work on *me*?

Nicky

I

May 1901
100 miles northeast of Orkney, Scotland

When Nicky came to, the room around her swayed, the musky scent of wood and lantern oil hanging in the air. For a moment she fancied she was at home in Faulkner Street, with Allan in bed next to her. She reached out a hand and felt hard wood. When she opened her eyes, she saw she was in a cabin on a slim hard bed, the whole room lilting a little as though it sat on springs.

"Ah, welcome back," a voice said, and she lifted her head to see a man standing next to her, a white apron daubed in old blood. Dr. O'Regan, she remembered, and with a dizzying rush the realization came that she was on the *Ormen*. Her foot had been bandaged, though it hummed with white-hot pain.

"Reid will help you to your quarters," Dr. O'Regan told her. A blond-haired boy of about fifteen stood warily in the doorway, his inky eyes shifting across the room. Dr. O'Regan pressed a palm against the small of her back to help her upright before handing her a cane made of whalebone.

One arm across the boy's slim shoulders, the other leaning on the cane, she hobbled out of the captain's cabin, back along the narrow deck to a small cabin at the opposite end of the deck.

It was no bigger than a cupboard, the ceiling barely high enough for Reid to straighten to his full height. A straw mattress and blankets on wooden crates wedged into a corner. A stained ceramic bedpan sat on the floor, a gnarly sea chest adjacent to it with a Bible on top. A brass oil lamp swayed from a hook on the ceiling. No window.

"This is a bonnie cabin," Reid said, helping her sit down on the mattress. "At least you won't be bothered by any snoring."

She nodded but couldn't return his smile. She reminded herself that she couldn't expect much more. It was temporary. And the thought of sleep was sublime.

"Do you share with many others?" she asked the boy.

"Six of us sleep in steerage," he said.

She winced. "Is it uncomfortable?"

"It's all right," he said. "If I ever make it to second mate, I'll get to sleep in a room like this one."

"I hope you do," she said weakly, sitting on the bed, and watched as he reddened.

"I'll bring you food in the morning," he said, turning to the door. "I can't promise it'll be what you're used to."

"Thank you," she said.

She listened to his footsteps as he headed to the kitchen. Inside the sea chest, she found some clothes—woolen socks, a fisherman's jumper, trousers. Her dress was still wet, and so she slipped it off and pulled on the dry clothes before lying down on the bed and covering herself with the blanket.

The waves outside beat against the hull, the noise of the men above ringing in her ears. She thought of Allan in the Transvaal, waiting in line for the mail delivery. Her father and mother and Cat would be worried. They'd wonder why she hadn't returned from the mill. She imagined the police rallying to her mother's shrill voice, a foot kicking in the door of her house on Faulkner Street.

She felt panic rise in her chest, the whole room beginning to spin. It felt like she might go mad, the thought of how much everyone at home would be worrying about her, believing her to be dead.

Strange, she thought, that the man in the park did not steal any of her jewelry. The fine gold chain she wore at her neck would have been easy to rip off and pawn, as would the gold wedding band on her finger. She touched it now, holding the metal between finger and thumb as though it might transport her to Allan.

Their wedding had been exhausting, a stiff, rote affair organized largely by her mother, Mhairi, and her new mother-in-law, Alison. The friction between the two women spilled over into almost every corner of the arrangements; Mhairi had wanted Nicky to wear her grandmother's wedding dress, which Mhairi had worn for her own wedding day. Alison, however, protested loudly, claiming that it was unfair for Nicky to wear both her grandmother's wedding ring *and* her wedding dress, and that she should instead wear the dress that Alison's mother had made for her almost thirty years before. Nicky worked hard to broker a truce between both women, offering to wear Alison's old-fashioned, oversized dress—a potato sack with a throttling collar—and invite all six of Allan's sisters to be bridesmaids, as well as her own younger sister, Cat. Three hundred guests were invited, the majority of whom Nicky had never met.

On the morning of the wedding, Mirrin, one of Allan's sisters, and Cat accused each other of taking the other's bonnet, and soon Mhairi and Alison had chosen sides. The bonnets were torn and lopsided, both girls wearing hand marks on their cheeks from where they'd slapped each other. Alison stormed off, refusing to participate in the ceremony. Just as the organ sounded, Nicky took her father's arm to be given away and her mother hissed into her ear—*If you go through with this, hell mend you!*—and so she took Allan's hand in marriage with her mother's glare burning a hole in her back, Alison's footsteps ringing down the chapel foyer, and an occasional sob rising from the bridesmaids.

That night, the heavens opened, the cobbled streets of their neighborhood soon awash with water. Allan dutifully carried her over the threshold and upstairs to the bedroom.

"Give me your ring," he said, when she started to undress.

She frowned. "Why?"

He was lying on the bed, naked to the waist. His eyes full of kindness. "Your ring, madam."

She was down to her slip—new, not borrowed—when she removed her wedding ring and handed it to him.

He looked it over, then squinted at the inscription. "Fourth of June 1832." He looked up with a furrowed brow. "Did we time travel?"

She sighed and sat down next to him. She had tried so, so hard to appease both her mother and her mother-in-law, but she had liked the idea of wearing a ring that had belonged to her grandmother, a stern woman who believed strongly in not sparing children the rod.

"It doesn't fit, either," she said. "I'll need to get it resized."

He put the ring in his pocket then.

"What are you doing?" she asked.

"How about we put your grandmother's ring in a box, and we put this one on your finger." Removing his hand from his pocket, he opened his palm to reveal another gold wedding band, bright and shining. Brand-new.

She gasped and took it from him, looking it over in the light. An eighteen-karat gold wedding band, with an inscription: *12 April 1895.*

"It's beautiful," she said, slipping it on her finger. The fit was perfect.

He stood up, lacing his fingers through hers. "I'm sorry the wedding was a nightmare," he said, kissing her neck.

"Your mother told me that weddings are for other people," she said, removing her hairpins. "I didn't think she meant it quite so literally."

"I suppose a single day isn't too much to ask," he said, lifting her slip over her head.

"What do you mean?" she said, and he paused, their faces close. His eyes were tender, softening as he looked down at her.

"I mean, the wedding was one day," he said. "But we've got the rest of time together. If you'll have me."

She smiled. "I will."

II

As the *Ormen* passed by the Orkney archipelago, the ocean stretched out, an infinite sheet of metal, no land in sight. At night, the shrieking wind and pounding waves were so loud she wondered if the ship was sinking. When the pills wore off and the wound in her foot flared again, she wished more than once that it would.

She imagined Allan's worry, the torment of it. How anguished he'd be. To think she had been worried just two days ago, when his letter didn't arrive. She had had to distract herself at the mill, and that was possibly why she was here . . . How did the man know she would be there? Or was it a random attack? She remembered how he'd searched her out, his eyes meeting hers through the crowd. Who was he? A disgruntled colleague, someone who had a bone to pick with Allan?

No—it was something to do with her father. He had told her to lie low. But he had also said that the company was folding, and yet the *Ormen* had set sail as planned. Why, then, had the surgeon known her name?

When she ventured out of her cabin and up onto the deck, she spoke to the crew, asking questions about their tasks, before steering the conversation to her attack to try to probe them for answers. The tactic had mixed results—some of the men, such as Ellis and Arnott, made lewd comments that embarrassed and confused her, and so she left them alone. The men made no bones about singing bawdy songs and telling crude jokes in her presence, occasionally using their genitals to demonstrate a punch line. They seemed equally fine about pissing and shitting in front of her, lowering themselves a little down the bow and using the end of a shared tow rope for cleaning. She would have confined herself to the small cabin, but it made her seasickness intolerable, and the wind on the upper deck soothed her injured foot.

Never in her life had she been exposed to such scurrilous behavior. There were no washing facilities, no practice of even rudimentary hygiene or manners. She had imagined sailors to have a loose tongue, but on deck, the men's language was incendiary. It had almost moved her to insist that they curb their tongue, but then she had heard the men discuss money, the lack of food in their homes, a child they'd had to leave behind with consumption, and their coarse language ceased to matter. Consumption, she knew, was fatal, especially so when a family hadn't the means to pay a good doctor. The conversations she overheard taught her that their wages were paltry, and often not paid at all, if a voyage made slim gains. Their wives and children had gone hungry, had died, as a result.

For a moment, she thought of her father bitterly. How often he had boasted of his profits from the company. How he had complained about his "sea dogs," the men that were working twenty hours a day in the most horrendous conditions, and spoken openly about trimming their provisions to the bare bones.

There were twenty men on board, including Dr. O'Regan and Captain Willingham. Reid and Anderson were the youngest crew members, smooth-faced boys whose voices had barely dropped. Reid's uncle, Daverley, served as boatswain. Then there were the boatsteers, McIntyre and Gray, both Dundee men around her father's age, perhaps younger—she well knew that the ravages of poverty ground the young old before their time. The harpooners were Ellis and McKenzie, who also served as the specktioneer. Skentelbery was the ship's cook, Royle and Arnott served as seamen, Lovejoy was the first mate, Wolfarth was the second, Stroud and Martin were landsmen, Collins and Goodall were coopers, Harrow was the skeeman, and Cowie served as a carpenter.

She etched all their names on her mind, filing away tidbits of information in case it linked any of them to her attacker.

One of the mariners had to have known. Someone had to have arranged it with the man in the park. She had watched the crew carefully to work out if she might recognize one of them, and when she didn't, she studied their interactions, and their relationships, for the man in the park couldn't have been working alone. The park was some distance from the docks, so it would have taken more than one man to get her on board the ship, and even then it could not have been done without witnesses.

She noticed that both Royle and Gray frequently rested their eyes on her, and when she looked back neither of them looked away. She wondered if they had worked alongside the man, perhaps, or if her memory served her poorly. No—the man who had attacked her had a bent nose, and his build was different than any of the crew.

Daverley and his nephew were quite close, she could see, with Daverley acting protectively toward him, helping him when he trapped his hand in the rigging, and when Lovejoy screamed in the boy's face she saw Daverley consoling him afterward.

As they sailed toward the Arctic, the ship's hierarchy became clearer—the captain was hapless when it came to ordering the men, preferring instead to leave such duties to his first mate, Lovejoy, a stout, pale-eyed man with a mouthful of broken teeth and greasy black hair that moved with lice. He was the only man to address her as Miss Abney, and she hadn't had the nerve to tell him that her maiden name had been abandoned six years prior.

Witnessing the ship's hierarchy in operation made her realize that they were far away from the authorities, or indeed from anyone who might protect her from being violated, or killed. The captain was perpetually busy, and the surgeon was disinterested. A few days into her ordeal, she approached Ellis, a short, stocky man with a thick ginger beard, and asked him how far they were from Iceland.

"Why?" he said. "Not thinking of leaving us, are you?"

She was suddenly wary of how close he was leaning in to her. In the corners of her vision she saw Lovejoy watching, and ahead of them, Cowie and Royle had turned to her. Her foot shrieked with pain.

"Thank you," she said, not wanting to stay on deck any longer.

Back in her cabin she swallowed several pills quickly, sinking into her bed as the room around her faded.

She woke to the sound of "Land ho!" and footsteps pounding the deck outside.

When she opened her eyes, she saw a familiar face above her, groaning and grunting. It was Ellis, and he was naked, thrusting inside her, a hand pinning her wrists above her head. She gave a scream, but immediately he clamped a hand over her mouth.

"Quiet!" he hissed.

She began to tremble, the effect of the drugs sharply tapering. Ellis got up then and wiped his mouth. He sat on the side of the bed, belching as he pulled on his shirt.

"You beast," she whispered, pulling the blankets around her.

A moment later, the door burst open. Lovejoy stood in the door with a face like thunder.

"You!" he shouted, lunging at Ellis and dragging him out of the room by his collar.

Dominique

I

December 2023
Skúmaskot, Iceland

I dream terrible things. I see myself on the mermaid rock in the bay, my throat burning with a mystical song. It's not a song of delight, but one of darkness—each note that leaves my mouth is like a curse sent out into the world. A long black tail flicks at the end of the rock instead of legs, settling into the groove in the rock.

I wake up with a headache, the rasp of the ocean outside making me fear that the wreck has cut loose and is being pulled out to sea. That would be a first.

I find my lantern and turn it on, sending the tent aglow, my little blue cocoon inside the cabin. The images in my mind swirl, grainy and sickening. I remind myself that I'm safe, that this is my tent, my sleeping bag, my water bottle, my gloves. I take a long, deep breath, then let it out.

I have no idea what is going on with my brain right now. Jens told me about the mermaid stone, and maybe it has freaked me out. Or maybe it's the darkness, and the strangeness of the ship. Sleeping on board has taken some getting used to. I've set up my tent in the cabin, for both the double insulation factor and the familiarity. But still, the creaking and the groaning of the hull is pretty loud at night, as is the ocean. Those waves are fierce.

"Score!" I hear Samara shout upstairs.

I head up to see what the excitement is about. Leo has lit the fire, and I see him busily carving the top off another similar oil can, presumably to create an additional source of heat. Samara is sitting on the floor pulling the contents out of her backpack. I see a laptop and a microphone beside her, and she looks over a pair of earphones with an expression of glee.

"This is the best day of my life," she says.

"What do you mean?" I ask, wary. She's pulling out her kit like she's never seen it before.

"Did you forget you packed those, Samara?" Jens says from behind me.

"What?" she says, looking up. "Oh. Yeah. Yes, I did. *So* much stuff I forgot I brought."

"Is this your recording equipment?" I ask, picking up a shiny black box with a mic attached.

"Yes," she says, happily, looking it over.

I watch her carefully, unsettled by her behavior. *Is the equipment stolen?* I wonder silently. She's looking at it like she's never seen it before.

I don't say anything to her about what I overheard last night. She is wrapped up in the gear she forgot about, murmuring to herself about the things she will record. It reminds me to check the battery packs, and try again to set up the internet terminal.

"What have you got?" she asks Jens, and I turn to see that he's holding what looks like a model airplane.

"A drone, by the looks of it," Leo says.

"A drone," Jens repeats.

"Can you sort one out for me, too?" Leo asks me. I watch as he unzips his rucksack near the cabin door, unsure of how to answer. Is he accusing me of theft? He pulls out a laptop and a small camera with a headstrap.

"A headcam," he announces, putting it on and fiddling with the buttons. "That'll do, I guess." He angles his face to me and grins, that same jaw-splitting grimace. "It's just like Christmas. Thanks, Santa!"

"Leo," Samara says, a warning in her tone. She flicks her eyes at me warily.

Santa? I don't understand Leo's sense of humor, or even when he's being serious. He heads outside, and a few moments later I see him racing across the sand, breaking into a series of backflips and twirls like a gymnast.

"Parkour helps him deal with it," Samara tells me when she sees me watching.

"Deal with what?" I ask.

She hesitates. "The isolation," she says finally. I can't help but feel she was going to say something else.

"What's the deal with the three of you?" I ask carefully. "Are you all in a relationship?"

She pauses before breaking into a loud laugh, her head thrown back.

"No," she says. Then, pulling a face of disgust. "God, no. We're . . . colleagues."

"Colleagues," I say. "For this trip, or . . . ?"

She shrugs, her face darkening again. "For the foreseeable."

The weather this morning is foggy and cold, which is to be expected in December in Iceland, but when it feels like knives across my skin I can't help but wish this site were farther south, or closer to civilization. While the sky is light and the snow isn't falling, I decide to go for a walk along the beach toward the caves, filming content: the shipwreck from a distance is an incredible image, and as the light goes it looks black-and-white, no filter needed. The rocks are packed with birds and nests, black birds with long red beaks. They squeal above the cliffs, circling and diving. I watch for a long time, growing strangely emotional. The sight of them struggling to survive out here in such a savage environment makes me sad, and yet the sign of life is moving. Maybe the cold is starting to get to me.

I search the horizon for the horses I heard the other night, but there's no sign of them.

II

It's dark when I return to the *Ormen*.

There's a mood in the cabin when I enter, as though I've interrupted a conversation, or an argument. Leo is fixing another two-by-four on one of the cabin windows, hammering aggressively, as though trying to channel his anger. I feel myself tensing—all the good feelings I was starting to have about the three of them begin to fade. Maybe I need to leave. Maybe I should grab my gear and leave right now. There's no reason to stay on the ship. I could camp outside, build my own goddamn fire.

But I remember I wanted to film the ship, to explore the cabins. There might be things I find here that tell her story.

I hang my coat up, then finger the long row of cuts in the wooden post. "Did you see these?" I ask Samara when she looks up.

She stares, so I tell her what they are, how I counted them.

"I think they're marks someone made to tally the number of days they stayed here."

"Two hundred eleven, right?" Leo says in a flat voice.

"You counted them?" I ask.

He looks up as he positions the last piece of wood against the window frame.

"Obviously."

I'm trying my hardest to set up the internet terminal, but it won't connect. I move to a different spot close to the bookcase, re-plugging the cable into my laptop. The others are quiet, just the sound of the fire crackling in the background, and the waves beyond. I feel like I might cry—if I don't manage to connect to the internet, the project is ruined.

I watch the screen of my laptop, praying silently as the terminal lights up. My web page stutters before connecting to TikTok.

"Yes!" I shout, punching the air with my fists.

"What?" Samara says, approaching with a smile.

"We're online," I tell her, clapping my hands to my mouth in excitement. "I got it working."

"Really?" Leo says, skeptical. "How far will the signal reach?"

"It won't extend much beyond the ship," I say, clicking through to the project TikTok account. "But we can film outside and upload to the project social media accounts. I'll show you."

I show him the TikTok account for the project. It's the first time I've been on it for a few days and I notice my followers have gone up. "I have four hundred followers now," I say, showing her the tally on the top of the screen.

"Wow," Samara says, taking the seat next to me. "People are interested?"

"Of course they're interested," I say.

I have this dream, albeit a recent one, that this exploration will make it possible to continue exploring. Urban exploration isn't a hobby—it's a lifestyle. Of the urban explorers I've met, I don't know a single one who has a career, or a demanding job, because to be able to drop everything at a moment's notice and spend a month in an abandoned mall in China, or trawl a Nazi bunker in eastern Germany, you have to work zero-hour contracts.

"My goal is for the project to hit ten thousand followers," I tell Samara. "We have more chance of going viral then. And hopefully we'll all end up with more subscriptions on our individual channels."

I turn to Jens and Leo. "We have one chance of telling the story of the *Ormen* before she gets destroyed," I tell them. "And if we're going to do it properly, we need to rethink how we document her story. How we structure the narrative."

I want to say that filming endless amounts of stuff and then hoping it'll all coalesce into something interesting is too slapdash and time-consuming, but I hold back.

But then the web page glitches before crashing altogether. I reboot the terminal, my heart in my mouth. It says there's a problem and refuses to open the page. Why is nothing working? I try not to show my frustration, or my fear that the terminal is dead.

"We need to film the *Ormen*, obviously," Samara says, sitting down at the dining table. "But we need to tell the story of Skúmaskot, too. Like, I had no idea there would be so many buildings here."

"Wasn't this place a shark fishing village?" Leo says, taking the seat opposite her.

"Up until the turn of the twentieth century," I say. Samara pulls out the seat next to her and I take it, setting my laptop in front of me. Finally, it logs back on.

"They ate sharks here, right?" Leo says.

Samara nods. "It wasn't like they could grow crops. Way too cold, especially back then. Fishing was the only way they could stay alive."

"So why did they leave?" I ask.

Samara pulls my laptop toward her and types into a Google search bar. *Why did the villagers leave Skúmaskot?*

She finds a Wikipedia page. "It says the trade for fishing Greenland sharks died out when the demand for shark oil decreased," Samara says, scrolling. "Which makes sense, right?"

"Skúmaskot is cursed," Leo says darkly. We look over at him and he shrugs. "That's what I heard."

"So folklore, in other words," Samara sums up.

I glance at Jens, recalling what he said about mermaids. "You heard about a local legend, didn't you?" I ask him.

He glances from me to Samara. "Not really local. It was a folktale related to Iceland. Icelandic folklore is savage."

"I guess it would have to be," Leo says.

"Why's that?" Samara asks.

"You've got to be tough, living out here," Leo says. "Especially in the olden days. Brutal winters. Can't raise kids to be soft and then expect them to cope."

"My mother taught me an Icelandic lullaby," Jens says.

"Your mom?" Samara says. "She was from here?"

"Not this region," Jens says. "But yes, she was born in Iceland. She moved to Orkney as a child, which is where I was born."

"What's the lullaby?" Leo asks.

"The translation is something like this: 'Sleep tight, be kind, and do no wrong, lest mermaids wound you with their song, prayers and penance do not postpone, lest they trap you by their stone.'"

The air in the room feels charged.

"Fuck, that's weird," Leo says, breaking the silence.

"'Lest mermaids wound you,'" Samara repeats in a low voice. "Am I missing something? I thought mermaids were pretty and shit."

"In Iceland they're savage," Jens says.

"What's the last part about?" Leo asks. "The stone?"

"Is that something to do with the mermaid's chair out on the bay?" I ask, and Jens nods. He tells the others: "A mermaid's stone is where she sits and sings and braids her hair, and all those who haven't repented are chained to the stone for the rest of time. And actually, the first part—'Sleep tight'?"

"Yeah?" I say.

"It means death, not sleep as we know it. It's a warning to the dead not to be wicked."

"Shit," I say.

"So the throne is hell, basically," Leo says.

"The entrance to Valhalla," Jens agrees.

"Great," Samara adds. "Not only is there no Wi-Fi here, but it's right next to hell."

"All of this is good," Leo says, drumming his fingers on the table.

"Really?" Samara says. "How is it good, exactly?"

"Well, we're here to make content, aren't we?" he says. "To tell the story of the whaling ship, and of Skúmaskot."

"You're right. There's so much more here than I expected," Samara says with a sigh.

"In what way?" I ask.

"I mean, the history, and that lullaby . . . I went out first thing this morning to record some sound. It usually takes days, weeks, even, to pick up the kind of tonal textures of a place that tell its story. But this place . . ." She shakes her head. "As soon as I put my headphones on, I could hear so many different registers. It's like poetry."

Leo gives an amused laugh. Maybe he's thinking the same thing as I did when I first heard it—that all Samara's evangelizing about sound is a bit woo-woo.

From her pocket, Samara produces her spiffed-up audio recorder and sets it on the table, then bends down to her backpack and fetches a small round speaker and a cable. She plugs one into the other, then presses a button. The room is suddenly filled with what sounds like the ocean moving up the beach, but beneath it is a rhythmic popping sound that's hard to place.

"It sounds like . . . fireworks?" Leo says.

"Is it stones?" Jens says. "You were standing on the beach and the sound is the waves hitting stones?"

Samara shakes her head. "I used a hydrophone mic in the bay. This is what it sounds like underwater."

"Wow," Leo says. "I thought underwater would sound a lot more . . . wet."

We all hold our breath, listening hard. Slowly, I can hear that the rushing sound isn't like the ocean at all—it's almost synthetic, the bassy pulse of a rave.

"You're sure you recorded that here?" Leo asks, and she nods.

"I told you," she says. "Sound tells a story different from the one you can see."

"Maybe we're approaching this all wrong," Leo says. He chews the inside of his cheek, thinking.

"Do you mean we shouldn't film it?" Jens says.

Leo shakes his head. "No, I mean . . ." He pauses. "Maybe we need to approach this differently. If it's for social media, I mean."

"Differently?" Samara asks him, her eyes narrowing.

He shrugs. "Like, give all these followers a reason to really tune in. A contest."

"A contest?" I say, and he nods.

"Yeah. With teams."

I think back to last night, when I heard Jens say *I'll work on her.* I feel my cheeks burn a little. "There's a lot to uncover about the shark fishing industry here," I say. "Why the villagers *really* abandoned this place, and why people are still scared of it."

"We should explore the houses here," Samara says. "Along the bay."

I boot up my laptop and start writing a list. "And we'll do a story on the shark fishing era of Skúmaskot," I say.

"What about wildlife?" Samara says. "Sharks?"

"You planning to go scuba diving?" Leo says with a laugh.

"We might see them from one of the cliffs?" Samara says. "Loads of bird's nests there."

"I'd like to do some parkour episodes, too," Leo says.

"You could do some tutorials," I say, nodding at Leo.

"I'll stick with the trails," he says, shooting me down, and I feel my cheeks burn.

"Jens," Samara says. "What do you think?"

"I could explore the geography," he says. "Take my drone camera and film as much as I can. Some really old rocks around here."

"I think a contest will work," Leo says. "We form two teams. One team will gather information on the whaling ship era, and the other will try to find information on the research ship era. And Dom, we tell everyone following your project TikTok feed that they get to judge which team wins."

"Imma warn y'all right now," Samara says, before I can answer. "I am *super* competitive."

"Oh yeah?" Leo says, cocking his head. "I'm an ESTP."

"What's an ESTP?" Jens asks, side-tracked.

"It's the Myers-Briggs personality test," Leo says. "ESTP stands for extraverted, sensing . . ."

". . . thinking, and perceiving," Samara finishes, nodding at Leo. "Also known as the Dynamo. Yeah, I'm also an ESTP, thank you."

"Oh my God," Leo says, high-fiving her. "Two ESTPs on one ship. That's like finding two nuclear bombs inside a shoebox."

"I think I saw a book about Myers-Briggs on the floor earlier," I say.

"It's probably been used as firewood," Jens says, almost too quickly, folding his arms.

"I'd say you're an ENTP," Leo tells me.

"Definitely," Samara says.

"What's an ENTP?" I ask.

"You're a Visionary," Samara says, throwing me a wink. "You're a creative, an innovator. Da Vinci was an ENTP. I read about it."

I smile, the tension in my shoulders fading a little.

"Folks, this is riveting," Jens says. "But can we get back to the topic at hand?"

"Yeah," Samara says. "Sorry, Jens. The contest."

"The *Ormen* has two main stories, right?" Leo says. "The era when she served as a whaling ship, circa 1890 to the late 1950s. And then her research ship era, circa 1960s until 1973."

I feel the hairs on the back of my neck prickle. This is changing the whole scope of the project. He's dominating, taking over. And I feel like there's a reason for it.

"So what's the criteria for winning?" Samara asks.

Leo holds up his phone. "We let the followers vote. And the winner gets to . . . open the door to the captain's cabin!" he says.

"Wait . . ." I say.

Jens cuts in. "The captain's cabin is sealed shut. Hardly much of a prize, is it?"

"We'll cut it down. It'll be dramatic," Leo says.

Jens still doesn't look convinced. "We're going to get into teams and find stuff out about the ship. How do we do that, exactly?"

"We're explorers, aren't we?" Leo says. "So, we explore the ship. The ship *is* the story. There will be clues, relics we've not found yet. We've found stuff already . . ."

"And we search online," I say. "We all have laptops, don't we?"

"We do, thanks to you," Leo says with a smile. Again, I have no idea what he means, but he still unnerves me too much to ask. So I smile nervously back and he winks.

"So," Jens says. "Who's doing the era when the *Ormen* was used as a whaling ship?"

"I will," Samara says, raising a hand.

"I'll join you," Leo tells Samara. They fist-bump and look at me and Jens.

"And you two will do the research era," Leo says.

"We get four hours of daylight," I say, "so we'll have to plan everything to find inside those hours."

"Four hours," Samara repeats with a sigh. "What a shame they couldn't decide to destroy the wreck during the summer."

"Maybe we could time travel," Leo says. "Ask the wreck very nicely to land somewhere like California. Or the Maldives."

"Leo," Samara says, irritated at his sarcasm.

"Hey, did you know what Skúmaskot translates as?" Leo asks me.

I shake my head. "I didn't think to translate it."

"'A dark and sinister corner,'" Leo says, triumphant. "Isn't that just so fucking perfect?"

"Godless," Jens adds. "That's what this place is."

"I would say it's more Lovecraftian," I offer.

"What did you say?" Samara asks after a beat.

"Lovecraftian," I say. "You know, after the style of the writer H. P. Lovecraft." Samara's eyebrows raise, and she glances at Leo.

Suddenly, Leo claps his hands together and gives what sounds like a shout of joy.

"Lovecraftian!" he shouts, his arms pumped high above his head. "Did you guys hear that?"

"I don't understand," I tell Samara, but I can see she has a look of excitement on her face. She glances at Jens, who reads her look before turning away.

Leo leaps up and runs to the top of the room. Then, by the post with all the nicks in it, he crouches down, fingering the line of cuts. I stare, wondering what the hell he's doing. Near the middle, he taps one of the cuts and says, "Aha!"

He straightens, then takes his seat by the fire again, like he's just won a prize. He lifts his glass and salutes Jens. "You were right, my friend."

"I'm sorry, right about what?" I say, turning from Leo to Jens.

"It's nothing," Jens says, but I watch Leo closely, the way he turns and glances at the post lined with cuts. He walks up to Samara and high-fives her.

"Different this time," he says to Jens. *"Different."*

"Did you make those marks?" I ask.

He takes a drink before answering. "No," he says. "Of course not."

But the lie is written all over his face, and when I look over at Jens and Samara, I see their faces hold the same look.

A knowingness. Like they've just achieved something.

What is it they're not telling me?

Nicky

I

May 1901
Skúmaskot, Iceland

Nicky curled up in the bed, her legs pulled tight to her chest, her wounded foot beginning to bleed afresh through the bandages. The shock of waking to find Ellis raping her seized her like a cage of thickest iron bound tight against her skin . . . She felt like she'd pitched from one nightmare into a deeper one, a horror beyond words. A thousand needles scratched against her skin, the air turned to smoke, too heavy to breathe. She could hear Lovejoy roaring at Ellis on the deck outside, Ellis squealing like a stuffed pig. *Not yet*, Lovejoy was shouting. *You weren't supposed to yet.*

Dragging the chest across the small room, she pressed it tight against the door, then sank down, barricading it with her weight. On the upper deck, the rig creaked and the anchor clanked, suggesting they were pulling into port. *Iceland*, she thought, suddenly. *The whaling station.*

This would all soon be over. A dark memory.

It was dawn when the ship finally stopped, a heavy rocking toppling the blanket from her bed as the ship moved close to the shore, the engine shuddering to a halt. The deep moan of the ship pulling into port, the high-pitched whine of the pulley lowering a rowboat, the gurgle of the bilges emptying.

She waited until the footsteps faded, the men's voices dying down, before getting to her feet. Her head felt like spun cotton. Although the bleeding had stopped, her foot felt hot and frightfully painful. She would seek help at the whaling station. She would crawl, if she had to, and have them send a telegram to her father. She would find the courage to tell them about Ellis's shameful, cruel assault. Two brutal attacks from two different men in just over a week, her foot destroyed and her strength depleted from appalling food and sleepless nights. She would leave this ship as a different person altogether.

As she moved the chest away from the door and pulled it open, Allan's face was vivid in her mind, telling her to be strong. That she would see him again. That the horrors of the last week would someday be nothing, absolutely nothing.

II

Wrapping herself in a blanket, she stepped out onto the deck, steadying herself with a hand on the wall as she moved up the steps and through the hatch to the upper deck. The sky was vivid gold, a new dawn gilding the hills in the distance. She felt tears of relief pricking her eyes. Iceland had always struck her as a strange place, a mythical land of fire and ice in the distant north, but she had never been gladder to see it.

She glanced across the deck for any sign of Ellis, or the captain, but they were nowhere to be seen. The ship had not pulled into a port as she'd thought, but was docked about half a mile from the

Icelandic coastline. She saw a black sand beach ahead, the land behind rising into the steep apex of a volcano. A little to the right was a large bay filled with boats, houses on either side. No sign of another ship yet, but she could wait for one. Even if it took months, she would get off here and wait.

"Forgive me for asking," a voice said. "But are you all right?"

The boatswain, Daverley, stood next to her, running a loop of rope into a coil. He had seen that she was crying, and she tried to swipe the tears from her cheeks.

"I'm getting off at Skúmaskot," she said. "At the whaling station. When do you expect we'll pull into port?"

He cocked an eyebrow. "The whaling station?"

She nodded. "I expect to arrange a transfer. My father will pay, so money isn't a problem . . ."

"There's no whaling station at Skúmaskot," he said.

"There is," she said, her voice growing louder. "I heard my father talk about it. They built it a couple of years ago . . ."

"They *did*," Daverley said. "But then the villagers burned it down."

"What?" she gasped.

He nodded, searching out the remains of the station.

She looked back at the land beyond the boat in alarm. Cowie and Royle stepped out of the rowing boat and tethered it to a boulder.

"Where are they going, then?" she asked in disbelief.

"They're collecting fresh water," Daverley said. "The villagers are no longer keen on whaling ships, though, so they'll need to be quick."

Just then, she heard shouts from the bay. Cowie and Royle were hefting barrels onto the small rowing boat, and behind them a group of men were racing up the pier. They began to throw rocks at them, then at the ship, though the stones landed far off the hull. Their anger was visible, even from a distance.

At the stern, she could see Lovejoy gesturing at the sails.

"Bo'sun!" Lovejoy called, and Daverley raised his arm in reply.

"Aye, sir," Daverley called. Then, to Nicky: "Excuse me."

The crowd of angry Icelanders had swollen on the shoreline, a shower of stones landing in the water near the rowing boat and the ship. One of the rocks struck Arnott, who slumped over the oars, and another hit one of the *Ormen*'s sails, landing on the deck.

"Bastards!" Lovejoy roared, picking up the stone and flinging it back. It landed not thirty feet into the navy sea between them.

The *Ormen*'s engines roared into life, and as the crew winched up the rowboat the sails unfurled, fattening quickly with wind, driving the ship forward.

As they pulled away from Skúmaskot she watched, horrified, as a line of men formed on the beach, gesticulating and shouting. There was a structure on the far edge of the bay, the blackened wood suggesting that it had been subjected to a fire. In a moment, it was less a structure than a blotch in the distance, a dark stain erasing what chance she'd had to escape.

III

"Captain? A word, if you please."

She found Captain Willingham in his cabin, seated at a broad mahogany desk, his pipe sending an earthy spiral of smoke into the air.

"What ails you, woman?" he sighed when she stormed in, her despair having transformed to simmering fury.

"You told me that I would be able to depart at the whaling station," she said, tears in her eyes. "Why, then, are we sailing away from Skúmaskot?"

"The whaling station was destroyed," he said, pausing to cough into his fist. "The villagers claimed that whalers were wrecking their industry. So they set fire to the station."

"Two years ago," she said forcefully. "Two years! You *knew* there was no chance I could leave."

He lifted his eyes to her in a liquid gaze. "I'm afraid we need to negotiate some new terms. Please, have a seat."

She was shaking all over as she took the seat in front of his desk. "Negotiate? No, Captain. Turn this boat around immediately and return me to Skúmaskot."

"You saw what they did to our man Arnott," the captain said. "He's unconscious. May never wake up. They'll do the same to you."

"I'll take my chances," she said.

The door swung open; Lovejoy entered, a broad grin forming on his face when he saw her. "The Icelanders are a fearsome lot, aren't they?"

She wanted to burst into a scream. "I care *not* if the Icelanders are fierce," she said, trying to control the urge to cry. "Captain, you well know who my father is. One of your men raped me in my bed in the night. My father will have you and your crew hanged when he learns of it."

They were words of anger, but a moment after she said them she saw that they had not struck the fear she had anticipated.

Lovejoy stood next to the captain, the two men sharing a glance. "That's as may be," Lovejoy said at last. "When your father learns of it. Maybe we'd be best just throwing you overboard."

"You would not," she said in a low voice.

"You'll have heard about your father's finances being in a bit of disarray," Captain Willingham said.

Her father's face came to her mind. The awkward, flushed look on his face. *Lie low.* "And what of it?" she said.

"What of it?" Lovejoy parroted with a mock-casual shrug. Then again, "What of it?" Stepping toward her, he repeated it over and over again, each time in a different tone and with exaggerated hand gestures, as though the statement were a conversation, a journey through ignorance and injustice leading all the way to raw fury. She saw it in the men's faces as he ambled around the room: *this* was where the nature of her entrapment lay. *The men were angry at her father.* Captain Willingham, Lovejoy . . . she had found herself in the crossfire of a dispute—about their wages, perhaps, or the precarity of their work. The conditions of the ship . . . Suddenly, she understood that the potential reasons for why these men wanted to take revenge on her father were vast.

She found her anger dissipating, then, as she glimpsed the terrible reason for her internment here on the ship. She was a prisoner. There would be no court, no law above the men who stood leering in front of her. She was theirs to do with as they pleased. Her anger vanished, and in its place, she felt terror.

"Please," she whispered, feeling fearful. "I just want to go home . . ."

Lovejoy positioned himself against a wall, a hand on his chest, his face pulled into a thoughtful expression. It struck her that he was in control, here, and he knew it.

"Have you heard the tale of the selkie wife?" he asked after a moment.

She shook her head, swallowing hard.

Lovejoy pursed his lips and whistled. "Oh, it's a good 'un. And there's a moral to the tale, if you'll listen closely."

Bile curdled in her stomach as Lovejoy prepared himself to share the tale, removing his cap and setting it on her lap, designating her its temporary keeper. Then he licked his palms with a long tongue before running them across the greasy sides of his hair. He positioned himself in front of the fire, like a circus master poised to call in the lions.

"Once," he said, gesticulating with his hand, "when the whaling first began, folk of a certain island realized that their ships could not withstand the wild tempests that lashed the shore. They became skilled at building stronger ships, and sharpening both their harpoons and their aim, but when a hundred men drowned at sea in their efforts to feed the town, a clever woman decided to visit the sea gods and ask what could be done.

"The sea god appeared to her and told her, 'Be ye a Selkie Wife, and the seas will be calm.' The clever woman felt confused. 'A Selkie Wife?' asked she. 'I am wife to my husband, that is all.'

"The sea god explained that if she were to accompany her husband on his next voyage as wife to both him and the sea god, one night in the husband's bed, another in that of the sea god's, the men would be spared, and their hunt would feed their town for a season. The clever woman agreed, understanding that, in order to share the bed of the sea god, she would be changed for a time, part fish, in order to survive the depths, returning at dawn both to her former self and to her husband's bed.

"As promised, the hunt yielded more flesh and blubber than ever before, and the people lived long and prosperous."

Lovejoy fell silent, frozen in a pose with his hands held high, as though he had concluded the performance of a stage play for children, awaiting a round of applause. Nicky felt the room tilt, her stomach in a tight knot. She was panting loudly from fear, now, unable to hide it.

"As you'll no doubt have noticed," Lovejoy said, approaching her slowly, his gaze darkening. "We're missing a selkie wife on the *Ormen*. And I'm sure the tale has illustrated how much we need one."

"Please," she said, her eyes dropping to his feet. "I have a husband. My family will be worried . . ."

"You have more than one husband now, selkie," Lovejoy said, as though she had won a prize. "You have a whole ship of husbands."

"Captain," she said, pleading. "Surely your honor forbids you from . . ."

Just then, Lovejoy bent toward her, leaning his hands on the arms of the chair and drawing himself close until his nose touched hers.

"A selkie wife does not speak," he said. Then, straightening sharply, he struck her hard across the face. He caught the bruised part of her cheekbone that still ached from where the man in the park had struck her. The room spun, and she gave a loud cry of pain.

Drawing a trembling hand to the smarting cheek, she looked in horror at Captain Willingham. Was he going to allow this? She watched, her stomach dropping, as something skidded across his face. A wariness.

"You will be fed while you are on board," he said, a slight apology in his tone. "And Reid will assist you with obtaining fresh water for bathing and drinking."

She broke down then, the reality of what lay ahead pulling her apart, bone by bone. *Yes*, she thought. *He will allow this. He is party to it.*

"You may say 'Aye, Captain,'" he said, a little louder.

Her father's eyes flashed in her mind. The bird trapped in his palms. Its sooted wings.

She took a breath, the words like burning coals in her throat.

"Aye, Captain."

IV

That night, when the pain in Nicky's foot grew so intense that she wanted to howl for hours, she found the bottle of pills that Dr. O'Regan had given her. The effects were quick—a soft mist seemed to bloom in the cabin, distancing the pain as though it were a memory of an injury, something she could only recall with her mind.

She took off the shirt and heavy fisherman's trousers and replaced them with her dress. It felt warm, and she felt less exposed than she had been in the shirt and trousers. Then, too woozy to stand up any longer, she lay back in the bed, tugging at the gauze around her foot. It felt too tight, so she unwrapped it entirely, staring hazily at the wound just beneath her ankle, on the instep. Dr. O'Regan had stitched it roughly, leaving huge gaps between each stitch, so she could see the bone beneath.

Except, when she looked again, it appeared that her ankle bone had darkened, the wet white sliver between the folds of raw skin now dark gray. She moved closer to the lamp, arching over it. She could feel no pain, now, and it was likely the drugs making her wound appear different. But even so . . . she stared down, noticing that her toes seemed different, too. They were still bruised and swollen, but they were folding in toward each other, the skin shimmering.

Like the pelt of a seal, growing beneath her skin.

Dominique

I

December 2023
Skúmaskot, Iceland

I think I've managed to fix the internet terminal, but it is *very* temperamental. We stand in front of the shipwreck and film each team—me and Jens, then Leo and Samara—explaining how we're going to research the two different eras of the ship and then present our findings, and they get to judge which of the two research projects is the winner. Jens throws a bit of a curve ball while we're filming, offering two voters a thousand pounds each.

When Leo stops filming I confront Jens, alarmed at what he's promising.

"We don't have that kind of budget," I say. "We don't have *any* budget."

Jens holds up his hands. "I never asked you to contribute to it. I'll pay for it, okay?"

"Like, how will you choose which voters to give the money to?" Samara asks.

"At random," Jens says with a shrug. "We'll set up a poll for everyone to vote on the research teams. The voting will be anonymous, but we'll set up a place for everyone who voted to tag themselves. And then we can run it through a random selection app and give the prizes to the winners."

"Fair enough. It's his money, I suppose."

We've also made a plan to help us cope with the lack of sunlight. Every morning, we get up at eight, make coffee, and exercise. The exercise part is important to help us cope with the cold and the dark, which Samara says will drive us mad if we don't learn to adjust. Jens likes to run up and down the beach, I guess because the snow isn't as bad there, and Samara does press-ups against the rocks that Leo uses for his parkour. He does it over the top of the *Ormen*, which is amazing. We film it three or four times and people love it.

Our follower count is skyrocketing now. I think most of them have followed just for Leo's stunts. And it turns out that Samara is great behind the camera, much better than me, though she'd argue otherwise. She's funny and warm, whereas I'm awkward and come across a bit unfriendly, a bit cold. It's a shock to the system, because I don't see myself as unfriendly and cold. Maybe it takes practice. In the meantime I'm fine to take a step back and let her talk to the followers.

At nine, we begin preparing firewood, or bashing doors, as I call it—we're using the old doors of the ship for firewood, but they're a bugger to break up. Yesterday, Samara made us film her doing it and she was *fabulous*. She should have been a TV host or something, because her personality comes right through the lens. Samara has that rare mix of dorky and intelligent and smooth. Few people can make breaking an old door apart look dignified and even funny, but she manages it.

At ten, more coffee, then it's research until three, when it's properly dark. After that, we have personal time until seven, and then we meet up in the main cabin for dinner.

The fire bucket has made a huge difference to our camaraderie; in the evenings, we all sit around the fire with a bottle of wine and talk, and it has helped us bond as a team. We've even filmed some of that and uploaded it to the Whale Ship TikTok and it went down well.

The next day, while the sun gasps out a few rays of thin light, I suggest that we do some livestreaming while we have the battery power.

Jens films me climbing down the ladder of the *Ormen* to update our followers on the research progress.

"Hi, folks, how are you all this morning? Here in Skúmaskot it's bloody freezing, but gorgeous. We've not had much of Iceland's famous wind lately, just a lot of fog, which is wrapping us all in a big blanket. Anyway, vote Team Research Era! Jens and I have learned that Skúmaskot was not just a fishing village but a *shark* fishing village, back in the eighteen and nineteen hundreds, and for reasons we don't quite know, everyone up and left at the turn of the twentieth century. So, tune in later on when we'll be uploading all our fabulous content!"

Jens signals to me a thumbs-up and logs off.

"How many viewers?" I ask.

"Eighty-five," he says, and I frown. "It's actually not bad, considering the time of day and how short that snippet was. We've had a lot of new followers on the Whale Ship TikTok."

"How many?" I ask, pulling out my own phone to check.

"Four hundred new ones overnight," Jens says. "And some new subscribers on the Patreon."

Thank God, I think.

"That's amazing," Samara says, high-fiving Leo. Then, catching the look of confusion on my face: "Leo uploaded some parkour footage, didn't you see it?"

"I'm just seeing it now," I say, flicking through six new videos. They are brilliant. I was a bit worried that the snow would prevent Leo from doing anything parkour-ish, but he's got cool footage leaping across the rocks at the top of the *Ormen*, cutting between Samara's camera and a headcam.

The sun is already low and a heavy fog blots out what remains of the light. The water in the bay isn't frozen over completely, but there are sections along the beach that are frozen solid, so Samara shows us where she drilled a hole about an inch in diameter to record the sound. She crouches down, holding a pebble in one hand and a microphone in the other. Then she plugs a set of headphones into her recorder and hands them to me.

"Listen," she says, holding up the pebble and angling the recorder at the hole. And then she drops the pebble down. It makes the most incredible sound, not what I expected at all. Like lightsabers, with the whipcrack of lightning.

"It's the reverberations of the stone off the ice," she says. "Pretty neat, huh?"

She lets Jens listen in, then Leo, and we all have the same reaction.

"Told you," Samara says, smiling. "The sounds of the dead."

"Like anything is dead there," Leo says, teasing. "It's ice, for God's sake."

"This is *dead* ice," Samara says. "Look it up. It's ice that isn't moving."

We watch as she throws another pebble down, the same strange echoes calling back through the earphones. I give a shiver this time, realizing a moment later how Samara's explanation has affected me. *The sounds of the dead.*

"Speaking of sound," Leo says then. "I could have sworn I heard someone singing last night."

Samara cocks her head. "Singing?"

"Outside," Leo says. "A woman's voice." He glances at me. "Wasn't you, was it, Dom? Singing us all a lullaby."

I feel an icy chill up my spine, recalling my first night here. Those rising five notes, clear as a bell. "Of course not," I say, keeping my eyes on the ground.

"I'm going to set up a Spotify link for the sound documentary," Samara says, changing the topic.

I tell her it's a great idea. I had no idea that sound could do so much. But I'm fast becoming a convert, what with the ideas that Samara is bringing to the project. She explained what a field recording can offer in capturing a sense of place, how everywhere place is porous and filled with echoes.

II

We decide to explore the abandoned village of Skúmaskot on the other side of the bay. It takes us almost an hour to walk there. It's not actually that far, maybe a half-mile loop, but the snow is deeper on the far side than it is on the beach, nudging right up to the shore. Fresh virgin white that comes up to our waists, huge chunks of ice floating in the bay.

It isn't completely frozen, though, as the sea cuts rivulets through, so we can't skate across. We have to climb up the side of the volcano to find a pathway, and even there we're forced to zigzag up and down the valley to avoid the geothermal steam pumping out of the earth.

When we finally make it to the village on the other side, we discover that there are about thirty buildings, not just the ten that I had counted from the other side of the bay. The older buildings are traditional *torfbæir*, turf houses, constructed out of flat stones and turf, with grassy A-frame rooftops that are doused with snow—more like igloos than turf houses. Leo is able to climb up there and film the old turf beneath the snow.

Snow has clogged the doorways, though we could enter some of the tin huts that were still standing. They're empty, save some bits of turf. We manage to pull some of it out and carry it back to the ship for the fire.

The next morning, it's foggy, and the air inside my cabin is so cold it stings my face. Leo lights the fire bucket and Samara makes hot tomato soup for breakfast, dishing it into our plastic bowls. I don't question it. It's a relief to hold something warm in my hands, and the flames that begin to lick the sides of the oil can feel so good that I think for a moment about the fire gods worshipped by ancient tribes. I would worship this oil can, and this soup, simply because they bring respite from the biting cold.

We eat in silence, too cold to speak. But after a few moments, Jens gets up and says he's going outside for a walk.

"Are you off to do some filming?" I ask.

He shakes his head, not making eye contact. "Just a walk. Got to stay fit."

"If you're not taking your drone," Samara says, "could I borrow it? Just for a little bit?"

Jens raises his eyebrows, and I wait for him to say no.

"I was going to film more of Leo's stunts," Samara explains. "But I kind of thought it might be cool to alternate between the headcam and the drone this time."

"Sure," Jens says. "Do you know how to use it?"

Samara nods. "I think so. I'll look after it, I promise."

He takes out the controller and sits down next to her, giving her the lowdown on how to maneuver it.

"How about I film from the ship?" I say. I'm feeling warmer now, and outside the fog is beginning to lift. "We can cut between the three shots. Get some wide shots to create more perspective."

"Sounds great," Leo says.

Samara and Leo head off toward the rocks at the far end of the beach. It's still light, though just barely. I'm glad I suggested filming from the stern of the *Ormen*—the waves are spectacular, rising up to the deck like charging horses before spreading across the black sand as a fine white lace, and the trio of lava rocks sticking out of the sand look epic against the purpling sky. They look like guardians, watching over the ship. A dramatic canvas for a dramatic scene, in other words.

I wait while Leo stretches his calves and Samara sends the drone farther up the bay, capturing landscape footage before he starts.

I set my coffee mug on the ground and begin filming; my thinking is that I will capture more than I need and edit accordingly.

When I press record, I notice a third figure on the beach, about ten feet away from Leo. A woman, judging from the slight curve at the waist and the long hair.

I stare and squint, determined not to lose sight of her. It's *her*, the woman I saw the first day. I open my mouth to call out, then decide to keep filming.

Leo has stopped stretching, his hands on his hips, his face turned to her. Samara turns back, too, clutching the controller and the drone. I watch with intensity. They're talking to this woman. I give a small laugh. Thank God. I'd thought I was seeing things before.

She's not wearing a hat or coat, though, and it's freezing. I can see her dark hair and what looks like a pale jumpsuit or dress. I lower the camera quickly, wondering if I should go and help. But then Leo turns to me and waves, like he's inviting me to come and join them. Maybe the woman needs help.

I head across the deck quickly and climb down the ladder, my mind racing. Who is she, and how long has she been out here? How has she managed to survive these temperatures without proper clothing?

By the time I climb down the ladder, the woman is no longer there. Leo and Samara are walking back toward me, chatting. The woman is gone.

"Did you get it?" Leo says when I reach them.

"Oh my God, tell me you got that backflip off the big rock," Samara says to me. "I think I messed up with the drone. It was incredible, wasn't it?"

I open my mouth but realize I'm too confused to answer.

"You okay?" Samara asks. "You look like you saw a ghost."

I give a nervous laugh, and their faces fall. "Who were you talking to?" I ask.

"Who?" Samara says.

I tell them both what I'd seen, just minutes before—a woman standing between them. They looked like they were all chatting. I thought maybe she needed help. She wasn't dressed like the rest of us, all wrapped up in puffer coats and woolly hats. She was wearing a long, pale dress, no hat.

Leo and Samara turn back to stare at the spot on the beach with the rocks.

"When?" Samara says. "Where is she?"

I feel awkward, and I see Leo's gaze hardening.

"But you got the footage, right?" he asks.

"She was literally right here," I say, "where you both were standing by the rocks." I pull out my phone to show him.

I rewind the footage right to the beginning. Leo and Samara

appear on the screen but there's nothing of the woman. I try again, then zoom in.

"Where?" Leo asks.

I can feel myself growing flustered. Samara and Leo are sharing looks while I rewind the footage. Where the hell is it?

"I really did see someone," I say. "It looked like you were all talking. I have no idea why it didn't film . . ."

Leo's expression darkens. "Are you fucking with me?" he says.

I snap my head up. "No, I'm not."

I feel so confused. I keep rewinding the footage, as though the woman will appear again. Why isn't she there? I saw her on the screen. I *know* I filmed her.

Samara puts a hand on his shoulder to reassure him. "How about we go back and I'll get it from the ship?" she says.

Leo looks up. "The light will be gone soon. We can do it tomorrow."

"I must have been mistaken," I say quietly, my cheeks burning. Leo throws me a look of disgust before turning and heading to the *Ormen*.

Inside, I feel embarrassed all over again. Jens is back from his walk and is making a coffee.

"Hey," he says. "You get the footage?"

"No, we fucking didn't," Leo says, and storms off to his cabin.

"I think I'll go for a walk," I say.

"You want company?" Jens asked.

I still feel too embarrassed. "I'll be fine," I say. "I'm just heading along the beach."

The truth is, I have a small torch in my pocket, and I am heading back along the beach specifically to check out the big rocks where I saw the woman next to Leo and Samara.

I don't know what I'm looking for, exactly. But I know I saw something. I suspect I'll find that the rocks are angled in a way that creates a shadow, and even though it's getting dark I have this urge to see it up close and piece together the puzzle.

The sea is roaring and hissing, the powerful waves punching down on the sand. I try to keep clear of the tide in case I get dragged out by a rogue wave—I know the drill—so it takes a while until I can step up onto the rocks and check them out.

Up close, they are exactly as they appeared from the *Ormen*, only bigger and rougher, no sign of shadow casting or hidden contours.

I understand a little more now why Leo was disappointed that I didn't capture his backflip; they're huge—one fall and he'd have broken his neck.

I walk back to the ship, defeated and angry at myself. Leo hates me now, I'm pretty sure of it.

I brought my motion sensor module, which attaches to the camera and forces it to turn toward movement; I usually use it when there are predators about.

Now I set up my camera on a tripod and position it at the window of the main cabin that overlooks the beach. The sensor is super sensitive, and it makes the camera record the first ten seconds of whatever it picks up. I think I've done this for myself more than anything else.

"What's that for?" Samara asks when she sees what I'm doing.

"To film the horses," I say. "I saw them the other night, galloping across the beach."

"Really?" she says. "I've not seen any."

The truth is more sinister than horses.

I need to prove to myself that I saw what I saw.

Nicky

I

May 1901
90 miles north of Skúmaskot, Iceland

The storm struck as the *Ormen* crossed the Arctic Circle.

Waves tall as houses reared up at the bow, pummeling the deck so hard the crew feared the ship would capsize. Water thundered down the stairs, flooding both decks. Hens carried into cabins, all the lambs plucked from the hold, tumbled like wet cloths.

Nicky was an open wound, the burning agony of her foot slamming through her bones. She followed the men up to the top deck, where the scene of white-crowned squalls greeted her, a forest with teeth, watery oaks swaying in the gale. The wind flung anything that wasn't tethered down.

"Get back downstairs!" Lovejoy roared at her, but she decided she needed to see the tempest. She was freezing cold, wearing only a dress. But if she was going to die, she wanted to see the sky again.

And the storm—it was a divine punishment, the beautiful and terrible end of the world, as though the *Ormen* were crossing the River Styx and taking them all to hell through a valley of monstrous waves. Nicky managed to tether herself to the rig as the nightmare unfolded in front of her—the hands frantically hauling the sails, two of them torn and jagged above, the hold officer and harpooners heaving buckets of water from the deck while the surgeon and steward hefted an injured crewmate from the ground and hauled him to the surgery. She saw blood and vomit pooling on the deck, only to be washed clean by a wave that came punching down, ripping one of the crew from the rig and carrying him far off to sea.

The ship made a sound like a bear growling, listing for a moment at a terrifying angle, sure to plunge into the deep. Stanchions, davits, kegs, and a try-pot all showering down from the deck into the ocean. The sound of screaming beneath the deafening roar of waves, a man's voice calling out the Lord's Prayer.

Nicky felt herself being hurled upside down against the rig, the power of the water flipping her like a rag. Her head collided with something hard, and everything fell into silence.

Olav

September 1902
Skúmaskot, Iceland

He was known as a belligerent drunk and for leaving dark marks on his wife's face on market day, when invariably takings were slim. The villagers of Skúmaskot had long memories and held longer grudges, and so he was the first in a long line of horse breeders to struggle to feed his children.

The night Olav saw the creature, however, he was feeling rather at peace with the world, and with his lot in life. His horses were healthy, the yield of new foals larger than last year's. Forty-eight foals, thirty of them already sold at market. Money had been tight for years but now he felt he could breathe a little easier. He could afford to clothe his children and fix the holes in the walls of their small home. His son, Gunnar, had been asking for a pet dog. He would buy a pet dog.

He decided that Skúmaskot in September was the most beautiful place in the world. The evening was warm, and he had drunk mead at the home of his friend Ragnar before heading off home via the beach. He liked to check on the horses, make sure none of the wilder ones had broken free from the field. More than once he had found the two copper ones racing along the beach. His father had punished such horses with a whip, but he prided himself on taking a gentler hand. Besides, an injured horse sold for less at market.

The midnight sun was often torturous, especially when the children were young, but tonight he greeted the tide with resolve and contentment, the soft blush of the sun and the downy heather lifting his heart.

And then he saw her.

Before him, the shape of a woman, lying on a rock. He squinted, puzzled. Her arms were raised up over her head, her face buried into the sand. He could see that she was naked to the waist, a streak of pale wet skin catching the light.

He staggered toward her. She had likely gone for a swim. Perhaps she had fainted, or drowned. Either way, he was aroused.

Standing over her, he felt his jaw drop. Where he expected to find two slender legs was a thick black tail, like a seal, a set of flippers deep in the sand. When he recovered, he reached down and grabbed one of her arms, pulling her roughly over. Two black eyes flung open, the mouth pulled back in a snarl. He caught sight of the teeth, sharp as a shark's, the gray gums, before stumbling backward with a shout.

He found himself on all fours, shaken to the core. He looked up, expecting to see her sitting upright, primed to attack. That face. A demonic, inhuman face. And the tail . . .

But she was gone. He jumped again in fright, scanning the beach on either side. No sign. No marks on the sand. He rose to his feet, only to stumble backward with confusion. She had been right there. He had seen her. He had seen *it.*

Olav was not the same after that. How could he be? He had touched the creature. He felt possessed. He drank every night and used his fists on his wife, and when Ragnar intervened he took a swing at him, too. He was losing his mind. He visited the oldest woman in Skúmaskot, Katla, who was said to be a white witch.

Tell me, he asked her. *Am I cursed? I touched it.*

She looked him over with her pale sharp eyes, and nodded. *Yes. She cursed you. As she will curse others. Beware.*

Some years later, he saw her again. In the field with the horses. A moment, and there she was again. In his home, by the hearth. In place of his wife in his bed.

He found himself holding a knife in one hand and his foot with the other. It made sense, the impulse. Somewhere in the darkness, someone was singing. He should make his feet like flippers in order to swim to her swiftly. The song told him this plan.

His wife saw the blood and locked her children's doors, then her own, leaving him to it.

At the shore, he dropped to his hands and knees, crawling. He had cut his feet to the bone, blood and muscle trailing in the sand behind him. His feet split between the second and third toes.

He saw her head bobbing above the water, and lunged into the cool waves. Her black eyes, watching him. The dark water, swallowing him whole.

Dominique

I

December 2023
Skúmaskot, Iceland

I am in Skúmaskot, but something is different.

It is summertime, but I recognize the volcano and the beach, and the three rocks at the far end. No snow, gleaming fields, green as malachite, a leathery sea against the black sand. The bay is brimming with boats, the row of turf houses bright with lights and noise. People move busily through the fields behind the volcano. Several of the fields contain horses. Dozens of Icelandic horses with their distinctive shaggy coats and stocky build. I see a child riding one of them, a boy of about ten, a man walking behind. They are moving the horses to a gated entrance overlooking the bay.

I know without any doubt that the man and boy can't see me. I feel filled with rage, absolutely burning with it. As the man opens the gate I start to sing, each note of the melody carrying my craving for revenge into the wind. None of the people hear me, but the horses do. The one carrying the boy rears up, blond mane flying, a loud whinny drawing the man's attention. He races to help the boy, who has fallen off, but as he does so the rest of the horses bolt toward the gate. They have been spooked by my song, sent into a wild stampede. The gate is unlocked, and so they run loose down the fields.

As the man helps the boy to his feet, he spots me, just for a moment. Wide-eyed terror skids across his face as he sees me, a shape in the mist. I feel suddenly conscious of myself, and how I appear to him—I wear a long, ragged dress, seaweed fronds braided through my hair, and my feet—no tail this time—are naked. I bare my teeth at him, revealing my black gums and my pointed teeth, sharp as a pike's.

And I don't stop singing, not even when the horses plunge off the side of the cliff, down, down onto the rocks below.

I wake with a gasp, the walls of the cabin filled with shadows, reminding me where I am. My sleeping bag feels damp, and for a moment I think I've pissed myself. No—it's sweat. I am absolutely soaking with sweat, my heart pounding.

What is *wrong* with me? Why am I having such crazy dreams?

I get up and fetch my flask, sipping the cool water slowly. Outside, the rush of the sea is rhythmic, a kind of *wash-wash* on repeat, and I focus on it.

It felt more than a dream. That's what is freaking me out here. It felt like a vision.

I head upstairs and make a pot of coffee, then decide to crack open my pancake mix and make an apology breakfast for the others. I feel vulnerable, in need of company, which is bizarre. I feel scared.

"Wow, smells amazing," Samara says when she surfaces through the hatch a half hour later.

"Come and sit down," I tell her, and she's followed soon after by Jens and Leo.

"I wanted to apologize," I tell Leo. "I honestly didn't mean to fudge the recording."

He shrugs. "That's okay. I probably overreacted. I'm a bit of a hothead, in case you hadn't noticed."

I feel a weight slide off my shoulders. "And Jens," I tell him. "I snapped at you the other day, about the contest money. Sorry."

He gives a small smile. "Hey, no problem."

"Speaking of," Leo says. "How's the research?"

I sigh. "I've barely started. I got excited when one of the links on the Wikipedia page took me to a paper published by someone who had carried out research into Arctic Sea ice in 1973. They mentioned the ship and referred to it as 'a former whaler, named the *Ormen*.'"

"That's encouraging," Samara says. "It must have brought up some websites? Or research papers?"

"I found some links to academic papers on Google Scholar," I say, "but they all cost a fortune to purchase. Like, twenty-five quid per download."

"I can split it, if you want?" Jens says, and I nod, grateful.

After breakfast, Jens and I venture down into the hold. We take solar lanterns and set them up on the stairs while we wade through the disgusting, ice-cold water. It's my first time down here and I hide how unnerved I am, how anxious, and I don't know why. I mean, of course it's dangerous—the decks above could suddenly give way and collapse on top of us, or there could be toxins down here that Leo didn't encounter, or we could get stuck and die of hypothermia . . . take your pick. But my anxiety is placed elsewhere. It's the feel of this place. It holds something, a feeling. Of course, I say none of this to Jens because he'll think I'm crazy.

I concentrate instead on sorting through the personal effects that I find there, some of them in barrels and containers, spared from the water. So many books, a mixture of novels and academic texts about Arctic Sea ice and geology.

One of the books has a message written inside—*para Diego de tu Abuela, Navidad 1970.*

"Look," I call to Jens. "You think this belonged to someone on board the ship?"

He wades over to me, shining his torch down on the inscription. "For Diego from your grandmother, Christmas 1970." He wipes his face and squints down again. "We should google it and see what comes up."

"Not much to go on," I say. "Not even a surname."

"I should show you what I found about the research era," he says, turning and flashing his light at the hatch. "About the ghost ship."

"Wait, what?" I ask, reeling. "What ghost ship?"

He turns back to me and furrows his brow. "You don't know about the ghost ship?"

II

"You must have read somewhere online that the crew went missing?" Jens says.

"The ship was abandoned," I say. "It drifted over the Barents Sea . . ."

"Yes, but they never found the crew. They literally vanished." He takes a breath. "Except for one man. The coast guard found him."

"That's not what I read," I say. "I read that no one was on board. That the crew got off the ship and instead of spending money dismantling an old ship, they just let it drift across the ocean."

"What you read was whitewash," Jens says.

"Whitewash?"

He nods. "It was a cover-up. I'll show you."

I follow him through the hatch to the lower deck, where we head into our respective cabins to get dried and changed. A few minutes later, he knocks on my door.

"Am I okay to come into your room?"

"Sure," I say, though the only space is inside my tent. He steps inside and sits down on the floor beside me, his iPad on his lap. "Show me what you found. About the ghost ship."

It isn't a news article that he finds, but a 2012 scholarly article making a case for uncrewed vessel technology.

The highlighted line says: *. . . and the 1890 barque-rigged steam hybrid known as the* Ormen, *found floating in the Barents Sea in 1973, the crew completely vanished and never located . . .*

I look at him, astonished. "Can we find some more on this? Like, how and why, and so on?"

"Already done it," he says, clicking on a tiny column in the *New York Times*.

Missing Crew Still Not Found, August 31, 1973

> A research team based off the coast of Svalbard is still missing after the coast guard located their vessel adrift and unmanned in the Barents Sea. Families are working with authorities in the High Arctic to provide information about letters sent home and details of the crew's last moments.

"Shit," I say, reading it over again. "I thought the crew just left the ship. Surely they found out what happened?"

He shows me his search history, a long scrolling list of websites. "I've not found anything that suggests that," he says. "It all seems pretty ominous, right?"

I start to shake, still cold after wading through the icy water in the hold.

"Are you all right?" Jens asks.

"I keep having dreams," I say.

"What kind of dreams?"

I rub my forehead, which has started to throb. "Nothing."

"Don't dismiss it," he says. "Tell me."

I sigh. "Just crazy nightmares. Like mermaids with these hideous faces. I dreamed about Skúmaskot. About horses . . ."

"Horses?" he asks.

"I saw them diving off a cliff, because I possessed them." My throat tightens with a knot, squeezing my voice into a sob. "Oh God," I say, clasping my hands to my mouth. "Sorry. I'm emotional because I'm not sleeping properly."

"I'll give you some sleeping pills," he says. "And make sure you go outside when the sun is up. Icelandic winters are not for the faint of heart."

I nod and say I will, but when he leaves, I zip up my tent and curl up in my sleeping bag. And of course, I dream—about an empty ship, floating on a vast ocean. Blood trickling from a wall onto the floor below, and a bird pecking at a faceless corpse.

III

I don't know how long I sleep for, but I wake to laughter. It's a pleasant sound, bringing me out of my dreams with relief.

Upstairs, the others are in the main cabin, the oil cans burning brightly. They're all a little drunk.

"Come and have a seat, Dominique," Leo says. His voice is slurred, but there isn't the usual nastiness buried in his tone. I take a seat opposite. He hands me a bottle of wine, but as I go to take it, he pulls it back.

"First, you have to tell us something."

I glance nervously at Samara and Jens. "Okay."

"What is it you want with us?" Leo says.

I try to get the joke. "What do I want with you?"

"Yeah, like—when's it all going to stop?"

I blink, waiting for the punch line. "I don't get you, Leo."

This makes Jens laugh, which in turn sparks Samara's laughter, but they both sound forced. "No one gets Leo but Leo."

"I want a hot shower," I tell him, "clean clothes, and a glass for my wine. And a steak."

"Medium rare?" Jens asks.

"Exactly."

"That isn't what I asked," Leo says, his smile fading. The sharpness in his eyes is back. "I asked what do you want *with us*."

"Come on, Leo," Samara says, tapping his leg. "Play nice."

"I'm fucking done playing this game," he snaps.

"What do you want with *me*?" I ask, playfully. "I was here first, remember?"

He lifts his eyes to mine, a snarl forming on his face. "You don't want to know," he says, and I flinch. Leo's moods are like storm clouds passing through the ship. He makes me want to shrink into myself.

"Well, I would like you to pass the wine," Samara says to me, deflecting Leo's surliness with a light tone.

I try to steady my hand in order to pour myself a tumbler before handing it to her. The fire is soothing, and the wooden boards that Leo pinned to the windows are holding up. I allow myself to breathe deeply, grateful for food and warmth.

"Seriously, though," Samara says thoughtfully. "If I could have anything, I think I'd have one day with Lenny."

"Lenny?" I ask.

"My dog," she says. "I found him while I was at college in a box behind a dumpster. He lived until he was thirteen, and then he died."

"You'd ask for just one more day?" Leo says. "Why not a lifetime? Or like, forever?"

She nods, her eyes moistening. "Forever, then. Forever *and* a day."

"My old home," Jens says then. "That's what I'd ask for."

Leo bristles. "Who is it we're asking this stuff for, exactly?"

"The one I shared with my wife," Jens continues, ignoring him.

I stare at him, shocked. I hadn't figured Jens was married.

"Your wife?" Leo asks, a surprised laugh in his voice, as though he's thinking the same thing as me. "God, Jens. You have a *wife*? Since when?"

"She's dead," Jens replies in a flat voice. "Our house was by the river. She used to sit in the side garden looking out, sun in her face. Beautiful row of terraced houses, that whole block. I turned up a few years ago, hoping to remember her. Maybe lay a bouquet at her favorite spot. They turned the whole block into an indoor trampoline park."

"God," Samara says, disgusted.

"That's rough," Leo says.

"I'm sorry," I tell him, thinking of how sad his eyes are.

"Eilidh," he says, his face aglow as he stares at the fire. "That was her name."

"Eilidh," I repeat.

"Do you think I'll ever see her again?" he asks. It takes me a moment to realize he's asking me.

"I don't know," I say, stumbling over my words. "I mean, I hope so, right?"

"But if it were up to you," he says, turning to face me. "What would you say?"

What would *I say*? "I'd say, absolutely," I tell him, and his face lights up. “Absolutely, you’d see her again. And Samara would be with her dog. And Leo would be with . . . whoever or whatever Leo wants to be with.”

“Lucas,” he says hoarsely.

“With Lucas,” I say, raising my glass. Samara does the same, and we repeat their names.

With Lucas. With Lenny. With Eilidh.

But I don’t add my own. That space in my mind is a blank, and it puzzles me.

Why isn’t there someone, or something there? I can feel there is. But I can’t remember their name.

Nicky

I

May 1901
20 miles northwest of Skúmaskot, Iceland

Clouds.

A blue sky.

The sound of someone vomiting.

She came to on her back by the try-pot, which had somehow been flung back onto the deck, though now upside down. Next to her was the body of a dead lamb, and one of the men. Collins, she recalled, from his black neckerchief. Daverley approached with Captain Willingham, their faces drawn as they lowered to inspect Collins. His head was turned and his eyes stared ahead, fixed on her, his right arm reaching out.

"Where's Ellis?" Daverley asked Reid, who shivered next to him, soaked to the bone but otherwise spared. He shook his head, and the captain grimaced. Two men gone. And the storm wasn't finished with them.

"You best get downstairs to your cabin," Daverley told her. He pointed grimly to a dark line on the horizon. "There are more of those waves coming, bigger than before. Go to your cabin and lock the door."

He said it with enough urgency to persuade her to obey. She nodded, then made her way quickly down the stairs to the deck, which sat in three inches of water. A brown hen floated past, seemingly content to brood on the water, and in a corner a cow ate from a burst bag of oats. Outside the captain's room was a row of sandbags, preventing water from entering. If the maps got wet, they were done for.

She went into her room and made to shut the door, but just then a hand slapped on the wood, stopping it. Lovejoy stood there, that horrible, grimacing grin on his face, close enough for her to see the black holes in his teeth.

"What are you doing?" she said. Then, braver: "Why aren't you up on the deck helping with everyone else?"

"Ellis is dead," he said, looking her up and down. "You must be happy."

The pills made her reactions slow and sluggish, so as he reached out to touch her cheek, she found she could do no more than freeze to the spot, her eyes on his.

"*My* selkie wife," he said, stretching a smile across his black teeth.

II

The first night, he stayed with her a while, after. The length of him on the small bed, insisting that she lie with her arm across his round chest, his filthy hand gripping hers. She felt drenched in shame. In guilt. In disgust. She felt like the most integral part of her had been scooped out. She felt like she wanted to fold inward, in, in, never to return. She was in two places at once. On that hideous bed and elsewhere, floating, screaming, both at the same time.

Lovejoy talked as though nothing had happened, as though they had always been confidants, and not strangers, she held hostage to his dark desires. He told her about his childhood. About his sons, Ben, Arthur, and Philip. Scoundrels, he said, picking his teeth. In and out of prison, one of them locked up now for good. Murder. Another child in the highlands from a relationship in his youth. His own years in prison, and the beatings he meted there.

She began to hum. It was half intentional, a bidding of her body to close out the very fact of him, his gravelly voice, the rasp and wheeze of his chest under her ear. The stubborn thud of his heartbeat.

"What's that you're singing, selkie?" he asked.

She didn't answer, not verbally. Hymns she had sung in church and school, lullabies her mother had sung to her as a child . . . they spilled out from her now, soft, wordless. An involuntary response to what had happened. To what he had done.

He grew angry when she didn't respond, tightening his grip on her arm and making threats, then pushing her off him and storming angrily out of the cabin.

In the darkness, she curled the bedclothes around her aching body. The melodies continued in her head, seeping from her memories, until sleep rescued her with its wild and dreamless silence.

Dominique

I

December 2023
Skúmaskot, Iceland

The weather becomes what Jens calls "wolf weather," meaning that the elements want to eat us.

It reaches minus nineteen, the kind of cold that threatens to peel off your skin, or turn your digits into charcoal from frostbite. Sometimes the dark is that velvety midnight blackness, and around lunchtime it fades to a moth-light, owlish and ethereal, softening the lines of the hills in the distance and the zigzag of the turf houses on the other side of the bay. The desalination tank provides fresh water for drinking and technically washing, but we've all avoided washing in case it runs dry. It's so cold that we all live in our outdoor gear pretty much all the time now, except for the evenings, when Leo gets the fires going.

We have five oil-can fires, three dotted around the main cabin and two in the corridor in the lower deck. It's a workout, keeping them all lit. It's a fire hazard, quite literally, and I have dreams about the ship burning down with us inside it. We prop them up with old metal hooks from the upper deck, otherwise the wind finds a way inside and knocks them over.

I had the same experience as I did earlier in the week. I went downstairs to use the bathroom—a pot, whose contents that we throw into the sea, nothing glamorous—and when I was coming back up the stairs into the main cabin I heard whispering. Leo, mostly; Samara saying something back in somber tones. When I popped my head up through the hatch, the whispering stopped, but I heard it.

We're trapped, remember?

Leo's voice this time.

I pretended I hadn't heard anything when I emerged, covertly reading the room to deduce if anyone was going to fill me in. But of course, they didn't, and I've been trying to work out what he might have meant.

I have no idea. If he means they're trapped by the weather, I think it's an exaggeration—the snow is still heavy and the winds are savage, but trapped? Not exactly.

I've put the whole thing down to eccentricity. He's a weird guy. I'm going to keep out of his way until the project is done.

The next day, there is no proper sunlight, and we start talking to our battery packs, willing them to charge, urging them on like small children. The project social media accounts are glitchy too. My phone takes ages to connect. It's got to be the internet terminal, but it's a pain—we're relying on follower engagement to get word out there about what we're doing.

"Guys, guess what I found?"

Samara's voice sounds from the cabin, and I rush back upstairs.

"What is it?" Leo is asking, and we approach her as she sits on the sofa with her iPad.

"Has anyone got a camera with battery life?" she says, glancing up at us. "You need to film this."

"I do," Jens says, and he pulls out his camera.

Samara is beaming, and I see on the screen of her iPad that she has what looks like a document. She looks into Jens's camera.

"So I managed to hack into an academic research journal that has legit *thousands* of old newspapers and articles and photographs from the whaling era. Anyway, I did some searching and found some scholarly papers that mention the *Ormen*, and I've got some info for you all."

Leo claps his hands together, then glances at Jens and me with a shrug as if to say *Sorry, losers.*

Samara high-fives Leo, then holds up her iPad. "So there's quite a bit to get through, but already I've found out that the *Ormen*, this very ship we're standing on, was built in Dundee in 1890. It was owned by a number of companies right up until the 1960s, but it was a big deal when it was first built because of its auxiliary steam engine. It says here, 'In a time when whaling ships were powered mostly by wind and muscle, and subsequently ended up becoming crushed by pack ice, a ship that had the capacity to power its way through an ice-choked Arctic was regarded as a state-of-the-art vessel, and the solution to the single most perilous challenge faced by one of society's most important industries.'"

She looks up and pulls a *wowzers* face. "The ship was named *Ormen*—the Norwegian word for 'serpent'—because of her ability to wind through icy paths as easily as a snake. Her first owner was the Abney & Sons Whale Fishing Company, led by George Abney, and he ran it from 1890 until 1901."

She pulls another face at the camera, darker this time, then turns back to her iPad. "There are some footnotes and links here to numerous newspaper reports of the *Ormen*'s voyages in the Arctic. I've actually got a list of the first crew who sailed here. The *Ormen*'s crew were regarded as heroes of Dundee, so they all got a full mention in the newspapers." She pauses before looking up at us. "Should I read their names out?"

Jens nods. "Go for it."

"Okay. So we have twenty crew members. Captain Jonathon Willingham, Dr. Edward O'Regan, followed by P. Arnott, T. Collins, E. Cowie, J. Daverley, Y. Ellis, A. Goodall, F. R. Gray, G. Harrow, D. Lovejoy, F. Martin, N. McIntyre, B. McKenzie, S. Royle, L. Skentelbery, T. Stroud, V. Wolfarth, and two unnamed ship hands."

She looks up. "Ship hands?"

"Deckhands," Jens says. "Cabin boys. Usually in their teens."

She nods. "So, most of these men made ten journeys to the Arctic between 1891 and 1901. Probably some of them died on the voyages too, though. They spent up to nine months on board and then had three months at home with their families."

We all fall silent, our excitement eclipsed by the dawning meaning of what Samara has discovered. After a moment, Leo says, "Hearing their names like that is so powerful."

Samara nods, her smile replaced by a thoughtfulness. "It makes me remember they were real people. And up to nine months at sea in the Arctic. We're only here for a few weeks. *And* we have solar chargers and shit."

Jens stops filming and gives a thumbs-up.

"Thanks," Samara says, the buzz a little flattened. Her smile returns when she looks at her iPad. "Honestly, guys, there is *so much* stuff here, just in this one article. The contest is *over*, I'm serious. Take me to the captain's cabin, that door is *mine*."

I give Jens an "Oh yeah?" look. "I'm hacking that academic website," I tell Samara, half joking. "I see your boring crew list and raise you a shit ton of info on the research era."

"You're on," she says, fist-bumping me.

II

This afternoon, Jens announced he was going for a walk. He left at three and it's now gone eight o'clock. It's pitch-black outside, and it feels like moving through treacle, a viscous kind of dark, so we've been taking it in turns to stand on the deck to keep an eye out for him. Leo spots his headlamp in the distance and races out to greet him.

Jens looks pale when he comes into the cabin, a wide, liquid gaze and his shoulders rounded.

"What happened?" Samara says when he staggers into the cabin.

Leo gives us worried looks. "I think he's dehydrated."

Jens's eyes fall to my water bottle on the coffee table, and I hand it to him, reading his gaze as desperate thirst.

"Where've you been?" Samara asks. Then, "You didn't take a water bottle with you?"

Jens drinks deeply, wiping his mouth roughly on his sleeve. He steps forward, but stumbles, and Leo catches him.

"Whoa there. Come and sit down."

Leo and I support his weight as he sinks down onto the couch. The three of us trade *oh shit* glances. What the hell is wrong with him?

We all take our seats near him, waiting for him to say what happened. He doesn't seem to be injured, no blood or bumps, just badly chapped lips and a wind-whipped face. It's treacherous weather, minus twenty. He's bloody stupid for going out in it.

Samara grows impatient. "Jens, whatever it is, spit it out."

"I was out walking," he says, his voice hoarse.

"We kind of know that," Leo says. "You were gone a long time."

"I was exploring the caves."

My mind flies to the rocks that run all the way from the volcano into the distance. We've scoped out the area enough to know that there are four main entrances to the cave, but the one he seems to be referring to—the largest of the four entrances—isn't that far away.

"That took you five hours?" I say.

"I got lost," he says, gasping. "I just kept moving in circles."

He swallows hard and draws a hand to his mouth, like he's going to be sick.

"For God's sake, Jens," Samara said. *"What?"*

"Bones," he pants. "Skeletons. In the cave."

"Oh my God," Samara says. "Are you kidding?"

Jens lifts his eyes to her. He looks haunted. "I wish I were."

"What kind of bones?" Leo asks.

"Horses," Jens says. I thought of the horses I heard the first night I arrived. "And markings on the cave wall," he says. "They looked . . . satanic."

"Jesus," Leo says. Then: "Is it weird that I want to see?"

"Did you film it?" I ask, and Jens shakes his head.

Samara shrugs. "Well, we're here to explore. Let's explore."

We get dressed quickly, throw on our coats and hats. Outside, the wind is wild, the sea slamming the ship so hard that we almost fall off the ladder. I grip the sides tightly and try not to look down as I feel for the rungs with my feet.

We walk across the beach, the black sand glistening with frost, sand snakes rippling toward us.

Jens leads us to the cave, a black maw in the belly of the cliffs. At the entrance, I feel a raw, primal fear in my gut, and I want to grab

Leo and Samara and ask them whether they trust him. If we should let him fly his drone in there and show us the horses on a screen. But I know what the answer will be—we've already walked some distance and Jens has told us that he's reluctant to fly his drone in caves. Too much risk of damage.

"What if it's anthrax?" I call after the others.

Jens turns, and I notice he glances at Leo and Samara to check their reaction. "It isn't anthrax."

"I'm not sure I want to see it, actually," Samara says, frowning.

We all trade looks, weighing up if we should leave the skeletons alone.

We follow Jens inside the cave. The mouth is like the entrance to a French cathedral, an arched opening of those basalt columns I admired the day after I arrived. Absolutely stunning, especially where the snow sits on top of the shorter columns like white caps in perfect hexagons. The ocean doesn't reach inside the cave—we check the tide to be sure—but it is very damp, the poor light eroding our sense of depth.

"It goes all the way back," Jens says, turning on his headlamp, though the beam melts into the distance. "The length of the headland and then some. There's probably a network of caves throughout this whole section of the coastline."

"All right, let's not freak ourselves out," Leo says. "We've all seen some scary shit in our time, right?"

I do wonder why Jens didn't film it before. Not even on his phone. But maybe he was too freaked out. Jens is always so bloody straight-faced and stoic that I feel more unnerved by the fact that Jens is unnerved, of all people. Nothing seems to rattle him, but this has.

Samara and I flick on our hand torches and draw the beams of light over the damp cave walls. The rock pattern that I saw on the entrance continues inside, concealed in some places by moss and the calcium deposits that spiral down like fangs from the ceiling. The cave narrows as we press on, and I feel conscious of my heart, which is starting to gallop.

I pull out my phone and begin to film, doing a three-sixty turn to capture the mouth of the cave and the beach beyond. My light falls on Leo and Samara behind me, wrapped up in thick winter coats and hats and face masks, emerging from the snow and mist into the darkness of the cave like astronauts stepping out of the fog of a spaceship to explore a distant planet.

"So right now, Jens is taking us to see something he discovered in this cave." My voice sounds reedy with fear as I do the commentary. "Not sure if you can see, but the roof is about thirty feet above me here, and the width about fifteen feet. It smells disgusting. I think there are bats up above, or something flitting. Leo, are there bats in Iceland?"

"No," he says, shining his torch up to the cave roof, though the light is blunted by mist. "I mean, they might have been artificially introduced as a foreign species, but they're not native here. And I dare say it's too cold this far north for them to survive."

A loud rustling sound overhead makes us all stop in our tracks.

"It's just birds," Samara calls back.

"Or cave people," Leo says. "A vampirish human-mole hybrid species that survives by eating urban explorers."

"Leo!" Samara snaps. "Shut the fuck up!"

Just then, I spot something at the mouth of the cave behind us.

I glance back and see a figure standing there in silhouette. The woman. I give a shout, a loud "Oh!," as though I've stubbed my toe. Samara asks me if I'm all right and I stand like a deer in headlights staring at the mouth of the cave, frightened out of my wits. I had swung my phone around to film it, but in that moment the figure is gone, melted into the white glare of moon on the cave entrance.

"Did anyone see that?" I say.

"See what?" Leo says. "You saw something behind us?"

I turn back to check, the hairs on my arms standing on end. "I . . . I think so."

Samara and Leo exchange looks, and I swallow hard, reminding myself of when I saw the woman standing next to Leo when he was doing parkour. *The ghost, ghost, ghost*, I think, trying to imprint the word into my mind, the possibility of it. The only thing worse than a ghost, after all, is madness allowed to gallop unchecked.

I close my mouth, relieved that the conversation has moved on while I composed myself.

My hands are trembling as I lower my phone and stop the recording, then run it back to see if I've managed to film the figure. I haven't. Of course. Every time I see her, the others don't. It's unbearable.

"How far in do we have to go?" I ask, my voice catching.

Jens turns and glances back at us. All three of us are hesitant now. "Just a little farther," he says.

We walk farther, the width of the cave expanding and the pattern of the rock changing. Leo stops and holds up a hand.

"Guys."

He bends down and lifts something slowly.

"What is it?" I ask.

Leo doesn't answer, but as I turn my camera and zoom in, he raises something in his hand. I see a round thing at the top of the object, a kind of knob.

"It's a femur," Leo says.

"Holy shit," Samara says. "Put it down."

He sets it back down, then takes out his torch and directs the beam at it. I film it all. The femur is too big for a human, which is a relief.

"A horse bone," Jens says.

"Is this what you saw before?" Samara asks, and he shakes his head. "I think the first skeleton was just by that stalactite," he says, sweeping his torchlight over a four-foot mineral dagger hanging from the cave roof. The roof is lowering here, which is starting to make me freak out. What if it collapses? What if we can't get out?

"Here," I call out, stopping by the stalactite. I can see a shadow on the ground, a large rock, I think. But then Leo's torchlight reveals a pleated pattern, and I realize it's not a rock. It's ribs.

"Oh God," Leo says, jumping back. He crouches down, covering his mouth. "You're right. I think that's a horse. There's a mane attached to the skull. Look."

He lifts a small stone to scrape away some of the dirt. The long shape of a skull appears, thick bunches of what look like coarse jute visible in the earth.

Jens walks on ahead, then stops and waves back to us. "Another one here."

"God, do we have to?" Samara says.

I press on, silently filming, until I reach Jens. At either side of me are more and more bones, far more than I'd expected. Images flash in my mind. The dream. The boy on the horse, the man leading them and the rest of the herd to the entrance of the field. The song, and the horses bolting to the edge of the cliff.

III

Outside, the wind has grown fierce, whipping up the sand in frightening black columns that spiral around us like a thousand crows.

We head back to the *Ormen*. Inside, Leo makes us all cups of tea while Jens sets about lighting the fire to warm us up. Samara is pacing and murmuring to herself, saying over and over how she can't, she can't.

"Dom?" Leo says. "Dominique?"

"Yeah?"

"I've asked you four times if you want milk in your tea."

"Uh, no. Thanks."

In my mind, I keep seeing the horses falling over the cliff, that terrible whinny.

A part of me feels angry at Jens. What did we gain by encountering the horses for ourselves, other than being scared witless?

Unless he wanted to make a point. Unless he wanted *me* to see them. I told him that I'd heard horses the first night I was here. And I'd told him about my dream.

No, I tell myself. It isn't like he planted the bones. He's as shocked as the rest of us. But that feeling returns, the one that rested inside me when I arrived here—caution. An instinct to be guarded around him. Around all of them. Though maybe it's too late for that.

Samara finally sits down close to the fire. Jens throws a blanket across her shoulders and Leo passes her a cup of tea, then crouches down in front of her.

"You want to talk about it?" Leo asks her with uncharacteristic tenderness.

She wipes a tear from her cheek. "I can't," she says, her voice shaking. "I can't go through with this. I can't."

"Can't go through with what?" I ask her. "The contest?"

She doesn't answer. Leo is rubbing her hands, urging her in soft whispers as she shakes her head. "A night's sleep and you'll feel a lot better," he says, glancing at me.

"No, no," Samara says. "It's never been as bad as this. You said it would work but it's worse this time. I want to leave . . ."

"You know we can't, Sam," Leo says. "Let's just stick to the plan, okay?"

I feel a prickle on the back of my neck. The plan?

Just then Samara stands up and marches across the cabin toward the door.

"Samara, come *on,*" Leo calls loudly after her, holding up his hands. "It's Armageddon out there. The wind will fuck you up."

Samara yanks her coat off the hook and spins around. "It doesn't matter how long ago it was," she shouts, her voice shrill. "You were wrong, Jens. This isn't working. I can't go through with this!"

Leo is trying to calm her, taking her hands again and telling her to repeat a mantra, but she pulls away.

"Can't go through with what?" I ask, because there's a horrible feeling in my stomach, and a strange sense of déjà vu. Samara looks up at me, her face full of fear. I turn to Leo and repeat it. "Can't go through with what?"

Leo ignores me. "If you want to bail, we can do that," he tells Samara. "Okay?"

Samara is nodding and wiping her eyes, but she's unraveling.

"This is all too crazy," she says. "Too, too much. I mean, what does it mean?" She looks up at Jens. "I can deal with the research thing, I can, really. And the laptops and the wine . . . but I cannot deal with this . . . *mindfuck.*"

Her eyes travel to mine, and I do a double take at the look on her face when she sees me. She looks terrified of me. *Why of me?*

"Samara," I say. "It's okay."

I reach out to touch her arm, but she pulls away.

"Don't fucking touch me," she hisses. *"Witch."*

I reel. She called me a witch?

"You did this," she says. "You killed them!"

I stare at her, horrified. Why is she saying this? She's distressed,

I can see that, and the room is charged with emotion. Outside, the wind howls, a loud, high-pitched shriek that bangs against the cabin. One of the Perspex windows blows in, and Jens rushes to catch the sheet as it drifts across the room toward the fire bucket.

"Somebody help?" Jens calls from the blown-in window. I rush to help pin the Perspex sheet into place, but the wind is too strong. Finally, Leo picks up a sheet of wood and leans in against the gaping space, and the cabin falls into silence.

"Come on," Leo tells Samara. "A good night's sleep will help, okay?"

Jens looks at me but says nothing. I feel completely alone. I feel sick. The look on Samara's face when I touched her . . . it was pure terror.

I head down to my cabin and close the door. There's a mark on the floorboard near the door that looks like another bloodstain. I feel my skin crawl.

There's malice in the persisting midnight, a cruelty. I know this makes no sense. I sound paranoid, out of my mind. But that doesn't make it any less real to me. And Samara is right.

I *am* a bad person. If I could change the things I've done, I would. But I can't. I can't.

PART TWO

The Mermaid Stone

Nicky

I

June 1901
near Cape Farewell, Greenland Sea

A month had passed since Nicky woke up in the stinking hold of the *Ormen*. Her injured foot did not heal but seemed to grow infected, though Dr. O'Regan swore it was not. The infection was spreading up her leg, a dark bruise. He claimed he could not see it, but the evidence was there, and so she kept it bandaged.

The sea disappeared beneath a vast mosaic of ice. Thick slabs thudded against the ship, and Nicky feared they would breach the hold. The knocking of them, the blinding whiteness as far as the eye could see—she wondered how any boat could sail through such dense matter. But they did.

The weather calmed after the storm that took Collins, Ellis, and the lambs. The crew buried Collins at sea, despite misgivings. According to Daverley and several others, a sea burial resulted in a vexed and vengeful spirit, one that might haunt the ship. They had no choice but to lower him into his watery grave, a stitch at the nose to keep the soul inside the shroud. Ellis's body was never recovered.

Captain Willingham asked Nicky if she would write a letter to his wife, capturing Ellis's labors on board before he died.

She wondered if she'd heard him correctly. Ellis had raped her, and now he was asking her to redeem him in writing? "I will do no such thing," she said.

"You write that Ellis was a good whaleman," Captain Willingham said, lacing his fingers together. "An elegant rendering of his part in the capture of whales and such like."

She cocked an eyebrow. "How about I write it, and you turn the ship around and take me back to Dundee."

Captain Willingham produced a jar of sweets from a secret store. Pear drops, Highland toffees, and apple sours. "That's the best I can do," he said.

In the end, she agreed.

They faced other problems, including the destruction of the sails. The mariners replaced and repaired where they could, but the ship would have to rely on its steam engines to power through heavy ice.

One by one, the mariners started making their way to her cabin. Gray, who walked with a limp; Wolfarth, who never spoke a word to her; McKenzie, who told her secrets about his wife; Stroud, who sometimes cried. They arrived at her door with sheepish looks, forewarned about her tendency to sing strange songs. She kept her eyes on the door as they grunted above her, melodies that Allan had played on their old piano in Faulkner Street spilling from her lips. Often the men begged her to stop, but she didn't, not even when threats were made. Some of the men resorted to filling their ears with bits of rag.

The captain's wedding ring glinted in the amber lamplight, an apology folded in his silences. She spied the man behind the title, a quivering thing, buckled by too many years at sea. His command was sloppy, his words liquefied. He smelled of rum and shame.

And still she sang.

She came to expect a knock on her door at dawn each morning, the captain's early-morning visit, his silent apologies diminishing like arpeggios. She learned quickly that the key to survival—while she still believed in it—was to ram the fear that threatened to consume her right down into a tight box of hell deep in her heart, to lock it shut with a fake smile stretched across her face like a rictus.

There was a palpable dynamic at the heart of her role as selkie wife that cut through the fear. The men grew jealous of one another, and their jealousy spurred a bizarre protectiveness over her that she understood was no more than a sense of proprietorship. McIntyre in particular was a nasty and prolific drinker, given to picking fights with the younger men, such as Royle and Wolfarth. Her body was a territory, just like the ship, and each of them wanted to stake a claim.

She understood it was only this jealousy and proprietorship that spared her from violence. Lovejoy seemed to be the man in charge when it came to who ventured to her cabin; even McIntyre deferred to him. She considered it bitterly ironic that a man named Lovejoy was so utterly incapable of love and an antidote to joy. Some of the men were sympathetic, asking about the injury to her foot and the bruises on her face. The bruises had faded, but her foot had not healed, or rather it had healed with chimerical effect; like a limb transfigured by flame is often useless long after the bleeding has stopped, perhaps withered, so her foot was not the way it had been. It was no longer human. The gray pelt she had spied forming beneath the skin had continued up her ankle, fading at the calf. She asked Dr. O'Regan for fresh bandages, applying them herself so he would not see.

But it was only a matter of time. And Allan—what would he think? How could she ever return to him like this?

II

She thought of the day she went into labor, how her mother had wanted her to give birth in Larkbrae but the plans fell apart when it progressed too quickly.

"What should I do?" Allan said when she woke him with a yell. She had felt the pains earlier in the night but thought nothing of it. She wasn't due for another month, and her mother told her to expect the last weeks to be painful. "The body prepares itself for labor by faking it," she said.

But by the time she realized that this wasn't fakery, her waters had broken.

"Get Dr. McGill," she said through heavy breaths, and so Allan pulled on his trousers and raced off to the doctor's home two miles away.

The relief of pain during childbirth was considered sacrilegious, and therefore forbidden, on account of the Old Testament pronouncement *In sorrow shalt thou bring forth children.* Even Dr. McGill, who had delivered her and her sister, held fast to this rule, worried that she and the child might be cursed if he disobeyed.

Allan occupied himself in a stupor, following the list of chores Nicky's mother had provided—light the fire, open the windows, boil towels and blankets. Ready the crib, and the cabbage leaves, and the leeches. He completed his tasks and took to holding Nicky's hand and dabbing her forehead as she screamed.

"You're doing well," he whispered by her head. "You're a champion, Nicky. A champion."

She felt as though her back were breaking, the child presenting with its spine against hers. Dr. McGill resorted at last to forceps, a fearsome contraption that drew a gasp of concern from Allan.

"Surely that will only hurt the bairn?" he asked.

"Better an injury than a corpse," Dr. McGill grunted. "Or two corpses." He threw a meaningful look at Allan, who turned pale. He gripped Nicky's hand and nodded at Dr. McGill, who inserted the mechanism between Nicky's legs.

A moment of tugging, then a shrill cry. The baby covered in chalky vernix, placed on Nicky's belly. Its cone-shaped head, bruised and misshapen from the forceps. The placenta removed, and the leeches placed on her cervix to stem the bleeding.

She remembered the impossibly small fingernails, the lines on the palms. The delicate feet, identical to Allan's.

The birdlike mouth, searching for milk. And against all odds, alive.

III

The pristine shores of Greenland pricked the horizon, towering jags, crisp as broken glass, mantled by feathery haar. The air glittered. Absinthe-green patches peeked up through the ice slabs on the surface of the ocean, and glassy lozenges bobbed against the hull, thick and solid as concrete. The combination of colors was striking—alabaster white against cornflower blue and polished silver.

A small pod of grampuses grew curious of the ship one morning, their slick black bodies plowing the sea. Longer and darker than dolphins, they huffed in a single file like a sea serpent weaving the waves. Dolphins traveled in pods of thirty, sometimes more. They liked to race the ship, the younger mariners tapping the side of the hull to encourage them. She spotted sea eagles flying overhead, their wingspan longer than a man. And on the sheet ice, walruses with fangs the length of her forearm barked at them, while smaller seals darted through the blue water.

She woke one morning to the blare of bagpipes. Harrow, one of the oldest of the crew, liked to stand on the poop deck on slower days playing Scottish tunes, waving a saltire and taking requests. In between tunes he'd announce that the bagpipes were weapons of war, hailing from the Battle of Culloden when Scottish pipers roused their troops against the redcoats, and banned thereafter by the British.

"Aye, we know," McIntyre shouted back.

"We're Scottish too, you dunderhead," Gray shouted, flinging a becket at him.

Harrow was undeterred. "The Highland Clearances began with the silencing of the national instrument. When we play the pipes, we echo the voices of our ancestors, lads! We defy our oppressors!"

"We're in the Arctic, you nugget," Lovejoy bellowed back. "The only oppression here is the lack of whisky."

Harrow asked Nicky what she'd like to hear, and she hesitated. She wasn't keen to join in with the men's play, certainly not in any way that might indicate her consent to being held captive like she was. And the bagpipes had marked almost every occasion of her life—her wedding ceremony and every Burns night her father employed a piper to address the haggis. The last thing she wanted to hear was a tune that might disturb a sacred memory.

After a while, she suggested "The Parting Glass," a song she had never heard on the pipes.

Harrow gave a bow and played it with feeling. The call of the pipes amid the loneliness of the polar expanses brought the men to contemplative silence. "Play 'Scotland the Brave'!" Lovejoy shouted after a while, and the plaintive mood that had settled across the ship was broken by a rousing melody.

The first whale they caught was a bowhead whale, female, forty feet long. It had seemed enormous in the water, almost the length of the boat. Nicky had heard the men shouting and headed up to the top deck. About thirty feet from the side of the boat she could see the line of a leviathan cutting through the waves. McKenzie and Gray were already lining up the harpoon cannon, but Lovejoy called out to them, ordering them to hold fire.

"We've not dunked a man," he roared. He whistled at Cowie, then nodded at Reid. "Chuck him in, lads."

Reid looked startled as the two men laid hands upon him, before heaving him over the side and into the dark water below.

"I'm not a strong swimmer!" Reid shouted from below. "It's . . . it's too cold!"

Daverley stood on the side of the rig glancing down, stricken at the sight of Reid thrashing in the dark water below. He pulled off his boots and hat before jumping feetfirst into the water near Reid, who was paddling frantically at the water with his hands.

"Why on earth did you do that?" Nicky asked Cowie as she watched Daverley drag Reid to the anchor rope, pulling them both up on deck again.

"Bad luck to start fishing without dunking a member of the crew," Cowie said.

As the boat turned toward the whale, she saw another, smaller fish in the water next to it—a calf. She waved up to McKenzie, calling out for him to stop, but just then the harpoon shot out from the cannon with a force that she felt right through her feet up to her neck. Instantly, the dark water reddened, bubbles of it rising and turning the side of an iceberg pink.

The calf didn't swim away, didn't make a sound, but Nicky imagined the helplessness of it as it watched its mother bloat with air from the harpoon, floating to the surface like a hot air balloon. "The red flag's flying!" Cowie shouted, as the water around it began to spew with blood.

The men hauled the whale alongside the hull for flensing, the tail held fast by a fluke-chain and the fins fixed with a fin-chain. Wolfarth fastened a blubber hook to a second fin-chain and pronged it on the upper lip, the lower jaw hanging open, the fringed baleen riffling in its enormous mouth like a lace curtain. Lastly, Arnott threaded a chain through the blowhole to stop the weight of the beast's body from tearing it free.

Wolfarth, Royle, and McKenzie set to the carcass with long-handled axes, with Lovejoy overseeing the process of stripping the flanks and hacking at the blubber that lay like a hot mattress underneath. From a distance, it looked like they were stripping a tree of its bark. She made herself look at the parts of it that were mammal, the navy eye buried in bloated eyelids. The air around it steamed with the heat of its body releasing into the cool air.

The men were tiring and drenched in blood. Reid and Anderson's job was to fetch fresh buckets of seawater to rinse the deck, while Stroud, Arnott, and Daverley stacked and hefted barrels filled with blubber into the bowels of the ship.

"Five and forty more!" Stroud shouted, meaning that the last piece of blubber had been swung inboard.

And then the boiling of the blubber in the try-works, the brick ovens abaft the forehatch containing try-pots, two enormous cauldrons, where oil was removed from the blubber for storing in casks.

Feeling the heat beating from the ovens, Nicky moved closer to warm herself, one eye on the calf moving in the white foam ruffling at the ship's side. To the distant east, she had spotted three black fins, though they slipped away as quickly as they reappeared, each time in a new position, as though they had sped up underwater.

"Orcas," Daverley told her, appearing by her side, wrapping a length of rope between his palm and elbow. "They'll come for the calf. Put it out of its misery."

"Why didn't you just kill the calf, then?" she said. "If it's going to be killed anyway?"

"Not my call. Captain's orders."

She felt her feet grow wet and looked down to see that a tide of blood had swept across from the butchered whale while she was searching out its calf, drenching her feet and soaking the bandages.

Daverley was still there, making a serving with string and a mallet as he glanced over the side. Usually he was high up the ratlines, checking the ropes for frays, or slathering foul-smelling tar across the rig. She sensed he wanted to speak to her. Next to him, behind a row of barrels, was a rusted metal cage, too large for fish. A length of heavy chain was attached to the top, and inside she could see long spikes angling down.

"What is that?" she asked. She'd never seen it on board before.

He turned and glanced at it. "It's a brig," he said.

She searched her mind for the term. A brig was a whaler jail for rowdy crew, but it was usually a small cabin in the ship with a set of chains and a padlocked door.

"We use the ship's brig for storing meat," he said. "So the cage takes its place."

She frowned at the spikes, long as her finger. "What's the chain for?"

"If any of the men break Captain's rules, they're put in the cage, and then the cage is thrown in the water and dragged behind."

"That's barbaric."

"Nothing warm and cozy on a whaling ship, as I'm sure you've found."

"I suppose you'll be visiting my cabin next," she snapped, kicking the blood off her feet.

"I will not," he said quietly, his eyes still on the water below. "And neither will Reid."

She felt relieved. The sound of footsteps had started to make her heart race with fear. She had come to associate the sound with the first sign of a man outside her cabin door.

"But you're content with what your crewmates are doing? Taking a woman prisoner?"

"Prisoner?" Daverley looked puzzled. "You're getting paid, aren't you?"

She laughed bitterly. "Paid? You call that vile slop 'payment'?"

"Why did you come, then?" he said. "I mean, why come on board if you don't like it?"

She was shocked. He thought she was a prostitute. That she was here by agreement. Her stomach dropped as she thought of Ellis, and the lewd comments the others had made. Lovejoy's tale of the selkie wife. Surely the men had all known that she was taken, plucked off the street because of her father's company? That she was collateral?

"I was kidnapped," she said. "I'm not here because I want to be."

He narrowed his eyes, processing her meaning. Wolfarth and Anderson were nearby, sweeping blood off the deck.

"Did you know about it?" she pressed, stepping closer to Daverley. "I mean, it must have been planned. Did the captain call a meeting with the crew? Why was I attacked like that?"

He lowered his eyes to the ground. "Whatever the situation is, I want no part of it. I work, I get my wages, and I go home to my wife."

"Is that what the others think?" she said, feeling sick. "That I'm . . . a common prostitute?"

He lifted his eyes to her, and his look told her that they did. "I don't care about your line of work," he said simply. "A woman's bad luck on a ship."

"Rubbish," she said. "And in any case, I didn't choose to be here. So I can't exactly bring bad luck." She watched him look over at Reid, who gave him a wave.

Daverley tied the end of the rope in a knot, then slipped the hoop of it over his shoulder. "He's my sister's boy. She passed this last Christmas."

She heard the catch in his voice. "I'm sorry."

"I got him this job. He's almost sixteen. He needs to make his own living now."

Her own sister floated to her mind, Cat's slim form at her usual spot in the round window on the landing at Larkbrae, holding her beloved dogs. A lump formed in Nicky's throat. How could she tell Allan about what had happened? How would he look at her, knowing how many men had violated her?

"My father owns this ship," she said. "George Abney."

He nodded. "I know."

"You honestly believe the daughter of George Abney is a common prostitute?"

Daverley crouched down to set a dozen grommets in a bucket.

"What did you hear?" she pressed, gritting her teeth.

"It's not my place to say."

"I swear on my life," she said, a catch in her voice. "I was kidnapped. A man attacked me in Dawson Park. My husband will be worrying about me."

A flicker of something passed across his face, and she tried to recall what she had said to spark it.

"Please," she said. "Tell me what you know."

"What does it matter?" he said hastily. "The captain has said you're here for the remainder of the voyage. That's all I know. Happy?"

Just then, a voice called "Daverley!" and she saw Lovejoy stomping across the deck, his face twisted in a scowl. Nicky shrank into herself, lowering her eyes, but not before she saw the way Lovejoy looked from her to Daverley.

"You two have something to chat about?"

"We weren't chatting," Daverley said.

"Not what it looked like to me," Lovejoy said, raking his eyes over Daverley. "If you're not interested in swyving you'll stay well clear, aye?"

"Aye, sir," Daverley muttered.

Lovejoy squared up to her, his eyes tracing the claret stain on her bandaged foot.

"Downstairs," he said. "Now."

As she moved toward the stairs, she risked a glance at Daverley, who flicked his eyes at her. Something had shifted during their conversation, she had felt it. Perhaps he believed her. Or perhaps he was no better than the other men. Even the most grandfatherly of the crew, like Harrow and McKenzie, the ones who had been tender with her, eventually found their desires overwhelming their decency. Harrow often offered the crook of his arm to help her when she struggled to limp across the upper deck, and McKenzie had been nothing but courteous and even sympathetic whenever she came across him. Even so, they arrived at her cabin, shame-eyed, only to leave with a flushed radiance that they'd somehow found beneath her skirts.

She would ask Daverley again. He knew something. She would persist until she found out the truth.

In her cabin, Lovejoy undid his belt in haste. She could read him now, the rush to take her emerging from the exchange he had witnessed between her and Daverley. She feared Lovejoy, but she well knew how pathetic he was, how much he needed to feel he owned her. The kind of man who would beat a cow for not producing the amount of milk he desired. Usually he ordered her to strip naked, but this time he threw her skirts over her head and thudded into her, blaring out like a stuck pig a handful of seconds later.

Afterward, she limped down to Dr. O'Regan's cabin to have her bandage replaced before the blood from the culled whale infected her wound.

She lay down on the bed, wincing as he took off the old dressing and dabbed the wound with a clean linen soaked in alcohol. In the mirror opposite, she could see it—her foot was no longer human, but the fin of a cetacean, dark and slick as ink, bringing fresh revulsion every time she looked at it. If Dr. O'Regan saw it too, he said nothing, but then he wasn't interested in her foot. He looked at her with heavy eyes, and before she could move from the bed, he had slipped his hand down her top.

"It's been so long," he whispered, cupping her breast. "So long."

Sigrún

March 1914
Skúmaskot, Iceland

The old woman looked over the bodies of the dead horses with a heaviness in her heart. Yes, the loss of so many horses would affect the family purse. But the way that they had stampeded off the cliff was greater cause for concern. And her grandson, Kristjan, had told her a strange tale of a hideous creature singing by the field. A face like a fox, a tail like a seal.

It was a devil, she knew that. A devil that had driven the horses mad, sending them over the edge of the cliff to their deaths. There was only one way to treat such a thing.

By night, Sigrún instructed her son, Stefan, to burn the bodies of the horses. He was not to shave the luscious manes to sell them. Everything was to be burned, right down to the bone. The flames licked the walls of the cliffs, birds screaming and wheeling above.

When the job was done, Sigrún drew blood from the arms of Stefan and his children, until they grew faint. Smelling salts brought them around. They had a job to be done before the blood grew too cold.

She took them deep inside the cave.

"Here," she told them, handing them brushes made of horsehair wrapped around sticks. "I want you to dip these into the pots and paint what I show you."

On the walls of the cave and on the bones, they drew patterns, lines upon lines. Cages designed to trap the devils that lay inside the bodies, and perhaps the very bones. Then they painted themselves, and the archway of their homes. And in the hearth, Stefan chiseled another cage to prevent a demon from coming down the chimney.

Kristjan had once laughed when she told him about such things. But now, she watched as he painted himself in earnest, terrified by the thought of the creature who had bared such sharp teeth at him clawing her way inside him.

Wearing his skin.

Dominique

I

December 2023
Skúmaskot, Iceland

Samara is afraid of me, and I have no idea why. I try to tell myself that we were all freaked out by the bones in the cave, and exhausted from the walk back through the storm. But the way she looked at me . . . I hardly sleep, but instead sit in my tent in the darkness, contemplating whether it's time to go.

This has all got too much.

My head is bouncing as I head up to the main cabin. I had my heart set on telling the story of the *Ormen*, but I did *not* count on doing it with three strangers, one of whom hates me and another inexplicably afraid of me.

Outside, it's a bright day. Freezing, yes, but postcard-pretty—a clear blue sky, fresh snow twinkling over the heath, a layer of ice making the sand shimmer like a slab of black opal. The savage wind of the night before has relented, softening to a gentle ripple across the ocean.

Upstairs in the main cabin, I find that Leo has made a generous breakfast—pancakes with agave and chocolate sauce, coffee, orange juice, scrambled eggs from powder, and—God knows how—banana muffins. Samara is dark-eyed, a blanket wrapped around her shoulders, but she looks heartened by the food.

I don't want to upset her, so I take a seat near the oil can.

"Hey," she says. "Dominique."

I look up. She smiles. No sign of the fear she showed before. "I want to show you something."

I sit at the table opposite her and she swivels her laptop around to show me, pointing at the screen. "I couldn't sleep," she says, "so I thought I'd try and find out more about the horses and the cave."

Jens comes up through the hatch then, and she waves them to come over.

"These don't exactly look like photographs of horses," Leo says, setting a plate of food on the table.

"They're of the *Ormen*," she says. "I couldn't find anything about the horses and that cave, but I came across these."

I notice the word *Ormen* in old lettering. Two of the images are from 1899, and three were taken in 1901.

Jens starts filming her. "Tell us what you found, Samara," he says, zooming in on the photographs.

She turns her laptop to him. "Well, if I show you the two from 1899, they're really cool, but they're clearly press images of the ship leaving the docks in Dundee." The image on her screen is of the *Ormen*, taken from a distance. It looks majestic, the sails unfurled and masts standing tall, a large crowd watching on at the docks as the ship departs for the Arctic.

Samara swipes to the other photographs. "These three are kind of slice-of-life shots, taken on board during the 1901 voyage."

Jens zooms in on an image of the upper deck. A teenage boy wearing a neckerchief and flat cap is standing near the ship's wheel, a cigarette in his mouth. He is holding a huge albatross upside down by the feet, its head falling limply on the ground. The boy's head is raised as though responding to a shout. On the rig behind him, a man is in the process of painting the ropes, and there are figures moving in the background, too, blurred by movement.

"Who is that?" Leo asks, leaning in closer. He taps the screen with his finger at a figure almost out of the frame, their face blurred but turned to the camera.

Samara moves closer to it, studying it. "I dunno. Why? You recognize them?"

Leo looks now, and I see Jens falter, not sure whether to keep filming. He decides to stick with it.

"It looks like a woman," Jens says.

"Well, that's unlikely," Samara says, bringing up another browser. "I found this academic book. It says the crews from Dundee were always men."

"Looks like a skirt," Leo says, tracing the outline of something that fans out at the very edge of the photograph, and he's right—the image is faint, but it does look like a long, billowing skirt. "And the figure has long hair, too. There's the shoulder, and you see a flick of something that looks like hair."

"Jesus, Leo," Samara says, impressed. "Talk about the eyes of a hawk. I've never seen that before."

Jens says nothing, making sure to film the three of us in conversation.

"You really think it's a woman?" Samara says to no one in particular. I take another look, trying to see the image from another angle. The cabin is dimly lit by candles, but Samara toggles the brightness until the contrast is just right. The outline of the skirt appears, then a slim waist and shoulders. It's a feminine silhouette.

Something twists inside me, a sudden fear. I think of the figure I saw on the beach. The woman.

"Are you okay?" Jens says.

I nod. "Yeah. Fine. I think it is a woman."

"Just because it looks like a woman doesn't mean it's a woman," Leo says.

"I very much doubt that a whaler in 1901 is going to be wearing a corset and skirt," Samara says.

Leo shrugs. "I'm just saying."

"Could be one of the mariners' wives," Samara says with a frown. "I read that the U.S. whaling industry allowed wives to go with their husbands sometimes. Kids, too. But this book is pretty clear about how things were in Dundee . . ."

"We could search through the academic research site you found?" Leo says. "Find out more about what she's doing there?"

Samara nods, and I feel queasy. There is something about the woman in the photograph that feels familiar, and an icy shiver shoots down my spine.

She looks like the woman on the beach.

II

Jens and I step up our search of the missing research crew in 1973, though we're kind of limited—he's convinced that a lot of print media is still to be digitized, and we'd have better luck in a library with old print archives and microfilm. Nonetheless, I come across a blog that contains photographs of the *Ormen* from 1973, when it was carrying researchers studying glacial ice. For a while I forget the creepiness of the ghost ship, the fact that all the researchers vanished—poof!—into thin air, and pore over photographs from the period. It's cool to compare the two eras, with Samara's photographs from 1901 and the ones we've found from seventy years later. The ship looks much the same, but there are vivid differences in what the people are wearing and how the ship is laid out.

The four of us sit around the dining table and check out the blog, and sure enough, there are a ton of photos there, some with names of the scientists—I search hard for Diego's surname but he isn't mentioned. It is interesting to see the way the crew were dressed, and the cabin that we are all sitting in arranged as a research lab, long tables with maps and microscopes.

"Some of that stuff must still be on here," Leo says, writing down an inventory of things we've identified in the photographs. "I guess some of it would have got washed off during storms."

"Not the bloodstains," Samara says.

"And scavengers," Leo says. "I mean, we can't be the only ones who came on board."

"We know we aren't," Samara says. "The desalination tank was definitely put on board after 1973 . . ."

"Yeah, but I bet anyone who came to explore didn't take souvenirs," Jens says. "I bet most of it is all here. If we search all the rooms and the crawl spaces we'll find it."

"And the shoreline," Leo says. "I think we might want to trawl along the bay a little more in case we find anything."

The conversation spins off toward the contest again. I noticed on our TikTok that people had started talking about which team they were going to vote for. It sparks up conversation, and I tell Samara and Leo that I'm going to win.

But then Samara falls silent. She is staring at something on her laptop, another browser page full of old-fashioned newspapers.

"Guys, look at this," she says.

"What are we looking at?" Leo says, and Samara zooms in on a newspaper headline.

Daughter of Abney & Sons Still Missing, Reward Offered

3rd Oct, 1901

The oldest daughter of George Abney, owner of the troubled Abney & Sons Whale Fishing Company, remains absent, her whereabouts unknown. Abney's daughter, Mrs. Allan Duthie, known as Nicky, was last seen leaving the Camperdown Mill in Dundee on the evening of 6th May this year, and has not been seen since. Abney & Sons was the subject of much controversy in the Spring, due to sunken ships and creditors seeking reimbursement. The saga continues, however, in the form of Mr. Abney's recent death, and the hasty sale of the business by his widow, Mrs. George Abney, without consulting Abney's business partners. Notably, the company's single remaining vessel, the *Ormen*, is due back in Dundee later this month, when the crew will learn of the company's new ownership.

A reward of £80 is offered for information on the whereabouts of Mrs. Duthie. Anyone with relevant information should contact Chief Constable James Michie at Dundee City Police.

"That's sad," Leo says. "But—sorry if this is harsh—what does that have to do with the *Ormen*?"

"Well, this is when the *Ormen* changed hands," Samara says. "It doesn't say who the new owner is, but it seems weird that it was sold under such tragic circumstances. The daughter missing, the owner dead, the owner's wife forced to sell the *Ormen* off before it even got back from the Arctic."

"Was she found?" Jens says. "The daughter?"

Samara clicks on the search bar and types "Mrs Allan Duthie," but the search yields only a single newspaper article, which is the one she showed us. She tries again, typing "Nicky Duthie," but nothing comes up.

I feel a prickle along my spine when I see the woman's name typed out like that, as though each letter is stirring something.

III

I am on the *Ormen*, but she isn't a wreck. She is out to sea, frothy waves bobbing up the sides, white sails unfurled in a splendid grid. Absolutely glorious. But I see myself in the reflection of the water. I am that hideous woman again, my face fixed in a gruesome smile. Black gums, fox teeth, sharp as daggers. My hair braided with seaweed.

I stand on the deck and sing my song of revenge. I want to hurt everyone on the ship. I want them to suffer.

I wake up, gasping for breath.

Switching on my lantern, I unzip my tent slightly to let in fresh air. Upstairs, floorboards creak like someone is moving around. Probably just one of the others, getting a drink of water from the desalination tank.

I lie curled up in my sleeping bag for a while, heart thumping in my throat, hating myself. Why did I dream again? Why am I dreaming such horrible, sickening things?

A scratching sound starts up, and I grow worried in case it's rats, or something bigger, like the Arctic fox I spotted. I pick up my box of matches and a wad of scrunched-up paper spiked on the end of a pen. I figure I'll make a flaming torch if it is the fox, to try to scare it off.

Upstairs in the main cabin, the scratching grows louder. No fox that I can see, and no rats. Someone is crouched by the door, and I freeze, certain we have an intruder. I point my torch in the direction of the sound and see Leo's head. Thank God. It's only Leo. What the hell is he doing?

"Leo?" I call out.

Leo doesn't answer. I'm worried he's going to freeze to death. He's crouched down on the ground, stripped down to his boxer shorts, and kind of hunched over, one of his arms moving back and forth in a really weird way.

I approach him slowly, recognizing instantly that his behavior is super odd. He's clearly sleepwalking, and I've heard that you shouldn't wake someone too abruptly when they're in that state. But what the hell is causing the scratching noise? It has an odd rhythm. Sometimes slow, like someone dragging nails down a chalkboard, and then quick, like he's hacking something. All the hairs on the backs of my arms stand on end.

I take a step to the side and spy something glinting in the safety light. A knife. I freeze, more certain now that I've worked out what's happening here.

He's cutting himself.

My eyes scan the floor for blood. He shifts to the side and I step back quickly, hiding behind the bookcase. I'm worried in case he sees me. He doesn't, but he moves the table, and I notice that he has written something—or carved something—into the surface. He sits back on his heels as though to look over what he has done, before returning to it.

I don't know what to do. I'm wary of waking him, but I also feel unnerved by what he's doing.

Just as I'm considering a way to wake him gently, there's a noise on the lower deck. A moment later, Samara's head pops above the hatch.

"Will you *please* shut the fuck up?" she says, and Leo gives a loud shout, like he's burned himself. The knife flings out of his hand and lands somewhere by the door, and he falls back, flat on his arse. Samara laughs. She mustn't have clocked that he was sleepwalking, and she hasn't seen him scratching the table with the blade.

"Leo," she says testily, and I watch as Leo comes to. He blinks and glances around, clearly not sure why he's in the cabin.

"What's going on?" Samara asks, stepping up to help him to his feet.

"Nothing," Leo mutters hazily. He's so out of it that he doesn't even see me. I watch as he staggers toward the hatch and down the stairs, my heart cartwheeling.

What is it about this place that makes everyone do weird things in their sleep?

IV

I sleep in after that, exhausted from finding Leo upstairs and ruminating about it afterward.

At eleven, I head upstairs for breakfast and find Samara, Jens, and Leo up there, sitting at the table. They all turn to me when I appear.

"Hello," I say, suspicious.

"Good morning," Samara says, her fingers laced on the table. "Did you run out of paper or something?"

"What?"

She points at the surface of the table. I look down at it and see scratch marks that Leo made while he was sleepwalking. When I look closer, I realize they aren't random scratches. He has written something. A kind of broken, half-remembered poem:

When once its men
a wife ne'er again
the sea hearts to grieve
and sailors to their would
So upon her knees
prayed Lír calm the seas
Lír heard changed this night
my queen til first light
these seas cause thee strife
if you'll become my

It is difficult to read, some of the chipboard splintered, but it's clearly a poem of some sort.

"What is it?" I ask Leo. "Some kind of nursery rhyme?"

"You tell us," Leo says, a hard edge to his voice.

I do a double take. "What?"

"Shame it's unfinished," Samara says. "'Calm the seas.' 'My queen' . . . something about making a deal with Lír? Who's Lír?"

"I think he's the sea god in Celtic mythology," Leo says.

"'And sailors to their . . . would . . . ' weave?" Samara tried.

"It's an AA BB rhyme scheme," Jens offers, tracing the carved words with his fingertips. "Grieve, leave, sheathe . . ."

"Maybe *you* wrote it, Jens?" Samara says.

Jens cocks his head and smiles, but says nothing.

"Dom can tell us," Leo says.

I shrug, feeling the charge in the room. "I have no idea."

"Well, someone wrote it," Samara says.

"Jens said you've been having nightmares," Leo says, his eyes fixed on me.

I bristle, turning to Jens. "That was shared in confidence."

"When it impacts the rest of us, it's important that we share," Leo says.

"Okay," I say, trying to swallow back my irritation. "I *have* been having nightmares. But that doesn't automatically mean that I carved up the dining table."

"Who did, then?" Samara said.

I nod at Leo. "You did."

He gives an amused laugh. "Are you serious?" Then, when he realizes I am serious: "When am I supposed to have done this?"

"Last night," I said. "I came upstairs to see what the scratching was. You were sleepwalking. I didn't want to disturb you." I look at Samara. "I saw you come upstairs."

She shook her head. "No. I saw Leo, but there was no one else there."

"How can you not have seen me?" I say, my voice growing louder. "I was right there."

"It was dark," she says.

With a sigh, Leo reaches out to touch the carvings. "So, no one knows who carved a poem into the dining table."

"I think it's just sleepwalk-ramblings," I say.

He shakes his head. "It's a proper poem. Look at that rhyme scheme. I'll bet you a burger it's an authentic folktale."

"What's the last line?" Jens says. "If you'll become my . . ."

". . . selkie wife," I say. Everyone looks at me, and I raise a hand to my mouth. Where did *that* come from?

"Selkie wife?" Leo says. "That fits."

"I thought you said you didn't write it," Samara says.

I feel lightheaded. I said "selkie wife" before I had even thought of it, as though my mouth spoke of its own accord.

"'Wife' does rhyme with 'strife,'" Jens says.

"Do you know the rest?" Leo asks, but my heart is clamoring, and I've broken out in a cold sweat. Where did those words come from? Why did I say that?

Why do I know the words to Leo's goddamn poem?

"Let's google it," Leo says, and right as he types the words *selkie wife* on his laptop I get up and walk out of the cabin.

I go for a long walk across the beach toward the headland, until my calves are on fire and my lungs are working harder than my brain. Even so, I feel embarrassed, blamed for something I didn't do. This isn't just about who wrote the poem, or why. I feel that old injustices from my past are being poked and prodded, and it hurts.

I'm freaked out. I'm afraid to even think about the poem, because the more I circulate the words in my head, the more the blanks seem to come bubbling up from the depth of my brain.

All the secrets I've managed to keep hidden inside are being stirred by this trip. I sit down on a rock, pull the knife out of my trouser pocket, and cut a fresh line into my stomach.

It feels good for all of two seconds.

I should have known that Jens would follow me. The minute I spot him—about twenty feet away to my left, his head cocked—I hate myself more than I hate him right then.

"Does that do it for you?" I shout. "Creeping around after people?"

He doesn't answer but walks slowly toward me. As he gets closer I can see he's looking at me warily, as though I'm holding a grenade. I pull my jumper quickly down over my bare flesh, but my coat is unzipped and I'm still holding the knife, which has a little blood on it.

"You want to talk about it?" he asks.

"About what?"

His face softens. "The fact that you're self-harming."

"I don't see it as a problem."

He looks out to sea. "Why do you do it?"

"It makes me feel better."

"Feel better about what?"

I look away. Images flash in my head. A man's face, frozen in a snarl. My fists pounding against a locked door. I feel my throat tighten, and the urge to cut myself rises up again, ferocious.

"Dominique?"

I snap back into the present, trembling. Jens is standing over me still, looking at me with concern.

"It's the dreams, isn't it?" he says. "You dreamed about horses, and then we found them. Is that what you feel guilty about?"

A sob rises up in my throat. I nod.

"What about the poem. Did you dream that, too?"

I get to my feet and start to run, the icy wind beating against my face. I can hear him calling after me but I have to run, as though all the whispering memories inside my skin can be left behind.

As though they'll someday stop hissing in my blood.

Nicky

I

July 1901
Karrat Fjord, Greenland

Days on the *Ormen* were spent in extremes—either the men would be bored and agitated, their chores finished by lunchtime and the sea around them scrolling like an endless blank canvas, or they'd spy a whale, and the hunt would occupy them from dawn until dusk, or sometimes until the next morning, leaving them drained and bloodied. The ship's harpoon was mechanized, sparing the men the ordeal of hunting by hand, using boats and old-fashioned, javelin-style harpoons. In years gone by, a whale took days to die, with the men having to stay out all night on their small boats in freezing conditions, waiting for the beast to give in. Now, the whole ship rocked as the harpoon cannon thrust out, spiking out of the leviathan and filling it with air so it would float to the surface. Even then, the task of flensing the blubber and carting it off in barrels to the hold was backbreaking.

The provisions from Dundee were dwindling, the meals supplied from the sea around them. She had never eaten seal or whale before, but now it made up almost every meal, the sight of albatross turning on a spit by the ship's wheel a constant sight. Royle and

McKenzie took to climbing the rig with pistols, then sling and stones, shooting the birds for supper.

Nicky spotted young Reid writing at a table in the galley one evening, and sat down next to him. The men who stayed clear of her cabin were relatively safe, in her eyes, and Reid was always pleasant to her.

"Would you have any paper I could use?" she asked. "I'd like to write to my husband."

Reid nodded. "I have a notebook. I'll tear out some sheets for you."

"A notebook?" she said. "You mean a logbook?"

Reid reddened again. "Nah. That's Wolfarth's job. I like to write."

"You send letters home?" she said, and he shook his head.

"I write for myself, mostly. Silly little songs. Sea shanties for the men when the hunting's not happening."

She straightened, surprised. There hadn't been the slightest hint of culture since she'd been aboard. "I'd like to read them," she said. Reid lifted his eyebrows, and she worried she'd offended him. "I mean, only if you don't mind."

He beamed, a small nod. "I'd be honored."

"You would?"

He dropped his eyes to his boots, but he couldn't wipe the smile off his face. "No one has ever wanted to read them. I mean, the men sing the shanties when they're bored, but I don't tell them it was me who wrote them."

She smiled. "I'll look forward to it."

II

She chatted with Reid most days after that, in the quieter periods when he could steal away for a short while to write. She made sure to stay out of Lovejoy's sight, and it brought a small comfort to build a friendship with one of the crew. He was her sister's age, and although he had left school at twelve his writing skills were good.

"Did you always want to be a whaler?" she asked one afternoon, when he had helped the men haul a thirty-foot sperm whale onto the boat. He was spent from the effort, and agitated by the animal's death. Reid struck her as a sensitive lad, unsuited to this life.

He shrugged. "Didn't think much about it. I need to earn money. It's this or the mill. And my cousin died in the mill, so I prefer this. Especially since I don't get seasick. My da says I've got good sea legs."

"When did you start writing?" she asked.

"I can't remember," he said, scratching his chin. "I've always liked a good story. *Macbeth* is my favorite."

"That's a play," she said.

"Aye, but it's still a story."

"Have you ever seen it staged?"

He scoffed. "What, at the theater? Naw. No money for things like that. Do you read Rabbie Burns?"

She nodded. "Of course. 'Wee, sleekit, cowrin—'"

Reid clapped his hands together in delight, finishing her sentence. "'—tim'rous beastie, O, what a panic's in thy breastie.' That's one of my favorites. I've memorized loads of his poems."

"We were forced to memorize them at school," she said. "I suppose it took the joy out of them a little."

"Oh, I love him. Could read him all day. No books on a whale ship, though. That's got me writing, actually, more than I do at home."

"That's understandable."

"I think I'd like to write a song," Reid told her. "For the men to sing." He looked at her meaningfully. "Could you help me?"

She nodded. "Of course."

They wrote several shanties together, he offering the themes and the opening lines and she helping him swap words to make the rhyme and rhythm stronger. He wrote shanties mostly to make tasks easier, such as hauling the bowline and flensing a whale, which the men could sing while performing their duties.

It lifted the men's spirits to try to learn a new song when the days stretched out. Wolfarth played Reid's tunes by ear on his fiddle and memorized the words, before leading any willing crew members in a singsong. Even Lovejoy joined in, his face lighting up as he clapped and sang along.

She watched the men carefully as they sang, tankards and spirits high, many of them still drunk from the night before. She wondered if whaling didn't breed men like this, debase them—men who might have exercised dignity and morals in some other form of employment, but out here, forced to slaughter such majestic beasts of the ocean, they became, stroke by stroke, little more than animals.

It wasn't just work that made monsters of men, but guilt. That, after all, was something she understood only too well.

She thought of the small shoes she first bought Morag, the red leather laces she taught her to tie. She liked to play hopscotch in the garden, a handful of sticks laid out to mark the boxes. Every trip to the park became a search for treasure in the form of the perfect hopscotch stick—straight, not too thick, a foot in length. A game that involved song was her favorite thing in the world.

Daffodils, baby birds.

She once found a robin's blue egg and begged for a dress in the same color.

When Morag died, Nicky's mother advised her to get rid of it all—every toy and shoe, and especially the dresses.

But the blue one, the silk dress the color of robin's eggs—she kept it to remind her. To remind her of what she had done.

Dominique

I

December 2023
Skúmaskot, Iceland

I'm on the upper deck watching the snow swirl down, melting as soon as it hits the tide. The ship moans and burps, the waves sucking at the debris on the sand. It snowed heavily last night, all the green patches of heath filled in with a blanket of blinding white snow. We've been filming it all morning, the snow. This is nothing like the kind of snow I've seen before. There are these weird ice formations all over the ship that look exactly like a crown of silvery hair with a center parting, as though there's a body emerging from the hull. The more regular kind of snow has mushroomed along the masts and the gunwale, and we have to push it off the roof of the cabin with kitchen utensils in case the weight of it brings the whole thing crashing down.

I hear the cabin door open and shut, Samara pulling on her green beanie as she approaches.

"Hey," I say.

"Hey." She stands next to me, her arms folded across her. "Can we take a walk this morning? Just you and me?"

I feel something inside me tighten. "Sure."

We climb down the ladder and walk along the beach, away from the buildings across the bay.

The beach is kind of grizzly today, a ton of seaweed dumped on top of the sand and snow. We reach the turning point of the bay, where the turf houses line the shore. There's one in particular I like, the house with a red door. The rest are in darker colors—blue, gray, black. The snow has covered them all, but the red peers through like a heart in the midst of so much white.

She sees me looking. "That's your house," she says.

I look at her, puzzled. "My house?"

She looks away, and I see it again—the look on her face that says she's hiding something.

"Look, Samara," I say. "I wanted to ask you . . ."

Our voices eclipse. ". . . wanted to ask you . . ."

She stops, and we both laugh. Mine is a nervous, brittle laugh. I think of when she called me a witch. The way she feared me.

"You go first," I say.

She stops, eyes fixed on the bay, biting her lip. "Jens told me," she says carefully. "About your self-harming."

I feel my cheeks burn, the sting of shame rising up in me. "Okay."

"You want to talk about it?"

I shake my head.

"We can't support each other if we don't know what's really going on," she says. When I don't answer, she places a hand on my upper arm.

"I'm your friend," she says gently. "I know you've been alone . . ."

"It's a release thing," I say. "When I'm stressed."

She nods. I suck my teeth, reluctant to say more. But she's waiting for it.

"And usually I'm fine. But sometimes I have . . . thoughts. And it gets too much. Cutting makes it feel better."

"Thoughts of what?"

I pause for a long time, and she waits, patient.

"I think I was attacked," I say.

"Attacked?" she says. "When? By who?"

I feel my skin crawl and my throat tighten.

"They . . ." I say, but I can't finish the sentence. The memory is there, but it's too murky to put into words. It's a scream that runs right through me.

"They?" she says. "There was more than one?"

I can't speak, can't even nod. My whole body has gone rigid, as though I'm turning to stone. I squeeze my eyes shut. I can't bear the images. I can't bear them.

She touches my arm. "Oh God, Dom. I'm so sorry."

I try to slow my breathing, remember to take it from my diaphragm, but it's useless. My head is light, and I can feel myself trying to dissociate. Like an internal mist blanking everything out, including my sense of self.

"Do you want to talk about it?" she says.

I shake my head, and she steps back, as though she's pushed me too far. "It's not that I have a problem with telling you what happened," I explain slowly. "It's just that . . . I don't have the words for it. That's why I cut myself."

She nods, and I can see she's trying to understand, even though she doesn't. No one ever does.

"I mean I literally don't have the words," I say. "Maybe you'll get it, being into sounds and everything. It's like, some things that happen to a person are so awful that they exist outside language. Am I making sense?"

I turn to her, noticing that her eyes have softened. "You're making complete sense," she says with a smile.

We stand in silence, looking out over the bay. But it's not an awkward silence, and I've stopped shaking. I feel like a weight has lifted inside me, just a little.

"Thank you for telling me," she says finally. "Anytime you want to talk, I'm here."

"You're welcome," I say, on autopilot and regretting the words as soon as they're out. But then, this is my point—words are meaningless. They're used up and secondhand and they never, ever capture the truth of an experience. They're just a keyhole. Never the full picture.

"Next time you feel the urge to cut," she says. "Come and talk to me instead."

I nod, relieved, because this means she isn't going home. And suddenly it strikes me—I've spent so much time and energy convincing myself that I'm fine being alone.

But I don't want to be alone anymore.

II

"Samara, tell us what you found."

Samara sits at the dining table, her face lit up in a smile. She looks very pleased with herself; we all are. I'm filming her, not live, but I'll edit and upload tomorrow morning. My battery is at nineteen percent and I'm silently praying that it doesn't run out, because we will never be able to recapture the sheer excitement vibrating off all of us right now.

She throws a massive, all-teeth smile at the camera, beaming with excitement. She's not even told the rest of us everything that she found, and now I see why—it translates better on camera if she's kept it to herself.

"Okay, first some backstory," she says. "I've been having some crazy dreams since coming to the *Ormen*, but I'm thinking now that maybe there's something more than my imagination to these dreams. I dreamed that I heard someone singing, right here on the shipwreck, right? And in the dream I was searching for them."

She pauses for dramatic effect, and my palms begin to feel clammy.

"I went into this little crawl space on the lower deck," she says, "and I saw some floorboards that were out of place, with something poking up underneath. So, the next day, I thought I'd check out the lower deck, right? Just to see if there was an actual crawl space like the one in my dream. And there was."

"Oh my God," Leo says. "Tell me you didn't find that box there."

She holds a finger to her lips, and I want to be sick. "So, right where the floorboards were all out of place in the dream, I found—guess what?"

"You found floorboards," Jens says.

"And something poking up from underneath," Samara says, gesturing at the box.

"Holy shit," Jens says.

"It was the muse calling," Leo says.

"Yeah, seriously," Samara says. "I lifted some of the floorboards, and I saw something underneath, covered in dust. And it was this."

I start to shake, and the image in the viewfinder begins to wobble. I want to scream at them all to run, to leave the tin box and run, but instead I do my best to keep completely still, panning slowly to the tin box on the table next to her. It's the size of a shoebox, still filmed with dust and cobwebs, the corners crumbly with rust.

She lifts out a bundle of old papers, dusty and fragile, and lays them across the table.

"Oh my God," Jens says.

"Are you fucking kidding me?" Leo says, clapping his hands together.

"There are some old maps," Samara says, holding up a folded map.

"Get the date," Leo says, pointing at some writing at the bottom of the cover. It says 1885.

"They're super delicate, so I don't really want to unfold them. There's a gorgeous vintage cigarette box here too. It's so pretty, I want to keep it." She lifts it up and I zoom in on the design. The box is dotted with weevil holes. The inks are faded, but I can make out a British flag on the front, old-style lettering that reads *Redford's Navy Cut*. Samara lifts the flap gently, revealing eight cigarettes inside, in pretty good nick.

"That must be super valuable," Leo says. "This is why we explore, folks," he says into the camera. "You come across stuff like this. Not cleaned up and in a museum. Straight from the source."

Samara and Jens hold the opposite corners and unfold it super slow across the table. It's a map of a place called Baffin Bay.

"This is where the ships sailed," Samara says as Leo moves his camera up close. "I looked it up online."

"Baffin Bay?" I say. The name sounds familiar.

"Greenland," Leo says, pointing at the name written in capitals along the map.

I draw my camera slowly across the shapes of the land while Jens holds a torchlight over the map to pick up the faded writing. I can make out some place names. *Lancaster Sound. Prince Charles Island. Clyde River.*

"And . . ." Samara says suspensefully, lifting out a small envelope.

"Holy shit," Leo says. "Is that a letter?"

She nods, gleeful. "There's no stamp, and it's never been opened." She fingers the edges of the envelope like a dark secret. It's clear that the envelope has been exposed to water, the writing faded and blurred by damp. She looks up at the camera, and we all pause. "It seems wrong to open it, doesn't it?"

"Can you make out more of the address?" Jens asks.

She squints down at the writing. "I can't fully make out the name. It starts with an *E*, I think? And the surname ends with a *D*?"

"That's not even the best part, is it?" Leo says, grinning.

"Seriously?" Jens says. "There's more?"

I watch my battery light flash, pleading with it to last. "Maybe you should film this, too," I tell Jens. "Just so we have a copy."

He nods and pulls out his own phone to film.

Samara waits until he nods, signaling that he's recording. "I found a notebook," she says, her smile widening, "and I believe it is actually a mariner's diary or logbook from when the *Ormen* was a whaling ship."

She holds up an A5-sized leather-bound notebook, weathered at the edges and the brown leather worn thin. Inside there are notes in old-fashioned cursive letters. None of us can read the writing, but we can make out several pictures inside a ship and whales. And the year at the top of the pages is discernible—it says 1901.

"Or maybe one of our followers could help decipher the writing?" Leo says.

Samara wags her finger at Leo as though he's a naughty schoolchild. "Ah, my dear Leo. I am one step ahead, baby. One step ahead."

She visibly prepares herself and turns to the camera. "So as you all know, I hacked into an academic journal," she says. "And I found a paper from 1962 from a professor at Dundee University. He was convinced there was someone else on board the *Ormen* in 1901."

"What does that mean?" Leo says. "Someone else on board?"

"A stowaway," she says. "He said he had analyzed several crew diaries, and one of them mentions a *siùrsach*, which is Scots Gaelic for 'whore.'"

"So you're saying . . . what?" Jens says. "That there was a prostitute on the ship?"

"It could have been a male prostitute, right?" Leo says, but Samara shakes her head.

"*Siùrsach* is a specifically female term."

She nods, then lays out the logbook on the table, carefully turning to a page that she's marked with a bookmark. "As you can see, the writing is super difficult to make out. It's mostly tallies and things I don't understand. But I did find the official crew list, with a date. This is from the beginning of May in 1901."

I zoom in on the names of the men as Samara points to them.

"There are twenty names there," she says. "Remember that number, okay?"

We all watch as she turns the pages slowly to another section, which is dated May 1901. At the top of the page is a tally:

𝍸
𝍸
𝍸
𝍸
|

"What does that mean?" Leo says.

"There's twenty-one people on board," Samara says. She turns over to another page, dated 30 July.

𝍸
𝍸

卌
卌 //
|

"What are the two leaning lines?" Leo asks.

"Two dead mariners," Samara says. "But even if you include those in the tally, there are twenty-one people."

Another, from September of that year, has the same tally. Only this time there are three dead mariners.

"That's a high percentage of deaths for one voyage, isn't it?" Samara turns to them all to ask.

It's Jens that responds. "Aye," he says, with a confident authority that takes me by surprise. "But you never know what's going to happen on a whaling expedition. Especially when there's a woman." He was staring at the notebook but didn't say anything more.

"Well, how sure are you?" Leo asks, skeptical, breaking the silence that followed. "I mean, this is all speculation, isn't it?"

"Thanks," Samara says flatly. "I worked really fucking hard to check my facts."

"Sorry," Leo says, pressing his hands to his face. "It's just . . . wow. We saw that photograph of the person in the skirt, too. That was from the same time, right?"

Jens nods. "Yes. 1901."

Leo shakes his head. "My mind is blown."

"That's some incredible detective work," Jens says, high-fiving Samara. My battery is at eight percent and my mind is racing. How did Samara learn the location of the box from a dream? And what about my own dreams? They've seemed so real. What if they're a form of control? What if the woman I keep seeing is possessing us? Is that what happened to Leo when he sleepwalked? I tried to shut my mind off, remind myself I'm being ridiculous. But I can still see the woman even when I close my eyes. Her long black hair, hanging like seaweed over her shoulders. Her ragged dress, the color of dusk. Her hands by her sides, clenched in fists.

"You heard it here, folks," Samara tells the lens as my battery flashes. "A female stowaway was aboard this ship in 1901."

Nicky

I

July 1901
near Devil's Thumb, Greenland

As they pressed farther north, something new appeared on the white shores of Baffin Bay.

Inuit.

Nicky was mesmerized by the men and women who appeared there, dressed in coats and boots made of deer hide, all of them healthy and happy in appearance. They greeted the ship waving and cheering, and she looked around eagerly for any sign of a ship. But they had none—their homes were tents that they erected and dismantled just as fast, moving to whichever part of the Arctic they wished to explore and hunt. They had pipes, she noticed, made of whalebone, and long rifles. As the ship drew closer to the water's edge, she saw that some of the children were fair-haired and pale-skinned. She had heard of this—whaling crew fathering children in the Arctic. And here was the evidence.

Royle and Arnott took rowing boats to the land for fresh water and returned with two young Inuit women, about sixteen years of age, long black hair to their waists. The arrangement seemed consensual, and when ardent sounds of lovemaking sounded in the cabins above, Nicky wept with relief. Perhaps the new installments would quiet the traffic in her own cabin. All but four of the men—Daverley the boatswain, his nephew Reid, Anderson, and Cowie—were regular visitors to her cabin now. The men were always sheepish at first, then more brazen, expectant.

The arrival of the Inuit girls sparked fights among the men. Each day the rowing boat that ventured to the shore for water returned with freshly replenished buckets and several new Inuit girls.

On the fifth day in Baffin Bay, she heard footsteps on the deck outside a little after midnight. A knock on her door. She froze. She could hear the voices of several men, and suddenly she feared they would all come into her tiny room. They were drunk, she knew that. She was terrified of what they would do in this state.

"Open up, selkie!" Lovejoy shouted, and her heart pounded in her chest. She stared at the door handle as it shuddered in the frame against the weight of fists pounding against it. "Open up!"

She reached forward and unlocked the door, holding her breath. Lovejoy and Wolfarth stood there, holding Reid roughly by his shirt.

"Good evening, selkie," Lovejoy said, his pale eyes lit with excitement. "This boy here became a man of sixteen at the stroke of midnight."

He shoved Reid inside with a yell. "A virgin on a whale ship's a curse on all our heads!"

Reid fell at her feet with a clatter. Lovejoy and the men behind him stood and laughed, the sound of it booming off the walls. They'd been drinking, but Reid's terror had sobered him up.

"Are you all right?" she asked, once the door was closed.

He shook his head, then slowly sat upright. She knew he wasn't going to hurt her. He seemed more afraid of the other men, and embarrassed.

"Come and sit down," she said, and he sat with her on the bed.

"I should never have come on this godforsaken voyage," he said after a long silence. "If my mam was still alive I'd be at home. But I have to earn a wage."

She found herself putting an arm across his shoulders. "You're earning a wage, though," she says. "That's good, isn't it? Once this is all over you can go home after all. And you'll have something to show for it."

He wiped tears from his cheeks and nodded. "I wish I could go home," he said. "I didn't think it would feel so long, being away."

A lump formed in her throat. She knew exactly what he meant, and although her situation was infinitely worse than his, she knew he was tender in years. "Everyone feels that way, the first time they leave behind everything that's familiar," she said. "The trick is to remember that you can get used to anything."

He looked up, his eyes red. "Even this?"

"Yes. And much worse."

He took her hand, recognizing that she spoke from experience. "I'm sorry."

She nodded and smiled.

"We caught something today," he said after a moment. "Do you want to see?"

She followed him out the door, along the corridor, then downstairs into the hold. A memory flashed brightly in her mind of the day she had woken in that dark space, when a barrel tipped over on her foot, a nail piercing her skin and creating the wound that was now transforming her leg entirely. She shuddered at the thought of it.

There was barely enough space in the hold now for them to enter, rows of barrels stacked there, the air thick with the sour stench of blubber. She started at a noise—a low growl.

"Come and see him," Reid said.

"Who?" she said.

He lifted the oil lantern and nodded at a cage in a corner. "We caught him today, Daverley and I," he said. "When we rowed to land for fresh water."

She squinted into the shadows cast by the amber light of the lantern. Something moved inside the cage, something with white fur. Too small for a polar bear. Perhaps a cub. She felt uneasy.

Reid made a tutting sound as he moved toward the cage. He lifted the lid off a barrel nearby and found some meat, then slipped a piece inside the cage. A bushy tail lifted, a glint of two red eyes.

A white fox.

"An Arctic fox," Reid told her. "Very hard to catch, these guys. The fur is worth a fortune back home. God blessed us."

She looked at the fox squatting low as it chewed the whale meat, watching them anxiously.

"You won't kill it, will you?" she said.

Reid's smile faded. "How would we skin it if we didn't kill it first? Be a bit cruel, no?"

She opened her mouth to say that maybe it would be kinder to the animal to set it free, but then she thought of Reid, and where he came from. She had seen the squalor in Dundee, and the hungry children who came to the mill, day after day.

It was cruel to kill the fox, but it was also cruel to deprive Reid of the money that would come from the sale of the fur. But as she watched the animal swallow the last of the meat, that thick, pristine fur like a cloud, her mind turned to the man who had attacked her in the park, and the conversation with her father the morning she was kidnapped.

An endless chain of purchase, the blood that tinged the waters around the *Ormen* a reminder that the new world of electric light and consumer goods cost murder and bloodshed in Arctic waters.

If her capture had purchased something she did not yet understand, what would her freedom cost?

II

Allan coming home from the mill, pulling off his clothes. The smell of jute under his fingernails. She prepared the bath by the fire, washed his back.

The line of his neck, the curve of skin from his ear to shoulder. His hand reaching for hers.

He left the house at dawn six days a week and returned after dark. One night, she woke to feed Morag and found that he was pacing the hallway, restless. He'd been up for hours, clearly, an open ledger in the front room suggesting he was still working.

"Allan?"

He turned to her, his eyes dark.

"What's the matter?"

"My mind is wandering, is all. Go back to bed."

They'd barely spoken for weeks, passing like ships in the night. She felt anger rise up—he had taken on extra work, by the looks of it.

"You want to work *more*," she said. "When you already work every hour under the sun."

A cry sounded then, the sort that made her breasts leak milk. She turned to fetch the baby, holding her for a feed in the armchair by the window. Her breasts burned, and she felt pummeled. She lowered Morag into the crib, but she screamed again, her face scrunched up and her legs drawn to her stomach.

A thumping started on the walls: Mr. Baird, telling them to quiet the baby.

Nicky pounded the wall. "Be quiet, yourself!" she shouted angrily.

Morag wouldn't be consoled. Nicky plucked her up from the crib and held her upright, but the wailing continued.

"I don't know what's wrong with her," she told Allan. "She does this all day, every day. Feeds then cries until she's exhausted. Then wakes and repeats it all."

Allan took the baby from her, rubbing her stomach. Slowly, she quieted. Nicky felt relieved and frustrated that she couldn't manage to console the baby.

"They lowered my wages," he said. "And our rent is due."

She looked him over, realizing how thin he'd become. He wasn't eating, either. So much had changed since the baby came. They were exhausted, wrung out with cares. It had been weeks since she kissed him.

He laid the baby back in her crib, the silence stretching, delicate and sweet. He made to go back to his work, but she took his hand.

"Come back to bed. You need your rest."

He made to turn, but stopped, the touch of her hand rooting him there. She stepped forward and took his face in hers.

"I'm here," she said.

"I'm here," he said back. Then he followed her back into bed, wrapping his arms around her. Curling into each other in the dark.

Dominique

I

December 2023
Skúmaskot, Iceland

After Samara's discovery we've had messages from our followers. The others are over the moon. We've been getting lots of comments and likes, but *messages* are a whole other level of engagement. And everyone's so excited about the discovery of the logbook and the letter.

I ask Samara about her claim that she dreamed about the location of the tin box, and she's less confident about it this time. The story a little less defined. She sees how relieved I am and laughs.

I'm even wondering now if the items are real. The tin box seems genuine enough, but the map and the cigarette box and even the logbook... Samara could easily have planted those to drum up a bit of theater for our followers. If that's the case here, great. I can stomach a fraud easier than I can the idea that she legit dreamed about singing that led to her finding some genuine material from over a century ago.

It is disquieting, downright stomach-churning, the idea that nudges at me. That we're all being influenced by something here.

First my dream of the horses, then finding horse bones. Then Samara saying she dreamed of singing. I'm sure I've never told her anything about my own dreams about someone singing. So that's two coincidences.

I hope, I *hope* the tin box story is false.

Jens and I still haven't had much luck with our own research. The internet continues to be super glitchy, but when I can log on I decide to start looking into Skúmaskot and the reasons why the villagers left. I find a Facebook group set up for people with ties to Skúmaskot and ask to join, and in the meantime I look at old photographs posted online from the early twentieth century. There are kids standing on the pier and boats in the harbor, and there's a mention in several blogs of a school.

I get approved for the Facebook group, so I run a search for any mention of a curse. Nothing comes up. A thread from 2014 pops up:

Gunnar Einnerson
Hi there, anyone know why the villagers left Skúmaskot so abruptly?

Ella Boyce
My great-great-grandma was born in Skúmaskot in 1898. Her parents moved the family to Hólmavík when she was 4, and she said it was because there was a fire. Not sure what kind but that was the story I heard.

Hildur Magnusdottir
You're right, there was a fire in Skúmaskot. Early 1900s, I believe. The villagers burned down the old whaling station pretty much as soon as it was built. Skúmaskot was historically a shark fishing village and the villagers said the whaling station would destroy their income because the whales scared off the sharks. I think

that's why people left. People started fishing out of Hólmavík, which had more amenities. And when that town grew, people stopped traveling to Skúmaskot.

Olaf Urwin
Retrospective BS. Skúmaskot still had a school in the 1960s.

I search the terms *shipwreck* and *Ormen* and the threads are so numerous I spend an hour trawling through them all. One stands out, and I notice it has forty-five likes:

Esther Watson
My father-in-law worked for the coast guard when the wreck washed up in Skúmaskot in the seventies. He was one of the first people on the scene to view it. And you're right, @olafurwin—there was a school there in the 1960s and the town was thriving. But after the wreck washed up, everything changed. *That's* when people left. The government wouldn't move the ship and people were freaked out. My FIL had violent nightmares for weeks. He's seen all kinds of things on the coast but the *Ormen* had a super nasty vibe. One of his workmates said he saw a woman on the beach every time he visited and he was so freaked out he asked for a transfer. Stay well clear, folks.

I pause at the mention of nightmares, and the woman. Many commenters claim that Skúmaskot was an otherwise normal, uneventful fishing village, winding down after friction between rival companies deepened. But a few mention that the *Ormen* was the real catalyst, and not just because of the spectacle of a crumbling ghost ship close to the bay. Anyone who ventured out to see it experienced nightmares or a feeling of being watched, and some people said they saw a specter. A woman.

I really want to believe that Skúmaskot was deserted because of infrastructure, but I find myself searching out those comments that mention a woman. It is majorly coincidental that Samara has a theory about a woman being on board the *Ormen* and loads of people claim to have seen a ghostly woman on the beach here. And there's the woman I have seen here, too . . . I suppose you could argue that the female stowaway was local knowledge. Samara's research paper from the 1960s—the one that mentions the *siùrsach*—proves that someone had already theorized it decades ago, and possibly folk mythologized a ghost on the back of that rumor. I've seen this happen time and again with abandoned places. People love to make up stories, and especially when it concerns ghosts.

But on the other hand, I've seen the woman with my own eyes. I've dreamed her. The singing I've heard . . . I could swear it's a female voice. And I can feel it, the sense of malice that lingers in this place. You just get a feeling from places. Sometimes there's a sense of peace, and sometimes there's even humor. But Skúmaskot is a place of cruelty.

I can feel it as strongly as though the rocks are shouting it.

II

I'm crawling across the beach, a heavy black tail beneath my dress. It's dark, and I can see the wreck of the *Ormen* in front of me. I hate it with every fiber of my being.

I want it to burn. I open my mouth and let out a long scream. Black birds shoot out of my mouth, flying up over the shipwreck before pummeling down like darts to their death.

I wake up sobbing, clawing at my mouth. I can still taste the feathers, their texture. I can hear the cry of the birds all around me.

I bolt out of my bedroom, then stagger upstairs and throw up into the sink. It's still dark.

Samara is sitting on the sofa.

"Are you okay?" she asks.

She looks upset, like she's been crying. She's wearing her pajamas and her beanie, her knees drawn up to her chest.

I wipe my mouth and approach her. "What's wrong?"

With a sigh, she takes her audio recorder from her pocket and taps the screen. She holds it to my ear and I listen. It sounds like gunshots. Just like the first recording she ever played me did, too.

"I recorded it last week," she says. "It's from the ice in the bay."

"It sounds like someone's pumping rounds out of a shotgun," I say.

She nods and taps her recorder, then holds it up to my ear again. A similar sound bleeds into my ear, the crack-sound more like a pistol this time. "Everything I record sounds like this," she says. "This whole place is just filled with the sounds of gunshots."

She plays another track and tells me it's from the turf houses. She spent two hours in one of them, not moving, just recording ambiance. For a moment I can't hear anything, but then there's a noise like the slowed-down blast of a rifle in the distance, the echo continuing for ten seconds.

"I don't understand," I say, sitting down next to her. "How the hell do you get gunshots from an empty turf house?"

She shrugs. "I mean, it's sped up. But I'm freaked out. *Everything* I'm recording sounds like gunshots. It's triggering me." She rolls her eyes. "No pun intended."

I stare at her. "Why is it triggering you?"

"It's like you said," she says, slipping the audio recorder back into her pocket. "Some things exist outside language, right?"

"Right."

Samara looks out the window at the ocean like liquid amethyst, a black line of horizon separating it from a bank of lilac clouds.

"I was shot," she says finally. "By a guy I'd been kind of flirting with. That's why the gunshots are freaking me out."

I watch her as she keeps her eyes away from mine, sounding out the words.

"I'm sorry," I say.

She nods and wipes a tear from her face. "I've blanked out most of it. Before and after. That's the basic fact. But the sound of fireworks, poppers, any loud noise at all . . . It has always triggered me." She turns to me, her eyes softening as she looks at me. "It's like you said. Us explorers always have a story. It's why we come to places like this, right?"

I nod. "Did he get put away?"

She shakes her head and looks at the ground. "He turned the gun on himself straight after."

"God. I'm so sorry."

"I wasn't the only one he hurt." She says it like she's remembering it for the first time, like something she has buried deep in a secret part has suddenly come loose.

"Is that why you were so upset about the horses?" I ask.

She bites her lip. "I need to ask you something," she says then. "About your past."

I stop. "My past?" I say.

Just then the cabin door opens, and Leo bursts in.

"You want to see something?"

Samara wipes her eyes and throws me a look that tells me at once that she's grateful for the chance to share and that we'll not mention any of this to Leo. We get up and pull on our coats before heading out on the deck.

Leo is starboard, ocean side, looking down over the waves.

“There’s a seal,” he says. “It’s been hanging out by the boat for days. Just one. Usually they’re in a bob.”

“A bob?”

“The collective for seal.”

“Where is it?” Samara asks.

Leo points at a spot in the sea, about twenty feet from us. “There,” he says.

We stare for at least a minute, looking hard at the sea.

“Is that it?” Samara says, pointing at a white wave.

“No,” Leo says. “I can’t see it anymore. That’s a shame. I was watching it for a while, too.”

Samara encourages him to fetch the cameras, and we run back to the cabin to get them. Samara lifts the binoculars and pauses at the window of the cabin that overlooks the beach, in case she might see something. She scans the horizon, and I stand behind her, looking out at the sea.

Part of me is looking for a human head, and the outline of a shoulder.

Nicky

I

30 July 1901
Melville Bay, Davis Strait

The *Ormen* was deep in the Davis Strait, winding past islands and channels and surrounded by inky pyramids daubed with snow that knifed into a marbled sky. The ocean was still, no heaving waves, the surface blanketed by large chunks of clear ice that crowded around the helm like an insurrection. Farther out, icebergs sat large as mountains, a verdigris halo in the water marking their depth. Nicky had always thought heaven would be white, and therefore serene and comforting, but the whiteness here was menacing. Everything was angled and chromatic, and as the men scrubbed the deck Nicky could make out their breaths glistening with ice fractals, a row of icicles along the ratlines like fangs.

In the crow's nest Cowie stood huddled in an overcoat, his chin buried beneath his collar. None of the men seemed to be as awe-struck as she was—they barely looked up at the staggering scenery all around. But then, the Arctic was familiar territory to them. For a quarter of the year, they walked the streets of Dundee, just like her, but the other three quarters they lived in this otherworldly place, with its hoary cathedrals and murky waters under which shadows moved quietly, and the ocean transformed itself from a wilderness of squalls to a cracked window.

The *Ormen* turned toward an ice shelf that adjoined the land, some shrubs and heathland visible beyond, and a waterfall. She thirsted after fresh water, the thought of bathing in clean water a sudden compulsion. Nicky could see what looked like fallen tree trunks on the ice shelf, but when the men gathered on the deck with their rifles, she realized they were seals.

Finding fresh candles and a bedwarmer in the galley, she retreated to her cabin and wrapped herself with the bedwarmer beneath the blankets of her small bed. Outside, gunshots rang out, one after the other, followed by shouts of joy. It went on for hours, growing more distant, and the length of time between the gunshots drawing out longer and longer.

It was almost dawn when she returned to the top deck to empty her bedpan, and she found the light was as bright as it had been that evening, though the ice shelf was no longer pristine—instead, it was scrawled with garnet. The men laid out their haul on the deck, exhausted and bloodied. She counted twenty-nine walrus and more than sixty seals. Lovejoy was still on the ice, yelling at Reid and Anderson. When she looked down she saw that he was trying to bring a dead polar bear on board. It was just a cub, but even so the boys were so tired that they couldn't lift it whole.

That night, when three knocks sounded on her door, she found Lovejoy there. As usual, her stomach tightened at the sight of him, though she noticed he had combed his greasy hair in a side parting, and he was wearing a clean shirt. Also, he was holding something wrapped in a blanket.

"A gift," he said, when he closed the door behind her. "For a selkie wife."

He unwrapped it, and she saw it was a skull, yellow teeth as long as her thumbs angling down, sharp as knives. Nicky realized with a jolt that it was the upper half of the skull of the polar bear cub, cleansed with rubbing alcohol, that Lovejoy had killed earlier that day.

He told her to sit on the bed. As usual, she did not speak, but did what he asked.

"A crown," he said, placing it on her head. Lovejoy had padded the underside with cloth—a small mercy, to prevent the sharp bone digging into her head, and also to keep it in place. The skull of an adult bear would have been too large, the length of a man's forearm, and she suspected Lovejoy had killed a younger bear for exactly this purpose. There was something in his stare as he looked at her wearing the skull. A transfixed kind of murk.

"Undress," he said in a hoarse voice.

As Lovejoy grunted above her, his face shining with sweat, he kept his eyes on the skull, as though he were fucking the bear and not her. She wondered if he cared anymore about what she was becoming. She kept her foot bandaged, hidden out of sight, but the wound was still badly infected, spreading up her leg like a second skin. A pelt. As though her body was desperately trying to heal itself, using whatever means necessary—human, or animal.

As she hummed, she imagined herself swimming underwater, the bear skull on her head as a crown. Her tail flicking through the blue, her bare breasts cupped by shells, and an icicle in her hand, long as a spear.

Sharp enough to kill.

Dominique

I

December 2023
Skúmaskot, Iceland

Jens and I discover Diego's surname.

I find it in my cabin, of all places. In the morning, as I come out of my tent I drop my torch. It rolls under the old metal electrical box, and when I search there I put my hand on a dusty old book. It's a Spanish edition of a Truman Capote novel, *Otras Voces, Otros Ámbitos.* The cover has been torn off, but inside I see that someone has written their name: *Diego Almeyda.* I remember the book I found in the hold with *Diego* written in the front, how Jens had said we needed the surname. Here it was: Almeyda.

"Jens!" I call, and he comes running into my cabin, as though something was wrong. When he looks down at the inscription, his eyes go wide. "Google it," he says.

Quickly I open my laptop and connect to the internet terminal, expecting it to glitch again. But no, this time Google appears, and I type words into the search bar:

Diego Almeyda Ormen

Eventually I find a newspaper article in *Argentina News* about a man from Mendoza, but it's all in Spanish. I cut and paste it all into Google Translate:

Funeral Held for Mendoza Man Found Aboard Ghost Ship

21 December 1973

Today the family of Dr. Diego Almeyda, 28, laid his body to rest in his hometown of Mendoza. Dr. Almeyda was found on a research ship, the *Ormen*, which was found adrift in the Barents Sea. The search continues for the rest of his colleagues.

"Holy shit," I say, glancing at Jens to gauge his reaction. He looks every bit as shocked as I am.

"Search again," he says. "Different keywords."

I try *Diego Almeyda body found Ormen*. We click through twenty pages of searches but nothing seems relevant. I try *crew of Ormen 1973* and nothing comes up either. It feels disappointing, like we're on the verge of a huge find for our research. A thread that, once pulled, could unravel a seriously sinister mystery. This discovery might lead us to find the whole list of people who were on board during the time they went missing, and maybe even the cause . . .

"My bet is that they were researching something shady and got on the wrong side of some nasty people," I tell Jens. The Arctic has been contested territory for decades because the oil is worth billions. There are shedloads of military vessels and personnel, mostly Russian, dotted throughout, trying to extend their territory into the Arctic. The Russians even planted a flag on the seabed beneath the North Pole in 2007 to claim territory. Russia's Arctic territory accounts for a fifth of their economy, so it's no wonder. Some countries have been known to train whales to scope out submarines and other vessels with spy cameras and location instruments attached to their bodies. How ironic—during the whaling era, the Arctic was fought over for whale oil to light cities and factories and basically prop up mechanical production. And from the *Ormen*'s research era until the present day, the Arctic has been fought over for fossil fuels. Capitalism, in other words. The Arctic is the cradle of capitalism. So much has changed since Victorian times, and yet many things remain exactly the same.

A few days before Christmas, Leo suggests we should hold the contest vote.

"A good way to celebrate the solstice, no?"

"I thought we were waiting until next week?" I say.

"People will be focused on the *Ormen* being broken up," Samara says. "We should do it now. A surprise for the followers."

I'm still not convinced, but Samara's more media savvy than I am, so I decide to go along with it. I'm still super shocked by the revelation about Diego Almeyda. I can't stop looking at the marks on the floor of the main cabin. The bloodstains. The reasons for an entire crew—save one man, who was found dead—going missing on a ship are likely to be violent.

We sit down at the dining table and eat lunch while Leo sets up the internet terminal to do a livestream.

"Here we go," Leo says, lifting his laptop onto the table. He sets his phone on a small tripod and films the four of us. We wave at the screen like a team, like four friends, though the dynamic is still charged.

"Hey, everyone," Samara says. I see the TikTok counter start to climb. Fifty-four viewers. "We're opening the voting for our fun contest today, woo-hoo! Just a recap about what we're doing and what you'll be voting on. My buddies Dom, Leo, Jens, and I have been researching two different eras of the shipwreck we're living on right now. Leo and I have been researching the whaling era—say hi, Leo."

Leo presses his hands into his cheeks and makes a goblin face. "Hi."

"And Dom and Jens have been researching the period when the ship was used for research here in the Arctic."

Jens and I do a thumbs-up. "Vote for us!" I say.

"We'll leave the voting open until midnight," Samara says. "Have a look at the footage we've posted and make your decision. Remember, the winning team gets to open the captain's cabin! And we've got a super-duper cash prize for two fabulous voters, chosen at random. Get voting!"

Leo reaches for the phone on the tripod and cuts off the recording, and we all sigh with relief. I sense that we're exhausted by this exploration, drained by excitement, apprehension, and, at times, stone-cold fear.

II

It's twenty minutes to midnight.

We're all heading to the captain's cabin, Leo guiding us down the steps and along the lower deck with a flashlight. We've gathered our solar lanterns and laid them along the corridor, but the additional light of Leo's torch is necessary both for the live and because Samara is carrying the tin box containing the logbook, the maps, and the letter. The deck is still slippery.

Samara takes her position beside the ornate door that remains sealed, and the set of chisels that Leo found in the hold, which the winners are to use to unjam the door. Despite this plan, I'm nervous that we have promised our followers something that we can't fulfill, that we won't be able to break the door to the captain's cabin down. And part of me is also nervous about what lies behind it. It could be a trap. That's not just paranoia talking. Samara said so as well. Or if not a trap, the air could hold spores.

I don't want to be a killjoy, but the climactic end of our contest might be our own end if we're not careful.

Samara's going to open the letter and attempt to read the contents outside the door, just before the countdown. I've brought the Capote novel with the missing cover and a screenshot of the guy whose signature is scrawled there. Jens has brought some old science instruments he found washed up in the bay—a microscope, some old test tubes, and our pièce de résistance, a brass cylinder that turns out to be a research instrument used for icebergs, called a tiltmeter. We'd spotted it in the filthy water in the hold when we first went down there, but didn't think it was anything significant. According to Google, a tiltmeter measures an iceberg's basal melting, as well as tidal motion and changes caused by tremors, so it likely would have been used during the *Ormen*'s research era.

"I wonder if it still works," Samara says, looking it over as Jens holds it up to the light. We cleaned it up, bringing the brass to a decent shine.

"Even if it does," Leo says, "do any of us know how to use it?"

"We'd need an iceberg," Jens says. "Or a volcano."

"We've got a volcano," Leo says. "I don't think it's active, though."

"Are we ready?" Samara says, glancing at her watch, and we all nod.

Leo sets up the tripod with the camera and light fitting, then scoots back alongside us all for the livestream.

"Hey, everyone," Samara says to the camera. "We're about to announce the winners of our contest. You've still got ten minutes to vote, so we thought we'd reveal our very last discoveries for those of you who might be sitting on the fence." She turns to me. "Dominique? You want to go first?"

I nod, instantly embarrassed. Even without a visible audience I know how bad I am on screen. I hold up my Capote.

"I found a copy of a Truman Capote novel," I say, fingering the yellowed pages gently as I hold it closer to the lens. "It's missing a cover but you can see the title here. And I saw that the owner had written their name inside. Diego Almeyda."

"What?" Samara says.

"Diego Almeyda," I say again, and I see her face drop. "I googled him and it turns out he was one of the scientists on board the *Ormen* in 1973, right when the whole crew went missing."

Jens starts to clap. Samara looks stunned. Leo glances at her, nervous.

"Samara, you okay?" he whispers, and she looks paralyzed, utterly stricken. We all trade looks for a second, wondering what to do.

"Uh, yeah," she says finally, visibly attempting to snap out of whatever was running through her mind. She holds up the letter but seems to freeze again, her eyes wide and her mouth open.

"So we have a letter here," Leo says, stepping in. He takes the letter from Samara's hand and holds it up to the lens. "This was in the tin box that Samara found, *unopened.* We reckon it's from 1901. A little warning: this isn't the moment you want to scroll away, folks. I'm going to open this *hundred-and-twenty-something-year-old* letter right now, and read its secrets to you all watching at home. Ready?"

I squint at the viewer counter on the screen. It looks like we're at three thousand viewers, which isn't bad at all.

Leo slips a knife under the fold of the envelope and opens it carefully. Gently, he pulls out the letter. The ink is distorted by water damage, the letters faded and blurry. Leo tries to read it but can only make out a handful of words that don't make sense.

"I think that says 'mother,'" Leo says hopefully, and we all look at the word he points at.

"Could be," Jens says. "Or perhaps 'mottle'?"

Leo squints at it a while longer before giving up. "Sorry, everyone," he says. "Still, a remarkable document right here. And if you look at our previous posts, you'll see Samara talking about the logbook with its incredible reveal of a stowaway! How's *that* for a discovery?"

We have a few minutes left, so Jens holds up the microscope. "This is from the research era, obviously. It has a Leica lens and would be worth a bit, if it weren't for the bullet hole through the casing."

I turn to him. "Bullet hole?"

He nods. "Pretty sure." He turns the microscope upside down and shows us a round hole in the metal casing.

"Wow," I say, taking that in. "Maybe it broke and someone used it for target practice?"

Samara looks uneasy, her face dropping again. It's awkward, as this is a livestream and usually she's the frontwoman, talking nonstop and leading the dynamic. But she looks dazed.

"Okay, that's thirty seconds left," Leo says, and I silently sigh in relief. We all count down from ten, and when it hits midnight Leo shouts, "Voting stops!"

We gather around the phone and look at the results: forty-six percent of votes are for the research era, and fifty-four are for the whaling era. Samara and Leo give a shout for joy and wrap their arms around each other. Jens and I share a brief look. Winning means nothing to either of us, really. If anything, I'm relieved that I'm not the one who'll be opening the door to the captain's cabin.

Leo leans his shoulder against the door, giving it a test, just in case. It doesn't budge, so we all set about using the chisels that Leo found in the hold to hack into the frame. It should feel like sacrilege, but after bashing in so many other doors for firewood, this doesn't seem any different. Still, it's a shame that the beautiful hand-carved oak will be underwater in a fortnight. I watch everyone warily, remembering the weird sensation I had that first night here. The feeling when I turned the handle. I've been dreading this.

"That's it!" Leo says then, setting down the chisel and pressing his hands flat against the wood. "Can you feel that?"

Samara leans against it too. "It's definitely shifted," she says, glancing at me and Jens.

"Let me have another try," Leo says, and we clear a space as he steps back along the corridor, then takes a run at the door and, with a roar, kicks it.

I cover my mouth as the door creaks open, only a couple of inches, the hinges refusing to yield. Samara and Leo push against it, but I back away, too nervous to approach. After a minute or so they manage to shove it open enough for Samara to slide through the gap.

"A desk has fallen against the door," she calls back to us. "That's why it wouldn't open."

We hear the wail of wood against wood as she drags it back. Leo grabs the camera and heads inside. Jens turns to me.

"Feeling nervous?" he says.

I keep my sleeve to my mouth as I follow him inside.

"Here we are," Samara is saying to the camera. "The captain's cabin! Opened for the first time in God knows how long."

It's a large cabin, a window blocked up, a gaping hole at the far corner visible behind a bookcase. An old wooden desk is overturned, a chair toppled beside the bookcase. Samara opens the drawers and lifts out sheaves of paper, badly stained. From the ceiling, an old brass oil lamp hangs crookedly, covered in cobwebs and dust. I help Jens right the desk. I can tell it's the original desk from the nineteenth century. The old brass handles on the drawers, the black leather writing surface. When Jens shines his light down onto the leather I can make out impressions. I think of a man writing on this desk, over a hundred years ago. As I'm leaning down, running my eyes over the still-visible imprints of writing, I think of the words that Leo carved into the dining table in the main cabin, the poem about the selkie wife and sea king. A melody slips into my mind. It fits the words. It isn't a poem.

It's a song.

And I have no idea how I know this.

"As a special thank-you to our wonderful voters," Leo tells the viewers. Only five hundred are still watching. "I'm going to do a pretty epic parkour challenge across the bay next time we have enough light and battery to livestream. Stay tuned, folks! It'll be mega!"

III

We wake to sunlight. Actual light, a ball of pearly brightness cradled by the mountains.

"Holy shit!" I hear Samara shout, and I run out onto the deck to see her halfway up the stairs. "Do you see that?"

"See what?" Leo calls after her, only to yell when they see the streak of light funneling down the stairs.

We all race up to the cabin. It's eleven o'clock in the morning and technically we've all slept in, but the darkness has disrupted everyone's sleep patterns. When it's dark like this there is no day and night, only a round continuum of time.

I check the solar chargers by the window. The red digits read seventy-eight percent charged.

"They're at seventy-eight," I call to Leo and Samara. "One has charged all the way to eighty."

"Holy *shit*!" Samara shouts again, in a different tone. "That's amazing!"

"That's enough for the parkour," Leo says. "I'll do it now before the light changes."

I start plugging the cameras into the solar chargers to give the batteries as much charge as I can.

We hear the familiar sound of Jens climbing up the ladder. "What's all the screaming about?" he says. "Haven't you ever seen sunlight before?"

"Not for weeks," I say, holding up the solar chargers.

"We got enough charge for the Parkour Thank You," Samara tells him. She bounces to the kettle. "And I'm making coffee. Anyone want one?"

We all do. It's been a long few days without enough charge for a kettle.

Leo tells us he's going to parkour over the bay and needs us all to film. "We'll do a drone *and* a headcam live," he says. "And maybe two other angles from both sides of the bay."

Samara, Jens, and I share a look. The range of camera angles *would* be really cool, and we could edit the footage later to cut between them all. It *would* be cinematic.

Jens shrugs. "I'm up for it."

Leo tugs his red bobble hat down over his forehead before

heading toward the cabin door. "You better grab your cameras, folks, because I'm only doing this once."

"Shit," Samara says, scrambling for her camera. Leo's already reaching for the door. I flick on the internet terminal and log in to our project TikTok account. I hit "live" and turn the lens to my face.

"Hi, friends, we've got some exciting content coming up so stay tuned. It involves Leo, it involves parkour, and it involves *ice*. Are you ready?"

"I need to get my drone," Jens says.

"You better hurry," Leo says, pulling the door open.

We all rush after him, stepping out into the bracing air. The wind is kicking up the sand, sending it dancing across the bay like the inside of a snow globe, and I can't help but laugh with excitement. Doing a live is stressful at the best of times, because you can't control things, and certainly not the weather. Doing a live out here is like aligning the planets, and after everything that's gone wrong for us, this combination of good light, charged cameras, and Leo's eagerness to do an epic stunt all feels like a gift. I watch the numbers climb on the screen—we're already at four hundred.

We climb down to the bottom of the ladder. Jens fetches his drone while Leo stretches on the sand, raising his calves and circling his narrow hips, then windmilling his arms. I film it all, positioning myself so that I get the shipwreck and a good section of the beach into the frame behind Leo. The black sand against the thickening snow is gorgeous. Six hundred ninety. Seven hundred ten. This is phenomenal. By the time I've been filming for four minutes we're at a thousand.

"Samara's going to film from the other side of the bay," I tell the viewers. "And in the meantime, Leo's making sure he stretches out his muscles to prevent injuries. A really important part of parkour, right, Leo?"

"Damn right," Leo says, sinking down easily into a split. "A warm muscle is a safe muscle."

"I can't even touch my toes, folks," I say into the lens. "So don't feel bad if you too can't do the splits in minus-six-degree temperatures."

"Ready?" Leo says.

I look over at Jens. He has the drone set up and livestreaming on his own TikTok account, and I tag him into mine. Samara's green hat is visible at the bend of the bay in the distance, and I see her livestream on my phone. She's jogging and laughing into the lens, chatting away but so exhilarated I can't make her out. The closed captions can't either, nonsense sentences blinking up on the screen before her face.

I watch the view numbers, expecting them to decline, but they continue to climb until they reach 3,074. Bloody hell. Comments pop up, too, remarking on the landscape and the ship, and conversations break out—people who hadn't heard about our project beforehand are intrigued while older followers are informing them about it. *They're a group of explorers checking out a shipwreck in Iceland before it's hauled into the sea. It was an old whaling ship and apparently it's haunted.* Reactions flood up the screen like bubbles, thumbs-ups, and hearts and "wow" emojis.

I look around for Jens and spot a pink dot on the side of the volcano. His beanie. Leo has finished stretching out and signals to Samara on the other side, before turning to me. "Tell us what you're going to do, Leo," I say, holding my lens on him.

He points at the frozen water of the bay. "I'm going to parkour over that to the turf houses on the other side."

"Can you tell us a little about what parkour is?" I say.

"Parkour is a dark poetry, bitches," Leo tells the viewers, making a peace sign and pressing his face so close to the lens that I can make out his eyelashes furred with snowflakes. He leans back and rolls his neck from side to side. "Seriously, though, you have to move fearlessly. Parkour is moving without hesitation, like you could dodge a bullet. It's a combination of dance, gymnastics, and extreme mental resilience and determination."

Leo clicks on his headcam. I check that the livestream is showing up on his TikTok feed before tagging it for our viewers.

"We're livestreaming from four angles," I say into the lens. "We're calling this *Live Parkour in Four Dimensions*, right, Leo?"

"Right!"

I look over to Jens and hold up an arm, then give a thumbs-up to let him know that we're good to film. I can't see his drone in the sky, so I check his livestream. Instantly I see Leo and me from above, the two of us small figures on a bed of white.

The project livestream has 4,007 viewers. I screenshot to prove it to the others. They won't believe me otherwise.

"Okay, we're ready Leo," I say, stepping back to allow him space to get into position. Already the sunlight is fading, clouds thickening overhead. He pulls off his coat, leaving him with just a beanie, a V-vest, and gloves for warmth. And then he's off, bursting off the bank toward the bay, snow kicking up behind his heels.

We all click into action, Jens's drone lowering into view like a black cross against the white curtain of snow. I keep my camera steady, but Leo is barely visible now. On the headcam footage I can see the icy surface of the bay, and he's using the rocks and ice blocks to propel himself forward, lowering onto all fours, then spinning into a backflip. The image wheels as he somersaults, and Samara comes into view, standing on the pier. She gives a whoop as Leo dives past her toward the turf houses.

Leo makes it onto the roof in two leaps, and from there he hurls himself onto the next roof, then the next, like a panther in human form. Like he's literally unafraid of falling.

I watch, openmouthed, as he reaches the edge of the last turf house. There's a huge gap between it and the school, and for a moment I think he's going to attempt to jump it.

My heart rises into my mouth, and Samara must be thinking the same thing, because I hear her voice over the livestream: "Don't be an idiot, Leo."

Leo is a speck in the distance, almost blotted out completely by fog, but I see from his headcam that he's doing a handstand on the edge of the turf house, his hands planted on the lip of the roof and his legs held high in the air. Suddenly Leo springs backward, his body wheeling through the air. I can't bring myself to look, because I know what he's doing—Leo has sprung off the roof of the turf house into a midair backflip and is trying to land on the roof of the school. It feels like an eternity as he spins through the air, the footage on his livestream a blur of granite sky and white ground.

I can't look.

Samara lets out a shout. Leo has landed, a little wobbly, but he rolls into it before springing up again on all fours, leaping down to the ground.

Jesus Christ. My heart can't take much more of this.

Emojis of hearts and faces bubble up across my stream. I lower my phone and squint through the blizzard. Samara steps off the pier and runs toward Leo, and I can hear her laughing. She wraps her arms around Leo and on Samara's livestream I see her and Leo's faces, wet and smiling and encrusted with snowflakes. Their exhilaration is palpable. I want to run over and join in the celebration. I want to show them that we have almost five thousand goddamn viewers tuning in from every corner of the globe right now.

But Leo's on the move again. I flick to Jens's drone feed to work out where he's going—he is headed for the bay, close to the bend. I raise my camera to film, wiping the lens with my glove to clear the moisture from the snow. I should have brought a lens cloth. In a moment it clears, and I see Leo bounding across the ice, zigzagging toward the beach. We're at five and a half thousand viewers now, my phone pulsing with notifications. It's terrific, but also draining my battery. I pause and find the "settings" tab, then tap the button that lets me switch off the notifications. When I glance up again Samara has cut across the ice instead of looping around the bay, approaching Leo as he holds a handstand on the mermaid stone, straight and still as a lightning rod.

The light is fading fast, shadows blooming across the heath. Something stirs in the corner of my vision. A figure at the turn of the bay in the distance, about two hundred meters away.

Fear thumps in my throat, acidic.

It's the woman.

I turn my phone to film her, toggling the zoom. Desperation burns in me to catch her, to snare the proof of her existence. But she's gone, only shadows where she stood before. I zoom in frantically anyway, sweeping my camera across the whole of the bay.

A yell echoes across the plain. I turn back to Leo and squint into the murk. He's off the rocks, moving quickly toward the pier. From his movements I can tell he's running toward something. Where is Samara?

I flip across to her live feed and see that it is no longer capturing the whiteness of the bay but is a dark blue, a stream of bubbles and a hand reaching forward.

"Help!" Leo shouts. "Dom, *help*!"

Oh my God. Samara is underwater. She has fallen through the ice.

Jens's drone appears in the sky above, diving down over a large hole in the ice. I frantically check Samara's footage to work out where she is, but just then her footage cuts out, goes blank. I can't move, can't will my legs to run toward her. And then I see Leo racing across the ice, and I realize he might go underneath, too, and suddenly I'm running from the other side toward them, shouting at them to get off the ice.

I find myself kneeling by a square-shaped hole about the width of the hatch in the *Ormen*, shouting for Samara. Leo appears with a long plank of wood and lowers it into the dark water that laps up around my knees. My hands are so cold they won't work properly.

"Samara!" Leo shouts again, leaning down to the hole in the ice. He pulls off his hat and plunges his head underneath in a bid to see her but it's so dark, impenetrably dark, and it strikes me that she's been underwater for over a minute. I'm gasping and crying into the wet dark, pawing at the water in the hole in case I might somehow find Samara there.

Something pushes to the surface, the crown of a head glistening in the light. It's Samara, her mouth open as she gasps and claws at me. I reach out to her, grasping her shoulders, but suddenly the ice beneath me tilts, lightning-shaped cracks streaking across the pale blue surface. Leo gives a deafening shriek, and on instinct I push myself back from the ice that crumbles into the dark water beneath, widening the hole.

Samara slides back down despite Leo reaching for her, their hands clasping for a moment. I lunge forward, reaching down for her too. My hands hit something but I can't grasp her. Leo is screaming, "Samara! Samara!" and I see the ice beneath his knees begin to fold, a creaking sound indicating that it's about to give way.

The noise grows louder, and I realize it's coming from behind. I turn to see Jens running toward me, pulling off his boots and hat as he moves. He jumps feetfirst straight into the hole, sending the icy water sloshing around Leo and me. I watch him as if in slow motion, as though I am far away, distanced from the scene in front of me.

A sense of déjà vu is creeping through me, as though I know this scene, as though I have watched it all before.

My reverie is broken by Leo shouting my name. Jens's jump has weakened the ice shelf, and I manage to grab Leo's hand right as the ice beneath him collapses, pulling him toward me.

We cling to one another, our breaths pushing out like clouds into the darkness.

Stillness. Jens and Samara are underneath us, deep in the water. We've lost them both.

Then I feel something move beneath me, as though a hand is scratching at the ice. I feel sure I can see Jens's face staring up through the layers of ice. I move forward and plunge my hand into the water, splashing and yelling, "We're here! Here!" A second later, Jens bursts up through the surface, gasping for air, and I see he has Samara in the crook of his arm. Somehow Leo and I manage to haul him up onto the ice while he holds Samara, and he drags her awkwardly up, her body weighed down by water.

"Give her CPR!" I scream at Leo, and he hesitates before lowering, pushing air into Samara's lungs, then turning her head to the side.

Water dribbles from her lips, her eyes staring. Leo leans down and breathes air into her mouth, then straightens and presses down, down, and down.

Samara gives a faint cough, and I shout out.

"Yes!" I say. "That's it, Samara! Breathe!"

"We have to get off the ice," Jens pants. The ice is bending beneath our weight, water bubbling up through narrow cracks.

IV

The ice breaks a second after we lunge toward the pier, folding inward like a shattered window.

Leo and I carry Samara back to the *Ormen*, her body limp as a doll's. She is unconscious, her mouth open and the whites of her eyes showing, but she's hanging on by a thread.

Inside the cabin, Leo makes a fire hastily while I strip Samara of her wet clothes and dry her with a towel, before wrapping her with a thick blanket. Jens watches on, shivering and refusing to get changed. I think he's in shock.

"You have to take your clothes off," I tell him. "Jens! You'll go into shock!"

But he stands like a sentinel, watching on as I remove Samara's socks and rub her feet, finally lifting my shirt and pressing the soles against my belly for extra heat.

"We're on the ship now, Samara," I say loudly. "We're getting you all warmed up. Stay with us, okay? You just keep focused on my voice. We're going to get the fire going and you'll be right as rain really soon."

I think of the woman appearing at the edge of the ice right before Samara fell. There's no denying it now. There's no denying what she is. And every single time she appears, bad things happen. But I still can't bring myself to mention it to the others. Not now.

Oh God, the livestream is still running, my phone in my pocket. All of this has been seen. What will our followers think?

"It's my fault!" Leo groans. "I did this! I did this! She wouldn't have stepped on the ice if I hadn't have gone on it."

"The ice cracked," Jens says, a statement so obvious and yet so devastating that we all nod. "No one knows where or when ice will crack. It has nothing to do with you."

"No!" Leo shouts, and he repeats it, beating his fists against his head. I want to stop him, but I don't. I know Leo is shouting at the situation, at the fact that we can't turn back time.

"We have to get her help," I scream.

"How?" Jens says quietly, and Leo covers his face with his hands and breaks down into ugly sobs. I feel angry for no good reason, particularly with Leo. For crying. But mostly, I feel like I'm the one who's really to blame. I feel it so strongly, without really understanding where it comes from. The nagging, tormenting guilt.

We are at least six hours from help. Six hours on a clear day. We can't even risk venturing to the nearest town, because the snow is now falling so heavily we risk getting lost, or getting trapped.

We sit quietly, praying the fire won't go out. Praying that Samara will survive the night.

And no one is listening to our prayers.

Nicky

I

September 1901
Upernavik, Greenland

Nicky sat in the galley with Reid while he unfolded the piece of paper. His cheeks were flushed, and she saw that his hands shook.

"Are you nervous?" she asked him.

"A little," he said, lowering his eyes to the page.

"You've shared your songs with me before," she said.

"Aye, but this one's about you," he said shyly. "I hope you don't mind."

"About me?" she said, looking down at the words on the sheet of paper.

"Well, it's about the folktale, too," he said. "But I thought of you when I wrote it."

She felt something turn in her stomach as she looked down at the words written on the page.

When once a town lost half its men
a wife did swear that ne'er again

the sea would cause such hearts to grieve
and sailors to their wives would cleave.
So by the shore, upon her knees,
she prayed that Lir would calm the seas.
Lir heard and said, be changed this night—
part seal, my queen, until first light
these seas no more will cause thee strife
if you'll become my selkie wife

"It's fiction," she said, trying to raise a smile to match his.

"But you're the selkie wife," he said. "That's what Lovejoy said. Only . . . Daverley said I'm not to . . ." He saw her face fall. "I didn't mean to upset you."

"You haven't," she said, forcing a smile on her face. "It's just a song, isn't it? Why don't you go and teach it to the men?"

"Won't you come and listen?" he said.

She desperately wanted to say no, but she saw the look on his face, his childish eagerness to impress her. Reid looked upon her as someone he could talk to, and she found herself acting toward him as though he were a younger brother. When Daverley was distracted, she kept an eye out for Reid in case he got into trouble. He was a good boy, eager to help, and he often brought her extra portions of food from the galley.

"Yes," she said. "I'll come and listen."

She followed him up to the deck, bringing an extra blanket for her shoulders as Reid handed out the new sea shanty to the crew. Most of them were drunk, their limbs loose and their eyes moving across her.

"What's this, then?" Lovejoy said, lifting his eyes from the page to Reid in suspicion. "A selkie wife?"

Some of the men threw furtive glances at her, as though they'd worked out the connection between her and the shanty for themselves.

"It's my new sea shanty," Reid said proudly, standing before them. "I'm going to teach you the tune."

He sang it aloud, and the men repeated it. After several tries they'd managed to get it, and Reid lifted his arms to conduct them. The horizon was beginning to darken, a storm coming. She waited for a call from Lovejoy or the captain to bring in the sails. But no call came; the captain was out of sight, and Lovejoy was singing loudly with the men, his arms wrapped around Wolfarth and Harrow as they danced and kicked their legs out.

The men's singing outpaced Reid's conducting, faster and faster, the lyrics beginning to run together.

And then, with a loud cheer, the song finished, and the men burst into applause. It had started to rain. Nicky shrank back under the cover of the forecastle. She saw Daverley approach then, a bucket of tar in one hand and a paintbrush in the other. Reid turned to him, beaming with pride.

"Uncle," he said. "What do you think of my—"

Before he could finish his sentence, Lovejoy grabbed him roughly by the collar, yanking him toward Nicky.

"If you like her that much, what say you give her a poke with your stick?" he said. "Come on, now. Right here."

The other men laughed, but Reid's face had flushed red with humiliation. He looked like a child, radiant with fear. Lovejoy reached forward heavily and pulled at the boy's belt, as though to strip him of his trousers. The movement prompted an instinctive reaction from Reid—with a cry, he struck Lovejoy in the face, as hard as he could.

The men fell silent. It was quite a punch, coming from such a scrawny lad. Lovejoy staggered slightly, the blow catching him on the jaw, but it would take more than that to knock him down. He straightened and cocked his head, shrugging off Royle and Gray when they stepped forward to intervene.

"That's enough," Daverley said, his eyes settling on Reid. "All of you, back to your stations."

The rain fell hard, pelting the deck and bouncing upward. The boat had started to rock, ravenous winds clapping the sails. The men glanced uneasily at one another, but no one moved.

Lovejoy turned to Reid, and then Nicky, who had risen to her feet, outraged at the way he had seized the boy. She opened her mouth to shout at him to stop, but just then he raised his eyes to her, and she shrank at the look on his face. It was the same transfixed expression that came over him when he made her wear the bear's skull, as though degradation was a drug he couldn't resist.

"He's just a lad," Daverley said, approaching him.

"Maybe he's a eunuch," Lovejoy sneered. Slowly he removed a knife from his pocket and held it by his side. "We can make it so, if not."

"Put the knife down, Lovejoy," one of the other men called, and for a moment it seemed he'd realized he'd gone too far and would comply. He gave a great laugh, as if it were all a game, and the men laughed in echo. She saw Reid relax, his face loosening. But then Lovejoy lunged at Daverley, managing to shove him to the side. For such a stocky man he was surprisingly swift; in an instant he was holding the blade against Reid's smooth throat.

On the ground behind them, Daverley struggled to his feet. He had blood in his hair from where his head had struck an iron hook hanging from the mast.

"I think we've got two lasses on board, lads," Lovejoy hollered, holding Reid tight with his free arm.

"I'm . . . I'm not a lass," Reid stammered, his hands clawing at Lovejoy's arm held fast across his chest. Reid's eyes fell on Nicky. She held up her hands, signaling him to stay calm. Lovejoy's knife flashed in the sunlight, and a sudden movement might result in it cutting too deep.

"Prove it," Lovejoy said. "Prove you're not a lass. Go on." He lifted the knife and pointed it at Nicky, instructing her to move toward him. "Swyve her right here and prove yourself."

Lovejoy nodded at the rest of the crew to join in. A chant rose up: *Swyve her! Swyve her! Swyve her!*

Reid's face had crumpled. Lovejoy pushed him toward Nicky, the knife at his back, while Cowie and Gray tugged at the hem of her skirt, trying to lift it.

"Stop it!" she shouted.

She looked at Daverley, who was on his feet behind Lovejoy, trying to gauge how to intervene without worsening the situation.

"Captain!" he shouted. "Captain Willingham!"

Lovejoy nodded at the two men at either side of Nicky, and quickly they seized her, holding her in place. Lovejoy lowered before her, lifting the hem of her skirt on his blade.

"I'll make it easy for you," Lovejoy told Reid.

Reid hesitated, unsure of what to do. Liquid bloomed on the deck by his feet, and Lovejoy roared with laughter.

"He's pissed himself!" he yelled to the others. "So afraid of a woman that he's pissed himself!"

"You've made your point," she said angrily. "Put the knife down."

Lovejoy's smile faded, his eyes darkening. He moved the knife away, only to ram the wooden end into her face. She felt a hard crack against her cheek, the heat of blood rising quickly around her eye.

"You don't give orders," he said with a growl. "You don't speak. Got it?"

She cowered from his hand, raised again to strike her.

"You want to know how you came to be on this ship?" he said then, a cruel smile on his face.

She noticed that Reid had stepped backward, as though he wanted to run away.

"You were attacked in a park, correct?" Lovejoy continued.

"I was," she said, cupping her injured eye. "What do you know of it?"

"Oh, I know plenty," Lovejoy said. "And I believe Master Reid knows plenty, too. Don't you, lad?"

"I had nothing to do with it," Reid shrieked. "I had no say in the matter!"

Somewhere behind her she heard footsteps on the stairs from the captain's cabin. Her mind raced. Why was Reid reacting like this? Had he been involved?

"I think you'll find that Master Reid here was the one who assisted in carrying you aboard," Lovejoy said. "While you were asleep."

"I was *unconscious*," she spat.

Reid trembled, his eyes brimming with tears. She looked to him, unable to hide her confusion.

"I was only doing what I was told," Reid said, a sob in his voice. "I didn't know . . . I didn't know . . ."

"You knew plenty, lad. And you knew exactly why we were bringing a lass on board." Lovejoy glanced at her. "I don't know about you, selkie, but I'd be livid if I knew I was helping out the very lad who'd bundled me aboard a whaling ship."

She felt suddenly as though she were falling. Reid's face told her everything—that he had helped the man who had attacked her. Perhaps the man was Lovejoy, his appearance changed by the hat and clothing. Either way, Reid had placed her in the hold, where the barrel had fallen over and pierced her foot.

"Why?" she whispered. "Why did you do that?"

Reid covered his face with his hands. Whatever he said, she didn't hear through his sobs.

Lovejoy chuckled to himself, bending to the coil of rope by the mast. Daverley approached Reid, resting a hand on his shoulder. "Come on, lad," he said.

Just then, Reid gave a strangled cry of fury and charged at Lovejoy with his fists. In a single movement, Lovejoy sidestepped Reid's blow and swept his knife across, slicing Reid's left thigh. She heard Reid cry out as he staggered forward, falling on all fours.

A ruby-dark patch bloomed beneath Reid, and he fell slowly into it, like a bale of hay collapsing in parts. He made no sound, but the red puddle drew shouts from the men. His body spasmed and jerked with shock.

Nicky lunged at Reid quickly, pressing her hands against the wound to stop the bleeding. "Call Dr. O'Regan!" she shouted.

With a wounded yell, Daverley charged at Lovejoy, but in a moment Captain Willingham was there, ordering Stroud and Cowie to pull Daverley off Lovejoy. As they grabbed Daverley he swung an arm at Lovejoy, landing a heavy blow that streaked the air red.

"Get this man in the brig," Captain Willingham yelled at Daverley. "Back to your stations!"

But the men didn't move. They crossed themselves as Nicky leaned down close to Reid, her cheek against his, whispering the Lord's Prayer into his ear.

"Please," he said, grasping her arm. "Please don't let me be taken."

"I won't," she whispered. She felt the warmth of Reid's blood around her knees and on her arms. She clasped both hands tightly around his leg, until she felt she might squeeze the very bones. But the blood flowed from the cut like a tap, pumping vehemently through her fingers and revealing muscle through his torn trousers.

"Clear a path!" Dr. O'Regan shouted, and quickly he cut the boy's trousers to attend to his wound. "Thomas!" he shouted. "Keep your eyes on me, Thomas!"

But Reid had fallen still, his eyes staring up into the sky.

By the time Dr. O'Regan made the first stitch, Reid was already gone.

Dominique

I

December 2023
Skúmaskot, Iceland

I bring my sleeping bag upstairs to sleep on the floor next to Samara. I stoke the fires, making sure she stays warm. Darkness falls like a blade.

Exhaustion consumes me. I don't know how long I sleep for, maybe just a couple of minutes, because when I wake the fire is still hot. I reach out to check on Samara. She seems . . . different. Panicked, I put my hand to her cheek to make sure she is warm enough, and she is, but there is no breath against my hand when I move it to her mouth. I reach for her pulse. Nothing.

"Jens!" I scream. "Leo!"

Leo comes racing up the stairs and I show him.

"She's not breathing," I say, pressing both hands on her rib cage. I can feel the bones snapping with a terrible crunch. Jens is there, and he kneels beside her, taking her hand as I breathe into her mouth. Frantic, I slap her cheeks, turning her on her side and back again to breathe into her lungs. Her eyes are open and staring straight ahead, like stones. They didn't flicker in the torch-light.

"Please don't die!" I yell. *"Please!"*

Jens rests a hand on my arm and looks at me with those terrible sad eyes. "Enough," he says, but I don't stop slapping her until he pulls me away.

Leo is panting beside me, his hands pressed to his cheeks.

"What do we do?" he says to Jens. "Jens, this hasn't happened before. What do we do?"

I watch, sobbing, as Leo's voice rises into a panic. "This hasn't happened before, Jens! Where is she? What's happening?"

He grabs Jens by the upper arms and shakes him, but Jens simply holds him in a flat stare, sadness etched deeply on his features. Leo is spiraling now, screaming things that don't make sense.

"You said it would work! You said it would fucking work! What's happening? Answer me!"

Jens doesn't speak, doesn't react at all. He is so still and vacant that I wonder if he's having a heart attack. It sends Leo wild. He picks up a camera and hurls it at the wall, smashing it. Then his laptop—he throws it against the door, then picks it up and throws it out into the wind. He lunges at me, his fists bunched, but Jens reaches a hand out to stop him.

"You fucking cocksucker!" Leo screams at him, before staggering out onto the deck.

I stare at them. I know this is my fault, that I have done this, but I can't quite put my finger properly on where my feeling of guilt is stemming from. But one thought is racing through my mind, constantly flashing through on repeat: she is dead *because of me.* I plead with her not to be. I tell her I'd do anything if she came back. Anything.

II

Our batteries are all completely done. We try and try to power them, but *nothing* works. Darkness has closed in now and without light, we have no battery, and that means we can't call anyone for help.

Not that anything would help Samara now. We have covered her up with a blanket, her beloved green beanie and walking boots on the floor beside her.

It feels like the inside of my brain is coated in acid. Leo is outside right now doing parkour against the side of the boat and howling like he's lost his mind. None of us know what to do. Her body is still here, and we are all on this boat, trapped by ice and fog and dead phones.

I look at the tin box on the table, the letters and the logbook still inside. How excited and sickened Samara was by what she read there.

A woman kidnapped and held captive here on the *Ormen*. And the words of the poem, the *selkie wife*.

I pull on another coat and stand outside on the deck of the *Ormen*, watching my breath turn to ice fractals in the moonlight. Never have I been so desperate for the sun to rise, for the reassurance that the dark will pass.

Jens, Leo, and I haven't talked about what we'll do now. We're shell-shocked, robbed of words. I think at least two of us will have to walk to the nearest town and get help while the other stays with Samara. With the body.

I know what I saw, right before Samara fell through the ice. It can't be a coincidence.

Maybe I was wrong not to say anything to the others about the woman. About the ghost. I felt ashamed, and I worried about their reaction.

But it seems we're no longer exploring the *Ormen*.

We are being hunted.

Einar

November 1973
Skúmaskot, Iceland

Dawn; a hard light beating down on the bay, the dregs of a snowstorm flickering across the volcano. A crowd gathered around the scene, surveying the damage to the rocks and the fishing boats in the bay. At first, many of them thought they were under attack, the huge ship plowing into the mouth of the bay to be taken as a hostile act. But it became clear that the ship was a wreck, a remnant, adrift and uncrewed.

Einar was one of the youngest fishermen in the village and had grown up trawling the fishing grounds with his grandfather's fleet, filling their nets with cod and sleeper sharks. He knew how to extract oil from the sharks' livers and how to salt and hang the cod on the racks. He had heard the stories of the whaling station that his grandfather burned down to protect their village and their livelihood. This, he knew, was a whaling ship, and its arrival had damaged his neighbor Gunnar's fleet of small boats. But he was excited. The village was quiet and offered little for young men and women in the way of entertainment. He couldn't wait to explore the new arrival.

The enormous masts of the ship stood tall above, the thick beams of wood and the hooks striking awe in all the men who had a keen knowledge of shipbuilding, most of them claiming Viking heritage. This was an old ship, yes, but clearly one of the first to embrace steam. Many of their own boats still relied on wind and muscle alone.

"Stay away," his uncle Aron told him when he attempted to climb up the hull, but Einar tugged his arm free. In a handful of moves, he was on board, his arms raised on the top deck in triumph.

Einar and his friends found the vast new arrival to be a treasure trove, teeming with strange objects. Most of them were scientific, and they found charts and maps in the main cabin that would prove useful for their fishing routes. The microscopes were taken for the local school, and they found wine, which was quickly drunk.

The wreck had crashed into the old whaling station itself, ripping off the blackened roof and sending the weakened structure into the bay. The villagers were careful not to allow the bay to become polluted, but they let the station sink. A feeling of unease rippled throughout the town. And when it became apparent that the coast guard was in no rush to remove the wreck, they grew fearful.

At midnight, his mother, Hildur, called him outside.

"Hold the ladder," she said, propping it against the stone archway of their front door.

He watched as she painted a symbol, just as she had seen her mother do before her. A series of runes crisscrossed as a cage to trap demons.

It was as he was returning the ladder to the shed behind the croft that Einar saw a figure in the middle of the bay, by the rock they called the mermaid stone. A seat, his grandmother taught him, reserved for the creatures of the sea who passed between the realms of the living and the dead. Creatures of punishment. He was never to give any reason for the mermaids to approach him, and if he saw one, he was to look away and pass by.

But the figure was no mermaid. She was a woman and she was beautiful. A girl he had never seen before.

Quickly he swam out to her, and before long she was kissing his face, little pecks all over his skin that felt like butterflies, draping him with soft scarves. He felt alarmed when he saw drops of blood on his hands and on his trousers, but she was insistent, and he didn't want to stop.

And so he let her gnaw away his nose and lips, the scratches at his cheekbone like teasing tongues, the soft scarves she wrapped around his neck tightening until darkness took him whole.

Nicky

I

September 1901
Upernavik, Greenland

“It was the selkie wife, sir,” Lovejoy said. “She was the one who kindled the fray.”

Nicky stood in the captain’s cabin alongside Daverley, Lovejoy, and Harrow. Daverley’s arm had been bandaged, and Lovejoy wore a thick dressing across his broken nose. Daverley swayed slightly, his legs threatening to give under him. She could tell he was in shock after what had happened to his nephew.

“Is this true?” Captain Willingham asked Harrow. “The selkie wife kindled the fray?” Harrow’s eyes darted nervously at Lovejoy. She could tell that Harrow was wary of crossing him.

“Aye, sir,” Harrow said finally. “She tricked the boy into writing a song about her. It set the men off, sir.”

“Explain what you mean by ‘set the men off,’” Captain Willingham said.

Harrow flicked his eyes from Lovejoy to the captain. “Well, they were all stirred up. And then a skirmish broke out . . .”

“Between who?”

"The boy, Captain. And Lovejoy."

"What was this skirmish about, exactly?" Captain Willingham said.

"Jealousy," Daverley said quietly.

"I beg pardon?" the captain said.

A muscle twisted in Daverley's jaw. "I said, jealousy."

"Who was jealous?"

"Captain Willingham, if I may," Nicky said, her voice shaking. "The boy, Reid, was merely trying to lead the men in singing a sea shanty. Lovejoy goaded him."

From the corner of her eye, she saw Lovejoy turn to her, a threat in his stare.

Captain Willingham turned to Lovejoy. "Is this true?"

Lovejoy bristled, affronted. "I did no such thing. Ask any of the men."

"Lovejoy tried to force Reid on me," Nicky said. "To make him violate me on the upper deck in front of the rest of the crew. He did it to humiliate us both."

"She speaks the truth," Daverley said.

Captain Willingham looked over them all, his eyes resting on Lovejoy. "Is this true? You tried to force Reid on the lady before the eyes of the crew?"

Lovejoy cleared his throat. "The japes may have gone too far, Captain. But you've seen for yourself the way the lady has spent time with Reid, helping him write his sea shanties and poems and what have you. I think the jealousy referred to was the boy's jealousy toward me. He made to shiv me, so I defended myself. A hand attacking a first mate, Captain! There must be order aboard a whaler."

The captain murmured in agreement. He turned to Nicky, then Harrow. "Can you confirm this?"

Harrow shuffled his feet. He seemed reluctant to be addressed. "Aye, I can, Captain, but—"

"Enough," Captain Willingham snapped. "I've heard enough." He rose from his seat with an angry sigh. "Daverley, you'll spend the night in the brig for your part in this fray. The boy will be buried at sea."

Daverley groaned. "Captain—"

"What would you have me do, Daverley?" the captain asked. "Carry the boy's corpse on board with us for another quarter of a year?"

"A sea funeral's the surest way to trouble his ghost," Daverley said under his breath.

Captain Willingham straightened at that. "The old superstitions don't hold true. You know that."

"Aye, they do," Daverley said with a growl. "And a woman aboard's the oldest of them all. No wonder the boy's dead."

Nicky flinched. He was implying that she was responsible for Reid's death.

Captain Willingham rose slowly from his chair and glowered at Daverley. "You will address me as 'Captain' at all times."

Daverley raised his eyes, though they were haunted. "Aye, Captain."

"The lady will stay in her cabin until I decide how I wish to proceed."

Captain Willingham nodded at Harrow. "See to it that McKenzie takes over Daverley's duties until I set him free. Off you go."

Nicky went to her cabin, shutting the door behind her without a word. She felt numb with shock. Reid was dead. Just a boy of sixteen, dead on the deck.

The knowledge that he had helped kidnap her twisted in her gut, sharp and alarming. She reminded herself that he needed the money. It had not been personal.

And yet.

She thought of Daverley, sent to the upper deck to spend a night in the brig out on the deck. The old cage, she thought, barely large enough for a cat. The sea was rough, and it was freezing cold. It would be a tough night for Daverley. And he'd just witnessed the murder of his nephew.

Just as she felt herself drifting off to sleep, a knock sounded at the door. She listened hard to work out who it was. Usually she could tell from the rhythm of the knocks which man stood outside her door, but it was difficult to tell.

"Who's there?" she called into the darkness.

No answer.

She held her breath. What if she just didn't answer?

Another knock, just one.

"No," she said firmly. "Get away from me!"

Suddenly the door exploded open, whoever stood behind ramming their foot into the wood and knocking the old lock off its hinges.

"You bitch," Lovejoy growled, a heavy blow sending her to the floor. "Dare you challenge me?"

She curled up in a ball as his fists rained down, and as the boot of his shoe lifted again and again she imagined herself underwater, seeing the ship as though from the depths, pulling it down, down with her.

Dominique

I

December 2023
Skúmaskot, Iceland

I wake to the sound of screaming.

I race upstairs to the main cabin to find Leo tearing the place apart. God, it's a mess. The dining table is upside down, coats and books strewn across the floor, and the sofa that Samara was lying on is now on its side.

I scan the room but I can't see the body. The blanket we covered her with is on the floor, next to the sofa.

Leo runs up to me, his gaze liquid, stunned.

"She's gone," he says.

I stare. "Who's gone?"

"Samara," he says, turning to the coats on the floor. "Her beanie and coat are gone, too. And—oh God!—her boots! Her boots are gone!"

Leo's face breaks into an exhilarated smile and he shouts for joy, clapping his hands to his face. I take a step back, frightened.

"What are you talking about?" I say.

"She's *gone*!" Leo says, gesturing toward the sofa. "I can't find her anywhere! She's escaped!"

He breaks into a loud laugh, his eyes wide, and despite myself I start to laugh, too. It suddenly seems hilarious, the sight of Leo searching under books, lifting cushions as though Samara has mysteriously shrunk to the size of a thimble. We've lost a dead body! What next?

Samara's coat is gone, just as Leo said, and her boots. And her phone isn't on the table, but her laptop is. I run down to her cabin to check. It's just the same as it was. A couple of books on the end of the bed, her rucksack filled with clothes and food sachets. Her tent rolled up. If she wanted to leave, surely she'd have taken her tent?

I stop at the foot of the stairs. What am I thinking? Samara is *dead.*

We all witnessed her body. I felt her cold, stiff hands, and bent her arms a little forcefully to tuck her in to make it seem like she was sleeping. I closed her eyelids with my fingers.

I gave her the kiss of life.

There was no pulse.

I must have blacked out for a while because the next thing I know I am upstairs again, and Jens is there, his face twisted in wild confusion as Leo explains the situation to him in a shrill, hysterical voice. *She's gone! She's gone!*

I watch Jens try to take it in. The empty sofa, the missing coat and shoes. We all watched Samara die and now it seems that she had been fooling us all. I feel that nervous, wild giggle rise up in me again, and I want to throw my head back and roar out a wide-jawed belly laugh. Samara simply got up, like Lazarus, put on her coat and boots, and left! Hilarious!

"There's no way she just got up and walked off the ship," I say, pulling the door open and rushing outside. Leo and I follow, and we stand in the freezing snow scanning the bay. The wind is so wild it's as if it wants to claw off our faces.

"She'll not be far," Jens says when we stagger back inside and close the door against the wind. I watch him closely, the guarded way he's handling Leo's enthusiasm, his certainty that Samara is gone. He must suspect Leo has done something with her. That he's hidden the body somewhere. That he's having a full-scale breakdown.

"You think maybe she's in one of the turf houses?" Leo says, pulling on his coat.

"Where are you going?" Jens asks him.

"Where do you think I'm going?" Leo snaps back, his voice breaking. "I'm going out to find Samara, that's what."

Leo looks at us both in disgust. The guilt that has driven through me at Samara's death pricks me once more, and I grab my coat.

"I'll come with you," I say.

Leo turns to me sharply. "The fuck you will. After what you've done?"

"I want to find Samara as much as you do," I say, a laugh of nervous disbelief in my voice. "Please, let me come with you."

Leo takes a step toward me, his eyes burning with hate. My mind wheels back to the night before, that terrible moment when Samara's head emerged from the square-shaped hole in the ice, her mouth gaping. Another flash: her body laid on the bank, limp and doll-like. We are all so tired and traumatized from it, and the dark is driving us crazy.

Leo lifts his fists like he's going to pound them on my chest, or on my face, and I watch him shake, as though the anger is so great it wants to burst out of him. I don't budge. "I'm sorry," I say, sobbing. "I'm so, so sorry."

I feel something release within me as the words tumble from my lips. But Leo backs away, his face twisted in disgust. "I know who you are," he snarls.

This isn't the response I was expecting. "What?"

Leo pokes a finger at me. "I know what you did," he shouts. "I *know*."

"She hasn't done anything," Jens says. "Let's work out a plan of action, okay?" He looks over the length of the room. "Is Samara's laptop here?"

I nod. "It's on the table."

"What about her phone?"

"I have no fucking clue," Leo says. "What difference does it make?

"Have you checked her cabin for it?"

Leo seems to right himself, visibly taking a breath and biting his cheek, thinking. Then he heads downstairs to check, and Jens shifts his eyes to mine.

"Do you think she left?" I ask, realizing as soon as I've spoken how stupid the words sound aloud. "I mean, she was . . . well, we all thought she was dead. I don't see how she was physically capable of leaving."

Jens turns and looks out the window. "We should go after her," he says. I wonder if he's worried that Leo might just be telling the truth.

I wait for him to offer an alternative to the theory that her heart started beating again and yet she still just walked out of the cabin. Perhaps her body was kidnapped? But that doesn't make any sense, because there is no one around for miles, and even if they could have somehow come aboard, there would have been footprints, a wet trail of snow on the floor of the cabin, such as Jens had left just then.

My head throbs from the chaos of it all.

Leo emerges through the hatch. "I can't find her phone."

We all exchange glances. Leo looks like he needs to run off more angst. He moves quickly to the cabin door, and I know he is going outside to see if there is any sign of Samara.

After a few moments, Jens says, "I'll go too." Leo tries to argue with him, telling him that *he'll* go, *alone*, that Jens should stay. Jens simply pulls on his coat and pink beanie and heads to the door.

He turns to me. "Stay here," he tells me. "We'll be back soon."

Nicky

I

September 1901
Upernavik, Greenland

Reid's body was kept in Dr. O'Regan's surgery until it could be prepared for burial.

Daverley was held in the brig overnight, as per Captain Willingham's orders. He had pleaded to stay with his nephew's body, promising to do two nights in the brig in lieu. His request was denied, and so he asked for one of the others to stay with the body. No one had come forward.

Nicky dabbed her face with a towel, wincing when the fabric touched her lip. Blood globed on her lip, her cheekbone bloomed with bruises. Her ribs ached, but it seemed that none were cracked. When Lovejoy drove his fist into her belly, she'd vomited all over him, and he fled.

After she cleaned up the pool of bile on the floor she crept out of her cabin with a blanket and made her way through the dark hallway to the surgery. Inside, she found the boy's body laid on the table where Dr. O'Regan had stitched the wound in her foot. *Thomas,* she remembered. That was his given name, the name that Dr. O'Regan had called him.

He was naked to the waist, his slim arms and bony shoulders luminous in the gleam of her lantern. His eyes had been closed, long black eyelashes against the delicate skin above his cheekbones, and his wound cleaned, though the bloodstain on his trousers remained.

She took his hand and found it was already hardening.

She found another bottle of pills in the apothecary cabinet and slipped one into her mouth. Then she sank down into the chair next to the boy's body, the pain dissolving slowly.

II

Morag loved horses. Nicky had been a keen rider since she was a child, and so she took Morag as often as she could to ride the ponies at her uncle Hamish's farm in Perth. The ponies were tame as house pets, following Morag around while she picked flowers in the meadow and allowing her to thread them in their manes. And on the streets of Dundee, she would stop by every carriage to greet the horses, asking her parents to lift her up so she could speak with them face to face.

It happened on a wet Tuesday night. She and Allan had ventured to Her Majesty's Theater to see *The Notorious Mrs. Ebbsmith.* It had been difficult when Morag was born, and for many months she had not wanted to leave the house out of both exhaustion and a strange fear that crept in whenever she thought of speaking to people. But now it was their wedding anniversary, and Allan had surprised her with tickets that morning.

"You look braw, Mammy," Morag had said from the doorway of her bedroom. She was clutching a teddy bear, her wet hair hanging in ringlets on her shoulders.

"Thank you, darling," Nicky said, turning to view her dress from the side in the long mirror. She was wearing a forest-green velvet dress with a lace neckline, her corset pulled so tight she could barely breathe. Before Morag was born, the dress was loose at the hips, but now it sat tight. She could manage it, so long as she didn't take long strides.

"Daddy and I are going to see a play," Nicky said. "Remember we took you to see the puppet show at Carolina Port?"

Morag screwed up her face. "You're going to see a puppet show?"

"No, but it's *like* a puppet show. A bigger version of that. It's on a stage and there'll be lots of people there."

Morag's little face brightened. "I liked the puppet show. And the fireworks after. Will there be fireworks at your play?"

Nicky laughed. "No, I'm afraid not. It's indoors."

"So what?"

"The roof would be set on fire, darling."

Morag's blue eyes went wide. "That's no' good."

Nicky fastened her pearl choker. "You promise you'll go to bed for Mrs. Mackie?"

Morag gave a woeful sigh. "I promise."

Nicky tugged up the skirt of her dress and knelt by Morag, dabbing her nose with the tip of her finger. "If you can't sleep, remember what Daddy told you to do."

"Think of horses jumping over a bale of hay and count them all."

"Exactly."

"Granny says I should count sheep, not horses."

"You can count whatever you like."

"I'll count horses, then."

Nicky leaned forward and kissed Morag on the cheek. Morag struggled to sleep in her own bedroom, plagued by dark imaginings and a curious mind that seemed to spark at nighttime, just like her father. "You be good for Mrs. Mackie, won't you?"

"Yes, Mammy," Morag said. Then: "Can I come to the play, too?"

"Sorry, love. It's a play for adults. But if you like, I'll take you to see a play for children. Would you like that?"

Morag nodded. "Yes, please."

"Well, you have to promise that you'll try very, *very* hard to go to sleep."

Morag took a deep breath and gave a solemn nod. "I promise."

She heard Allan answer the door to Mrs. Mackie downstairs and gave Morag another last peck on the cheek. "On you go, now."

"Ready?" Allan said from the top of the stairs. Then, seeing her in the dress she'd not worn for years, he said, "Good God. Maybe we should just get a hotel room instead."

She tutted. "There's a good chance I wouldn't be able to get the dress back on."

He approached and kissed the patch of exposed skin between her ear and shoulder. "You smell like glory."

"What on earth does glory smell like?"

"I have no idea. But I reckon it's beautiful."

She kissed him on the lips, leaving a trace of rouge. "Thank you."

The theater was resplendent and heaving with crowds, the shimmering lights and the gold balconies a welcome relief from the days she had spent at home alone with Morag. Allan clasped her hand and smiled at her; he worked so hard lately, such long days in the mill, that she had wondered if they might ever get a chance to spend time together again. And here they were, laughing at the play, holding hands, both of them dressed in their finest clothing. She never wanted the night to end.

When the play finished, Allan suggested they take a carriage home. He seemed anxious. "We should relieve Mrs. Mackie," he said. "She'll be tiring, no doubt."

Nicky felt crestfallen. She had one night and one night only to be her old self, to remember what it was like to be alone with her husband.

"Perhaps we might walk home?" she said. "Spend a little more time together?"

Allan hesitated, and she could see he was pained. But in a moment he nodded, and they took the path along the River Tay, admiring the lights on the water and the clear night sky. She felt light on her feet, and whatever had been bothering Allan had passed.

But as they turned into the main road near their home, she heard a commotion. In the dark, she could see that a carriage had toppled, and the crumpled heap at the side of the road was a horse lying dead. Nearby, the driver sat on a wall speaking to two policemen. As they drew closer, a howl pierced the air. A woman being taken into a police carriage. The wheels grinding across the cobbles.

"They've just taken her to the hospital," one of the men said. "Awful scene."

"Taken who away?" Allan asked.

The man nodded at the fallen horse, and Nicky saw that one of its legs had been broken. The teeth glinting in the light of the street lantern.

"The bairn," he said. "Ran straight out in front of the carriage."

Nicky felt a terrible chill race up her neck. "What bairn?"

"A lassie. Dashed out to see a firework. Driver couldnae do nothin'."

As the police carriage passed by, Nicky saw that the figure inside was Mrs. Mackie. Her eyes turned to Allan, his expression changing to horror as he realized. And when he raced after them, calling *Mrs. Mackie! Mrs. Mackie!* she couldn't bring herself to move. Didn't want to think of whose bairn had been struck by the horse.

They found Morag at the hospital, her little head wrapped in bandages. Her eyes closed, her curls shorn. Bedclothes drawn up over her broken limbs. A nurse had placed a cloth doll in her arms and encouraged them to speak softly to her.

"She might still hear you," she said.

Allan watched blankly, his face an open grave, as Nicky took her daughter's hand in hers and pressed it to gently to her lips. They whispered to her, told her bedtime stories as though she were simply lying in her bed at home, preparing for sleep. They told her they loved her.

When she had drawn her last breath, they knew, the stillness of her chest and the parting of her lips signaling that she had passed away before them. But still they whispered, as though the words might call her back, back to the ones who loved her most.

III

The day of Thomas's funeral, the crew gathered around the body. Like Collins, Thomas was wrapped in a sail and stitched tightly like a shroud, the last stitch through the nose to prevent the boy's soul from following the ship.

"All hands bury the dead, ahoy!" Lovejoy shouted.

Nicky watched from the forecastle as the men placed cannonballs into either end of the fabric, before Daverley and Royle lowered the body on a wooden slab into the ocean. Daverley looked haunted, his face dark. None of the men spoke as the shrouded body sank quickly, the gray water opening as if to accept him, before healing again, no trace left. A different kind of grave.

Three men dead. The human toll of whaling would never be measured, but in death it was felt most keenly.

She thought of what Daverley said about Thomas's soul being unable to rest if he was given a sea burial, how he might haunt the ship and seek revenge. She would have dismissed such a tale out of hand in the past, but her own secret, the wound that was somehow spreading up her leg, made her less skeptical. So she found herself turning to look behind the ship, studying the water there in case she might see Reid unfurled from the sail, angrily trying to catch them.

For a moment, she thought he would be justified. Perhaps, in his immortal form, the boy would have powers that would enable him to enact revenge on his killer. Lovejoy's claim of acting in self-defense was a bitter pill to swallow; even Harrow had seemed reluctant to agree. It should have been Lovejoy in the brig, not Daverley. She hadn't heard him speak a word since.

Her door was quiet for two nights afterward, and she felt relief at the men leaving her alone but also an overwhelming guilt at the cost of her peace. And she couldn't help but feel that she had played a role in the boy's death. Lovejoy had taunted Thomas by revealing his part in her capture; he had known that the boy would react.

Perhaps if she had not shown her dismay so nakedly, Thomas would not have lashed out the way he did. She had known, almost immediately, that Lovejoy's divulgence was not out of any wish to share the truth with her of her misfortune, but to goad the boy. To rip apart the relationship he had formed with Nicky. Lovejoy was jealous of Thomas's sea shanties, and his ability to write. He was jealous of the way he made Nicky laugh, at the way her face lit up instead of folding in disgust.

And that jealousy had cost Thomas his life.

IV

Three days after Thomas's funeral, a knock sounded on her door.

Cautiously, she opened the door just wide enough to let the amber light of the oil lantern in the hallway trickle inside. She had expected Lovejoy to be standing there, that vile grin on his face and his pale eyes running the length of her body. His fists ready to strike her if she displeased him.

Instead, she spotted the tall figure of Daverley. His shoulders were rounded and his eyes were dark. She reeled at his presence at her door, knowing what it meant.

She stepped back into her room, confused and saddened. She didn't like Daverley, but she had thought him principled. But now that Reid was gone she expected he didn't have to set an example. He was just like the others.

He closed the door behind him, the small room lit only by the candle that shivered on the sea chest next to her bed. She sat down, keeping her eyes fixed on him and her mouth closed. He remained standing, his eyes on the floor.

"Well?" she said when several moments had passed like that.

Slowly, he sank to the ground, his face twisted in pain. He drew his palms to his eyes. Around his wrist, she noticed the small bracelet made of rope that Reid had worn. *Reid*, she thought. *He's here because of Reid.*

Slowly she moved to the floor and sat next to him. After a minute she slipped an arm across his shoulders, and he moved into an embrace, letting her hold him. When she was sure he wasn't here for anything more than friendship, she sat on the bed and invited him to sit next to her. Then she lay down and held him, his arms around her, his tears dampening the sleeves of her dress.

"It's my fault," Daverley murmured.

"It's not," she said.

"He wouldn't have been here if it weren't for me."

She felt the sting of recognition at his words, a painful memory unfolding of the time she and Allan had held each other like this on the floor of the house on Faulkner Street. The devastation of their daughter's death should, perhaps, have drawn them together, but instead she found it housed Allan and her in two separate rooms, or in two different countries. She saw her daughter in Allan's face, and found herself hating that he was alive and she was not. The pain of Morag's death was a wound that drew across every inch of her heart, and she could not love while that wound was unhealed.

But, of course, it was an unhealable wound.

The pain Daverley held within, she knew well. It was still there, in her own body, as real and tangible as metal. Thomas's loss would live within Daverley forever now, that much she knew. There was no use telling him otherwise.

Dominique

I

December 2023
Skúmaskot, Iceland

Jens and Leo still aren't back. It's been forty-two hours since they went after Samara.

I'm so worried, I'm beside myself. What is actually going on? Samara died, and then she didn't. Jens and Leo said they'd go and look for her in case she *had* actually walked off the ship with a brain injury and needed help, but they've not returned.

And I can't stop crying.

Are they injured somewhere, or lost? Have they all walked off the project without telling me? Jens took his backpack, but his laptop is here. So is Leo's. I don't know whether to go and look for them or stay here and keep the fire going in case they come back.

It's probably a very unwise move, but I decide to use what's left in my solar charger to attempt to call Jens.

It doesn't connect.

I try Leo, then Samara. None of the calls connect. I click on the TikTok app. They've not logged on to any of their socials. Jens's TikTok seems to have been deleted. Or maybe it's glitching again.

I do a livestream to connect with the 5,098 followers who have logged on, no doubt eager to see more of the *Ormen* or Skúmaskot or the logbook we found in the crawl space.

"Hi everyone," I say, giving a little wave. My throat is tightening and I'm overwhelmed by the impulse to start crying again. Oh God. *Hold it together, Dom.*

"I have some news," I say, digging my fingernails into my palm to distract myself from the sob that wants to explode out of my throat. "First of all, Samara is okay. I know the livestream cut off super abruptly so you were all probably really worried. So don't worry! We'll be announcing the winners of the contest very soon, and filming the dismantling of the *Ormen*, so stick around! And tell all your friends!"

I give a cheesy thumbs-up, shamelessly mimicking Samara.

"I'm going to log off now," I say. "Because I need the battery to cook a meal. But I'll upload more footage tomorrow, I promise."

Heart emojis stream up the screen, and I see the battery begin to flash.

I make a peace sign and give what I hope is a strong, resolute smile. "Over and out."

I promised I'd be honest with my followers, but I can't do it. I don't want to admit that they've all abandoned the project. That they've left.

The cabin plunges into darkness. That's it—no more battery until the sun rises, though "rise" is inaccurate. A bright sun in the sky is a distant memory. Thinking of it now, I probably shouldn't have promised to upload tomorrow, because really, I'm at the mercy of the elements.

I reach for the wind-up torch and turn it quickly, relishing the brief reprieve from darkness when it glows faintly.

Outside, the wind sounds like someone is singing. I hold my

breath, listening as the melody deepens, a sound of humming. And then it fades to a whistle, the ship rocking in the wind's hands.

I wrap myself in a thermal blanket and hold my hands to the fire bucket, an exhalation of warmth rising from embers at the bottom. I so wish Jens had stocked up the wood supply before he left. We're pretty much out of doors, so either I start pulling up floorboards or I trek to the turf houses on the other side of the bay. But I'll have to, at some point, if I want to stay warm.

The fog is thick tonight, draped over the volcano like the neck of a dragon. I think of Jens with his backpack and tent—maybe he has managed to find somewhere to pitch it, and Leo is with him. I think of the glow cast by his camping lantern, transforming the tent into a lime-green dome against the dark sky. Maybe if I climb to the top of the cliffs, I'll spot it.

The thought gives me hope.

A voice in my head tells me I'm merely looking for a sense of purpose to distract myself from the terror of being alone, but I ignore it. I can't give in to that voice.

My knife is sitting on the worktop in the kitchenette, a flicker from the LED safety light running across the blade. I lift it slowly and feel the whispers beneath my skin growing louder, almost shouting now. I slip the knife inside the sheath on my hip, for safety, and the voices stop. It's a relief. Usually they don't stop until I draw blood.

Instead, the cabin is quiet and I feel reassured to have my knife in place, its protection right where it needs to be. I can go outside with confidence, as long as I have my knife. I can go to the turf houses and collect fuel for the fire. I think I'll make myself some porridge. I've not yet used the sachets I brought. I figured I'd spare them for an emergency, or for a time when I felt I needed a little boost. Some people use alcohol for a boost, I use porridge.

Outside, the fog lifts, and it's so beautiful I pull out my phone and feel my heart sink when I remember that the battery is dead. It is literally like being inside a snow globe, one of the posh ones with the fir trees and foiled robins, a polar bear wearing a gold crown. I hadn't expected to be so struck by the scenery; there's been so much fog lately that I suppose I expected the same murky grimness. But tonight is heartbreakingly gorgeous, a silk of snow across the volcano and over the bay. The sky is a bruise, moonlight parting the sea with a silver causeway. It's as though a great battle has been fought between Day and Night, the darkness showing off her regalia in triumph.

There are the most beautiful textures, too, as though we've had some kind of weird wind that has combed across the snow, lifting it slightly in tessellated formations. I don't mean to go on about it—actually, I do—but it's alarming how the same piece of land can look so different according to the light.

The light is a costume. A skin.

II

It's Christmas Day.

I have spent so many Christmas Days alone that it shouldn't bother me. But I feel utterly gut-punched today. I feel utterly confused by the Samara thing. By the fact that no one has contacted me. I managed to turn my phone on for a few minutes to check my messages and the TikTok account. For about a minute it looked like the project account had vanished. Nothing on there. I panicked. Had one of the others deleted it? We all had admin control. But then it popped up again. Jens, Samara, and Leo have gone dark digitally, too. They've not messaged me, and they've not posted anything on their own accounts. None of them.

If I'm honest, I feel abandoned, which I know is terribly self-pitying and childish, but there it is. It feels like there is more to this feeling, that it has *layers*.

The project TikTok has *tons* of messages from our followers, though, checking in on us all. Mostly, the comments are super nice. And we've got a lot of new followers. I didn't even count them, that's how low I feel about everything. Before, it really mattered to me. Now it doesn't. I don't even care if I never explore again.

I post some old footage of me and Jens researching stuff online from 1973 before my phone dies again. It's crap footage but at least it shows us doing something.

The knocking against the hull has started up again, and maybe it's my imagination but it has a rhythm that doesn't seem to be in time with the waves. It's starting to drive me insane. I've gone outside a couple of times to see if I can move the chain that's causing the sound, but the rocks are icy and if I fall and crack my head open . . . well, no one is coming for me.

I did see the chain and it was moving for sure, but it wasn't moving in a rhythmic, knock-knock-knock way. That's the rhythm of the sound from the inside. Three knocks, and a pause. Then another three, followed by another pause.

I'm sitting here listening to it and there's nothing I can do. I can't record it, can't contact anyone. I have the overwhelming sense that someone is outside.

I can literally feel them looking at the *Ormen*. If I close my eyes I can almost see myself inside, a little silhouette framed by the cabin window. As though I can see from two angles at once.

Stop it, Dom. You're being paranoid again. You have the feeling that someone is outside because the knocking sounds like someone is at the front door. Keep it together, will you?

I keep looking outside, partly to see if one of the others has returned, or in case I see the woman. Ghosts can't knock, can they?

I keep thinking of what Samara said so poetically about sound being a revenant, a trace.

No. The knocking is from the chain. Maybe in the morning I'll try to fix the chain so that it doesn't bang into the hull. Keep focused. Christmas Day is just another day, right?

III

It's still Christmas Day and I'm drunk. I climbed down into the hold to see if I could find some vodka. It took a lot of rummaging through debris and I went over on my ankle, but I got lucky. This bottle of vodka is absolutely gorgeous and has put a real shine on what was otherwise starting to feel like a proper pity party. Go me.

I've actually had a pretty productive Christmas. The project has almost ten thousand followers. Ten thousand! A month ago, that would have been my goal. I can't just up and leave, because I'll be ending the story before its natural conclusion of the ship being destroyed. I just have to make sure I have enough charge for when the breakers arrive. And I'll also need to think carefully about how to get close enough to film it all without getting arrested. Demolishers and breaker crews *hate* squatters. They're often briefed before going in on the possibility of environmental protesters, and sometimes they come with police. It's when they come alone that you have to be careful. They'll not even wait for you to be arrested—they'll just beat the shit out of you.

I'll need to hide. Maybe I'll leave the *Ormen* a day or two beforehand and hide out in one of the caves.

I also spent this afternoon setting up my sensor camera on the tripod here in the main cabin, where I'm going to sleep from now on. I want to see if I'm doing something in my sleep when I have nightmares. I want to record myself and get a clearer idea if something wakes me up or triggers me, and maybe I'll figure out how to stop it.

I put on my balaclava and coat and take the camera off the tripod mount to do some filming. A little bit here and there will give me enough to make a nice reel of Christmas Day alone here on the wreck. Some of the comments on the TikTok account said I was brave. I usually disregard that kind of stuff but actually, it made me feel better. Maybe this *is* a total badass thing to do. It's not my fault that the others left. They had the freedom to stay or go, and they left. Fine. I can choose to stay or go, and I'm choosing to stay.

And I feel like I'm confronting some personal stuff out here, too. I haven't told anyone about the rapes in . . . actually, I can't even remember a time that I told someone. And yet I told Samara. That took courage. Saying it aloud felt like I'd been punched in the chest. I know I'm not ready to go any further down memory lane, though. The whispers beneath my skin get too loud when I start to think of that, and I know what happens then. I'll need to cut, and I know it's not a good thing, the cutting. I don't like to cut when I'm exploring. I've become so good at stopping my memories, at blocking my mind from looking into the past at all, it barely feels like it's there for me anymore.

The sun is finally lifting into the sky, brightening the horizon with a weak dusk light. Thank God! Keep shining, sun! We're past the winter solstice now, so maybe we'll get a little more light during the day. I'm just thinking about my solar chargers. Every second of light counts.

Outside, snow is falling again. This is also a good sign—it's getting warmer, though it's still minus fourteen. I had started to worry that the temperature would continue to drop, and the fire wouldn't light. It would be game over, then. Plenty of explorers have been killed that way, especially now, with the weather being so extreme.

The deck is slushy, and I walk carefully toward the ladder, noticing the way the wind sounds like singing again. I pause and get my phone out of my pocket to record it, turning all the way around to get the top deck in a nice three-sixty spin. The singing has stopped, which is typical, so I put my phone away and head back to the ladder and climb down to the sand.

For a moment, it feels magical. I'm sure the vodka has helped, but I feel warm inside. The tide has pushed most of the snow off the sand, and so the black beach sits like an inky margin against the perfectly white snow, cottony and untouched. I climb up to higher ground, looking out over the bay to my left and the beach to my right. I wonder if I'll see the horses again. I haven't seen them since that first night. I wonder if the dead horses in the cave put them off coming here.

The walk to the turf houses sobers me up and gets me into a good sweat. I had almost forgotten how much a brisk walk helps clear my head. I must remember that—even when the weather is as bad as it has been, *get outside, Dom!* You know it works.

Carrying the turf back, though—I didn't think that through. I should have brought a sledge of some sort, a sheet of metal or plastic. I carry as much as I can, then leave it on the ground outside the *Ormen* and carry up as much as I need to get the fire going.

I break up the turf and feed it to the fire, then set a lid on it with the kettle on top of that. It'll take ages for it to boil, but I've got time, and it gives me something to look forward to. The solar packs will be full of charge tomorrow, now that I've got some light, and I'll be able to upload the footage from the last few days and film some new stuff. I'm looking forward to that. And I'm looking forward to seeing how many new followers I've got, and how many have subscribed to my paid content. Yes, Dom. There is *lots* to look forward to. Really, though, I'm itching to check whether Jens and Leo have contacted me. Whether they've walked back to the nearest town and have sent me a message, letting me know they've found Samara.

That they're coming back.

Shit, the snow has gotten really heavy. I need to get the rest of the turf before it gets too wet. I head outside, moving too fast across the slush. I manage to throw my arms out and stop myself from falling backward. At the ladder, I pause, sensing something nearby. It's not just the snow, or my pounding heart rate from the almost-fall.

There is someone standing right below, directly at the bottom of the ladder.

At first, I think it's one of the others. That would make sense, wouldn't it? They never left me! They went for a walk and got lost, and now they're back!

But it's not Samara, or Leo, or Jens.

It's the woman, her back turned to the ladder. Her wet shoulders glistening in the dark.

I give a shout and fall backward with fright, and there's a loud bang from where I catch my head on the sharp corner of the raised platform of the forecastle.

I hear the knock of feet against the rung of the ladder, one after the other.

And everything goes dark.

IV

I can't tell if I'm dreaming or if I'm underwater.

I can see shapes floating around me, a huge one above. At first, I think it's a whale, but then the shape of a rudder comes into view and I know it's a ship. I am instantly filled with rage, such hatred that it seems to burn inside me. I want to scream with fury.

I start to move toward the shape, and I know what I need to do. I need to get on board that ship and kill everyone on it.

I come to. My mouth is filled with something, and it takes a moment to realize that I'm not underwater but on the top deck of the *Ormen*, lying flat on my back with my arms spread out at either side and a mouthful of snow.

I pull myself slowly upright, the back of my head throbbing from where I fell. Muddy slush is all around me. Luckily, I'm wearing my waterproofs, so I'm dry, if very sore and annoyed at myself for getting drunk. Then I remember what caused me to fall—I saw something at the bottom of the ladder. The woman. She was standing with her back to me.

My heart racing, I look over the side, and instantly I see it—the shape of someone there. But then my eyes adjust, and I realize it's just a shadow. The moon has cast a shadow of the rocky outcrop and thrown it across the snow, and it looks very like a person standing there. Jesus Christ. *That* was why I fell?

A shadow?

At once relieved and annoyed, and still quite drunk, I head back inside the cabin, where the fire is throwing out a tremendous amount of heat. Oh, blissful heat! I pull off my hat and coat, then step out of my waterproofs. My fingers find a small amount of blood and a large lump, about the size of an egg, at the back of my head from where I fell. I must have been unconscious for at least a few minutes. I could have a concussion. But I feel okay, just sore, and suddenly ravenous.

I find one of Jens's fancy food packets on the worktop and decide to make use of it. Korean Style Beef and Rice. Oh my God—I rip open the packet and eat it cold, each mouthful the most amazing food I've ever tasted. Jens is not here to tell me otherwise, and it's technically still Christmas, for crying out loud. Forget turkey and trimmings—cold, vacuum-packed Korean Style Beef and Rice is the best goddamn Christmas dinner in existence.

The rest of the turf is still at the bottom of the ladder. So I know I have to go out there and get it, and I'll confront whatever waits for me. If it's a ghost, I'm going to laugh in its face. I'm going to tell it to go fuck itself.

I fetch my knife and fasten the holster around my waist, slipping the knife inside.

It has stopped snowing. The wind has died down on the deck. It was singing before, but now it's so completely silent. Only the wash of the sea, but even that seems muted.

I step carefully through the slush to the side of the hull and stare down at the bottom of the ladder. I can see the turf, half-buried in the snow. No footprints. No ghost.

I gather the turf and head back up the ladder, a shiver running down my spine. I still feel watched. Despite all my bravado, despite the knife in my sheath, I can't bring myself to turn around.

V

Research, that's the ticket.

Sorry, Samara, but you've left your laptop behind and it has fifty-three percent battery life, so I'm using it to check out the academic articles you've downloaded.

I've locked the cabin door, and my knife is out on the dining table next to me. I risk a glance at the window.

She's left a screenshot open. It's of the newspaper article from 1901 about the missing girl, the daughter of the first owner of the *Ormen*.

I stare at the name. Nicky Duthie. There's a scratch starting up in the back of my mind. I click on the bottom right, where the other open browsers are minimized. One of them is the photograph we all stared at, trying to work out if the blurry figure slightly out of shot was a woman. Leo said they thought the photograph showed a woman on the ship, which wasn't unusual. Ship captains sometimes brought wives along, though it was mostly a North American tradition, not common among Dundee whalers. My mind turns to the crew roster that mentioned twenty people on board when there were twenty-one, and the logbook that mentioned a prostitute . . . These were all from 1901.

I stare at the photograph of the figure, halfway out of frame. The scratch at the back of my mind intensifies. Nicky Duthie went missing in May 1901 and was still missing in October. The photograph on board the *Ormen* was taken in August 1901. It feels like a leap of imagination to even wonder if she's the figure in the photograph.

No. It's ridiculous. Why the hell would the shipmaster's daughter be on board as a prostitute?

It's midnight. My body clock is whacked, and I'm still tipsy, so I'm nowhere near ready for sleep. I pour some coffee from my flask and use a little of the solar charger to crank up the internet. No messages from the others, which makes my heart sink. Maybe I should stop looking.

Samara is still logged into the academic resource, so I search for info on the *Ormen* from the 1970s. Jens and I had been searching for information from 1973, but I decide to widen the dates until 1990. An article pings up from 1976, and I give a laugh of surprise. We'd made our search too narrow—that was where we were going wrong!

Letter Delivered Years Late Sheds Light on Crew's Disappearance

Laura Finlayson, 28, from Auburn, NSW, last saw her fiancé, Dennis Gordon, three years ago, when he boarded a research ship headed to the Arctic. Sadly, it was to be the last time the happy couple would set eyes on each other. Dennis sent letters home every week, and Laura began to worry when he failed to write.

"I knew as soon as the police pulled up outside my door," she says sadly. "I just had a feeling."

In 1973, Laura was informed that the ship Dennis had been on—known as the *Ormen*—had been located by the Russian coast guard. None of the crew had been located, however, and while searches were continuing, it was highly unlikely that anyone would be found alive.

Laura moved to the Gold Coast several months later. "I couldn't manage without Dennis," she said. "Our home became an excruciating place for me to live, so I needed to find a new place to make a fresh start."

This seems to be part of the reason why Dennis's letter didn't reach Laura until August 1976. The new tenant at Laura's previous address in Brisbane finally managed to forward Laura's mail, and among the mail was a letter from Dennis.

> "In the letter, Dennis mentions a guy on the research ship who had started to spend his days ranting and raving," she says, visibly upset by the memory. "He says this colleague was acting really out of sorts, not like himself at all, and that it was very upsetting and disruptive. He said that the chief [Dr. Andrea Karsen] had locked the guy in his room for safety reasons. That strikes me as very coincidental, given that the ship went off-radar just a day or so afterward."
>
> I ask her what she thinks happened.
>
> "Obviously, I can't be sure," she says. "But Dennis would never have shared something like that with me if he wasn't really worried, or even scared," she says. "I feel like he was almost writing it in case something happened, and then I'd understand that this was the reason for it. His letters never went into much detail about his daily routine and the people on the ship, so this really stood out. I do think it has something to do with the crew vanishing."
>
> Interestingly, the inventory for the ship when it was located adrift on the Barents Sea was missing a key object—a rifle, normally held in a safety box on the top deck. When the coast guard located the ship, they found that it had been damaged by storms, but most of the crew's personal effects remained on board.
>
> While speculation may not bring any of the researchers back, Dennis's letter and Laura's knowledge of her fiancé bring her some closure on a mystery that has torn at hearts for years.

My mind turns to the microscope that Jens found. The one with the hole in the metal casing that he said was a bullet hole. I get up to try to find it, but it's nowhere to be seen.

The battery is running out on Samara's laptop, so I do a quick check on three different search engines to see if I can find Dennis Gordon and Diego Almeyda linked together, but I don't find anything. It strikes me that it's worth trying the academic resource; after all, the scientists on the research ship probably published their papers. I type the names into the box marked *Author* and a single research paper pops up from September 1970: "Sea Ice Distribution in Franz Josef Land," by D. Gordon and D. Almeyda.

My heart quickening, I read the paper, which has been scanned onto the website. I can't make sense of it—lots about sea ice dynamics and the distribution of mean ice drafts—but I see that Dennis Gordon was a PhD researcher at the University of New South Wales, while Diego Almeyda was a geography lecturer at the University of Argentina.

The lead stalls after that, so I go out onto the top deck to search for the safety box mentioned in the article. The main cabin is really the only addition from the research era, but a rifle wouldn't have been stored in a safety box way back in the early 1900s. It might have been a box that was already there, but I figure I might find a modification of some kind, maybe an old lock that was from the 1970s.

Nothing.

But as I'm standing on the deck, finally a song comes into my head. The lilting melody that slid into my thoughts when I was in the captain's cabin, a tune that befits the words of the poem that Leo carved into the dining table.

these seas no more will cause thee strife
if you'll become my selkie wife

I think of the missing woman. Nicky Duthie, daughter of the *Ormen*'s owner. I feel the same scratch at the back of my mind start up again, the blurred face at the edge of the photograph flashing in my mind.

Samara's laptop battery is at twenty percent; my own is dead. Jens's and Leo's laptops are both password-protected. I kneel down to the internet terminal. Jens's solar charger has one bar left. Quickly I plug the internet terminal into it and log online, returning to Samara's laptop and logging back into the section of the academic resource where all the old newspapers are digitized. I search "Nicky Abney" and find a mere four articles, two of which are about another woman entirely. But one from late October 1901 mentions that George Abney's daughter has not yet been found.

Hat Found near Dock Suggests Foul Play;
Abney & Sons Latest

A hat that George Abney's wife claims belonged to their missing daughter has been found near the docks of Dundee.

Mrs. George Abney, wife of the owner of Abney & Sons, identified the hat on Tuesday evening, following the disappearance of her oldest daughter, Nicky Duthie. Mrs. Duthie's husband, Private Allan Duthie of the 1st Battalion Coldstream Guard, is said to have been killed shortly after Mrs. Duthie went missing, having sustained injuries at Fort Prospect in September.

Chief Constable James Richie of Dundee City Police says the discovery of the hat is a major step forward in the case, and has reiterated his invitation to the public to come forward with information. It is feared that Mrs. Duthie boarded a ship and set off for a new life while her husband was overseas.

Mrs. Abney is quoted as saying, "I have no reason to believe that my daughter left these shores freely. I plead again for information, and assurance of her well-being."

So she was a widow, and doubtless without realizing it.

The battery is at nine percent. I scan quickly through the articles on George Abney. There are dozens, many of them focused on the business, and some photographs. He is a stout, proud-looking man. His obituary indicates that he died by his own hand; the wording is a plea to God to spare his soul.

I stare at the photograph of him smoking a cigar with the prime minister, Robert Gascoyne-Cecil, the scratch at the back of my mind growing worse.

What did you do to her, you bastard? I think. *What did you do?*

Nicky

I

October 1901
Banks Bay, Greenland

Nicky remembered the weeks after Morag's death. It had felt as though the world itself had been ripped apart, a strange reality in which she and Allan had to relearn their own lives, their own selves. A reality in which nothing had meaning, or sense. She had thought she might go mad.

It was two months after the funeral when she had woken to find Allan on the small balcony of Morag's bedroom. He was naked. It was early, still dark.

"Allan?"

He was standing, his back to her, looking down at the garden below. She reached out to touch him and he spun around with a roar. She reared back, and he charged at her, ranting. His face taut with fury, a stream of expletives and accusations that didn't make sense.

"How fucking dare you! Don't you ever touch me again, do you hear?"

She had fallen to the ground, and he had stood over her, a hand raised. A terrifying moment.

"Don't," she had whimpered. "Please."

Her plea seemed to wake him up, his face softening, as though he'd returned to his own mind. He dropped the hand that had risen to strike her and staggered backward. Then he locked himself in the bathroom. She got up and moved tentatively to the door, pressing her ear to the wood.

She heard sobbing. Allan had never cried. She had never heard this sound. But she knew its nature. He was broken. He was a man without his daughter. He was expected not to mourn, but to carry on as though nothing had happened. He had worked the day after, as expected. She had witnessed the grind of it, but felt powerless to do anything.

"Allan, please let me in."

"I'm sorry."

She took a breath, steadying herself. "I know you are. It's all right. Please let me in."

Eventually, the door unlocked, and she stepped inside. She found him sitting on the toilet bowl, hands on his knees, his gaze on the floor.

"You frightened me earlier," she said.

"I know."

"I love you."

He didn't answer. Then, after a few moments: "I've enlisted to fight against the Boers."

She thought she'd misheard him. "What?"

"In the Transvaal," he said, looking up. His jaw tight. "My father was a soldier. It's my duty."

She laughed, thinking he was joking.

"I resigned from the mill yesterday."

"You *resigned*?"

"I told them why."

"Allan," she said. "You can't be serious."

"I leave in two weeks."

She was too stunned to answer. He was *leaving*? It felt like a punishment. She had blamed herself every single moment of every day for what happened to her daughter. If she had only listened to Allan and returned home earlier, if she had checked that the front door was locked behind them, if she had instructed Mrs. Mackie to check on her . . . so many things she could have done to prevent this gaping hole in their lives.

He was right to punish her. He was right to leave her.

And so she had walked out of the room and gone back to bed, saying little to him throughout the mornings and nights that followed, until one afternoon, she saw a suitcase and an army uniform on the bed.

She realized that she knew him less now than when they first met. Her husband, transformed into a stranger.

Over time, their letters to each other became warmer, friendlier, and she missed him. She sensed he missed her. They had both been changed by Morag's death.

But love, she thought, was a constant. Perhaps it would help them return to each other, in their changed states. Maybe it would be enough.

II

She vomited for a week before it occurred to her that she might be pregnant.

She hadn't bled since boarding the ship but had put it down to her usual irregularity and the stress of the kidnapping. At first, she had thought it seasickness. Or perhaps food poisoning. Her diet lately was seal entrails, dark, rubbery meat that she washed down with strong tea. She only ate when driven to it by ravenous hunger, and there was no telling if the meat was edible.

But she was still being sick, and now her breasts felt tender. A horrifying sign.

She climbed to the top deck in a daze. Should she throw herself overboard? The thought of giving birth to a child by any of the mariners brought bile into her mouth, hot and sharp. She hated every one of them, except now, a surprise even to herself, Daverley. Perhaps it was his kindness, his fatherliness toward her. Or their common grief.

How could she return to Dundee now? How could she ever face Allan? He would never shun her—of course not—but it would wound him, knowing that the child was not his. Knowing that it was conceived in such a horrific way. Would she give it up? How easy would it be to do this, given what they had suffered with Morag? To keep it, though . . . surely it was impossible. Whatever she did now would affect them forever.

She leaned over the side and vomited into the water below.

When she looked up, Daverley's gaze was fixed on her, contemplative. He was caulking a cask, glancing around to check that none of the other men were watching as he approached.

"Sea legs failing you?" he said.

She ran the sleeve of her dress across her mouth. "Must be something I ate."

"Maybe it's something you're carrying," he said.

"And how would you know about that?"

"I had a wife. She carried four of our bairns. Each time she looked every bit as peely-wally as you do now."

She looked down again, wondering how long would it take to drown if she slipped overboard. Perhaps minutes? Or perhaps the cold water would rinse the child out of her. Her grip tightened on the edge of the hull, and he saw.

"You see something in the water?" Daverley said, glancing down. "A mermaid, perhaps?"

She shook her head. "Where are your children now?" she asked him.

"Two of them are with my wife," he said. "In God's arms."

"I'm sorry," she said. "My husband and I lost a child. Our only child."

Daverley tipped his hat with a free hand. "My condolences." He turned back to the water below. "I've been watching for any sign of Thomas," he said. "That's why I asked."

"Thomas?" she said. Did he mean his body? Surely not—the lad was laid to rest many miles ago, weighed down so he would not float. Even if the weights had shifted there was no way his body would have traveled so far north . . . It struck her that grief played with the mind.

"The old tales have it that a body rested at sea does not permit the soul to rest," Daverley said, scanning the water.

"You've said that before. Why is that?"

"That, I know not. But the sea is where life began, and so the veil of death does not exist there." He threw her a searching look. "Surely you have heard these things, being the daughter of a shipmaster?"

"My father's a businessman, not a shipmaster," she said. "And he's certainly no storyteller."

He turned, pressing his back against the edge of the hull. "You've heard about selkies?"

"Too much about selkies," she said drily. "Selkie wives in particular."

"I heard some of the men call you that," he said. "But it's incorrect, the way they've used it."

She turned her gaze to him then, and he smiled.

"You want to hear the story?"

"Go on, then."

"For a start, a selkie wife is simply a selkie female, whether married or no. And when a person is drowned or buried at sea, their soul arrives in the kingdom realm of selkie folk instead of heaven. A selkie changes form because it can possess the living, slip inside their skin like you or me putting on a coat, ye ken?"

She studied him. "And you believe this?"

"I've seen it with my own eyes," he whispered. "Stouthearted sailors possessed by a selkie, driven to throwing themselves into the depths, or steering the whole ship into rocks. It's no' a folktale about sacrifice. It's a tale about giving the sea more souls, more selkie folk to do the sea god's bidding."

She tried to follow this. "So the selkie wife in the original story drowned herself to join Lír's realm, but then possessed the souls of the living so they would drown, too?"

He nodded. "It's a grim tale, indeed. But then, anyone who's ever spent time at sea will know that the ocean's a wild and savage place. And every time we take some of its fish for meat or whales for oil, old Lír sends his selkies out for revenge."

"God."

She found herself trying to explain the story away, her mind turning to other stories she'd heard over the years about the sea and its creatures. Sirens, mermaids, kraken . . . but then her foot twitched, and she remembered with a wrenching feeling the dark pelt that had formed over the wound. It had become infected, spreading all the way up her leg and transforming her foot into a flipper. She could barely bring herself to believe it, but each time she unwrapped the gauze, there it was, clear as day.

She had to get back to Dundee, to Allan. A doctor would help her. And the crew would be brought to justice for what they'd done to her.

"Can I ask you a question?" she said, lifting her eyes to Daverley.

"Aye."

She bit her lip. "Did you know? About Thomas's part in bringing me on the *Ormen*?"

He searched her face. "No."

"But you knew they were to kidnap me? You knew I was being brought on board?"

He shook his head without removing his gaze from her. "Lovejoy asked Thomas to assist with moving livestock on board."

"Livestock?"

"Yes. The day before we disembarked. We had to move the cows, the lambs, and the hens into the hold. He was gone for most of the day."

She nodded, taking that in. "That was the day I was attacked in Dawson Park."

He frowned. "By who? Thomas?"

"No. I've no idea who he was. An older man, late fifties, perhaps older. Stockily built, a dark beard. He was wearing a brown cap and a navy overcoat. Does he sound familiar?"

He shook his head. "Thomas never mentioned it. But then, he was under orders from Lovejoy. I'd wager Lovejoy told him he'd be punished if he said anything. Especially to me."

She searched his face, trying to work out if he was telling the truth. She supposed he had nothing to gain by lying.

He went to say more, but just then the watch started to shout. "Ship ahoy!"

She looked up and saw Wolfarth pointing north. For a split second, it seemed that nothing was there, but then the light shifted and she saw it—a ship, its white sails glinting in the sun.

"It's the *Erik*," Daverley said. "Another whaler. We pass each other frequently on these voyages. Sometimes we take home letters and suchlike to the crew's families, others they do the same for us."

"That's what Thomas told me," she said, excitement growing in her. "Do you think I could send a letter back to my husband?"

He hesitated. "We'd have to be discreet. If Captain Willingham were to hear I'm passing on messages on your behalf . . ."

"You could say it's a letter from Thomas. He was writing letters back to his siblings."

"What if they read the letters?"

"Do you think they would do that?"

"They might."

"Well, hopefully by the time they do that, they'll be too far away to tell Captain Willingham."

He shifted his feet. "Why would Thomas write a letter to be passed on to your husband?"

She hesitated. "My father, then. Maybe you can say it's his will? Instructions for his wages to be passed on in the event of his death?"

Daverley looked doubtful. She held him in a long, pleading look. At last, he sighed and looked away.

"I'll do my best," he said.

Dominique

I

December 2023
Skúmaskot, Iceland

I think someone else is on board.

I'm in my bedroom, holding my breath. Shaking like a reed in high winds.

With the exception of my camera and the sensor, all the batteries are dead. The last couple of days have been completely without sun. It's the end of the year and the bleakest one I can imagine. No electricity for the kettle or the solar lanterns, no internet. And the singing is back. It's driving me mad. Always the same melody, a humming on the back of the wind.

I feel like I'm losing my mind.

I wake at four in the morning. There's a noise outside like someone is climbing the ladder, feet pressing into rungs and the metal grips at the top of the hull twanging with the weight. I sit up, excited; it must be one of the others. I race upstairs, expecting to find Samara or Leo or Jens there.

But as soon as I reach the main cabin, the noise stops. I hold my breath, listening. Picking up my torch, I head outside and shine a light down across the ladder.

There is no one there. I feel so confused. I heard it. I literally heard footsteps coming up the ladder.

I head back into the main cabin, locking the door behind me and heading back down to my own cabin. There, I climb inside my tent and zip it up.

But now I'm shaking because, as soon as I zip up my tent, the sounds of the ladder start up again. I sit, stunned, wondering why I can hear this. Nothing else makes that noise. I know what the ladder sounds like. I've heard it a million times now.

I wait for the footsteps to rise to the upper deck. Oh God. Someone is walking across the deck. No, not footsteps. One footstep, then a dragging of something across the wood.

And now I hear the same rhythm across the floor of the main cabin. It's so clear I can pinpoint exactly where the person is.

They're right next to the stairs, about to come down to the lower deck.

II

I have spent the last hour holding the handle to my cabin door with one hand and my knife with the other. Outside the wind is singing, singing. The darkness is a blindfold across the world.

The step-dragging has stopped. Still, I listen, waiting for it.

Waiting for her to come.

III

I wait in the dark, my torch switched off, for the footsteps to continue down the hatch to the lower cabin. I am covered in sweat, my heart jackhammering wildly.

But the sound stops. I wait, shaking, until I feel like I'm going to claw my skin off from fear. I have to open the door. I have to *see* her.

My hand on the door handle, I open it slowly, slowly, holding my breath. The corridor is pitch-black, but I don't dare turn on my light. The wind outside is faintly singing. I'm so scared I think I might faint. I force my foot to lift and step forward, then another step, and another.

I take the stairs, super slow, my ears thrumming from my pounding heart.

The main cabin is empty, but I can feel her. She is here. Not in one place. She is the ship, every part of it.

My knife is sitting on the worktop in the kitchenette, glinting in the safety light. I know what she wants me to do. If I don't do it, she'll kill me.

I lift my shirt and stand in front of the fire for warmth. I need to be sure I cut in the right place—the shouting in my skin is so loud I feel I'm about to explode, my skin bursting with noise. Quickly I move the point of the blade to where the sound is loudest, which is across my ribs. I press it deeper than usual, a long, stinging incision that brings a moment of indescribable bliss.

Blood seeps down across my skin, but something feels different.

I can feel something literally moving under my skin, a stealthy squirm inside that makes me gasp and step back in surprise. It moves again, and I start to panic. Something is inside me.

All at once, a dark seam appears at the slit I've made in my abdomen, something protruding beneath the bloody film as though it wants to burst out. It seems to have a will of its own, pushing and writhing. I let out a scream, but the thing is insistent, the sharp sting rising as it begins to tear the slit wider. Oh God. A black snake, I think, crawling out of me.

An inky loop slips down, wet skin shining in the glow of the fire. With my finger and thumb I pinch the loop, then tug a little, my hand shaking. I want to be sick. My mouth opens and I want to scream but I'm too horrified to make a sound.

It's an eel.

It drops to the ground, coiling and thrashing for a few seconds before it falls still. I am trembling, my mouth wide, wide, and soundless.

An eel was inside me. Tears stream down my face and I struggle to breathe. An eel. An eel was inside me. I can't believe it. I daren't believe it.

I am howling now, crying *Help me! Help me!*

A slim black eel, about ten inches long, a fin along its back.

PART THREE

Attempt Two Hundred Twelve

Diego

June 1973
near Svalbard, Norway

Diego Almeyda was in the High Arctic, and he was feeling relieved. He had plucked up the courage to tell Lorna, his colleague on a postdoctoral fellowship from Yale, about the figure he kept seeing on the stern. Always the same figure, holding the same stance—a woman, her back turned to him.

"How do you know it's a woman, then?" Lorna had said.

"She was closer, last time," he said. "I could tell she had a waist and hips."

"If she was so close, why didn't you ask her who she was?"

"Because when I looked again, she was gone."

Lorna had laughed and accused him of trying to freak her out. Diego's English was limited and so he wondered if it was a cultural thing, or if Lorna and the others pegged him as a nervous Latino who believed in ghosts. His grandmother had had the gift of sight, had spoken of ghosts like they were members of the family. Even so, he had never seen one. Until now.

It had been twelve hours since he last saw the woman. He had taken to staying in his cabin. Professor Joffre had knocked on his door last night, asking if he'd like a chat over a drink. Diego shook his head. He preferred to stay in his cabin.

"Research doesn't happen inside a cabin, mate," Professor Joffre said. He was Australian and took no bullshit. "You either get out of there or you leave the trip."

They both knew there was no leaving the trip. They were docking at Svalbard in a week to collect ice samples from the Tunabreen glacier. Perhaps then he'd be able to muster the courage to go outside. He'd be able to leave the ship then.

He woke when it was dark, a thick, pulsing blackness that told him he wasn't alone. He flicked on his table lamp and gave a gasp. In the corner of the room, facing the wall, was the woman he'd seen on the stern, the familiar shape of her head.

"*Por favor*," he whispered. "Please. Leave me alone."

He wondered if he screamed, would anyone come? Would anyone believe him this time? And just then, he looked up again and saw that she was gone. A sigh of relief. But something caught his eye. The woman was on the floor, elbows bent and her head tucked down, and behind her was a long, black tail. He whimpered, and she looked up with a craven look, the mouth stretched in a too-wide smile, revealing black gums and small sharp teeth.

He opened his mouth and screamed, a howl that stirred the other researchers from their sleep.

The nurse came and sedated him, but when he woke, the woman was back. He knew what she wanted now. He would be prepared, next time. In the lab, he found a scalpel, then locked himself inside his room.

A day later, Professor Joffre kicked the door down. Diego was on his bed, unconscious from blood loss.

"Oh, mate," Professor Joffre said, rushing to Diego. But when he set eyes on what Diego had done to his feet, he fainted.

Svalbard sat on the horizon like a white stone when Diego went to the top deck. He had spent three weeks in the boat's first-aid unit, and though they'd saved his life, they hadn't managed to repair the damage done to his feet. The deeper damage, though, was in his mind. He knew there were guns in the poop deck, protection against polar bears and pirates.

He took both shotguns and slotted the bullets into the chambers, then found a pistol.

"Hey, Diego," a voice said. "What the hell are you doing?"

It was Dr. Karsen, a glaciologist from Montreal. Her eyes dropped to his feet, which were marked with terrible wounds, the middle toes on both feet separated by a long gash.

"Diego, what *happened*?" she gasped.

But the woman appeared behind Dr. Karsen, her long tail visible beneath her white dress. With a yell, he lifted the gun and pulled the trigger. He saw the glaciologist's head burst open, and it took a long moment for him to realize that his own bullet was the cause of it.

He saw a tail flick inside the main cabin, so he followed.

Inside, his colleagues were having coffee by the fire.

"Diego," someone called. Diego lifted one of the shotguns and pumped a bullet at the woman, but she slithered out of sight. Behind her, Dr. Jeong collapsed with a terrible scream. Blood splattered across the floor.

The girl Diego had liked, Dr. Morton, was stooped over the body, yelling "Leo!," and the professor was there, his arms up in surrender.

"Look, take it easy, mate," he told Diego. His face shone with sweat, the whites of his eyes reminding Diego of the cows that lived behind his house. "Come on, buddy. Don't do this. This isn't what you want, is it?"

Leo was screaming and Diego wanted it to stop. He went downstairs through all the cabins, blasting the gun furiously until there were no bullets left, then lifted the other shotgun and did the same. And when he ran out, he was astonished to see that all was still.

A full moon shone down on the deck, a black, velvety ocean rocking the boat like a cradle. The galaxies were heavy overhead, a streak of green marking the awakening of the aurora borealis. Soon the green lights would fill the sky, dancing overhead in vivid rivers. Diego returned to his room, a sickening fear swelling in his solar plexus. He felt the boat groan with a new weight, the floorboards sounding out the presence of the woman. She was on board, and she was coming to him. And when he saw the shadow in the doorway, a spark of delight rested inside him—she was no longer monstrous, but beautiful, lowering above him on the bed to kiss his face. Even when blood plumed warm on the bedclothes around him, he couldn't bring himself to make her stop.

When the coast guard boarded the *Ormen* a month later, they found it empty. It had been lashed by tall waves, and the sails were damaged. The coffee machine was still running, and the generators. The laundry bags waited by the doors of the cabin, half-written letters were found under beds. Someone had left a record on the turntable.

They expected the *Ormen* to sink. But she drifted on, cradled by the waves, a piece of lint on the steely expanse of the Greenland Sea.

On the morning of the fifth of November, 1973, the ship swept into Skúmaskot, Iceland, coming to rest in the knobbly grip of volcanic rock.

And in the darkness, something climbed out of the water behind her, slinking into the shadows.

Dominique

I

December 2023
Skúmaskot, Iceland

I run out onto the deck, screaming at the thing I've just pulled out of my stomach. I lean over the side of the hull and vomit down the ladder.

A hand reaches up and touches me.

I scream. It touched me. She touched me.

I fall back onto the deck, shrieking at her to get away. I curl up into a ball, feeling the song of the wind wrap around me, enter me, clutching me.

"Dom?"

A man's voice. A familiar voice.

I uncurl slowly and look up. A shape appears at the hull, a watery shape. Jens. He's in a bad way, almost losing consciousness even as he struggles to climb over the top of the ladder. Quickly I move forward and grab the shoulder straps of his rucksack and stop him from falling, holding him there until he finds the rungs and clambers up.

I'm elated and terrified and angry all at once. He looks terrible, his knees weak and his hands visibly shaking as he staggers across the deck to the cabin. The wind is ferocious, too, and neither of us speaks until we're inside.

No sign of the eel. The cut in my abdomen has stopped bleeding, a dark clot forming already along the line that I made with the blade of my knife. I find a dressing while Jens removes his rucksack and coat, then sinks down onto the sofa.

"Is Leo here?" he pants. "Samara?"

I manage to find my voice. "Just me."

He looks pained, but I'm relieved to have company again. I turn to the kitchenette and fill his water bottle with trembling hands.

"I thought you'd left," I say, handing him the bottle.

He takes it and drinks deeply. "We got separated in the storm."

"You and Leo?" I ask.

He nods.

"Did you find Samara?" I ask.

He looks down, and I hold my breath. We sit in silence, because I'm too scared to ask if they're dead.

"Why did you come back?" I say finally.

"I wanted to make sure you were okay," he says slowly, in between breaths.

I wonder if I heard correctly.

"You wanted to make sure I was okay?" I say.

He nods. "I promised I would."

"Who did you promise?"

He lifts his blue eyes to mine. "You."

I stare, trying to recall this promise.

"You don't remember?" he asks, and I shake my head.

"There's something I need to tell you," he says. His eyes fall to my fingers, and I realize they're covered in blood. My blood.

"What happened?" he says.

I open my mouth to explain, but I can't. A sob swells in my throat, and to my horror I start to cry. I can't help it. I can't remember ever crying in front of anyone, but suddenly I'm unraveling in front of him. He reaches out with his good arm and holds me to him, a feeling so alien and so comforting I can't let go.

Nicky

I

October 1901
Banks Bay, Greenland

The *Erik* was a whaler that set sail from Hull in the north of England, the crew every bit as leery and coarse as the *Ormen*'s shipmates. Lovejoy directed the men to sail the *Ormen* right up alongside the neighboring ship, close enough for the men to jump from one ship to the other and greet each other. Morning sickness made the tight space of Nicky's cabin almost unbearable, a sudden aversion to the closeness of the walls around her, and so she stayed on the forecastle with a blanket, watching as the men exchanged kegs of beer and furs.

It was clear that the mariners intended to stay for a few days, Inuit tents growing on the bank running parallel to the ships. She watched rowboats creaking back and forth between the tents and the ships, carrying female Inuit dressed in impressive fur coats and bringing food for the crew.

"Offerings," Daverley told her, handing her a piece of dried caribou. "The Inuit women bring gifts to entice our mariners to impregnate them." He watched her expression change and smiled.

"Aye, not many folk from home would find it acceptable, either. But we're not at home, are we? We're in the Arctic, and the natives don't live in the kind of world we do. Their communities need births to survive. And they need foreign seed to prevent inbreeding." He grinned at her expression. "The native lassies see us Scots as fresh meat."

She watched Lovejoy climbing onto the *Erik*, licking his palms to slick back his oily hair. "I suppose one woman's poison is another woman's fresh meat."

He followed her gaze. "You could also say that the seed may be rotten, but the flower can be fine."

"Every garden needs manure," she said dryly.

Daverley laughed.

She bit into the caribou and found that it was delicious, the gaminess of the meat a welcome contrast to the diet of whales, seabirds, and seals that now turned her stomach. He passed her a parchment bag filled with ripe purple berries that burst on her tongue. She ate the lot without speaking.

"I'd best see if I can get you more," Daverley said.

"Won't the Inuit women expect you to impregnate them?" she said, watching the women climb aboard the *Erik*. Wolfarth, Royle, and McKenzie all but fell over themselves in the attempt to reach the other ship.

Daverley grimaced. "I'm sure one of my colleagues will happily take my place."

She was puzzled at this. "Why aren't you up for it? You were married to a woman, weren't you?" She asked it delicately. Her brother Harry was, as he had once whispered to her, Achillean, which she took to mean after the Greek hero Achilles, whose relationship with his battle mate Patroclus was romantic in nature. Harry told her that a surprising number of men and women were of a similar ilk, but of course to be outward about it was to put oneself in mortal peril. She had imagined her father's reaction, if he had cause to suspect Harry's inclination. A Dundee whaler, born and bred? He'd have disowned Harry without blinking.

"I'm still married," Daverley said softly. "I didn't stop being Thomas's uncle when he died. And I didn't stop being Eilidh's husband when she died."

For two days, there was no hunting or whaling. Both the *Ormen* and the *Erik* were transformed into floating brothels, occupied by Inuit women who raced up and down the lower deck, naked, and Inuit men, who stood in their heavy caribou furs on the upper deck, smoking pipes, drinking Scottish ale, and playing cards with the crew.

Daverley promised to look after her, and he kept his word. He brought her food and fresh water from the land and traded his own tools for Inuit blankets to keep her warm.

The ship hummed with moans and squeaking beds, and it reeked of sex and caribou meat. Nicky found that her vomiting began to subside. As long as the ship didn't move and she ate the sweet Inuit berries and the smoked caribou, the vomiting stopped. Her strength began to return, and the crew of the *Ormen* were preoccupied with naked Inuit women.

One night, she saw a flash of white weaving through the try-pots on the upper deck. It was the Arctic fox, though that single flash was as much as she saw. It had escaped the cage and was doubtless making its way back to land, even as she marveled at how it had broken free. Had the ship been at sea the fox would have been doomed, but the Inuit women had stalled the voyage, providing an opportunity.

And perhaps she could do the same.

II

"I need you to help me."

Daverley looked around to check that they weren't being watched. Harrow was caulking a cask with a cinching iron, his gaze hard and cold on them both. Above, Anderson sat on the rig, glancing at them. And on the bow, Royle and McKenzie were removing whale oil from a copper cooler. She caught them looking at her before whispering to each other.

"I'll collect your letters later," Daverley said. "We're setting sail tomorrow at dawn. I'll pass your letters on to the captain, all right?"

"I don't want to send letters home," she said. "I need to *go* home."

He turned his eyes to her, realizing what she was proposing.

"The *Erik* is returning to Dundee, is it not?"

He nodded.

"I could hide away on that ship. Three weeks, maybe less, until I'm home. I could manage it. But I need your help."

Daverley lowered his eyes, and she feared he was going to refuse her.

"They killed your nephew," she said, her voice a little louder. "Surely you want your own revenge for that."

He leaned forward angrily, pressing his face close to hers. "What I want," he said, "is to get home to my sons in one piece. And if you think you're going to involve me in something that will prevent that, you've lost your mind."

He looked over his shoulder, and she saw the men glancing over. She thought to remind him of his promise, but she had to tread carefully.

"Please," she whispered. "I just need you to signal when it's safe for me to go on board the other ship."

He gave a small nod, and she kept her face turned from the men as she headed back to her cabin.

Later that night, she heard a knock at her door. She opened it to Daverley, a grim look on his face.

"Come in," she said, and closed the door behind him.

"You risk your life going aboard the *Erik*," he said. "If those men find you on board, you'll not have the same protection as you've had here."

She widened her eyes and gave a laugh. "Protection? Are you joking?"

"I know they raped you," he said carefully. "But if you weren't George Abney's daughter they'd have thrown you overboard by now, I can promise you that."

She gave an angry scoff. "What, are my services no good? You think they'd rather me dead than prostituting myself day and night?"

He held out a hand to keep her voice down. "It's still a three-week journey back to Dundee. You've not thought this through . . ."

"I *have* thought this through."

"How will you get food and water without being noticed?"

"That's the least of my concern."

He scoffed. "You nearly bit my arm off when I gave you a bag of berries and you think you can go three weeks without eating or drinking?"

"I'll find a way," she said, folding her arms.

He sighed. "Look, I know the crew on the *Erik*. I know what they're like. And if they find you on board their ship, they'll do much, much worse than what you've endured here."

She turned away, stung with a sudden frustration. What option did she have? She couldn't endure another three months on the *Ormen*. And if she went home to Dundee, she could possibly recruit someone to help her with the matter of the pregnancy. Perhaps Allan would still be in the Transvaal. She would never have to tell him. Her mother had once whispered that Mrs. Cross, the family housekeeper, had a sister who was a skilled abortionist.

If Nicky left it too long, she'd start to show. And perhaps she'd be beyond the point of help.

"As long as you know the risk," he said after a long silence. "If you come to the top deck at midnight, I'll help you aboard the *Erik*."

"Thank you." She leaned forward and kissed his cheek. He flinched, and she could tell he was embarrassed. With a nod, he turned on his heel and returned to his cabin.

III

At midnight, she slipped out of her cabin to meet Daverley. Fear crept up her spine and across her shoulders. A fresh mouthful of vomit raced up her throat, and she swallowed it back, stifling a cough as she made her way to the upper deck.

As soon as she raised her head through the hatch, she spotted Daverley, standing with a tankard of beer near the forecastle. He saw her and gave a loud shout.

"McKenzie! Have I ever told you about that time I swyved your ma?"

"Are you out of your wits, man?" another voice called.

Daverley appeared to be drunk, leaning his elbows on the side of the hull and taking a swig of beer. "It was the time after I swyved *your* ma," he shouted to Royle.

"What did you say?" McKenzie said, his voice closer. He had

climbed down from the rig to challenge Daverley. "Say it to my face, why don't you?"

"You heard me the first time." Daverley said.

"I'll have your guts for garters if ye mention my ma again."

"Leave him be," Royle called out. "He's off his head."

Daverley spat in Harrow's face. With a shout, McKenzie swung his fist for Daverley, who ducked out of the way, the blow landing on Royle's jaw. Royle lifted his tankard and brought it crashing down on Harrow's head.

"What the devil's going on?" a voice shouted. Daverley glanced quickly at Nicky, and she saw her chance—the crew were distracted by the brawl that had sparked between Daverley, McKenzie, and Royle, more and more of the men drawn in. She looked up at the watch aboard the *Erik*. His gaze was on the swinging fists at the stern of the *Ormen*.

Under cover of darkness, she made for the starboard side of the *Ormen* and pulled herself onto the neighboring ship.

The layout of the *Erik* was much the same as the *Ormen*. She had memorized the crawl spaces, those parts of the ship in which spare sails and coils of rope were kept. There would be enough space for her. The small storage room above the engine room was probably the safest and warmest. She planned to slip down into the engine room when possible to stretch her legs, and to eat. The hold would be best for that, though she would likely have to eat raw whale for the duration of her stay . . . but these were small matters compared to the next stage of the plan.

The familiar cries and squeaking bed frames told her that the crew were busy saying goodbye to the Inuit women. Only a fire or murder would draw them out of their cabins.

She moved quickly toward the stairs that led to the hold, but when she lowered to the next level she found that it was different than the *Ormen*.

For a start, the decks weren't as dark as the *Ormen*'s—wall sconces trickled warmth and light along the hallway, their small flames tilting as she moved quickly past. The cabin that was Dr. O'Regan's surgery wasn't there, and instead she found herself staring through a crack in the door that led to the galley.

The galley was larger than the *Ormen*'s. Clean pots and pans hung from an overhead rack, and a cook stood at a table peeling potatoes. Her mouth watered—there hadn't been potatoes on the *Ormen* for months—but she had to tear herself away and find the crawl space. The thought occurred to her that perhaps she should have found a reason to board the *Erik* as a guest in order to scope it out before escaping. But then, this was a last-minute plan, and so much hinged on it. Already she could hear the men returning to the rig and preparing the sails for their launch, and it was just enough to give her a boost of courage to keep moving along the deck.

And then she found it—a barely perceptible brass hoop laid flat into the wood of the floor. She pulled it up and found the crawl space beneath her feet. No sails, only a few dusty tar pots, a soothing warmth rising from the engine room below. A space about six feet by four, barely larger than a coffin. But the wood had gaps, and as she slid inside she felt a draft passing from the upper floor.

Outside, she could hear voices shouting, calling the men to their stations. She pulled the hatch door shut, tight, and lay down, a hand to her stomach. She thought of Daverley, starting a fray with his colleagues to draw attention away from her. Had he gotten into trouble?

She slept several hours before the sound of coal being shoveled in the room beneath woke her. She heard the whistle of the boiling water and the roar of the engine, more shouting. Feet pounded the wood above the crawl space. Sweat gathered under her armpits and along her spine. They were moving.

Closing her eyes tightly, she took slow, deep breaths, images of home beginning to slip into her mind. The noise of the jute mill, the children's voices and the women singing. Her sister's dogs, the fluster of paws across the parquet each time she came home. Sunlight on the Tay. The photograph of Allan on her dresser.

Footsteps. She held her breath as they paced up and down the deck, praying hard that they'd keep away. There was nothing of any obvious value in the crawl space, nothing anyone would be searching for, but that didn't mean they wouldn't check it. The footsteps moved away, and she allowed herself to breathe.

But then, light. The hatch lifted and a face looked in.

A grin.

"Hello, my lovely," McKenzie said. "So here you are."

IV

She sat before Captain Willingham's desk in his office, Stroud and Cowie standing close by her side, as though she might burst out of the room and run for her life. Her arms and legs burned from where they seized her, bruises on her shins from where they dragged her roughly out of the crawl space and took her, kicking and screaming, back to the *Ormen*.

She kept her eyes on the floor, fighting back tears of anger.

"Your father sent us a telegram via the *Erik*," he said. "That is why we searched for you and found you were not in your cabin."

"My father?" she said. A burst of hope, vivid as fresh flowers. "How does he know I'm here? What did he say?"

"It doesn't matter what he said," Captain Willingham said

tersely. He seemed irritated, bothered by something. "What matters is you were found trying to escape."

The mention of her father emboldened her. "You don't own me, Captain. I have every right to leave if I choose."

"We had an agreement," Captain Willingham said, the matter closed.

"An agreement?" she said. "Is that what you call it?"

"We had two telegrams from the *Erik* that you might wish to know about. The first was from your father, asking after you."

She opened her mouth, astonished. "But how does he know I'm here?" she repeated, her voice low and steely.

"We told him you were well," the captain said, continuing to ignore her question.

"My father will have you in the courts," she hissed, her voice quavering. "He'll have you hanged for what you've done to me."

The captain held her in a flat stare. "Oh, I don't think so."

She lifted her jaw, tears wobbling in her eyes. "I'll stake my life on it."

Captain Willingham cocked his head, the edges of his mouth beginning to curl in a smile. "I'm afraid that the second telegram was to inform us of an imminent change in the company ownership. Your father is dead."

Her face dropped, all the hope that had risen in her sinking through the floor.

"Dead?" she said.

Captain Willingham nodded, his eyes cold. Then, taking pleasure in the telling: "By his own hand."

Her mind filled with metal shards. Grief, noxious and bitter, fell on her like a boulder. The tears that came were raw, guttural. And now that her father was dead, she feared what the men might do.

They had no reason to let her live.

Dominique

I

December 2023
Skúmaskot, Iceland

The singing stops.

I tell Jens what happened, and he spies the blood on my stomach. No sign of the eel, but he doesn't question me when I tell him. Despite his own exhaustion he cleans the cut on my stomach and applies a dressing. Then he presses a sleeping pill into my hand and insists that I go to my tent at once and sleep.

When the sun comes up, I start to feel better. The wound on my stomach doesn't hurt so much, and the light today is strong for the first time in weeks. Jens has made a pot of coffee and is sitting by the back window overlooking the beach. I pick up a solar charger and try to go online to check for any messages from Leo and Samara, but it won't connect. I try again and again, until the power runs out. Frustrated, I put the charger back by the window to power up the battery again for another try.

"What do you think has happened to them?" I ask Jens, sitting down opposite. "Do you think they got lost?"

He nods. "I got lost out there for a long while. I'm going out again, after this cup of coffee."

"I'll come," I say. I force a smile to show I'm well enough.

He holds me in a long look. "I think it's time I told you something," he says then.

"That sounds ominous."

"I don't think it's ominous."

"Bad, then. Anytime someone says they need to tell me something, it's bad."

He falls silent, and I crane my head up to see his expression. He looks down at me, a deep line of worry slicing his forehead. He opens his mouth, then closes it, before striding across the cabin to the wooden post with the column of cuts.

I watch, utterly confused, as he runs his fingers over the nicks in the wood.

"Two hundred eleven times," he says. Then, pulling a penknife from his pocket, he cuts a fresh line at the very top. "Attempt two hundred twelve," he says with a sigh.

Have I missed something? "Attempt at what?" I ask him.

He turns and holds me in a look of such despair that I wonder if he's lying about Leo and Samara. Are they dead?

A loud knocking breaks the silence. The chain beating against the hull.

"What *is* that?" Jens says.

"It's just the chain," I say. "The wind catches it . . ."

We hold our breaths and listen as the knocking shifts. Two knocks, now. Jens gets up, glances outside. Light rests on his face and I realize I have lost track of what time it is. It must be daytime, about noon.

"Where are you going?" I ask.

"I want to see what's causing that sound," he says.

Outside, the deck has ripened with snow. An albatross the size of a chair is perched on the side of the hull, ruffling its feathers against the shining flakes that twirl in the air. The light is stronger today, hard on my eyes after days of darkness. Jens climbs down the ladder and I follow.

"Jens," I say, approaching him as he looks over the hull. "Tell me."

He stares down into my face. He hasn't forgotten our conversation. He was going to tell me something.

"We know each other," he says then. "From before."

I frown at him, suddenly wary. "That's what you wanted to tell me?"

He looks nervous and relieved, as though he'd been carrying around a secret that he had to get off his chest. "Do you remember me?"

I run my eyes over him, confused. Memories swirl in my mind. The men's faces above me. The rapes.

I back away, feeling foolish. The urge to cut myself nudges at me. But when I glance up at him again, I feel it—recognition. A duality to the knowing of him. Dizzying déjà vu.

And as though he can read my mind, he steps forward.

"You do remember me, don't you?" he says, reaching out. I pull away, instinctive, and he looks shocked.

"Dom," he says. Then, as though he's realized something, he turns and strides past me, right around the side of the wreck to the ocean. I watch, alarmed, as he wades into the tide, the waves thunderous.

"Jens!" I shout. "Don't!"

He keeps walking until I can't see him, and I cup my hands to my mouth. Iceland's seas are treacherous, but suddenly I'm wading in after him, the shock of the cold as it seeps through my clothing making me shout out.

I'm up to my neck before I see him—he is swimming toward the back of the wreck, heading for the stern, where a thick chain is clanging against the hull. The water is ice-cold, snowdrifts floating by like miniature islands. I pull off my coat, then close my eyes and push into the water. I start to swim, wheeling my arms and kicking hard, but waves slam into me, pushing me back. I can feel powerful currents pulling at me, insistent on taking me off course.

The illusion of the ship's closeness from land is laid bare by the length of the swim. But finally I'm there, panting with exhaustion and clinging to the metal rivets with my fingertips, feeling the ship groan and swell against me with the force of the waves.

"What are you doing?" I shout over the noise of the waves crashing down on the beach.

Jens holds up the chain, its black loops filled with solid ice. "There's something hooked onto this," he shouts back. "That's what's causing the knocking."

"Great!" I shout back sarcastically. "It doesn't matter! Come back to the ship!"

But then he dives under, and my heart stops. A moment later he surfaces, only to dive under again. What the hell is he doing?

The chain begins to move, stretching out toward the beach. I follow it, watching Jens's head bobbing up above the waves, waiting for the moment that he doesn't surface. I'm still so shaken by Samara's fall into the ice that I can't bear the thought of him going under, adrenaline flashing through me in case he doesn't come back up.

He has caught something, the thing the chain is hooked to. I swim quickly toward him, hard currents sapping my strength. I reach down to help him shift whatever he has found, my fingers finding a metal bar beneath the surface.

We drag it together onto the beach, then collapse onto the sand, utterly spent.

"Don't ever do that again," I say, gasping between words. He turns to me, silvery hair slicked across his forehead. The currents were frightening, and we both know we were lucky to make it back. Ironically, the thing we've dredged from the chain anchored us, helping us to shore.

After a moment he stands and shakes off his coat and shoes, then hefts the object at the other end of the chain out of the water.

"What the fuck?" I say.

Nicky

I

October 1901
Banks Bay, Greenland

They whipped Daverley first.

Twenty stripes with a strip of tarred ratline, each one lifting his skin in a livid welt. Nicky watched on from the forecastle as Lovejoy meted the stripes, putting all his muscle behind them. Her hatred roiled. Her father, dead. She was sure he was the reason she was on board the *Ormen*. How else would he have known she was here? She braced herself for what they would do to her. Throw her overboard, perhaps. Why would they spare her? They had nothing to gain from it.

Daverley sank to his knees, gasping, his back ablaze with bloody lines. The captain nodded grimly at Wolfarth, who pushed her toward the mast and tethered her wrists to it.

"Twenty lashes," Captain Willingham called out. She fixed her eyes ahead, seeking out the faint bar of the horizon in the distance.

A shrill snap as the rope unleashed behind her, again and again and again. The sea singing, an invitation. A war cry.

. . .

After the beating, the mariners let her be. She stayed in her room for several days, no desire for food or water. She had stopped vomiting, and there had been blood, dark and arterial. When the men carried her back after the flogging, her bandage unraveled. Now, stretched out on the bed in front of her, she saw what had become of her foot. Dark as coke, a layer of fine fur, her toes bruise-dark and flattened at the end of a thin curve. Her ankle bone swallowed by sooty flesh, the whole foot sinuous and slick. Her left leg was still human, but the skin between her thighs had webbed, a darkness spreading at the seam.

The transformation of her foot was something appropriately selkie-like, horrifying and familiar at once. She had seen more seals in the last three months than she had ever thought possible, dozens of them. But so many of them were captured, hauled onto the ship, a mass of dead things. Walruses piled like sandbags, dolphins, polar bears.

She was becoming like them.

To the mariners, she was prey, the division between the ship and the rest of the world cut by species, and now gender. The rape of the ocean was brokered by men like her father, like Lovejoy. Men who would take without impunity for their own gain, by whatever means necessary.

A noise outside her cabin door startled her as she lay there. She fixed the blanket across her legs and watched, stricken, as Lovejoy strode in. She could read his mood before she saw his face.

"Here she is," he said. "My selkie wife." He had the same smile he had worn while lashing Daverley. The cruelty she had clocked in his eyes months ago had crystallized into something monstrous and consuming.

He lowered to his haunches, moving closer to her. "What must you have done to be so worthless in the eyes of your own father?"

She kept her gaze on the ground. He wanted a fight. He wanted to provoke her.

"Your father offered you up, you know," he said. "I told him the men would walk without payment and he offered you." A cruel smile. "His own daughter."

She closed her eyes, a tear spilling down her cheek. *He is lying,* she told herself, but her mind returned to the morning before she woke up in the hold. Her father telling her to keep out of sight, that he had done something that he regretted . . .

"You didn't know?" He reached down and gripped her cheeks, turning her face to him. "Answer me."

She moved her hand to the bedclothes, nervous in case he saw her tail. What then? Would he kill her?

"His company or his daughter, that's what it came down to," Lovejoy continued, watching for her reaction. "The crew wouldn't sail without a woman on board. Says he, 'I have a daughter who I can offer as a selkie wife if the men will sail,' and so we did."

She shook her head. "My father would do no such thing," she whispered.

"Oh, but he did," Lovejoy said, lowering his face to hers. "Your own kin betrayed you. Your own *blood*." His grip remained tight on her face, and she didn't move. "You think anyone's missing you back in Dundee, selkie? You may as well stay here on the ship. My selkie wife."

He climbed onto the bed on top of her, lowering for a kiss. She kissed him, obedient, but she knew what was coming. He was unfastening his belt, and he would see her tail. Instinctively she moved a hand to the side of the bed to pull herself from under him, but her hand touched something familiar. The polar bear skull.

Lovejoy was reaching beneath, hauling up her skirts. Quickly she lifted the skull and raised it, a heavy upward swing that caught Lovejoy's jaw.

He fell backward against the door, his arms flung to the sides, and she lunged again, swinging the skull across her body.

It connected with the side of his head, a long split across his eye spurting blood as he dropped to the floor.

Dominique

I

December 2023
Skúmaskot, Iceland

It's a cage.

About three foot square, wrought of thick, sea-oxidized steel. Jens hefts it closer up the sand, and I lean my weight behind it, pushing it with him. Those couple of minutes in the freezing sea have left us wrung out. Even on the shore I can feel currents pulling at me, invisible hands snaking around my ankles, pulling me back, back.

Once the cage is free of the tide's reach, we sink into the sand and look over it in silence.

"It was hooked to the chain," Jens says, as though that explains anything. As though it explains why he was so desperate to find it.

"So this was causing the knocking," I say. We're both stunned, looking for answers.

I'm no expert, but it doesn't strike me as a standard fisherman's cage. For one, it's super heavy, and second, there are spikes on the inside, designed to wound whatever sits inside. Jens moves forward, tentatively, reaching out to check that the spikes are actually attached to the frame. And they are.

"Jesus," he says.

Something moves in the corner of my eye, and I turn to see a figure moving in the mist, about a hundred feet to my right. The ghost woman. My heart thuds in my throat, acidic, noxious fear. I grab Jens's hand.

"Tell me you see her," I urge.

"I see her," he says, rising to his feet.

I start. "You do?"

He squints. "It's Samara."

I turn, astonished. He's right—the figure stumbling toward us has morphed into Samara. Behind her, Leo emerges, his form hardening as he steps out of the fog. We both scramble across the sand toward them, laughing and shouting.

"Samara!" I call. "Samara!"

It's a miracle, an actual goddamn miracle. She's alive! I pull her close to me, my arms around her, weeping into her neck. A moment later, Leo collapses. In my excitement, I haven't realized the state they're both in. Leo's gloves are missing, his fingernails caked with dirt. Samara has leaves sticking out of her dreadlocks and there's dried blood around her mouth.

Jens looks up at me. "We need to get them indoors, quickly," I tell him.

II

By the time we reach the cabin, the four of us are quaking and gasping from the cold. Jens and I are soaked through, the skin on my hands raw and split open from hauling the cage. I don't even go down into my cabin—I stand in front of the fire, stripping off my clothes until I'm naked, before slipping inside the sleeping bag. Jens watches me briefly before doing the same, stripping down.

I watch in horror. "What are you doing?"

"We don't have much choice, do we?" he says, shaking off his trousers. He leaves on his boxers and climbs inside the sleeping bag with me. Jens feels like an older brother to me. The weirdness of it is only for a moment; soon, his skin against mine lowers my heart rate and helps me stop shaking.

Leo and Samara are curled up on the floor next to us, all of us trying to soak up the faint heat of the fire, huddled together desperately for warmth. Leo reaches for a piece of broken wood and, with a trembling hand, feeds it into the fire.

We must all fall asleep, because when I wake, Jens is sitting opposite, talking to Leo. He's dressed. I sit up, holding the sleeping bag to me. Samara is changed, too, holding a cup of something.

"Hello," Jens says to me.

I smile back. "Hi."

It's dark outside. The mood is quiet, shell-shocked. I can scarcely believe the events of today. Of the last few days. The dynamic between Jens and me has shifted entirely. And more important, Samara is here. I want to reach out and touch her to prove to myself that she's really here. That she's alive.

"Are you okay?" I ask, holding off my more existential questions until I find out where she's been.

Samara nods, though her eyes are haunted. She glances at Leo, and I follow her gaze, trying to read what they're not saying. "We were so worried," I tell Leo. "Did you get lost?"

Another glance between Leo and Samara. "I went after Samara," Leo tells Jens. I notice he can't look me in the eye, though maybe it's just exhaustion. No—he's still angry with me.

"I saw footprints in the snow, just outside the caves," he says. "So I kept heading in that direction. Eventually, I found her. She'd lost her footing and rolled down a ravine, close to the river."

Jens and I turn to Samara.

"But I don't understand," I say gently. "Samara, you were *dead*. I gave you CPR. I felt your pulse, and there was nothing. You were stiff, for God's sake."

Samara looks uneasy. She shifts her eyes from me to Leo, who seems to nod, as though consenting to a shared decision.

"I thought . . . that I was free," she says. "I thought I'd made it out." She presses her hands against her eyes.

"What?" I ask, astonished.

"You lost consciousness," Jens says, and I'm grateful he's here, saying sensible things. I'm reeling so hard that I can't think straight. "That hasn't happened before."

"I remember waking up here in the cabin," Samara says haltingly. "Then . . . walking through the snow, feeling lightheaded."

"You just woke up?" I say, interrupting. I'm keen to understand how the hell she came back to life.

She nods. "I kept walking," she says. "I wanted to get away from here."

"We walked for days," Leo says. "Both of us. When I found Samara, I had already passed the *Ormen*. I figured I'd messed up the path and turned back on myself. But then it happened again."

"*What* happened again?" I ask.

"Well, we kept going in circles, obviously," Samara says, her voice filling with anger. "No matter how hard we tried, we kept coming back here."

"Seventeen times," Leo says darkly. "We passed the *Ormen* seventeen times."

"We couldn't escape."

The room sits in silence. None of us can process this. If they passed by seventeen times, how come I didn't see them? Why didn't they give up and come on board? Why did they not want to return?

"It's a labyrinth," Leo tells me, as though explaining it has deepened his exhaustion. "The wreck is in the middle of a vortex. We can't get out. Not you, not me, not any of us. We are stuck here."

I give a small laugh, and instantly everyone turns to me.

"Sorry," I say, swallowing back another laugh. "I'm just . . . this is all crazy, isn't it? First you, Samara, looking like you'd died but then . . . not. And now you two getting lost."

"The *Ormen* will be sunk tomorrow," Jens says, his voice raised.

"We'll wait for the coast guard," I say. "And if we can't get out, we'll ask them to take us back."

It sounds like a reasonable plan to my ears, but I can tell that neither Leo nor Samara is paying me any attention.

Whatever they've gone through has been harrowing. Their minds are elsewhere.

Nicky

I

October 1901
Cape Hooper, Greenland

A gasp from the doorway made Nicky look up.

Daverley was there, his face like a broken window. Lovejoy lying facedown in a pool of glossy claret, the side of his head bashed in. She dropped the skull with a clatter and keeled forward, gasping for air. Daverley lunged forward, catching her as she fell off the bed.

"Are you hurt?" he said, kneeling beside her, and she realized her hands and face were spattered with blood, the hem of her dress soaked red.

She broke into tears. She had killed Lovejoy. It had been a momentary reaction. She was glad and not glad. Relieved, terrified.

Daverley leaned his ear to Lovejoy's chest, listening for a heartbeat. He rolled back on his haunches, crossed himself. "He's gone."

"Lovejoy said my father arranged for me to be on the ship," she said. "As a selkie wife. Did you hear anything about this? Did you *know*?"

He hesitated. "When you insisted you were no prostitute, I spoke to the men. To Reid."

"Tell me," she whispered.

"Your father didn't pay us last time," he said quickly. "He owed us all wages. He couldn't guarantee they'd be paid. Lovejoy told us he'd made a deal."

"What deal?" she said.

"He said he'd ask for a woman for the men. Your sister."

Her mouth fell open. "Cat?"

"Your father offered you instead."

The news knocked the wind out of her. She sank back against the bed, breathless.

"I shouldn't have told you," Daverley said.

"Did you agree to it?" she said. "The deal."

Daverley lifted his eyes to hers. "I didn't know you had been taken by force," he said carefully.

He reached out to hold her hand. She let him.

"God's wounds!" a voice said. Wolfarth and Stroud stood in the doorway, looking in horror at the scene—Daverley with his hand in hers, both of them sitting by Lovejoy's battered body.

"Murder!" Wolfarth screamed. "Murder aboard! Fetch the captain!"

The sentencing was swift, and without trial or record.

"In," Captain Willingham said, pointing inside the brig.

They were standing on the upper deck, hard rain needling down. The whole crew watching on. The sight of Lovejoy's body had stunned them all. She'd gone mad, Wolfarth said. The selkie wife was a murderer.

It could have been any one of them.

Wolfarth gave her a shove. She stepped toward the brig, her hands still stained with Lovejoy's blood.

The clang of the cage door. Her knees to her chin, her spine pressed up against the metal. A spike brushing her scalp.

Stroud and McKenzie hefted the cage starboard, a heavy chain hooked to the top of the cage. She saw Daverley hauled in chains toward a barrel, his right arm held out as Royle brought down an ax. One clean, brutal blow taking off his hand. He let out a cry that sounded like no human she had ever heard. A roar like a bear.

The chain knocked against the side of the hull as the men lowered her down in the brig. She saw the blue sky and the sunlight reflecting off the metal rivets, the distant shape of Anderson in the crow's nest above. Then, her own reflection in the waters below.

The water received her like it had been waiting, patient. Fetching her home.

She held her breath for as long as she could, fighting against the heavy bars of the brig. The spikes cut into her arms, releasing long red feathers of blood. Her fingers reached through the cage, clawing at the hull.

Shadows in the depths. A face with whiskers, curious at the cage.

Her body fought. She jerked and convulsed, her lungs burning and her hands wringing the bars of the brig until her palms bled. The spikes pierced her scalp, her cheeks.

And then, a honeyed glow.

An awakening.

Dominique

I

December 2023
Skúmaskot, Iceland

Today, the *Ormen* is to be dragged beneath the waves, sunk to the depths.

The light today is sublime. A crisp blue sky, fat, picture-book clouds, a generous spread of gelatinous sunlight ruddying the hills. A night's sleep has been good for us all. Jens makes breakfast, cracking open double the amount of his expensive sachets and encouraging us all to dig in. He makes a pot of strong coffee, produces sugar and dried milk. I had no idea we had these. He must have been hiding them—his emergency stash. Small luxuries that make an otherwise ludicrous situation a little more palatable.

I want to find the right time to ask him what he meant before, when he asked if I remembered him. Everything feels so fragile. Samara is here, alive. The *Ormen* is about to be destroyed. We seem to be trapped here. If I don't stay focused on small things—the weather, the food, the fire bucket—I'll go mad.

We take it in turns to keep watch for the breakers. We need to approach them to avoid their discovering that we've been living on board. If we present ourselves as hikers who have gotten lost, rather than urban explorers who have essentially been squatting on the wreck, we have a much higher chance of getting help. Jens says this is a better option than calling the coast guard for help. None of us want to be arrested, especially not in Iceland, and especially not in a part of the country where the nature reserves are protected. The penalties will be harsh. Better that we ask the breakers to take us back to civilization.

At midday, Jens gives a shout from the upper deck. "A ship!" he shouts, and we look outside. An orange coast guard vessel has appeared out at sea, moving swiftly toward us.

"They're going to tow it out," Samara says.

"Maybe we should film this," Leo suggests.

I fetch the solar chargers from the window. They have enough charge to allow the cameras to film this.

Jens comes inside. "They're almost here," he says. "We need to go outside."

Leo passes him his drone. "Get some drone footage," he says. "I'll film from the rocks."

"It's better if one of us approaches," Samara says. It makes sense—she's the most charismatic of the four of us, the one most likely to persuade the breakers that we're hikers who got lost.

We plan it—Jens will climb the volcano to get drone footage while Leo and I get shots of the breakers arriving. We put on our backpacks and say goodbye to the cabin. I click the TikTok app on my phone, but the project account isn't there. I try again, closing down the app, then reopening it. Still not there, and neither is my own personal account.

"Something wrong?" Leo says.

"I can't find the account," I tell him.

"Don't do a live," he says. "Upload it later."

I follow Leo up the rocky outcrop once we've got our footage, while Samara waits behind, waving her arms at the ship. It's growing closer, the insignia of the breaker company visible on the main mast. A mermaid.

Jens's drone buzzes overhead, and I scan the side of the volcano where he stands, controlling the drone. I hope he's right about the breakers. I hope they listen. Even if Leo and Samara are wrong about the path out of here, it's clear that neither of them has the strength to take on a fifteen-mile trek across lava fields.

I hold up my phone and film the ship, lifting my free hand to wave at them.

"Over here!" Samara shouts. "Help us!"

Leo drops something beside me—his camera, I think—and I lower to help him find it among the shrubs. But as I stoop down, I feel my arms being pinned behind me. In the corner of my eye I see Samara, and it takes a moment to register what's happening—she's binding my hands together. I hear the zip of a cable tie, the friction of plastic against my wrists.

"Samara, what the fuck?" I shout, but she pushes me forward, tying my ankles together with another cable tie. I give a shout as she pulls the tie too tight, the plastic nipping my skin. Leo ties a leather belt across my mouth, fastening it at the nape of my neck. My eyes bulge as I stare at him, pleading for him to stop. But my cries are muffled, and he doesn't let go.

He looks past me at Samara.

"We don't have much time."

II

Samara and Leo carry me down the outcrop, back to the *Ormen*. I squeal into the leather at my mouth but it isn't enough to rouse Jens, who has climbed high up the side of the volcano.

At the ladder, Leo throws me over his shoulder, then uses another cable tie to bind my wrists to my ankles, my arms thrown straight behind my head and my thighs bent until my feet are almost touching my head. I'm not flexible, and my shoulders feel like they're about to pop out of their sockets.

Inside the *Ormen*, they carry me down to the lower deck. I'm bewildered and frightened—the breaker ship is right next to us, the thrum of the engine in the water making the *Ormen* sway. Through the window I catch a flash of a man in a luminous boiler suit leaning out to tether the *Ormen* to the orange vessel with hooks and chains.

Samara is meant to be approaching him, asking for help to get us out of here. What the fuck is going on?

"Inside," Leo says, and they kick open the door to the captain's cabin. The ship sways violently as the tether to the breaker ship tightens, another roar of an engine as they pull us clear of the rocks.

They drop me roughly to the floor beside the toppled desk. Leo bends to me, anger etched into his face.

"This isn't just for me," he growls. "This is for all of them. Lorna, Dr. Karsen, Professor Joffre . . . every one of those poor bastards Diego shot."

"And Diego," Samara says, and she kicks me, hard, in the gut. I jackknife forward, gasping for air. She wipes her eyes, suddenly tearful. "For all the people you've cursed."

The door bangs behind them as they leave, the sound of footsteps moving quickly through the cabin. I hear the clank of the bow as the breaker pulls, again and again, the engine cutting out several times. I can't shift position, my legs bent behind and my arms stretched to the small of my back.

A dizzying bolt of panic—I can't get out. Jens is up the volcano. I'm going to drown like this. A couple of minutes and it's all over.

I roll over on one side, scanning the room for anything sharp that I might rub the cable ties against.

The ship sways heavily, the terrible whine of the bow deafening my screams as the breaker pulls the *Ormen* back.

And then, a deafening crash. It sounds like the bow has finally split, the whole floor tilting, flinging me hard against the far wall.

I can feel blood seeping through my hair, blood oozing quickly, the heat of it streaming down my face. The bookcase across the hole shifts, and it takes me a moment to figure out why my clothes are suddenly wet.

Black seawater is storming through the hole.

III

"Dom? Dominique?"

I hear my name from the upper cabin. Jens. Jens! I try to shout but the belt is too tight. Water laps up around my knees. A moment later, I see a set of shoes.

A knife, cutting me free. He pulls the belt from my mouth.

"Can you walk?" Jens says, and I nod.

"Good," he says. "But you'll need to swim."

He pulls me through the lower deck and up the stairs to the main cabin. We're three hundred yards from the shore, the ship tipped forward as water floods through the hole of the captain's cabin.

"Jump," Jens says when we reach the hull, and I do, I jump down into the freezing water.

I panic in the depths, the shock of the cold and the stream of bubbles making me flail wildly for what seems like hours. The undertow of the *Ormen* almost pulls Jens back with it, a current that feels too strong to escape. I see him drift, his arms outstretched and his mouth open. Reaching out, I manage to grab his collar and pull up, up.

And then I haul him to the surface, holding him alongside me.

IV

Sand, then ice.

No sign of Samara and Leo.

We watch the orange ship move farther and farther away. Our chance of rescue disappearing.

The *Ormen* limps into the fog, the front tipped forward as though taking a bow.

The light is fading. Neither of us has our backpacks, our supplies. Our tents.

Jens gets to his feet, scanning the bay. His eyes settle on the turf houses, and I know what he's thinking. It's snowing again. We're drenched, freezing cold. We'll go indoors and spend the night there. Light a fire.

I stand up and link my arm through his as we head toward the nearest turf house.

"Do you know anything about that?" I say. "Why Samara and Leo wanted to kill me?"

"They didn't want to kill you," he says.

"You reckon they were just having a laugh by drowning me, then?"

He shakes his head. "They can't drown you."

I stop. "What?"

He turns to face me. The look in his eyes is different, and I feel uneasy.

"Where did you buy your internet terminal, Dominique?"

"What?"

"Where?" he presses, shaking me. "You can't remember, can you? You can't remember, because you never bought one. You didn't set up a TikTok account. You didn't google, you didn't film anything. It wasn't real."

He's speaking so fast that the words are crashing into one another, his blue eyes wide and wild.

"Jens! Stop this!"

He claps his hands to my cheeks and pulls my face to his. "That thing I was trying to tell you? You're dead, Dominique. We're all dead. All of us."

I pull away from him. "What are you talking about?" I say. Then, angry: "Stop it. Stop saying this!"

"I know you remember," he says.

"What?"

He says it again, and I step back. "Why are you saying this?"

"You think you're still alive. But you're not. And neither am I."

"Fuck you, Jens."

I walk away, and when he reaches for my arm it might as well be a slap in the face. I pull away sharply, then spin around, my fists clenched. He sees.

"Nicky," he says. "You were born Dominique, but everyone called you Nicky. Your father was George Abney and your husband was—"

I hit him, then, a hard crack across the cheek. "Don't you *dare* talk about my husband!" A sob steals away the rest. But, too late—it's as though the balloon has been pricked, and now the air seeps out, all the memories spilling from his words into my mind.

My husband. Allan.

The faces of the men.

Ellis. Lovejoy.

Daverley.

"Let me show you," Jens is saying, his hand on my arm, and he is pulling me toward the pier overlooking the bay.

I'm asking him what he means by *let me show you*, until I realize that he has no interest in telling me. We are on the pier, the rotten wood making it difficult for my feet to find purchase. The force of the sea has ripped away most of the ice, carrying it in great chunks past the mermaid stone. If I slip, I'll fall in, and the memory of Samara seizes me.

"Let me go!" I scream, right into his face. For a moment, he looks at me with what seems to be tenderness. And then, in one sudden move, he shoves me in.

I feel my feet leave the ground, my body flying through the frigid air. I hit the water on my side, my feet catching a block of ice.

I'm under, the shock of it tearing through me. Freezing water gushes down my throat and up my nose, stinging my eyes. All I can think about is getting up, getting out, finding air, and warmth. My hands flail and I kick hard, but it's no use—the water is too cold, and soon my muscles won't work.

My lungs are screaming for oxygen, panic ripping through me, bright as a comet. I reach up but my hands find a block of ice instead of the surface.

And then I stiffen. I can do nothing. Can't swim. I can only hope Jens sees sense and tries to pull me out.

But I don't drown.

Somehow, the water is no longer cold.

I look around, suspended in the dark. The panic softens. My lungs remember.

Shadows move in the depths, seaweed swaying there. I see a tail, long and black, flicking in the distance.

And I remember everything.

The Selkie Wife

October 1901
Cape Hooper, Greenland

Like all lies, the tale that Lovejoy told of Lír and the selkie wife was woven with threads of truth.

The sea was conscious.

This was the first thing she learned, once she left her body. Silvery strands of light radiated out from her like jute fiber, connecting her to the seals and whales and seaweed that drifted by, a vast web that spanned the planet in its past, present, and future dimensions.

Is this what you want?

A question posed by the sea.

Stay, and take revenge? Or go, and have peace?

There was no hesitation in her answer.

Stay.

A moment later, she felt something rest on her head, and when she reached up her fingers met the hard bone of the polar bear skull that Lovejoy had made her wear, the long fangs slender and sharp between her fingers. On her shoulders, two black guillemot wings, silken to the touch. The leg that had been human before joined the other, fusing, a muscular black tail. It was powerful enough to burst open the cage.

She swam out, relieved that her lungs were no longer straining for air. Bubbles drifted from her nose, and she saw clearly in the water. Her tail lengthened behind, twice the length of her former legs. Fish swam alongside as she moved into the blue depths. Above, the long shadow of the ship appeared, and she followed it, careful not to breach the surface.

Remember, the sea whispered, *that revenge is a stone tossed into water. You can't direct the ripples.*

The wind had heard her songs, and the dark wishes folded inside them. In the currents of the sea they materialized, a scrim, a wraith unleashed, craving retribution.

I

Now

I'm in one of the turf houses, curled up inside the cage. How did I get here? How am I dry?

I look out through the bars of the cage. It's the same one that Jens dragged from the sea. He is sitting next to me in a chair, and as my eyes adjust to the gloom, I see Leo and Samara there, too. I lurch. A moment ago I was underwater. Did I pass out? Surely they didn't rescue me?

"Jens?" I call out. My voice wavers, fearful. "Will someone let me out?"

"We can't," Jens says. "The cage is in your head."

I grip the bars and shake, the cold metal firm beneath my grip.

A moment ago I was underwater, my head bleeding. I reach up and touch it. There's a faint pain there, but no wound. No blood. I grab the bars and shake the door. Nobody reacts.

"Well, she's here now," I hear Jens say. "You still want your revenge?"

"Yes," Leo says, right as Samara says, "No."

"What?" Leo says, turning to her. Samara clasps her hands together, and she looks tearful.

"Can someone tell me what's going on?" I ask.

"We're dead," Jens says flatly. "All four of us."

"We're not dead, Jens," I say, a sob in my voice. "We're all very much alive."

I just want him to let me out. I want to go back to the ship, and light a fire, and feel the safety of the cabin and the wood holding me close.

"Not in the real world," he says in a low voice. "Nice to see you're remembering things, though. Aren't you?"

I open my mouth to shout out *I'm not dead!* but I remember the smell of Captain Willingham's cabin, teak and the earthy tang of pipe smoke, the amber glow of his oil lamp on the desk, my own reflection staring back at me from the window behind him. Beyond that, a strip of ocean, black as night, and the thump of the waves against the hull. The sway of the boat churning my stomach.

You must have stowed away.

And then they violated me, over and over again.

When I killed Lovejoy, they put me in the cage and threw it into the water.

The dreams I had. They were my own memories.

Everything was different. Something had switched inside me. I could see that now. I didn't feel time the way I used to. I would go to sleep and wake a week or even a year later. I would look out of a window and watch the seasons change, the trees turning from green to red to black naked branches, stripped of their leaves by wind and rain. The world around me moved on a different set of wheels. I didn't change, didn't grow old. *But I still felt like me.* I saw my face when I looked in a mirror. I got hungry, and tired, and happy, and angry, and I had dreams.

Sometimes I met people who spoke to me, and I knew they were in the river of time that I was in. They were like me, in the world and not in it, moving at a different speed. Unseen, invisible, but here.

Dead.

I remember.

I remember the man in the park, and waking in the hold of the ship. I remember the apologetic smiles of the men who appeared at my cabin door.

I remember what happened next.

I remember Daverley's hand being cut off. They thought he had helped me kill Lovejoy, but he didn't. All he had ever done was try to protect me. He died from blood loss, never returning home.

I remember taking revenge on the residents of Skúmaskot for burning down the whaling station, for preventing me from escaping when I might have had a chance to return home. To return to Allan. To live the life we promised each other.

"Let me out," I say again, rattling the bars with my fists. "Please. We can just leave, okay? The four of us. It doesn't matter that the coast guard have left. We can use the drone to help find our way . . ."

"We can't get out," Leo snaps. "Like, ever. Skúmaskot is a labyrinth."

I stare at him. "What do you mean, a *labyrinth*?"

"I mean, you walk and you walk and you walk and you'll come back to the ship. You go any direction, you run as hard as you can, and you will always, always come back to the ship. Swim, walk, run, dig . . . always the same. Circles. Every cave, every current . . ." He stops, his tears shining with tears of anger. "It's because of you. *You* are doing it."

I shake my head. "I'm not. I'm promise you, I'm not doing anything . . ."

"I believe you," Jens says.

"Oh fuck you, Jens," Leo says, kicking the air in frustration.

"I do," Jens tells me, ignoring Leo. "I don't think you are consciously doing this."

"So, what—it makes it okay that she's doing it *subconsciously*?" Leo asks Jens. "We're all in her fucking self-created hell, her own personal Valhalla, and we literally *cannot leave* . . ."

"We're trapped in your nightmare," Samara screams, her voice bouncing off the hard surfaces of the room. "We're inside your fucking memories! The horses in the cave? They weren't real. They were your memories. The cameras, laptops . . . all in your head. And you possessed Leo. The poem on the table . . ." She starts to sob. "I didn't know a ghost could possess another ghost. Jesus Christ."

"She's not possessing anyone," Jens says quietly. "It's the legacy of what happened to her on the *Ormen*. Trauma is an element, remember?"

I listen, trying to make sense of it all. My heart is beating so fast, and I feel nauseated. How can any of this be real?

"I just want to go home," Samara says after a thoughtful silence. "Like, wherever we're meant to go. I want to move *on*."

Samara tells me she was a field recordist working on a research project in Svalbard. Her parents were so proud. They'd grown up in Jim Crow, and here was their daughter, getting a doctorate, then a postdoc for a project in the Arctic.

"We were on a ship. The *Ormen*." She squeezes her eyes shut. "There was a guy from Argentina, Diego. Another postdoc, really sweet. I liked him a lot, and we really hit it off. And Leo . . ." She turns her eyes to him, and I realize he was there, too.

"I'd felt on edge the whole trip," Samara says. "I kept having nightmares. I put it down to being seasick, being away from home. Then I started to hear Diego ranting. We all did."

"What was he ranting about?" Jens asks.

"He said he kept seeing someone, or something," Leo says. "A woman, or a mermaid. He stopped coming out of his cabin. Then Professor Joffre found him in his room half bleeding to death. He'd cut his feet apart. We thought he was having a psychotic episode."

"We called the station on Svalbard to see if we could arrange for him to go home," Samara says. "And then he had a gun. I remember him turning the gun on Leo." Her voice drops to a whisper. "Diego shot him.

"I remember trying to tie my T-shirt around Leo's leg to stop the bleeding," Samara continues, her voice trembling. "And then there were more gunshots, huge bangs, and everyone fell around me. Diego pointed his shotgun at me and I pleaded with him not to. I could see he was crying and mumbling that he was sorry. And he shot me."

I feel like someone is pulling me backward into an enormous hole, and then I'm falling and can't stop. I hear the gunshots, like the popping sounds of the ice through Samara's microphone. I remember Leo racing across the bay, leaping and ducking and diving, as though he's trying to dodge a bullet.

Eternally trying to dodge the thing that killed him.

"And then what do you remember?" Jens says.

Samara opens her mouth to speak, but the words don't come immediately.

My mind flickers with bright images, nauseating in their strength.

I haunted the horses, the prized horses of the men who owned the fishery, sending them to their deaths. I haunted the people who lived there, sending them running with fear, until not a single soul remained.

I hid in the wood, in the oil cans, in the hold of the ship, small as a knot. I changed form. I became.

I saw the explorers who stayed on the *Ormen*, heard their conversations. Picked up the shifting languages and turns of phrase, their technologies. Time moved in a staccato frenzy, whole years feeling like minutes. I was present and absent at the same time. I was a trace, a fragment. A haunted haunting.

Leo has calmed down, his arms folded and his chin to his chest like a scolded child. "Let me ask you something: what's the definition of insanity?"

"What?"

"It's doing the same thing over and over and over again and expecting something to *change*."

I blink. "I don't understand."

Leo throws his head back and laughs. It's a horrible sound, a forced laugh. The sound of torment.

"Do you even realize how many times we've tried to fix this?" he says. "How many times we've tried to get you to, I don't know, do whatever you need to do in order to let us leave?"

"No," I say.

"Two hundred twelve," Samara says in a low voice. "This is attempt two hundred twelve."

"You used to hang out in the turf houses," Leo says. "You would only come onto the ship at night."

"You spent the longest time in the cage," Samara says. "You were this . . . creature. A selkie. Half human, half fish, half wolf or fox."

"That's three halves," Leo says.

Jens looks up at me, tugging at his pink beanie. "And then, you changed. The tail went. Your face became more human. You became like this."

He runs his hands down in front of me. "Human," he adds.

Samara gives a loud, pained sigh. "It gave us hope."

"We hoped that the wreck being broken would change something," Jens says sadly. "And when you said something was 'Lovecraftian,' we thought that this time was different."

"About twenty years ago," Leo adds, "I showed you a book on the ship by H. P. Lovecraft, and we talked about things that were in his style. You know, *Lovecraftian*. It was a sign you were starting to remember."

Flashes of memory spool in my mind, erratic, a bombardment of smells and textures. Leo screaming at me to remember, to wake up. Samara on her knees by the pier, begging me to let her go. Countless times. I didn't know how to do what she asked.

I couldn't.

Finally, my thoughts turn to Morag, and it burns in me. The guilt of it. How can I ever make it right? The effects of guilt are stronger than any haunting.

It changed me, over and over and over again.

II

The cage melts away. In a moment, I'm sitting on one of the empty chairs with the others.

I look around, astonished.

"What happened?" I ask.

"The cage is only real in your mind," Jens says. "In this world. Or realm, whatever you want to call it. You must have done something."

"I didn't," I say.

"You did it without realizing, then," he says.

I look down at my hands, my knees. I still feel pain. I eat. I bleed.

I think of the woman I saw on the beach, at the bottom of the ladder, at the three rocks farther down the coast. It was me, traces of who I'd been as a haunting. My memories eclipsing, superimpositions of the past and the present. Present absences, with all the ruptures in time and space that they create. Like guilt.

"You killed me," Leo tells me, the anger burning in his eyes. "I fucking hate you. I've been stuck here for decades. I wanted to trap you in that fucking ship and sink you forever to the bottom of the ocean."

"Easy, now," Jens says.

Leo looks like he wants to kill me. He can't, I realize, but he can still hurt me. I don't know the rules here. In this realm.

"I'm sorry," I say, glancing at Leo.

He scoffs. "You're sorry? That's it?"

"Just . . . let us go home," Samara says, holding up her hands. "Whatever you're doing to keep us here . . . just stop, okay?"

I shake my head. "I don't know what I'm doing."

Leo lunges at me, but Jens reaches out to stop him, and his shirt falls away, revealing his stump. Osteosarcoma, he told me. Liar. He's Daverley. He risked his life on the *Ormen* for me. Jens Daverley. I hadn't realized that he had died, too, but I see it now, like a shared memory—he bled out when they cut off his hand. He never returned to Dundee.

I think of the way he spoke of his wife, Eilidh. I've kept him here. Maybe if he left, he could be with her.

Maybe it's too late.

"I'm sorry," I tell him. Then, turning to Leo and Samara, "I'm sorry about Diego. About everything."

I'm pretty sure it's not enough for what I've done. I have died a thousand times over. The girl who was drowned on the *Ormen* was filled with revenge. Delirious with both trauma and guilt, she drove the living to their deaths out of revenge. Some part of her was me, despite how much it hurts to admit it.

But I don't want revenge anymore.

Something has changed. I just want to go home.

III

We're outside now, the four of us standing on the rocky outcrop facing the sea. The orange ship is a smudge in the distance. The *Ormen* bobs above the surface, a hard triangle of metal against the liquid dark of the ocean.

Samara gives a gasp, and I turn to see a shape on the tideline. A wet head, shoulders. A long gray dress. Her back turned to us.

Fear runs through me, sharp and swift as a javelin. But this time, I don't shrink. I force myself to move toward her, keeping my eyes fixed on her in case she disappears again. When my feet reach the sand I break into a run, screaming for her to turn around.

Turn around! Turn around!

She doesn't move. I get closer, all the terror I felt before turning to fury. I need to see her face.

She doesn't turn, her slender back to me. Her pale dress is worn and stained with blood. I move in front of her, my fear electric, a vivid current pulsing through me.

Her jaw is stretched open in a frozen scream, her dark eyes creased and bright with anger. Her eyes are white, no pupils, seeing nothing.

She is a trace, a quavering memory clutched by time. A haunting.

She is me, then. A version of myself. A trace.

I step forward, pressing my face to hers, and in a moment I seem to absorb her. All the hate and fury fusing with the hope and sadness and grief I didn't even realize was inside me.

The mists swirl, black sand snakes in a flurry around my ankles.

She's gone. I hear a dog bark. Behind me at the outcrop, Samara is on her knees, her arms around a black dog. I see Leo running past her toward another man. He leaps on him, his legs wrapping around his waist, his arms gripping his neck.

Jens approaches, and as I turn to him the light shifts.

The *Ormen* has disappeared beneath the surface. Jens keeps his eyes fixed on the land ahead, and right as I ask him what he's looking for, a figure appears.

A woman. She has soft eyes and a face that melts when she sees Jens. I see him raise a hand to his mouth, his eyes softening.

"Eilidh," he whispers. He races toward her, glancing back just one last time, before disappearing into the mist.

I stand, watching the last of the sun liquefy into the hills. I'm glad for Jens, truly I am. And I'm glad that I had a chance to apologize to Samara and Leo.

But I'm alone. *That's* what's been different this time. This time I've felt alone. Felt *lonely.* Craved something that only someone else can give me.

The black sand stretches out at either side, the ocean like a toppled tombstone. I have been searching all this time for my home. But I could never imagine where that was.

It was never a place.

A shadow lengthens up the sand, a crestless wave. A head and shoulders.

And I recognize him, the lines of his strong form, the angles of his face.

It's Allan, heading toward me. Oh God.

The last of the light sweeps across his face. He smiles at me, and my heart leaps. I can tell he wants to go back to Dundee. To our home on Faulkner Street. Just for a while. To remember what it was like to be together in those early years of our marriage. To remember each other.

To remember our daughter.

Behind us, I hear the drumming of hooves. It is a low hum, growing louder as I strain my eyes to see into the fog. There they are: Icelandic ghost horses, untethered from the bodies that lie broken in the cave. I count two dozen of them, thundering their hooves against the sand, blond and chestnut manes flying up as they race across the bay.

Thriving in the dark.

Author's Note

Memory and trauma pervade all my work, but I wanted to write about them more consciously, or intentionally, than I have in the past. I have always believed that ghost stories examine memory and trauma, how the past inhabits the present, how our experience of time can be erratic and nonlinear, perhaps even a kind of disorienting spiral. Trauma disrupts our sense of the present even more drastically; in my own life, I've recognized patterns through the lens of generational trauma, repetitions that can be galling, flashbacks that can feel like a haunting—as though time is a prison.

I set myself a challenge to try and write about these ideas, or to write *through* them. As with my previous novels, the setting was important: place is how we forge meaning from time, the architecture of time chaptered by tide, stone, and wood. And of course, place can clutch memory; a site can haunt, tugging at the unconscious in uncanny ways.

A ship came to mind, both as a wreck and a moving vessel. I resisted this idea at first, knowing how much research it would take to write authentically about a whaling ship crossing the High Arctic in 1901. But then a link popped up on my Twitter feed, a news article from 1883 about a polar bear that escaped from a whaling ship after being captured during an Arctic hunt, prowling the streets of Dundee. It felt like a sign. And it felt like I should definitely use the newspaper article in my book.

I read nineteenth-century newspaper articles and researched contemporary scholarship on the history of Arctic whaling and the Dundee whaling industry. I interviewed people with knowledge of ships and polar exploration. Although I had been to Reykjavík—for a few days in 2019 to teach at the university—I felt I needed to explore the Icelandic wilderness to solidify the fictional village of Skúmaskot (translated as "dark corner") in my mind. Luckily, Creative Scotland awarded me a grant to carry out a short research trip, and in the spring of 2022 I drove to Iceland's south coast, visiting the famous (and dangerous) black sand beach of Reynisfjara, then up to the Snæfellsnes peninsula, where the glacier-topped stratovolcano Snæfellsjökull has sat for seven hundred thousand years. From there, via ferry, I went to the Westfjords (where the road transformed to a gravel path for about sixty kilometres), where I visited the wreck of the *Garðar BA 64*, an old whaling ship grounded at Patreksfjörður. Though this vessel differs from the *Ormen*, which I imagined as a barque-rigged sail-and-steam hybrid built around 1880, visiting the wreck was a pivotal moment. There is something about visiting a setting in person that always seems to knit the scattered tendrils of a story together; maybe this is all the more powerful after the lockdowns of 2020–21, when so much of our lives shifted to virtual spaces—being *present* is something I still don't take for granted. Without giving away any spoilers, exploring the *Garðar BA 64* helped me push my story deeper, and the risks I knew I wanted to take with my ideas of memory and trauma felt a little more possible. I had the unlucky experience of losing a month's work on the novel to a glitch in my laptop (an experience which has taught me to triple back up everything!)—I'll admit that I cried for a good few days! But being in Iceland helped return many of the ideas I thought had been lost forever. And when I returned to Reykjavík, I found myself standing on the word *Skúmaskot*, which someone had written across a pavement. It felt like a good omen.

The history of whaling is stridently masculine. Having researched the policing of female bodies for my previous novel, *The Ghost Woods*, and upon discovering the long-held superstition that a woman's presence—her body—on a whaler was a curse, I felt compelled to explore the feminine within that space, particularly in terms of the folkloric imaginings of femalehood. I find it intriguing that so much seafaring lore reimagines sexual transgression and the female body; the water's edge figured as a liminal space, a site to imagine those human experiences outside the norm. In many oral traditions, the mythical figures of mermaids, sirens, and selkies evoke notions of illicit desire and sexual violation, often in terms of a woman who is captured by a man for his sexual pleasure. In the legend of the selkie wife, a man steals a selkie's skin to trap her ashore, whereby she is forced to marry him and bear his offspring. Later, her seal skin is returned by her children, allowing her to escape to the sea. Violence and vengeance figure brightly in these stories, too; just think of the sirens in Greek myth who lure sailors to their deaths. I love how these myths explore chimeras and monstrosity, the way they seem to disrupt binaries of gender and species, and how they force us to contemplate our relationship to place, and to the past.

I should say that the tale here of the mermaid stone and selkie wife, including Reid's shanty about Lír, are my own inventions. As I imagined Nicky's story, I found myself reflecting on how traumatic experiences can leave us feeling altered ourselves, right down to our identity, perhaps at a cellular level. Trauma can feel like a theft of one's skin, leaving us vulnerable, uncannily *othered* from one's past self. At a time when language could not fully capture the effects of trauma, perhaps myth and metaphor served instead. Perhaps they still serve best.

C. J. Cooke, June 2023

Acknowledgments

I am so very grateful to everyone who helped me bring this novel into the world:

Alice Lutyens, my fabulous agent, for always being in my corner.

Lucy Stewart at HarperCollins UK and Jessica Wade at Berkley (US), and of course, Katie Lumsden, for collaboration and encouragement and zingy ideas that sent my brain alight, and for helping me find the best possible story in the quarry of possibilities.

Kimberley Young, Lynne Drew, and all at HarperCollins UK; the fabulous team at HarperCollins Canada; to Claire Zion and all at Penguin Random House US; to Deborah Schneider, my lovely US agent. Luke Speed (thank you for encouraging me to set this on a ship), and Anna Weguelin, Olivia Bignold, Caoimhe White, Samuel Joseph Loader, Liz Dennis, and all at Curtis Brown. Thank you all. I feel so unbelievably privileged to work with the absolute best in the business. Your talent and brilliance are both constantly inspiring.

Creative Scotland for funding a research trip to Iceland—finding the *Garðar BA 64* shipwreck in the Westfjords will forever be one of the best days of my life.

Carol Knott, fellow Moniack Mhor resident, who gave expert advice on the history of Dundee whaling, and to Natasha Pulley for ship talk—all errors are mine.

Professor Willy Maley at the University of Glasgow for sending fantastic scholarly articles on Iceland and Greenland whaling, and my colleagues in creative writing: Colin, Elizabeth, Zoë, Louise, Kerry, Jen, and Nicky. Thank you all for your support and friendship.

Angharad for the mermaid. She kept me going, you know.

My husband and children, for too much to mention here, but ultimately, for love.

Ralph and Winston, our darling dogs, for always being near (and often on top of me) while I wrote this book.

Booksellers, book bloggers, and readers who have championed my books—my absolute love and thanks to you. There were times when your messages fished me out of dark places.

Hjörvar, my Icelandic brother-in-law, who sadly passed much, much too young, during the writing of this book. I hope this would have made you proud.

Photo by C. J. Cooke

C. J. Cooke is an internationally bestselling Edgar®- and ITW-nominated gothic novelist. She is the author of *The Lighthouse Witches*, which is currently being developed for screen by The Picture Company for StudioCanal. Her books have been critically acclaimed for their atmospheric use of place and historical research, and have been published in twenty-three languages. Born in Belfast, Northern Ireland, C. J. has a PhD in literature and teaches creative writing at the University of Glasgow, where she also researches creative writing interventions for mental health. She lives by a river with her husband, four children, and two dogs.

VISIT C. J. COOKE ONLINE

CarolynJessCooke.com
CJessCooke
CJCooke_Author

LANGUAGE AND LITERACY SERIES

Dorothy S. Strickland, FOUNDING EDITOR
Celia Genishi and Donna E. Alvermann, SERIES EDITORS

Critical Encounters in High School English: Teaching Literary Theory to Adolescents, Second Edition
DEBORAH APPLEMAN

Children, Language, and Literacy: Diverse Learners in Diverse Times
CELIA GENISHI & ANNE HAAS DYSON

On Discourse Analysis in Classrooms: Approaches to Language and Literacy Research (An NCRLL Volume)*
DAVID BLOOME, STEPHANIE POWER CARTER, BETH MORTON CHRISTIAN, SAMARA MADRID, SHEILA OTTO, NORA SHUART-FARIS, & MANDY SMITH, WITH SUSAN R. GOLDMAN & DOUGLAS MACBETH

On Critically Conscious Research: Approaches to Language and Literacy Research (An NCRLL Volume)*
ARLETTE INGRAM WILLIS, MARY MONTAVON, HELENA HALL, CATHERINE HUNTER, LATANYA BURKE, & ANA HERRERA

Children's Language: Connecting Reading, Writing, and Talk
JUDITH WELLS LINDFORS

On Ethnography: Approaches to Language and Literacy Research (An NCRLL Volume)*
SHIRLEY BRICE HEATH & BRIAN V. STREET WITH MOLLY MILLS

The Administration and Supervision of Reading Programs, Fourth Edition
SHELLEY B. WEPNER & DOROTHY S. STRICKLAND, EDS.

"You Gotta BE the Book": Teaching Engaged and Reflective Reading with Adolescents, Second Edition
JEFFREY D. WILHELM

On Formative and Design Experiments: Approaches to Language and Literacy Research (An NCRLL Volume)*
DAVID REINKING & BARBARA BRADLEY

No Quick Fix: Rethinking Literacy Programs in America's Elementary Schools, The RTI Reissue
RICHARD L. ALLINGTON & SEAN A. WALMSLEY, EDS

Children's Literature and Learning: Literary Study Across the Curriculum
BARBARA A. LEHMAN

Storytime: Young Children's Literary Understanding in the Classroom
LARWRENCE R. SIPE

Effective Instruction for Struggling Readers, K–6
BARBARA M. TAYLOR & JAMES E. YSSELDYKE, EDS.

The Effective Literacy Coach: Using Inquiry to Support Teaching and Learning
ADRIAN RODGERS & EMILY M. RODGERS

Writing in Rhythm: Spoken Word Poetry in Urban Classrooms
MAISHA T. FISHER

Reading the Media: Media Literacy in High School English
RENEE HOBBS

teaching**media*literacy***.com: A Web-Linked Guide to Resources and Activities
RICHARD BEACH

What Was It Like? Teaching History and Culture Through Young Adult Literature
LINDA J. RICE

Once Upon a Fact: Helping Children Write Nonfiction
CAROL BRENNAN JENKINS & ALICE EARLE

Research on Composition: Multiple Perspectives on Two Decades of Change
PETER SMAGORINSKY, ED.

Critical Literacy/Critical Teaching: Tools for Preparing Responsive Literacy Teachers
CHERYL DOZIER, PETER JOHNSTON, & REBECCA ROGERS

The Vocabulary Book: Learning and Instruction
MICHAEL F. GRAVES

Building on Strength: Language and Literacy in Latino Families and Communities
ANA CELIA ZENTELLA, ED.

Powerful Magic: Learning from Children's Responses to Fantasy Literature
NINA MIKKELSEN

On the Case: Approaches to Language and Literacy Research (An NCRLL Volume)*
ANNE HAAS DYSON & CELIA GENISHI

New Literacies in Action: Teaching and Learning in Multiple Media
WILLIAM KIST

On Qualitative Inquiry: Approaches to Language and Literacy Research (An NCRLL Volume)*
GEORGE KAMBERELIS & GREG DIMITRIADIS

Teaching English Today: Advocating Change in the Secondary Curriculum
BARRIE R.C. BARRELL, ROBERTA F. HAMMETT, JOHN S. MAYHER, & GORDON M. PRADL, EDS.

Bridging the Literacy Achievement Gap, 4–12
DOROTHY S. STRICKLAND & DONNA E. ALVERMANN, EDS.

Crossing the Digital Divide: Race, Writing, and Technology in the Classroom
BARBARA MONROE

Out of this World: Why Literature Matters to Girls
HOLLY VIRGINIA BLACKFORD

Critical Passages: Teaching the Transition to College Composition
KRISTIN DOMBEK & SCOTT HERNDON

Making Race Visible: Literary Research for Cultural Understanding
STUART GREENE & DAWN ABT-PERKINS, EDS.

The Child as Critic: Developing Literacy through Literature, K–8, Fourth Edition
GLENNA SLOAN

* Volumes with an asterisk following the title are a part of the NCRLL set: Approaches to Language and Literacy Research, edited by JoBeth Allen and Donna E. Alvermann.

(Continued)

Critical Encounters in High School English

TEACHING LITERARY THEORY TO ADOLESCENTS

SECOND EDITION

Deborah Appleman

Teachers College
Columbia University
New York and London

National Council of
Teachers of English
Urbana, Illinois

Published simultaneously by Teachers College Press, 1234 Amsterdam Avenue, New York, NY 10027 and National Council of Teachers of English, 1111 W. Kenyon Road, Urbana, IL 61801–1096

Library of Congress Cataloging-in-Publication Data

Appleman, Deborah.
Critical encounters in high school English : teaching literary theory to adolescents / Deborah Appleman. — 2nd ed.
p. cm. — (Language and literacy series)
Includes bibliographical references and index.
ISBN 978-0-8077-4892-3 (pbk : alk. paper)
1. English literature—Study and teaching (Secondary) 2. Literature—History and criticism—Theory, etc.—Study and teaching (Secondary) 3. American literature—Study and teaching (Secondary) 4. Literature—Study and teaching (Secondary— 5. Criticism—English-speaking countries. I. Title.

PR33.A66 2009
820'.71'273—dc22

2009011059

ISBN 978-0-8077-4892-3 (paper)

NCTE Stock No. 09543

Printed on acid-free paper
Manufactured in the United States of America

16 15 14 13 12 11 10 8 7 6 5 4 3 2

For Martha Cosgrove

Best teacher, best friend

Contents

Preface to the Second Edition

In the preface to the first edition of this book, I wrote that I hoped to bridge the divide between secondary language arts teachers and college English professors over whether we should teach theory to secondary students: "On one side of that divide were my high school teacher friends, most of whom initially found my interest in contemporary theory to be somewhat suspicious, a sure sign that my high school teaching self was fading into those impractical ivied halls. They were even more doubtful of my claims that it might be fun and profitable to try to integrate theory into their literature classes. On the other side of the theory chasm were my college and university colleagues, literature and literacy education professors from a variety of institutions who, on one hand bemoaned the lack of literary knowledge with which secondary students came to college and on the other hand also deeply doubted that contemporary literary theory was within the intellectual grasp of most high school students."

Since the first edition's publication, in 2000, I have been gratified by the degree to which that gap has narrowed. More and more secondary teachers have incorporated literary theory into their instruction, and my college colleagues have revised their estimation of the remarkable abilities of high school students to use the multiple perspectives of literary theory to read texts and to read the wider worlds of their lives.

As I traveled around the country these past 8 years, working with teachers and their students, I listened carefully to them as they described the challenges of teaching and learning literary theory. Some teachers were challenged by the traditional theory terminology. For example, teachers reported that *gender* seemed to be a more accessible term than *feminist* and that *social class/power* might be less confusing than *Marxist*. While I could offer some theoretical reasons for preferring the ideological precision of the original terms, I embrace any suggestions that can make theory more accessible to adolescents and more useful to their teachers. For this reason, the chapters on feminist and Marxist theory have been significantly revised to reflect this change, with new activities in each. Also in responding to teachers' requests, I have added a brand-new chapter on postcolonialism.

A new introductory chapter as well as an additional chapter on diverse learners serve to counter one of the most common misconceptions about teaching literary theory in general and about the use of this book in particular. Literary theory can be useful and relevant for all students, not just those who are college bound or enrolled in Advanced Placement courses. Finally, I have included many new activities in addition to those that proved particularly successful from the first edition.

I hope that the approaches described in this book will continue to help teachers enrich their literature instruction by teaching contemporary literary theories. I also hope these approaches to reading literature will help all students learn to read from a multiplicity of perspectives and, most of all, will encourage young people to develop the intellectual flexibility they need to read not only literary texts but also the cultural texts that surround and often confuse them.

I am very grateful to many people. Thanks to Lois Marek for her insightful editing and expert manuscript preparation. Thanks to Krista Herbstrith for clearing the path for me on a daily basis. Thanks to Carol Chambers Collins for her support of the original project and to everyone at Teachers College Press, whose patience was tested this time around, especially Meg Lemke. Thanks to all the teachers and students who have been willing to try on the lenses. Thanks to the late James Mackey, who continues to inspire me to be the scholar and teacher he told me I could be. And finally, thanks to John Schmit, whose love and generosity make everything possible.

Introduction

> Often literary theories change our views of a work of literature by proposing new distinctions or new categories for looking at the work. This is a bit like putting on a new set of glasses: suddenly you see things more clearly.
>
> —Stephen Bonnycastle, *In Search of Authority*

It is the class period right after lunch. The students tumble in, distracted by their school's recent success in the state football tournament. The fluorescent light of the classroom is dimmer than usual; a threatening sky may bring the first blast of a long Minnesota winter. It is a smallish class, of around 20 students, and the atmosphere seems comfortable, almost intimate.

The students have been reading Henrik Ibsen's *A Doll's House*. Jessie, a confident and creative student teacher, is eager to put to use some of the contemporary literary theory that made her college English courses so interesting. She thought she might incorporate feminist/gender literary theory to highlight the role of women in Ibsen's portrayal of 19th-century Norwegian society. She thought that feminist literary theory might help her students really see Nora's plight as Nora struggles to make meaning of her drab and bounded life, a life at war with her imagination and ambition.

It hasn't been easy. The students haven't been at all captivated by the hand-me-down theory articles that Jessie pulled from her college notebooks. The students have never even heard the term *literary theory* before, even though their regular classroom teacher had clearly employed both New Critical and reader-response techniques. The students had even studied a variety of archetypes. But this—this *theory*—seemed new and strange. Worse, to some of the students it seemed artificial and contrived, a "teacher game" not unlike the transparent symbol hunts or the fishing for themes, designed to make reading literature even more complicated than it already was. It seemed a fancy tool that came without instructions. Some of the male students, in particular, were irritated by what they considered to be an unnatural forcing of feminist issues onto a difficult and burdensome text.

Announced as a special visitor from the neighboring college, I come armed with pink handouts, some cryptic notes on feminist/gender literary theory and a pair of Ray-Ban sunglasses. The lenses of the glasses have been specially ground for driving. I pass the sunglasses around; ask students to look through them; and when all have tried them on, ask them to comment on what they noticed.

"The reds stand out; look at Katie's sweater." Katie blushes and someone cries, "Look at Katie's face!" "The greens are way green," says someone else. "Do the glasses turn colors that aren't green or red into green or red?" I ask. "No," someone replies, "they just seem to bring out what's already there. Bring it out, so you won't miss it." After I tell them what the glasses are for, someone volunteers, "I get it—red and green, stop and go. The glasses bring out what's there 'cause you can't afford *not* to see it."

I shuffle the handouts on literary theory and tell the students that what the sunglasses did for the green and red, literary theory does for the texts we read. They provide lenses designed to bring out what is already there but what we often miss with unaided vision. Like the sunglasses, contemporary theories highlight particular features of what lies in our line of vision. If used properly, they do not create colors that weren't there in the first place; they only bring them into sharper relief. And, like the sunglasses, they have purpose outside the classroom. There are things we can't afford *not* to see.

I put away my Ray-Bans and ask the students to open the pages of their Ibsen. "There's a critical lens I'd like you to peer through," I say. "Let's see what we encounter."

Critical Encounters in High School English

• C H A P T E R 1 •

What We Teach and Why: Contemporary Literary Theory and Adolescents

> The paradox of education is precisely this—that as one begins to become conscious one begins to examine the society in which he is being educated. The purpose of education, finally, is to create in a person the ability to look at the world for himself, to make his own decisions. . . . But no society is really anxious to have that kind of person around. What societies really, ideally, want is a citizenry which will simply obey the rules of society. If a society succeeds in this, that society is about to perish. The obligation of anyone who thinks of himself as responsible is to examine society and try to change it and to fight it—at no matter what risk. This is the only hope society has. This is the only way societies change.
>
> —James Baldwin

> Everything we do in life is rooted in theory.
>
> —bell hooks

More than 7 years ago, in my introduction to *Critical Encounters in High School English: Teaching Literary Theory to Adolescents* I made the following statement: "We live in dangerous and complicated times and no one is more aware of it than our teenagers" (Appleman, 2000, p. 1). It's ironic to note that when I wrote those words, the 9/11 attack hadn't happened, the war in Iraq hadn't begun, and Columbine had just heralded the era of mass shootings in schools. Now, almost a decade later, the times we live in have become considerably more dangerous and even more complicated. We are all, in the 21st century, submerged in ecological, economic, and political crises. It has become more and more difficult to navigate our way through an increasingly ideological world.

In addition to being affected by the crises wrought by war and both natural- and human-made disaster, we are bombarded with messages, slogans, and pleas from the political Left and Right. The radio airwaves, the Internet, print and television ads, and films and documentaries all compete for our attention as they attempt to sell us their version of the truth. While this cacophony of ideologies can be deafening to adults, it can be absolutely overwhelming for young people. The charge for those of us who engage with adolescents through literacy, as Paulo Freire (Freire & Macedo, 1987) has pointed out, is to help students read both the world and the word. Our job is not simply to help students read and write; our job is to help them use the skills of writing and reading to understand the world around them. We want them to become, in the words of bell hooks (1994), "enlightened witnesses," critically vigilant about the world we live in. To become enlightened witnesses, young people must understand the workings of ideology.

IDEOLOGY

What *is* ideology? Bonnycastle (1996) offers an adolescent-friendly definition:

> In essence an ideology is a system of thought or "world view" which an individual acquires (usually unconsciously) from the world around him. An ideology determines what you think is important in life, what categories you put people into, how you see male and female roles in life, and a host of other things. You can visualize your ideology as a grid, or a set of glasses, through which you can see the world. (p. 32)

Bonnycastle rightly emphasizes the unconscious quality of ideology. One is reminded of Leo Lionni's classic *Fish Is Fish* (1974), in which a tadpole's lively description of what he observed on land is translated by his fish listener into mental pictures that all look like fish-cows, fish-birds, even fish-humans. The fish is unaware that everything he hears is translated unconsciously into his own limited, fishy paradigm.

While Lionni's depiction is playful and points to the foibles of limited experience and imagination, Mark Ryan (1998) offers a somewhat more sinister definition of ideology:

> The term ideology describes the beliefs, attitudes, and habits of feeling, which a society inculcates in order to generate an automatic reproduction of its structuring premises. Ideology is what preserves social power in the absence of direct coercion. (p. 37)

In other words, when we teach the concept of ideology to young people, we are helping them to discern the system of values and beliefs that help create expectations for individual behavior and for social norms. Although ideology can be individual, it is generally a social and political construct, one that subtly shapes society and culture. As history has taught us, ideologies are not always benign or harmless and they need to be questioned and sometimes resisted. Although ideological constructs help each of us learn how we fit into the world, like Lionni's fish, for us ideology is often invisible and transmitted unconsciously. It is what Norman Fairclough (1989) has dubbed "ideological common sense." He writes,

"Ideological common sense is common sense in the service of sustaining unequal relations of power" (p. 84).

I was recently on an airplane when a woman in a pilot's uniform boarded the plane. The gentleman sitting next to me whispered, "That's the copilot." As a frequent flyer on the airline, I recognized the pilot's uniform and knew that my fellow passenger was mistaken. His ideological common sense kept him from seeing that a woman was the pilot. While this example may seem trivial, ideological common sense also influences who we think are trustworthy renters, likely friends, college-bound students, or plausible presidential candidates.

IDEOLOGY AND THE STUDY OF LITERATURE

A literature or language arts class at the secondary level is an ideal place to help students learn to read and, if necessary, resist the ideology that surrounds them. In our literature classes, we teach texts that are full of ideology. As Fairclough (1989) explains:

> Ideology is most effective when its workings are least visible. . . . Invisibility is achieved when ideologies are brought to discourse not as explicit elements of the text but as the background assumptions, which, on the one hand, lead the text producer to textualize the world in a particular way, and on the other hand, lead the interpreter to interpret the text in a particular way. Texts do not spout ideology. They so position the interpreter through their cues that she brings ideologies to the interpretation of texts—and reproduces them in the process! (p. 85)

When we read Robert Frost's "The Road Not Taken," we attend to the assertion that "taking the road less traveled by" makes all the difference. From Fairclough's perspective, the text "positions" us to embrace the American ideologies of individualism and nonconformity. In Mark Twain's *Adventures of Huckleberry Finn* the racialized portraits of Huck and Jim normalize a particular kind of America, whose ideology of inequality was unquestioned for too long. Our responsibility as literature teachers is to help make the ideologies inherent in those texts visible to our students.

LITERARY THEORY AND IDEOLOGY

The best way to uncover and explore these ideologies as they are found in literature is through the explicit teaching of contemporary literary theory. Literary theory provides readers with the tools to uncover the often invisible workings of the text. Many people consider literary theory (if they consider it at all) as arcane and esoteric. It's dismissed as a sort of intellectual parlor game played by MLA types whose conference paper topics are the annual object of ridicule by the *New York Times*. As Terry Eagleton (1983, p. vii) put it, "There are some who complain that literary theory is impossibly esoteric—who suspect it as an arcane elitist enclave somewhat akin to nuclear physics." What could poststructuralism, new historicism, deconstruction, social class/Marxist, and gender/feminist literary theory possibly have to do with the average adolescent, just struggling to grow up, stay alive, get through school, and make the most of things? It sounds as if I'm promoting a sort of theoretical fiddling while the Rome of our sacred vision of successful public education burns.

Teachers, too, may not be convinced of the relevance of contemporary literary theory. High school literature teachers often feel distant and detached from recent developments in literary theory. Literature teachers find it difficult to see, at least initially, how contemporary literary theory can inform their daily practice. They are already overwhelmed as they juggle curricular concerns as well as the varied literacy skills and needs of their increasingly diverse student body. Students and teachers alike find it hard to believe that something as abstract and "impractical" as literary theory could be relevant to their lives, both in and outside the classroom. Nothing, however, could be further from the truth.

Literary theories provide lenses that can sharpen one's vision and provide alternative ways of seeing. They augment our sometimes failing sight and bring into relief things we fail to notice. Literary theories recontextualize the familiar and comfortable, making us reappraise them. They make the strange seem oddly familiar. As we view the dynamic world around us, literary theories can become critical lenses to guide, inform, and instruct us.

Critical lenses provide students with a way of reading their world; the lenses provide a way of "seeing" differently and analytically that can help them read the culture of school as well as popular culture. Learning to inhabit multiple ways of knowing can also help them learn to adapt to the intellectual perspectives and learning styles required by other disciplines. When taught explicitly, literary theory can provide a repertoire of critical lenses through which to view literary texts as well as the multiple contexts at play when students read texts—contexts of culture, curriculum, classroom, personal experience, prior knowledge, and politics. Students can see what factors—whether a character from a text, an author or literary movement, an MTV video, a shampoo commercial, peer pressure, or the school system in which they find themselves—have shaped their own worldview and what assumptions they make as they evaluate the perspectives of others. As Stephen Bonnycastle (1996) points out, studying theory

> means you can take your own part in the struggles for power between different ideologies. It helps you to discover elements of your own ideology, and understand why you hold certain values unconsciously. It means no authority can impose a truth on

> you in a dogmatic way—and if some authority does try, you can challenge that truth in a powerful way, by asking what ideology it is based on. . . . Theory is subversive because it puts authority in question. (p. 34)

In the past decade or so, critical theory has played an increasingly important role in professional conversations between college literature professors and has become more visible in college literature classrooms as part of what it means to study literature. James Slevin and A. Young (1996, pp. ix–x) regard theory as the site of some of our most profound professional reexaminations as we reconceptualize what it means to teach literature: "the new directions in literary theory and criticism that mark the last two decades can be seen as responses to these very concerns, reexamining the assumptions that underlie literary study."

Similarly, Bonnycastle (1996, p. 20) writes: "Literary theory raises those issues which are often left submerged beneath the mass of information contained in the course, and it also asks questions about how the institution of great literature works. . . . What makes a 'great work' great? Who makes the decisions about what will be taught? Why are authors grouped into certain historical periods? The answers to fundamental questions like these are often unarticulated assumptions on the part of both the professor and the students. . . . Literary theory is at its best when it helps us realize what we are really doing when we study literature."

In the early 1980s, Terry Eagleton (1983, p. vii) wrote, "Not much of this theoretical revolution has yet spread beyond a circle of specialists and enthusiasts; it still has to make its full impact on the student of literature and the general reader." More than a decade later, the presence of literary theory is more clearly (some might argue, oppressively) present in the college literature classroom, yet these new developments in theory and the reconsiderations of curriculum that have been generated have not, for the most part, been introduced into the high school literature classroom. As Arthur Applebee (1993) points out,

> The certainty of New Critical analysis has given way to formulations that force a more complex examination of the assumptions and expectations about authors, readers, and texts as they are situated within specific personal and cultural contexts. The challenges to New Criticism, however, have taken place largely within the realm of literary theory. Only a few scholars have begun to give serious attention to the implications of these new approaches for classroom pedagogy . . . and most of that attention has been focused at the college level. It would be fair to say that, despite the recent ferment in literary theory, the majority of college undergraduates still receive an introduction to literature that has been little influenced by recent theory. (pp. 116–117)

In fact, Applebee (1993, p. 122) found that 72% of the high school literature teachers he surveyed in schools that had a reputation for excellence "reported little or no familiarity with contemporary literary theory." As one high school teacher put it, "These [theories] are far removed from those of us who work on the front lines" (p. 122). In one of the few texts about theory written explicitly for secondary teachers, Sharon Crowley (1989, p. 26) agrees: "The practice of teaching people to read difficult and culturally influential texts is carried on, for the most part, as though it were innocent of theory, as though it were a knack that anybody could pick up by practicing it."

While it is not widely reflected in the practice of secondary teachers, the notion that literary theory can be useful has gained greater voice in the field of English education. In *Literary Theory and English Teaching*, Peter Griffith (1987) describes the tension between presenting literature as cultural artifacts or literature as a vehicle for transmitting ideology. Additionally, the aim of many progressive educators is to use literature as a vehicle for self-exploration and expression. Griffith points out that the teaching of literary theory to secondary students is a useful way to bridge this gap:

> Certain applications of literary theory can lay bare what the text does not say and cannot say as well as what it does and, as part of the same process, to make certain aspects of the context in which the reading takes place visible as well. . . . To be able to offer pupils this sense of power over their environment seems a desirable goal, especially if the sense of power is more than a delusion and can lead in some way to an effect on the pupil's environment. (p. 86)

Dennie Palmer Wolf in *Reading Reconsidered* (1988) urges us to reexamine our notions of what literacy is, of what students should read, and of what it means to read well. She encourages us to teach students ways of thinking about texts. She writes, "Not to teach students these habits of mind would be to cheat them just as surely as if we kept them away from books written before 1900 and burned all poetry" (p. 4). Wolf reminds us that reading is "a profoundly social and cultural process" and urges us to provide all students with deeper and richer ways of thinking about literature, using terminology such as "holding a conversation with a work," "becoming mindful," and "reading resonantly" (p. 9).

In *Textual Power: Literary Theory and the Teaching of English*, Robert Scholes (1985) argues that there are three basic textual skills: reading, interpretation, and criticism. Although there are many secondary English teachers skilled in all three, all too often they relegate only the reading to their students. It is they, rather than their students, who determine the appropriate critical approach for each literary text. After their critical stance has been articulated, the teachers either allow students to create interpretations within the context of that critical approach or they provide a single privileged interpretation for the students. While the teacher may be well schooled in theory, the students are not and are therefore limited in the interpretive choices they can make.

THE CALL TO THEORY

The call to theory has just begun to be heard by secondary school practitioners. As he contemplates the "shape high school literature should take in the coming years," Bruce Pirie (1997) also invokes Scholes (1985) as he calls for a repositioning of the study of literature that "clarifies its relationship with the rest of the world." Critics such as Scholes have pointed out that contemporary literary theory opens the barriers between the literary text and "the social text in which we live" (Scholes in Pirie, 1997, p. 31). It is at his intersection of text and social context that the explicit study of contemporary literary theory can help adolescent readers make meaning of literary texts.

Kathleen McCormick (1995), a scholar notable for her unique ability to gracefully straddle the theoretical world of the university and the seemingly more pragmatic world of reading instruction in elementary and secondary schools, argues for the relevance of contemporary literary theories, especially those she calls "culturally informed theories," to the development of pedagogies in the schools. She writes:

> While so often the schools and universities seem quite separate, it is primarily the research carried on in the colleges and universities that drives the reading lessons students are given in the schools. If feminists, theorists of race and gender and cultural studies, teachers, and researchers in the universities were to begin to engage in more active dialogue with the developers of reading programs and the teachers who have to teach students—young and older—"how" to read, it might be possible to begin to change the dominant significations of reading in the schools—so that more students could begin to learn to read the world simultaneously with learning to read the word—so that readers can begin to see themselves as interdiscursive subjects, to see texts as always "in use," and to recognize that different ways of reading texts have consequence. (p. 308)

McCormick's suggestion that theoried ways of reading have significant consequences for our students of literature echoes an eloquent plea Janet Emig made more than a decade ago for the teaching of literary theory. In a conference paper as president-elect of the National Council of Teachers of English, Emig (1990, p. 93) wrote, "Theory then becomes a vivid matter of setting out the beliefs that we hold against the beliefs of others, an occasion for making more coherent to others, and quite as important to ourselves, just what it is we believe, and why."

Emig underscores the power of the approach to teaching literature that I present in this book. The purpose of teaching literary theory at the secondary level is not to turn adolescents into critical theorists; rather, it is to encourage adolescents to inhabit theories comfortably enough to construct their own readings and to learn to appreciate the power of multiple perspectives. Literary theory can help secondary literature classrooms become sites of constructive and transactive activity, where students approach texts with curiosity, authority, and initiative.

BUT ISN'T IT TOO POLITICAL?

There are those who may say that they signed on to teach English, not social studies, and that this approach is too political. I have two rejoinders to that objection. First, teaching is essentially a political act, a political stance—a stance that advocates for the literacy rights of everyone, a stance that acknowledges that when you give someone literacy, you give them power. Second, even our seemingly neutral reading of texts is political. In our literature classes, then, we should focus on helping students read texts with an eye toward the ideology that is inscribed in those texts. An African proverb puts it this way: "Until lions tell their stories, tales of hunting will glorify the hunter."

Our canon has been filled with tales of the hunter. Recently, tales of the lion, in works by authors such as Toni Morrison, Alice Walker, Louise Erdrich, Sherman Alexie, Amy Tan, and many others have begun to fill our schools' libraries and our students' sensibilities. In addition to hearing from the lion, we can continue to teach tales of the hunter but with the remediating lens of literary theory—a postcolonial lens for *Heart of Darkness*, a gender lens for *The Great Gatsby*, and a social-class lens for *Hamlet*, just to name a few possible examples.

For those who say that we should simply teach the literature "neutrally," I offer the perspective of literary scholar Shirley Staton (1987):

> Contemporary theory holds that there is no such thing as an innocent, value-free reading. Instead, each of us has a viewpoint invested with presuppositions about "reality" and about ourselves, whether we are conscious of it or not. People who deny having a critical stance, who claim they are responding "naturally" or being "completely objective" do not know themselves. (p. 43)

We could continue to uncritically teach *Adventures of Huckleberry Finn* or *To Kill a Mockingbird* because they are classic pieces of literature, without regard for the problems engendered by the use of culturally offensive customs and terms. That decision privileges the arbitrary literary value of a canonical text over the significance and relevance of a changing student demographic. It ignores the deeply politicized history of the word *nigger*, for instance, and how it differently affects different populations. Teachers often make these kinds of decisions, teaching the same texts in the same way without taking changing classroom demographics into account. That, too, is a political decision, as much as offering a postcolonial analysis or reading the texts through the lens of critical race theory.

THE IMPORTANCE OF MULTIPLICITY

With these considerations in mind, it is very important that we don't offer only a single theory to our students, for that truly is dogmatic or propagandistic teaching. It is the monotheoretical approaches of most secondary English classrooms that drew me to the notion of multiple perspectives, as an antidote. Even a reader–response lens is limiting if it is the only possible theoretical frame in which one can produce a reading.

Offering students several ways to look at texts does more than help them learn to interpret literature from multiple perspectives; it also helps them develop a more complex way of thinking as they move from the dualism of early adolescence to the relativism of adult thinkers (Perry, 1970). F. Scott Fitzgerald (1964) perhaps most notably stated the virtue of this kind of thinking:

> The test of a first-rate intelligence is the ability to hold two opposed ideas in mind at the same time and still retain the ability to function. One should, for example, be able to see that things are hopeless and yet be determined to make them otherwise. (p. 69)

These multiple ways of seeing have become vital skills in our increasingly diverse classrooms as we explore the differences between us, what separates us and what binds us together. As Maxine Greene (1993, p. 16) has eloquently argued, "Learning to look through multiple perspectives, young people may be helped to build bridges among themselves; attending to a range of human stories, they may be provoked to heal and to transform." Attending to multiplicity, to the diversity that has come to characterize our interpretive communities, has caused some scholars to reconsider the role that literary theory may play as we acknowledge our need to learn to read across and between cultures (Rogers & Soter, 1997). As Laura Desai (1997, pp. 169–170) points out, "Literary theory reminds us that we do not live in isolation, nor do we read and interpret in isolation. We understand what we read through some combination of ourselves as readers and the text with which we interact, but this is never free of the multiple contexts that frame us." Desai further argues that literary theory can provide for young people the tools necessary for interpreting culture as well. "Literary theory allows us to recognize our own reactions by providing the contexts we need to understand them. In this complex world, cultural forces are clearly at play in the lives of young people." But young people will remain powerless over these forces unless they can recognize them: "How can we judge culture's impact if we cannot define what it is that is influencing our reactions?" Literary theory provides the interpretive tools young people need to recognize and "read" those cultural forces.

THE CHANGING TIMES

> As we begin a second century of teaching literature, it is time we examine these enduring characteristics of literature instruction, asking which are appropriate and essential and which have continued because they have remained unexamined.
>
> —Arthur Applebee, *Literature in the Secondary School*

In the past few decades, the relatively stable (some might even say staid) and predictable practice of teaching literature has undergone changes from many directions. At the prompting of scholars; practitioners; and perhaps most important, the changing nature of our students, we have considered and reconsidered the texts, contexts, and pedagogical approaches that constitute the teaching of literature. Our canons are loose, our pedagogy is shifting, and our profession seems to be challenging every assumption we have made about the teaching of literature since 1920. For example, we have reconsidered the relationship of texts to readers, of readers and teachers to authors, of texts to theories, and of course of teachers to their students. Multicultural literature has largely been embraced by many teachers, but the complexity of teaching such works to both diverse and homogeneous classes is just beginning to be confronted. Our profession is challenging its assumptions about our literary heritage, our students, and even who is included in the pronoun *our*. This reflection demands that as we challenge the hegemony of the sort of "cultural literacy" proposed by Alan Bloom or E. D. Hirsch, we also challenge the notion of a single theory, perspective, or "truth" about what literature we read together and how we teach it. As Slevin and Young (1996) put it:

> If texts no longer organize the curriculum, then what does? If the professor is no longer the privileged agent of education then who is? . . . These pressing questions . . . contemplate the end of coverage as a model, the end of the canon as an agreed-upon certainty, the end of the professor as the agent of learning, and the end of the classroom as a place where education is delivered. These "ends" have been much contemplated, indeed. But what arises in their place? (pp. ix–x)

CONCLUSION

In the end, by teaching literature along with theory, we help students learn to decipher the world inscribed within the texts they study as well as help them learn to read the world around them. They can become the enlightened witnesses that bell hooks (1994) calls for, as they discern how power and privilege are inscribed all around us and learn to read both texts and the world with a nuanced and critical eye. Our students can become, with our help, truly educated in the way James

Baldwin (1985) envisions, able to critique their own society intelligently and without fear. This kind of teaching is difficult. It requires a willingness to give up one's ultimate authority in the classroom. It reminds us, as Peter Rabinowitz and Michael Smith (1998) suggest, that we are not teaching readings but teaching ways of reading.

This book challenges current theoretical and pedagogical paradigms of the teaching of literature by incorporating the teaching of literary theory into high school literature classes. The guiding assumption of this book is that the direct teaching of literary theory in secondary English classes will better prepare adolescent readers to respond reflectively and analytically to literary texts, both "canonical" and multicultural. I argue that contemporary literary theory provides a useful way for all students to read and interpret not only literary texts but also their lives—both in and outside school. In its own way, reading with theory is a radical educational reform!

Teaching literary theory is also, as Lisa Shade Eckert (2006, p. 8) points out, a way of teaching reading. "Teaching students to use literary theory as a strategy to construct meaning is teaching reading. Learning theory gives them a purpose in approaching a reading task, helps them make and test predictions as they read, and provides a framework for student response and awareness of their stance in approaching a text." Similarly, Robert Scholes (2001, p. xiv) offers the notion of the "crafty reader," explaining, "As with any craft, reading depends on the use of certain tools, handled with skill. But the tools of reading are not simply there, like a hammer or chisel. They must be acquired, through practice."

This kind of teaching changes our conception of what we teach and why. We are no longer transmitting knowledge, offering literature as content, as an aesthetic experience, or as neutral artifacts of our collective cultural heritage. Instead, we are offering our students the tools to view the world from a variety of lenses, each offering a unique perspective sure to transform how adolescents read both words and worlds. As Lois Tyson (2006) writes:

> For knowledge isn't just something we acquire; it's something we are or hope to become. Knowledge is what constitutes our relationship to ourselves and to our world, for it is the lens through which we view ourselves and our world. Change the lens and you change both the view and the viewer. This principle is what makes knowledge at once so frightening and so liberating, so painful and so utterly, utterly joyful. (p. 11)

This book offers instructional approaches that begin to meet the important challenge that Emig (1990, p. 94) offered to her fellow teachers: "We must not merely permit, we must actively sponsor those textual and classroom encounters that will allow our students to begin their own odysseys toward their own theoretical maturity."

QUESTIONS ADDRESSED

This book addresses some of the following questions:

- Which contemporary theories seem best suited to or most age appropriate for high school students? Are some more "teachable" than others?
- What are some specific strategies that teachers can use to encourage multiple perspectives as students read literary texts?
- What does a teacher need to know about theory in order to be able to teach it?
- Is theory really relevant to marginalized students or reluctant learners, or is it only appropriate for college-track classrooms?
- Can the study of literary theory help students understand, question, and bridge cultural differences?
- How does the teaching of theory change classroom practice?
- What sorts of texts can be used in teaching contemporary literary theory?

ORGANIZATION OF THE BOOK

This book combines theory with actual classroom practice. It combines argument with narrative. Classroom examples illustrate the practice of teaching literary theory. Portraits of urban, suburban, and rural classrooms help make the case for particular theories. Throughout the book, actual lessons and materials provide ways of integrating critical lenses into the study of literature. A number of texts—"classics" such as *Hamlet*, *The Awakening*, *Of Mice and Men*, *Heart of Darkness*, *Frankenstein*, and *The Great Gatsby* as well as titles that have been more recently included in our secondary literature curriculum such as *Beloved*, "The Yellow Wallpaper," *The Things They Carried*, and *Native Son*—are used to illustrate a variety of critical lenses.

In Chapter 1, I set forth the reasons for teaching critical theory. In Chapter 2, I argue for the importance of multiple theoretical perspectives as we read and interpret literary texts. Four very different classroom vignettes illustrate the power of multiple perspectives. Through the vignettes I offer specific strategies for introducing the notion of multiple perspectives to students (and to teachers) through several short stories and poems. These introductory activities, designed for Grades 9 through 12, can be used at the beginning of a semester, trimester, or yearlong course, or at the beginning of a specific unit on critical analysis. The focus of the activities will be on the power of viewing literary texts from a variety of perspectives, not on specific literary theories . . . yet. The emphasis on multiple perspectives and multiple ways of viewing texts helps set the stage for the introduction of theories that are addressed in the rest of the book.

Is reader response an appropriate interpretive strategy for all students? Is it useful or appropriate for all texts? In Chapter 3, I explore what happens when students are taught how to apply the basic tenets of reader response to their own reading. By describing what happens when students are given interpretive tools that are explicitly named, I demonstrate in this chapter that when we make our teaching strategies explicit to students, we strengthen their interpretive possibilities. I also challenge some of the common assumptions and practices of response-centered teaching, especially as they relate to diverse classrooms.

In Chapter 4, I explore the political prisms of literary theories grounded in issues of ideology, class, and power. I make the case for the importance of political theory to help students learn to understand and read, and perhaps even resist, prevailing ideology. Using texts such as *Of Mice and Men*, *Black Boy*, *Native Son*, *Hamlet*, *The Great Gatsby*, and *Beloved* I analyze how these theoretical lenses help us understand the political, social, and economic dimensions of the world in which we live.

Gender theory is the focus of Chapter 5. Here I present classroom situations in which students learn to interpret texts such as *A Doll's House*, *The Great Gatsby*, *A Room of One's Own*, *The Awakening*, "The Yellow Wallpaper," *Frankenstein*, and a selection of poetry using the gender lens. I also address the resistance that both male and female students have to reading literary texts through a gender lens. In addition to exploring this resistance, I illustrate how students can also learn to read both texts and the world through the refractive light of gender theory.

Chapter 6 introduces a lens that was not included in the first edition. Postcolonial criticism gives students the tools necessary to interpret a literary text within the context of European colonialism and imperialism. It allows them to see how commercial and military power have advanced Western ideologies among colonized peoples through examination of literatures from both sides of the colonial divide. An analysis of these differences allows new interpretive possibilities for both canonical and postcolonial texts.

In Chapter 7 we tackle the more difficult and more rarely used contemporary theory of deconstruction. Students will contrast the purposes of critical theories that are structural and linguistic to more political, extrinsic critical lenses. In using these theories, students are encouraged to focus on the specific language used in literary texts (mostly poetry) and apply recent postmodern theories to those texts. Again, several specific lessons are provided for teachers along with a discussion of the potential value of these approaches to high school students.

Chapter 8, also new to this edition, focuses on three very different readers, describing theoretical predispositions that these readers began to develop when given a choice of interpretive perspectives. This chapter provides especially useful information for teachers who are interested in accommodating their instructional approach to different kinds of students in heterogeneous classes. The three readers are presented as case studies, and I chronicle their prior attitudes toward reading; the resistances and predispositions they brought to their literature class; their backgrounds, abilities, and interests; their written and oral responses to several literary texts; and the degree to which a multiple-perspective approach enhanced their responses to literature. I also consider issues of cultural diversity as I focus on relatively homogeneous suburban classrooms as well as heterogeneous urban classrooms.

In addition to concluding remarks, Chapter 9 gives specific suggestions on how teachers might implement the teaching of literary theory in their literature classes, whether they be yearlong required courses or electives. The chapter includes an expanded discussion of the importance of reading cultural texts, using examples from contemporary media. I also summarize the central thesis of the book: that literary theory can and should be taught to secondary students. Using literary theory as they read texts, students become theoried and skilled readers with a variety of interpretive strategies and theoretical approaches. They become constructors of meaning, with multiple literary visions of their own. They become adept at reading the world around them.

• CHAPTER 2 •

Prisms of Possibilities: Introducing Multiple Perspectives

A man with one theory is lost. He needs several of them, or lots! He should stuff them in his pockets like newspapers.

—Bertolt Brecht

PRISMS OF POSSIBILITIES

As a former high school English teacher who knows something about literary theory, I've been pressed into service by a colleague who teaches at an urban school in Minneapolis. Stephanie is keen on the idea of introducing literary theory to her 10th-grade, mixed-ability American literature class, but she doesn't exactly know how to begin. I volunteer to get things started for her, figuring that I'd better be able to walk my talk. I bring each student a set of literary theory cards (see Appendix; adapted from Lynn, 2007; see also Beach, Appleman, Hynds, & Wilhelm, 2006). The cards are fastened together by a metal ring, which the students immediately begin to pry apart. I also bring the poem "Mushrooms," by Sylvia Plath, but the title has been removed from their copies:

Mushrooms
Overnight, very
Whitely, discreetly,
Very quietly

Our toes, our noses
Take hold on the loam,
Acquire the air.

Nobody sees us,
Stops us, betrays us;
The small grains make room.

Soft fists insist on
Heaving the needles,
The leafy bedding,

Even the paving.
Our hammers, our rams,
Earless and eyeless,

Perfectly voiceless,
Widen the crannies,
Shoulder through holes. We

Diet on water,
On crumbs of shadow,
Bland-mannered, asking

Little or nothing.
So many of us!
So many of us!

We are shelves, we are
Tables, we are meek,
We are edible,

Nudgers and shovers
In spite of ourselves.
Our kind multiplies:

We shall by morning
Inherit the earth.
Our foot's in the door.

—Sylvia Plath

This poem has been used extensively with reader response approaches (see Beach, 1993; Appleman, 2000; this volume, Chapter 3), but now I enlist it for a different cause. I ask the class if anyone has ever heard of Sylvia Plath. Thanks largely to a 2003 film starring Gwyneth Paltrow (*Sylvia*), five students raise their hands. "Great," I say, "you are our biographical group." I clump the remaining 24 students into groups of four and assign each group the labels of reader response, gender, and social power. I then pass out the Prisms of Possibilities handout (see

Appendix, Activity 8) and ask the students to create a reading of the poem based on their assigned perspective, using just the theory card, their own background knowledge, and each other.

I circulate in the room, answering questions and repeating my admonishments about the metal rings that hold the theory cards. We reconvene, in ragged circles, each group reporting its findings.

"You can tell she was really depressed," the biographical group reports. "Her husband made her feel invisible."

"All women feel invisible," a gender group explains. "Look at the language in the poem about serving and about being subservient."

"It's not just women," the social-power group retorts. "It's about any group that feels at the margins: workers, poor people. Immigrants, maybe? People without full rights. But look at the last two lines: 'We shall by morning inherit the earth.' There's gonna be a revolution!"

"Man, our group didn't get so . . . political," says the reader response group. "We tried to guess what the poem was about, and then we, like, focused on the woods and stuff like that. Jonah's done a lot of hiking in the Boundary Waters Canoe Area wilderness and it reminded him of that."

"Well, who's right?" some students ask. "Which group got it?" "Can there be more than one right answer?"

"Oh, yes." I respond with a smile. "There certainly can!"

WHAT KIND OF WALTZ?

My Papa's Waltz

The whisky on your breath
could make a small boy dizzy
But I hung on like death
Such waltzing was not easy.

We romped until the pans
Slid from the kitchen shelf
My mother's countenance
Could not unfrown itself.

The hand that held one wrist
Was battered on one knuckle
At every step you missed
My right ear scraped a buckle.

You beat time on my head
With a palm caked hard by dirt
Then waltzed me off to bed
Still clinging to your shirt.

—Theodore Roethke

Joe, a 10th-grade language arts teacher in an urban school, distributes this frequently anthologized poem to his mixed-ability class of high school juniors. He asks them to read the poem to themselves several times and waits for the silence to be broken by the stirring of students ready to talk. In a series of gently prodding questions, he asks the class to construct an oral reading of the poem that conveys its meaning. One student, Mark, offers that it is a wistful remembrance of a young boy's affectionate kitchen romps with his deceased father. The teacher asks the student to read the poem aloud with this interpretation in mind and he does so. His changing voice does not betray him as he reads gently and affectionately, stressing words like *papa*, *waltz*, and *cling*.

Complimenting the student on his reading, Joe turns to the rest of the class and peppers them with questions. "Is this the definitive reading?" he asks. "Is this what Roethke meant to communicate? Would all of you have read the poem the way Mark did, or are there any other ways this poem could be read?"

Slowly, hesitantly, a hand rises from the corner of the room. Marnie, a serious and quiet student, says firmly, "I don't think this poem is about a happy childhood recollection at all." Then under her breath, almost inaudibly, she asserts, "I think his dad was a drunk who beat him." Some members of the class murmur in assent. Mark silently shakes his head in vigorous disagreement. Joe pushes. "How would the poem sound if that were the case? How would it be read? Does anyone care to try?" There are more than a few students who seem willing to take on this reading. Marnie is not one of them.

Josh begins to read forcefully, emphasizing words like *beat*, *death*, *battered*, *missed*, *dirt*, and *whisky*. After the reading, some students in the room seem to shudder visibly from the effect of Josh's reading. They also seem a bit unsettled. Hadn't they already heard a convincing and sensible reading?

"Which one is right?" one student asks. "How do we know which way to read it?"

"Could they both be right?" Joe asks.

"Not at the same time," one student replies.

"Not to the same person," another one offers.

"But do they both seem to make sense? Do they offer two plausible perspectives?" Amid general murmurs of assent, Joe continues, "There clearly seems to be more than one way to read this poem, more than one way to read the situation. This may turn out to be true for many of the texts we read together, as well as for many of the things that happen to us in everyday life." Joe smiles and hands out another poem, "Thirteen Ways of Looking at a Blackbird," by Wallace Stevens.

INTRODUCING MULTIPLE PERSPECTIVES

Bob, a veteran of 20 years of teaching, surveys his class of restless 10th-graders, an assortment of adolescents very different from the Advanced Placement students he is generally used to teaching. In the class are hardworking students who hope to go to college, a few students who are struggling to pass their classes, and a few underachieving students who long ago decided to get off the train going on the college-prep track.

The students have read a short piece by essayist Russell Baker titled "Little Miss Muffet" (see Appendix, Activity 1). Baker recasts the familiar fairy tale of the unfortunate Ms. Muffet and the intruding spider by retelling it through a variety of perspectives, through the eyes of, for example, a psychiatrist, a teacher, a militarist, and a child. The students respond ambivalently to the essay. They are surprised that anything as childish as nursery rhymes is being introduced by a teacher who has a schoolwide reputation of "making you think without making you sweat." Bob arranges the students into groups. He then asks them to select a nursery rhyme and recast it from several occupations or roles. The students do so and come back to class the next day with fanciful results. Here are three examples:

"HUMPTY DUMPTY": PROSECUTING ATTORNEY'S POINT OF VIEW

> This whole incident is obviously a conspiracy. There is no way Mr. Dumpty would just fall off the wall. Being in the fragile state that he was, he would have been extremely cautious while up on that wall. He was obviously distracted by a diversion so he wouldn't notice the suspect creeping up behind him, ready to push him off at just the right moment. It was just an "innocent fall," or so the members of the palace would have you believe. The fact of the matter is, all the king's horses and all the king's men are suspects. They all had a motive. They were sick and tired of the egg getting all the attention. And the fact that they couldn't put Mr. Dumpty back together is very suspicious, since they were all trained in egg lifesaving. So far, they've come up with an alibi, but it won't hold. There are almost as many holes in their stories as there are in Mr. Dumpty's poor broken body. (Maggie)

"THERE WAS AN OLD WOMAN WHO LIVED IN A SHOE": DEMOCRAT'S POINT OF VIEW

This is, no doubt, a serious concern of ours in the United States of America. We are no longer living in a middle-class suburban home with a father, mother, two-and-a-half children, and a family pet. This poor woman needs the federal government's help. With a welfare check every so often, maybe she could feed her children something more nutritious than broth. And she's living in a shoe! What is happening to low-income housing these days? The government should raise some taxes so that she doesn't have to live in a shoe! Something that is so truly heartbreaking is that this poor mother is single and stuck with the burden of the children with no support from the father. We need to catch these absentee fathers and make them pay child support. Welfare, not workfare, is the answer to all of the Old Woman Who Lived in a Shoe's problems. (Mandi)

"JACK BE NIMBLE": FIRE CHIEF'S POINT OF VIEW

This is a textbook example of what happens when fire is in the hands of careless children. Children should never play with fire. It's a cardinal rule. Everybody knows that. This isn't play. No, it's much worse than that; fire is not a toy. What we see developing is a blatant disrespect for the animal which is fire. We may be looking at a future arsonist of America. And, what's that candle doing on the floor in the first place? It's a fire hazard, people! (Eric)

When the reading of these new versions of nursery rhymes winds down, Bob reads aloud *The True Story of the Three Little Pigs by A. Wolf* (Scieszka, 1989), a children's book that retells the familiar tale from the point of view of the wolf. It begins: "Everybody knows the story of The Three Little Pigs. Or at least they think they do. But I'll let you in on a little secret. Nobody knows the real story, because nobody has ever heard *my* side of the story." And it ends: "So they jazzed up the story with all of that 'Huff and puff and blow your house down.' And they made me the Big Bad Wolf. That's it. The real story. I was framed."

Amid giggles and chatter, Jessie blurts out what many of his classmates were thinking: "Why did we do this, Mr. B? It was fun, but it seemed pointless."

"We did it to demonstrate one very important point—that the same story, even a simple story such as Little Miss Muffet, can take on very different meaning depending upon who is doing the telling. So, when we read, the meaning depends on who's doing the reading. Meanings are constructed; we create meanings that are influenced by who we are and what we are culturally; historically; psychologically; and, in the case of the Baker version of Miss Muffet, vocationally. If we can construct and change the meaning for something as simple as Little Miss Muffet, can you imagine the changes, the variations in meaning, that occur among us as we read poems, short stories, and novels?"

"What if," Bob wonders aloud, "*Adventures of Huckleberry Finn* were told from the perspective of Tom Sawyer or Jim; *To Kill a Mockingbird* were told from the perspective of Boo Radley or Tom Robinson; *The Diary of Anne Frank* from the point of view of Peter, Miep Giess, or Ann's father? How does a story change when the narrator changes? How are the basic elements of that story transformed? Is it the same story, or narrative, told from a different point of view, or does it become, at some point, a different story?"

Bob raises some questions that are fundamental to the study of literature, questions he would like to pursue with his students through the use of literary theory. How can we read a narrative from a single perspective and be able to trace the influences of that perspective on how the text is shaped? Given one perspective, how might we be able to imagine how other perspectives could change the telling of that narrative? In other words, how can we see the wolf's side in the pigs' story? Further, how can we deconstruct the singular vision that is represented by one story? And how can we extrapolate from that single tile of vision to the mosaic of other human experiences and perspectives?

Imagine! All this from fairy tales and nursery rhymes!

FAMILY STORIES

Rachel is in her 1st year of teaching in a small rural community. Overall, her teaching has been going fairly well—she feels that she is well planned and well prepared, and, for the most part, she's been able to maintain the interest of her 9th and 10th graders. Each day brings her a greater understanding of the contrast in sensibilities between those of her small town students and those she experienced in her own adolescence in a large, metropolitan city. Rachel admires the feeling of community and camaraderie among her students. There seems to be more unanimity about issues than she ever imagined could have been possible in the diverse urban high school she had attended. While she embraces the harmony of her students' common outlook, she finds the homogeneity of opinion tends to stifle class discussions—as happened today.

After reading *The Scarlet Letter*, Rachel held a final discussion that she hoped would arouse some controversy. Throughout the reading of the text (mandated by the district's curriculum), Rachel tried to present a variety of contestable issues. What is a moral code? Who were the characters they most and least admired? Did Hester deserve her fate? What motivated the townspeople—cruelty, morality, both? What is innocence? Who was using whom? Do we have absolute moral codes in today's society?

On various occasions, she threw out several provocative statements, playing devil's advocate and even offering some possible interpretations that she knew her students would find implausible. But her playful questioning was returned by either silence or halfhearted acquiescence. She tried extending one student's commentary by asking if anyone disagreed, but there were no takers. Finally, in desperation and probably not her finest teaching moment, she cried, "Isn't there *any* other way to see this? Do we only have only one point of view out there? How can that be? Counting me, there are 31 of us. There has got to be more than one opinion among us!"

Rachel wants her students to be able to understand that there is usually more than one side to any issue. Events, in literature and in life, are multifaceted and have different sides, cast different light, depending upon the viewer. She wants to change the monochrome of students' vision; she wants them to see other perspectives. She hopes that by the end of their year together, students will be able to do more than walk around in someone else's shoes. They should be able to see things from other viewpoints, heartily argue positions that they don't believe in, inhabit other ways of being or habits of mind. She wants her students to analyze their lives and texts, not just from the inside out but from the outside in. Eventually she hopes that the students will be able to take different theoretical stances toward literary texts as well as toward other things. But now, at the very least, she wants them to see that every story, every position, has more than one side. But where should she begin?

She decides to use a lesson on family perspectives. She tells a story about a little black puppy that came to her family as a stray. She says that when she compares notes with her siblings and her parents, each person has a different memory of who found the dog first, who named it Pickles, and how long it was in the family. She asks students to consider a retelling of "The Three Little Pigs" from the wolf's perspective. Then she asks students to tell a family story from their own perspective (see Appendix, Activity 3). Finally, she asks them to have another family member tell his or her version of the story when the students go home that evening.

The next day, Rachel leads a discussion on the different versions and introduces the concept of "perspectives." She tells her class that the notion of perspectives is very important to consider as one reads literature. She begins with the idea of being able to consider a story from perspectives other than that of the protagonist. For Rachel, this is not simply an important step in interpretive reading; real life also means looking beyond one's own point of view to understand the point of view of someone else. Rachel chooses a story by John Updike called "Separating." It's a typical Updike story, set in suburbia, told from the husband's point of view—and told as if there were no other point of view that mattered. This myopic narration is particularly relevant to the story line (as well as to Rachel's larger purposes); the husband has decided to leave his wife, but neither his wife nor his children are aware of the decision.

After her students read the story, Rachel asks them to consider the plot from the perspective of the other characters, such as the wife or the children (see Appendix, Activity 2). Rachel and her students move the discussion of point of view (something they've done since seventh grade) into a discussion of worldview, or stance. She tells her students that stories are often told from a vision as singular as the husband's; it's just not always so painfully obvious to us. She tells them that for every text they read, there is another tale wanting to be told. Our job is to invoke those other voices, always on the lookout for the betrayed wife, the neglected child, the overarching commentary about manicured lawns and culs-de-sac. She tells them to think about how tales could turn on the teller as they read their next book together, *Catcher in the Rye*.

STAR WARS AND MULTIPLE PERSPECTIVES

It is a crisp September morning and the school year is only 2 weeks old. The students in Martha's 12th-grade Advanced Placement class have just finished reporting on their summer reading. They are beginning to get to know each other and their teacher and are trying to figure out how this last year of high school English, how this Advanced Placement class, may be different from their previous study of literature. Or will it be? In *Literature in the Secondary School* (1993) Arthur Applebee reports on how little has changed in curriculum and instruction in most high school literature classrooms, especially among the upper-track classes. Are Martha's students simply in for more of the same?

On this particular day, the classroom is darkened and the students absolutely cannot believe their good fortune. The teacher has popped *Star Wars* into the VCR. She asks them to jot down a few things that strike them as particularly interesting or important as they view the film. Despite the block scheduling, the film spills into the next period and Martha feels a little guilty. After all, this *is* Advanced Placement and the students' parents and administrators seem to impose a different level of accountability on the class.

When the film is over and the lights come on, Martha waits for the students to piece back together their location in the classroom world of fluorescent lights and chalk dust, light years from the intergalactic battles they've been cheering on. Martha distributes a discussion sheet titled "Theory Wars" (see Appendix, Activity 7). Together they discuss the first two questions. They discuss the relative merits of seeing a movie and of reading a book more than once. They weigh the advantage of the surprise and spontaneity of a first reading or viewing to the ability to see things you didn't see the first time during a second, more considered reading. They also discuss the relative inequities that often exist in most classroom settings when students are encountering a text for the 1st time and the teacher may be encountering it for the 10th or 13th (Rabinowitz, 1987).

Martha leads the students through a brief discussion about archetypes, and the students are visibly gleeful about how easily the archetypes they learned last year in their British literature class seem to fit the characters of *Star Wars*. Martha takes a deep breath and hands out a sheet called "Literary Theories: A Sampling of Critical Lenses" (see Appendix, Activity 5 or, for alternate definitions, see Activity 4) as well as a stack of theory cards, index cards with short definitions of literary theories (see Appendix, Activity 6). This handout contains brief synopses of some of the major literary theories she hopes to include during the rest of the year. It is a dynamic document, changing each year with a collective reconsideration of theory by Martha and her students. At this early stage of their time together, Martha does not want to either overwhelm or overfeed the class; she simply wants to give them a preview or taste of the theories to come. She will reintroduce them later, weaving them into the curriculum as the year progresses.

Generally, none of Martha's students has heard of literary theory before. Even though many of them have been in classrooms that favor either a New Critical or a reader response approach, their responses have never been explicitly articulated or "named." Their study of literature has, to this point, been atheoretical. One could argue that, even for this upper track, their entire education has been atheoretical. That is, the biases that frame the particular perspectives of their learning—be it scientific paradigms, historical school of thought, or approaches to literature—have never been admitted. To be sure, however, they are at play in the presentation of knowledge as truth. The students deserve to know that. They also need the tools that will help them recognize and evaluate the ideologies through which their education has been funneled. As Stephen Bonnycastle (1996) points out:

> The main reason for studying theory at the same time as literature is that it forces you to deal consciously with the problem of ideologies. . . . If you are going to live intelligently in the modern world, you have to recognize that there are conflicting ideologies and that there is no simple direct access to the truth. (p. 19)

Martha knows the dangers of teaching didactically; she tends to prefer a more inductive or a discovery approach, but this brief but explicit introduction of a sampling of literary theories is part of her grand plan. She hopes to briefly introduce all the literary theories at once, to just let them simmer in the students' minds as she introduces the readings and texts one by one over the course of the school year. Martha and her students will return to this sheet again and again as they reframe their reading into the multiple perspectives that are suggested by the theories. Herein lies the optometrist's gold—the treasure trove of different colored lenses that can alter our vision. Martha and her class have taken the first step on their theoretical odyssey, an odyssey that is at the very center of her curriculum for her Advanced Placement students and the center of this book.

WHAT'S NEW ABOUT THEORY

The previous five scenarios, although they take place in separate classrooms distinguished by significant differences in teachers, students, and curriculum, provide the opening salvos to the concept of multiple perspectives. The activities themselves can be used individually or they can occur consecutively in any classroom. I tend to use all five when I introduce the topic of multiple perspectives and do them roughly in the order in which I present them here (Appleman, 1992). Encouraging multiple perspectives provides a conceptual introduction to considering the different "readings" of a text that literary theory can provide.

Taken together, these activities help students understand that literature can be read from different perspectives. This pluralistic approach indicates that the sources of these different perspectives do not always spring from personal experience. It encourages students to hold texts up to the light, as they would a prism, just to see how many colors might be cast. Or, to return to the opening metaphor from the prologue, it introduces readers to various tinted lenses through which they can view things differently.

At first blush, the experienced literature teacher may wonder if we are really offering anything new. For example, many teachers may have used "My Papa's Waltz" to teach tone. Activities such as rewriting nursery rhymes or considering other characters in the John Updike story help teachers convey age-old literary devices such as point of view, protagonist, and characterization. Similarly, archetypes, such as those embedded in Martha's *Star Wars* activity (see Appendix, Activity 7), have formed the anatomy of our literary criticism for years.

Further, the notion that there are several critical stances, or perspectives, from which texts can be viewed is not new in the language arts curriculum, especially in a literature curriculum that has been duly influenced by Louise Rosenblatt, Robert Probst, and other notable proponents of reader response. Reader response clearly claims that the meaning of texts changes from reader to reader; that there is no single "correct" interpretation; that it is created by the transaction of reader and text; and that every reader may create a different interpretation of a text, given our different backgrounds and orientations. Yet all reader responses, regardless of how they may vary from student to student and reader to reader, are really variations on a single theoretical theme: that personal experiences provide the lens that colors the reading of the text. There is, of course, some unassailable truth as well as pedagogical promise to this claim. But most contemporary theoretical approaches, other than reader response, are rarely used in secondary literature classrooms. Further, as literature teachers we may want to move students beyond their own personal response into the perspective of others. As Pirie (1997, p. 23) points out, "At some point, examination of their own meaning-making will probably lead students to recognize limitations in their current perspectives—that's a characteristic of growth, after all—and engender new appreciation of many things, including perhaps Shakespeare."

Teaching multiple approaches to literature through contemporary literary theory promotes what many in the field of literacy education have come to regard as a constructivist approach to literature. As Applebee (1993, pp. 200–201) defines constructivism, "Instruction becomes less a matter of transmittal of an objective and culturally sanctioned body of knowledge, and more a matter of helping individual learners learn to construct and interpret for themselves." Applebee goes on to say that "the challenge for educators is how in turn to embed this new emphasis into the curricula they develop and implement." When teachers introduce literary theory into their literature classes, they invite students to construct both interpretive method and literary meaning into their study of literature. No longer will students respond within a preselected theoretical paradigm. They construct the theoretical context as well as the content of their meaning-making.

THE END OF THE BEGINNING

After these initial introductory activities, some teachers might want to offer students some straightforward explications of literary theory, such as Stephen Lynn's (1990) "A Passage into Critical Theory," an essay in which Lynn interprets a story by Brendan Gill about working at *The New Yorker* from various theoretical perspectives. The essay nicely iterates the structure of the Baker piece but pushes students more firmly into the direction of theory. Excerpts from *The Pooh Perplex* by Frederick C. Crews (1965) provide a more elaborate variation on the same theme. These pieces whimsically demonstrate how different theoretical perspectives cast light differently on the same text, even an "innocent text" such as *Winnie-the-Pooh*. And they remind all of us of the potential absurdity that can result when we overreach with our criticism:

> The fatal mistake that has been made by every previous Pooh-ologist is the confusion of Milne the writer with Milne the narrator, and of Christopher Robin the listener with Christopher Robin the character. These are not two personages but four, and no elementary understanding of Pooh is possible without this realization. We must designate, then, the Milne within the story as "the Milnean voice" and we must call the Christopher Robin who listens "the Christopheric ear." With these distinctions in mind, Pooh begins to make perfect sense for the first time. (Crews, 1965, p. 6)

The presence of humor and grace are important in this enterprise, for the introduction of theory needs to be approached gently and with care. Students already suspect that we English teachers meet together at conferences and make up terms such as *tone*, *symbol*, and *protagonist* just so we can trick them on the next test, wreck something that was just starting to seem like fun, or complicate something that was just starting to get more simple. If theory is going to be believed and used by students, if it is somehow going to become an integral part of their repertoire of reading, then it needs a chance to make a case for itself, even if that means beginning slowly and subtly with activities such as the ones used by Joe, Bob, Rachel, Martha, and me.

Clearly, not every theory should be used with every text. Reading with theory can become as mechanistic and arbitrary as some of the other kinds of literary apparatuses we've been collectively guilty of overusing in the past. Applying theory should be neither mandatory nor automatic. In fact, as Susan Sontag (1969) has argued, the reading of some texts should be done without any theory or interpretation at all. I sometimes go weeks without directly applying theory, letting it lie fallow as we go about our reading in the usual way. More often than not, as we read together, a student may bring up a particular lens. When that happens, I know that his or her theoretical journey is progressing, that it is the student and not I alone who helps construct the theoretical framework of the classroom.

While a teacher may chart the theoretical journey anywhere and with any theory or combination of theories, in this book we begin our study of theory with the one with which students may have the most practice—reader response. Although in many classrooms students have become socialized into sharing their personal responses to texts, rarely have they heard of Louise Rosenblatt or have any idea that their responses lie within a particular theoretical framework. In addition, reader response is often unconditionally presented to students as the most comfortable and familiar way into a text, even though many teachers, like Rachel, have some understanding of the limitations and perhaps even dangers of this particular pedagogical approach, what Pirie calls "the cult of the individual." It is time to pull back the curtain on the workings of reader response.

• CHAPTER 3 •

The Lens of Reader Response: The Promise and Peril of Response-Based Pedagogy

> What a poem means is the outcome of a dialogue between the words on the page and the person who happens to be reading it; that is to say, its meaning varies from person to person.
>
> —W. H. Auden

> We must keep clearly in mind that the literary experience is fundamentally an unmediated private exchange between a text and a reader, and that literary history and scholarship are supplemental.
>
> —Robert Probst, *Response and Analysis*

> A poem is the map of a dream.
>
> —Kevin, Grade 12

> This poem has no meaning to me. Because I get no meaning, it is not poetry.
>
> —Jesse, Grade 12

A few years ago I served as an outside examiner for an International Baccalaureate program in an urban high school in Minneapolis. My role as an "invigilator" was to help students demonstrate their understanding of several canonical texts (*Oedipus Rex*, *Macbeth*, *Hamlet*, *The Grapes of Wrath*, *The Scarlet Letter*) by asking them first to prepare a brief explication of the text and then to respond to a series of questions.

Particularly memorable was one discussion I had about *The Scarlet Letter* with a 16-year-old student named Leah. Leah spent two or three sentences on plot summary and then exclaimed, "You know, if my man ever treated me the way Hester's man treated her, he'd be out of my life before you could say 'the scarlet *A*.' I can't believe the crap Hester took. Actually, last week my boyfriend Rob and I almost broke up. Okay, well, it all started when . . ."

Try as I might, I couldn't move our conversation back to Hester or to anything specifically textual about *The Scarlet Letter* or any of the other texts she had read for her IB English course. I felt that she had dived off the springboard of personal response into an autobiographical wreck (apologies to Adrienne Rich). Leah's inability to craft a response that was textual in any way might have been inadvertently facilitated by her skilled and well-meaning teacher, who encouraged personal responses to literature and de-emphasized more traditional forms of textual analysis. While this anecdote may exaggerate the "worst-case scenario" of the personalized approach to literature, it does point out some of the potential weaknesses in how that approach has come to be practiced in secondary schools.

In this chapter I review some of the basic tenets of a *reader-centered* approach, discuss some of the many advantages of this particular lens, and explain how its practice may have become diverted from its intentions. I then explore some of the limitations to the approach that have emerged recently as both students and canon have become more diverse. Finally, a close look at reader response activities in two different classrooms reveals that we can use reader response with our students more fruitfully by (1) teaching it more explicitly, and (2) teaching it as one of a variety of theoretical approaches rather than as the only possible approach. This multiplicity of approaches will be further explored in subsequent chapters.

THE BENEFITS OF THE READER-CENTERED APPROACH

There can be no denying the power and purpose of a reader-centered approach to literature and the degree to which it has positively informed our practice. It has made the enterprise of literature teaching more relevant, immediate, and important. It has forced us to rethink what we do when we teach literature, why we do it, and whom we do it for. There is ample evidence of the soundness of the reader-centered approach; its advocates are influential and articulate—from Louise Rosenblatt's efferent reading to aesthetic reading, to Judith Langer's engagement with literature, to Robert Probst's elegant and elegiac meditations on the importance of personal response. The value of the lens of reader response to literature study in secondary classrooms simply cannot be denied. And no one would want to.

As we look back at literature instruction over the past 50 years, it is easy to see how reader-centered teaching fit perfectly with the goals of constructivist education and with the progressive-education movement. At the center of the educational enterprise was the student. No longer was the text itself or the author the most salient part of literature study. No longer could students' individual responses to texts be considered "mnemonic irrelevancies," as I. A. Richards had claimed. Instead, the reader was the creator of meaning through a "never to be duplicated transaction" between the reader and the text (Rosenblatt, 1968, p. 31).

This new focus on the reader indisputably enlivened and irrevocably altered the teaching of literature. It changed, or supposedly changed, the power dynamics in the classroom and the role of the teacher, and it clearly changed what it was that we asked students to do when they read texts. The paradigmatic shift from a text-centered to a reader-centered pedagogy also changed our consideration of the kinds of texts we used. We found ourselves sometimes considering whether a particular text was teachable by the degree to which it might invoke personal responses from our students. From the point of view of most observers, at least, these were all changes for the better.

Five-paragraph themes gave way to reading logs; recitations of genre or structural aspects of the text gave way to recitations of personal connections to the text; and the traditional teacher-in-the-front formation gave way to the intimate and misshapen circles with which many of our students and many of us are familiar. Of course, knowledge of the text was still important, but personal knowledge seemed in many cases to be privileged over textual knowledge. Rather than seeking out biographical information about the author or historical information about the times in which the text was written or took place, teachers began to spend time finding personal hooks into the texts they chose and frequently began literature discussions with questions that began "Have you ever?"

A CAUTIONARY TALE

We met Rachel in Chapter 2. Rachel was an enthusiastic, if relatively inexperienced, practitioner of reader-centered pedagogy and had become increasingly frustrated as she watched her students measure, by their own limited experiences, the predicaments and decisions of Hester Prynne, George and Lennie, Daisy Buchanan, and Atticus Finch. On the one hand, Rachel is grateful that they can find connections between their own lives and the lives of these literary characters. She knows that personal experience often provides the coattails that students ride into a book. She also knows enough about reader response approaches to the teaching of literature from her college methods class to realize that using one's personal experiences to connect to the text can be a fruitful way for students to make meaning. She knows that personal response is the hook that many teachers favor for good reason. In fact, some of her colleagues contend that it is the only way that really works.

And still . . . There is something about this personal approach to literature with which Rachel feels uncomfortable. Yes, she wants her students to read literature to gain insight into their own lives, to gain perspective into their own situations. Yet there is, Rachel believes, something limiting about that position, something that might trivialize the importance of the real differences that exist between the students' world and the world of the text. Are we *really* all the same? Is the purpose of studying literature only to clarify our own existence and underscore our unique personal attributes? We know the personal connection and engagement with literature that is gained when students measure the relationship of

Hester and Chillingworth through their own dating experiences, or issues of adultery with contemporary scandals involving American politicians. But what is lost?

Rachel is not the only one who has been reconsidering the relative merits of reader response. Perhaps one of the most biting reappraisals of an individualized reader-centered approach is offered by Bruce Pirie in *Reshaping High School English* (1997). In a chapter tellingly titled "Beyond Barney and the Cult of the Individual," Pirie reflects on the practice of valorizing individual responses in the literature classroom and the inherent dangers and complications of that approach. He argues that our focus on individuals may be overly simplistic. Even our definition of *individual* may be flawed; it does not acknowledge the contextual factors that help to make us individuals. As English teachers, we may have been guilty of overprivileging and romanticizing the individual at the expense of considerations of context. Pirie warns, "We now need to question the limits of the doctrine of individualism before our classroom practices harden into self-perpetuating rituals" (p. 9). This is, in part, what James Marshall (1991) refers to when he calls reader response our new orthodoxy.

Pirie notes Applebee's (1993) observation that we shuttle between valorizing personal response as an end in itself or using it as a hook or motivation to get students interested in more serious literary analysis. Pirie (1997) also questions whether a personal-response approach to literature is justifiable from the perspective of academic rigor: "I am, however, suspicious of the suggestion that just expressing your personal response is a satisfactory educational attainment, or that such a response could be evaluated for its authenticity" (p. 120).

This failure to critique readings is also lamented by Michael Smith (Rabinowitz & Smith, 1998) when he says, "I think it's important for readers and teachers to have a theoretical model that allows them to critique readings" (p. 121). In their provocative book, *Authorizing Readers*, Rabinowitz and Smith remind us of the importance of authorial intention. If reader response is a transaction, at the very least we need to acknowledge that the text is an equal partner in that transaction. Meaning is a result of a kind of negotiation between authorial intent and the reader's response. It is not simply the question "What does this mean to me?" that captures the essence of reader-centered theories. How can literature foster a knowledge of others when we focus so relentlessly on ourselves and our own experiences? Without some attention to authorial readings, Rabinowitz and Smith remind us, we give up the power of the text to transform.

BE CAREFUL WHAT YOU ASK FOR

Perhaps the excesses that alarm even some of the originators and strongest supporters of reader-centered pedagogy have to do with how atheoretical its practice has become. Students are not exactly sure what it is they are supposed to do when they respond to a text; they just know they are supposed to respond *personally*. A cynical 10th grader once confided, "My teacher likes it when we get gooey and personal—the gooier, the better." They sometimes even overreact by making such remarks as that of Nathan, in an 11th-grade discussion of *Snow Falling on Cedars*: "You really can't tell me anything about this book, since my *personal* response is the only thing that counts." We may have "balkanized" the response-based classroom, thus preventing the ability to discuss or share our personal experiences. Since our responses to literary texts are particularly and uniquely ours, then what is it that anyone, teacher or classmate, could offer that would either enrich or contradict them? Perhaps it is this phenomenon that frustrates Rachel so much when she tries to get a discussion going. Her students' attitude seems to be, "If my response is uniquely mine, then what can anyone else tell me about it?" This also leads to the sort of autobiographical diving that Leah did with *The Scarlet Letter* in the anecdote that opened this chapter. Bonnycastle (1996, p. 174) addresses this issue of reader response when he writes, "If each of us only pays attention to individual experience, the communal basis for the discipline will disappear and literature classes will have nothing to hold them together."

Then, of course, there is the matter of students who may be uncomfortable with personal response. This may be more than a question of learning style; it is in some ways a privacy issue or perhaps a cultural one. The sharing circle that characterizes much of our practice is also culturally determined (Hynds & Appleman, 1997). It makes assumptions about the amount of trust that students have in each other and in their teachers. It makes some assumptions about their relationship to the institution of schooling and whether they have experienced school as a safe place. Perhaps most important, it makes some assumptions about the degree to which students' lives are in "sharable shape." And, of course, underlying all these assumptions is our belief that the sharing of personal responses in the public sphere of school will bring students to a greater understanding of themselves and each other rather than underscore the depths of the chasms, of the inequality, that often divide us. This is the essence of the false promise of democracy in the literature circle.

CONFESSIONS OF A TRUE BELIEVER

As a high school teacher during the 1970s and 1980s, I was an enthusiastic practitioner of reader response. I tirelessly sought the personal connections that would engage my students with a text, whether it was *To Kill a Mockingbird*, *Of Mice and Men*, *Ordinary People*, *Black Boy*, *The Hobbit*, or *The Great Gatsby*. Like the teachers I described above, I began more than my share of literature discussions with that "Have you ever?" opening. I have to admit, however, that while I considered myself to be a true-blue reader response teacher for about 10 years of high school teaching, I never once explained to the students that what we were doing was called *reader response*. While I'm sure I explained or paraphrased the concept of a "transaction" with a literary text in general terms, I never was explicit about what exactly we were doing and why.

Sometimes the students themselves, noticing the tone of our classroom yet not being able to name the difference they felt, would refer obliquely or disparagingly to Ms. Engstrom's sophomore American literature class or Ms. Debarge's 11th-grade British literature class, in which there was clearly *one* meaning to a passage or even an entire text and feelings were *never* discussed. The students would reminiscence bitterly about memorizing quotations, preparing for nitpicky objective tests, and embarking on wildly elusive symbol hunts. Even then I wasn't clear about what was different in this class. Neither did I name the competing traditions of literary study or admit to myself and to my students the validity and potential advantages of a more text-centered approach. As I prepared my reader-friendly lessons, journal assignments, and essays, I vilified the New Critics, making them the evil strawpeople of single-minded interpretations. Ben Nelms (1988) stated it well in this description:

> I learned to think of the literary text as an edifice. Almost as a temple. Complete, autonomous, organically whole, sacrosanct. We approached it with reverence. We might make temple rubbings and we were encouraged to explain how its arches carried its weight and to speculate on the organic relationship between its form and function. But it was an edifice and we were spectators before its splendors. (p. 1)

I congratulated myself that I could never treat my students as "spectators" or the texts as "temples." I felt comfortable and confident—superior, even—in my reader response pedagogy. Looking back, from the viewpoint of multiple perspectives, I realize I was guilty of imposing a theoretical framework with no room for deviation. In my own way, though I could never see it or admit it then, I was as narrow-minded and singular in my theoretical vision as Ms. Engstrom or Ms. Debarge and their single-answer worksheets and symbol hunts.

I would like to be able to claim that I somehow saw the light and eventually learned to teach explicitly and theoretically while I was a high school teacher, but that is simply not the case. It was only when I began teaching about teaching that I started making response-based teaching explicit with my own version of "the naming of parts." For those preservice and in-service teachers who had never been pricked by the needles of "porcupines making love" (Purves, Rogers, & Soter, 1990), I began to think strategically about how to make the lens of reader response explicit. In other words, I didn't simply want to encourage my students to respond to literature within a classroom context that was never articulated; I wanted to teach them about the theory of reader response and then encourage them to respond to literary texts with those responses enriched by their metacognitive awareness of that theory.

PULLING BACK THE CURTAIN

I began to pull the curtain back on reader response with my secondary preservice teachers and realized, as I had with many other instructional strategies, that I had been withholding from the high school students themselves the power of being able to name what it was that they were doing. It was rather like wanting students to reach the upper levels of Bloom's taxonomy but never teaching them about the taxonomy itself. I sometimes felt as though I had been teaching high school like the Wizard of Oz, trying to create magic and illusion, asking students to ignore the man behind the green curtain when all the time it would have been more illustrative and perhaps even more magical without the illusion, if I had only trusted them enough to take them backstage.

Taking them backstage wasn't very hard. While there are many different forms and variations of reader response—as Beach (1993) categorizes them: textual, social, psychological, cultural, and experiential—I decided to focus primarily on a version of Louise Rosenblatt's transactional approach. It is, in many ways, the most straightforward, sensible, and comprehensible to secondary students. And, thanks to the wonderful "translations" of Robert Probst, it seems to be the version of a reader-centered approach to literature with which most secondary teachers are familiar. Rosenblatt views literary reading as a transaction between reader and text. She views responding to literature as an "event." As Richard Beach (1993) explains:

> In contrast to the textual theorists who are interested in the competent or ideal readers' knowledge in general, Rosenblatt focuses on the uniqueness of a particular momentary transaction. While the textual theorists are concerned with achieving interpretation consistent with knowledge of appropriate literary conventions, theorists adopting Rosenblatt's transactional model are open to exploring their responses as reflecting the particulars of their emotions, attitudes, beliefs, interests, etc. (p. 51)

In his useful volume, *A Teacher's Introduction to Reader-Response Theories* (1993), Beach illustrates some of the principles of reader response theory by using the poem "Mushrooms," by Sylvia Plath, a poem discussed in Chapter 2. The poem is so oblique and ambiguous that it can nicely illustrate some of the basic tenets of reader response to secondary students. It can become an important part of a lesson designed to help "pull back the curtain."

As Beach reports, readers respond with marked variety to this text and construct a wide range of interpretations. When the poem is presented to students without its title, even more interesting variation can result. For example, some students divine that the poem is about some kind of vegetation (from moss to trees) while others, especially female students, have mentioned that they think it's about unborn babies. Some students have suggested that it's about people who are oppressed—either people of color or, perhaps, women. One student ingeniously suggested that the poem was about rabbits and provided a line-by-line explication using words such as *multiply*, *silent*, and *edible* to prove that it was so. A few others reported magical and mysterious walks in the woods with their fathers or mothers. A few even noted a trace of mental illness in the poem.

Here are some of the responses of 11th- and 12th-grade students after they were asked to write their response to the poem on an index card:

> This poem is about conformity and how it jeopardizes our individuality.
>
> This poem is about an oppressed group of people. They are beaten, ignored, abused, used. There is some hope of things being okay for them. It comes in inheriting the earth. They are almost there.
>
> These are slaves, escaping from plantations. They were just mindless tools before; now they are individuals.
>
> Snow.
>
> About a class of unnoticed underdogs who will come together silently and rise against the present power.
>
> White carpenter ants.
>
> I think this is a dream. A dream is the uninhibited imagination and a poem is the same thing put to words. A poem is the map of a dream.
>
> Insects, cockroaches . . . It made me think of how they say that if there is ever a nuclear war, it would just be cockroaches left to cover the earth.
>
> Mushroom-rotting fungus plaguing the earth.
>
> It's about woodland mice.

As these statements demonstrate, the range of responses to this poem is extraordinary, although some kind of cohort pattern can sometimes be detected—more women tend to see the unborn babies, college students seem to be more likely to see oppression. Students are usually amazed at the diversity of responses, and the activity itself makes the case for the notion that our responses to literature are almost as individual as fingerprints.

It is at this point, after they've responded to "Mushrooms," that I introduce the reader response diagram to secondary students (see Figure 3.1). This diagram graphically illustrates the principles of Rosenblatt's transactional theory of reader

Figure 3.1. Reader Response Diagram

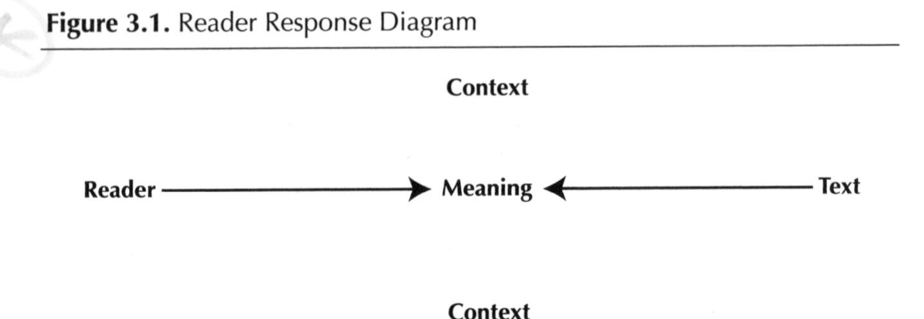

response in the following ways: First, students are asked to consider what personal characteristics, qualities, or elements of their personal histories might be relevant to their reading of a particular text. We stress that the relevant personal qualities or attributes they choose are dependent upon the particular text. For example, it is obviously relevant that I have red hair when I consider my response to *Ann of Green Gables*. However, the fact that I have red hair is irrelevant when considering my responses to *A Separate Peace*, *All Quiet on the Western Front*, or *The Awakening*.

On the right side of the diagram, students are asked to consider the textual properties that might affect their reading or response and to list those properties. They might, for example, list the presence of vernacular or other aspects of vocabulary, the length of sentences, use of punctuation or italics, or the narrative structure. I point out to the students that all these factors do contribute to a reader's response to a particular piece, but they are characteristics of the literary work, not of the individual reader.

In addition to considering both textual and personal characteristics, students are asked to consider what contextual features may have influenced their reading. In some respects, adolescent readers seem to have a difficult time differentiating between the contextual and the personal, a fact that would not surprise most observers of adolescents. The lack of boundaries between self and other typifies the kind of adolescent egocentrism that David Elkind (1986) has described. In this case, the word *context* is used in a fairly narrow sense, referring not to the sociocultural context, which may indeed be imbedded in all three of the other categories, but to the context or conditions under which the book was read. For example, people read differently under the fluorescent light of the classroom or on an airplane in close proximity to a stranger from how they do when they are in the comfort of their own home and in their favorite reading place. The amount of homework, what one has been required to do as part of reading, and what else may be occurring at school or at home are all factors that contribute to the reading context.

Next, we apply the reader response diagram to the students' responses to the poem "Mushrooms." On the left, or reader, side of the diagram, students often list their affinity or lack of affinity for nature, their comfort and experience with reading poetry, their awareness of being part of an oppressed or marginalized group, and whatever prior knowledge they might have about the poem. On the right, or textual, side of the diagram, students may list the following textual properties: There are only one or two words per line, the language is very concrete, the poem doesn't rhyme, it's "modern" and imagistic. Sometimes they mention that the poem is written by Sylvia Plath and offer some biographical information or insights (just the kind of thing that drove those New Critics crazy).

After we describe the mechanics of the transaction or dialectic between reader and text, we further discuss how that dialectic created individual responses for the readers that enabled them to construct their own personal meaning for the text. Given the range of responses to "Mushrooms," it is easy for students to see how they have imprinted their own experiences and understandings onto the text itself and rendered interpretations as diverse as their own life experiences. At this point, the case for reader response generally makes itself. Now, let's see how pulling back the curtain plays out in two different classrooms with two different texts.

READER RESPONSE AND *RUNNING FIERCELY TOWARD A HIGH THIN SOUND*: "I AM NOT A LESBIAN; I AM NOT A JEW"

Carolyn Bell's Advanced Placement (AP) class quickly forms the large circle that is the de rigueur formation for them. Located in one of the most diverse high schools in the city of Minneapolis, the class of 30 doesn't fully reflect the heterogeneity of the overall school population, but it is more diverse than many of the AP or college preparatory classes elsewhere in the state. Juniors and seniors, males and females, preppies and goths, White students and students of color, students with brown hair, those with blue hair, those with yellow hair, jocks and poets, gays, straights, and bisexuals, they all assemble in their delicious and unpredictable individuality. Their regular teacher is a skilled and imaginative veteran with a taste for offbeat literature and a deep faith in her students' ability to be engaged and adventurous readers. When she is called to jury duty, she generously allows me to have her class for a week. The novel that the students will be reading has already been selected, since a visit from the author, who lives in Minneapolis, had been previously scheduled.

Never one to teach only the canon, Carolyn had introduced her students to a variety of literature, mixing some predictable AP or college-bound choices with more surprising ones. They have read *As I Lay Dying*; *Beloved*; *Stones from the River*; and now this, *Running Fiercely Toward a High Thin Sound*, a first novel about a Jewish family that is divided by the mental illness of one sister and the jealousy of the mother. Mental illness, family dysfunction, lesbian relationships, and Jewish family history and values are all salient themes of this book set in New England in the mid-1970s. Its uniqueness of theme, form, and content make the discussion of this novel particularly suitable for a reader response approach, since students are bound to have visceral and highly individualistic reactions to the work.

While Carolyn's taste in literature is contemporary and unconventional, her pedagogy is a bit more traditional and is highly effective. The class itself generally focused on some of the more traditional forms of literary analysis that they would be expected to use on the year-end AP exam. The class had been briefly introduced to reader response by a student teacher, but the students seem to prefer a more text-centered, teacher-led approach to literature. To deepen their collective repertoire of ways of interacting with literary texts, I decide to spend my week with the students using a reader-centered approach.

We begin by reviewing some of the basic tenets of reader response with a handout (see Figure 3.2 and Activity 34) adapted from an article by Lee Galda (1983). Then I introduce the transactional diagram described in the previous section and very slightly adapted for the novel (see Appendix, Activity 10). I ask the students to fill out the diagram at home and to bring a completed diagram to class the next day. I then ask them to write some "meaning statements" on the back of the handout—one or two sentences that describe the meanings they constructed as a result of the transaction between themselves and the text.

We discuss the reader diagrams the following day. Under the reader heading, students had listed some *reader characteristics* (or lack of characteristics) that they felt were important to their reading of the novel:

I have a pushy mommy.

My family has communication problems.

My father is not always present in my life.

I have friends who are gay; I know lesbians, how they live and what they are like.

I am morally opposed to homosexuality.

I feel completely exasperated and helpless with my mother.

I am not Jewish.

I am not a lesbian.

I don't like reading about any kind of sex.

Figure 3.2. Reader Response

What Is Reader Response?

"A reader makes a poem as he reads. He does not see an unalterable meaning that lies within the text. He creates meaning from the confrontation" (Rosenblatt, 1968).

Philosophy or Rationale

Reader response advocates stress the interaction between the reader and the text. Reading is recognized as a process in which expectations operate to propel the reader through the text. Readers bring to the text their own experiences, morals, social codes, and views of the world. Because readers bring their meanings to the text, their responses are different. Response-based teaching pays close attention to the reader, respects the reader's responses, and insists that the reader accept responsibility for making sense of personal experiences.

Response to Literature: Theory

In *Literature as Exploration* (1968), Rosenblatt presented her alternative to the belief that a text carries a precise meaning, which readers must try to discern. She proposed that a literary text was simply symbols on a page and that the literary work, or "poem," as she later designated it, existed only in the interaction of reader and text. She defined the literary experience as a "synthesis of what the reader already knows and feels and desires with what the literary text offers" (p. 272). This transaction between reader and text consists of a reader's infusion of meaning into verbal symbols on a page and the text's channeling of that meaning through its construction.

The realization of a literary work of art requires an active reader who constantly builds and synthesizes meaning, paying attention to the referents of the words being processed while aware of the images and emotions experienced. The text does not embody meaning but rather guides the active creation of meaning. Thus within this theory, it becomes impossible to discuss literature without reference to the reader.

Based on Galda, 1983.

Interestingly, on the diagrams most students seemed to focus more directly on what they were not than on what they were, a case of negative identity. I wondered whether this would have been true with any text or whether the students were particularly interested in disassociating themselves from being Jewish or lesbian.

The following *textual characteristics* were most commonly offered:

The book contains a lot of Yiddish words.

Explicit and graphic lesbian sex.

Going through mirrors, a surrealistic quality to the prose.

All the stereotypes of the radical lesbian.

Magical worlds.

Multiple narratives or perspectives.

After the students list both the reader traits and the textual characteristics, they are asked to compose several *meaning statements* that arose from their "unique transactions" with *Running Fiercely Toward a High Thin Sound*. These meaning statements were impressive in their range as well as their gravity:

Books don't have to have redeeming, happy endings, because a lot of lives don't.

Sometimes what you perceive is not always the truth.

Mothers do not innately love their children. Society only thinks they should.

Homosexuality is real and important but it is not the book's most important theme.

You can't force your children to be what you want.

Forgiveness is not always possible.

Accepting other people for who they are instead of what you want them to be is important in family relations.

You really have to love someone before you can hate them or truly be cruel to them.

I found little meaning in this book at all as it didn't apply to me.

CONTRAST OF TWO READERS

What then happens in the reading of a literary work? Through the medium of words, the text brings into the reader's consciousness certain concepts, certain sensory experiences, certain images of things, people, actions, scenes. The special meanings and, more particularly, the submerged associations that these words and images have for the individual reader will largely determine what it communicates to him. The reader brings to the work personality traits, memories of past events, present needs, and preoccupations, a particular mood of the moment, and a particular physical

> condition. These and many other elements in a never-to-be-duplicated combination determine his response to the peculiar contribution of the text.
> —Louise Rosenblatt, *Literature as Exploration*

If we are to give credence to Rosenblatt's account of what happens in the reading of a literary work, we would expect that the individual characteristics of students would really come into play as they read a novel such as *Running Fiercely*, one that is so clearly marked by definitive personal qualities, unusual lifestyles, and unique family history. We might, for example, expect students to have a wide range of responses to such an unusual text, given the diversity of the class. In addition, we might expect students whose "personality traits, memories of past events, present needs, and preoccupations" bear some resonance and similarity to the characters and events of the text to have a markedly different response from those students whose life experiences and memories stand in stark contrast to those that are represented in the novel. The student-response diagrams seem to call these assumptions into question. Although the text is not at all obviously theme driven, many students seem to have similar transactions with the text, not at all like the never-to-be-duplicated combination that Rosenblatt predicted.

While most of the students had enjoyed the book, two seemed unable to make meaning from it or to have a positive transaction with the text; let's take a look at them. Of course, it is not particularly surprising that some students failed to respond to the book; as English teachers, we know that that happens all the time. What is surprising, however, is how different these two students are. Their personal qualities are almost diametrically opposed and yet they experienced a similar response to the novel. Their shared resistance seems to call into question some of our assumptions about the relationship between personal qualities and their relevance in how they might influence our responses to a literary text.

Mark

Mark is perhaps the most recalcitrant student in Carolyn's class. He is intelligent and competent, if somewhat surly. His air of passivity and lack of emotion didn't seem to waver during the reading of the text, even when the author herself came to visit our classroom in all her radical lesbian splendor. Like many of his classmates, Mark listed the relevant reader characteristics in the negative. As a reader, he described himself: "not Jewish, heterosexual, introvert, small family." In terms of the textual features that would influence his response, he mentioned "technique: metaphor, social ideas, Yiddish, and sexual content." See Figure 3.3.

Mark speculated that the novel might be about what he called the "inevitable conflicts between introverts and extroverts" and acknowledged the possibility that the author was telling a metaphorical story that meant something to her, that she was trying to educate the reader about an issue. Yet in the end Mark

Figure 3.3. Mark's Reader Response Diagram

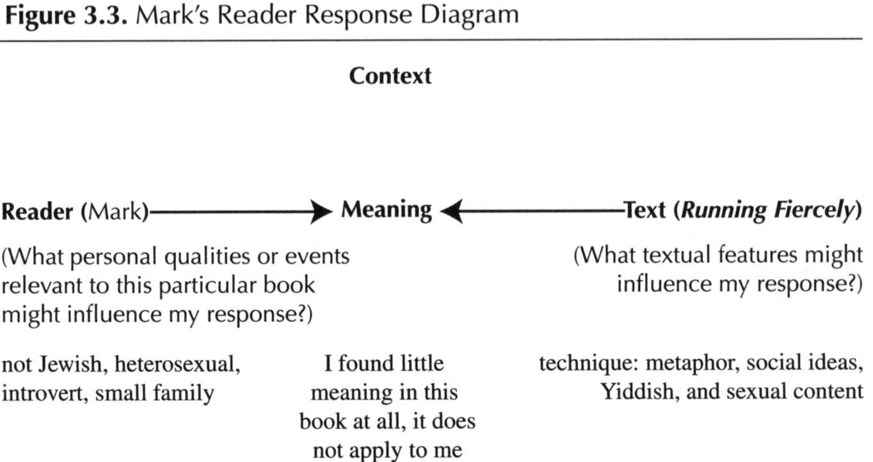

came up relatively empty-handed in his transaction: "I found little meaning in this book at all; it does not apply to me."

It would be easy to dismiss Mark's inability to find meaning in this text as having something to do with how different he is from its characters and his difficulty in relating to them. But Mark's classmate Ellen's reaction to the same text cautions us against making such a simplistic, if superficially sensible, explanation.

Ellen

Unlike all her classmates, Ellen is Jewish and speaks Yiddish. Further, she believes that her parents are very much like the selfish, jealous, woefully imperfect parents of the protagonist. Ellen doesn't find the family dynamics of the novel strange; she recognizes them as being very much like those of her own family. Ellen claims that the mother is bitter, jealous, and mentally unstable (see Figure 3.4). One might think that Ellen's shared characteristics with the characters and situations would make the text especially relevant for her. At the very least, we might expect that her response would be significantly different from that of a classmate who is as dissimilar from the characters as she is similar. This is not the case.

As did her classmate Mark, Ellen seemed to have an unfulfilling transaction with the text. Like Mark, she dismissed the author's motive as being more writer based than reader based: "I think Judith Katz wrote this as therapy. I could tell it was based strongly on her life. She wanted to pull out everything that pissed her off and write about it." Ellen failed to map her own experiences onto the text and

Figure 3.4. Ellen's Reader Response Diagram

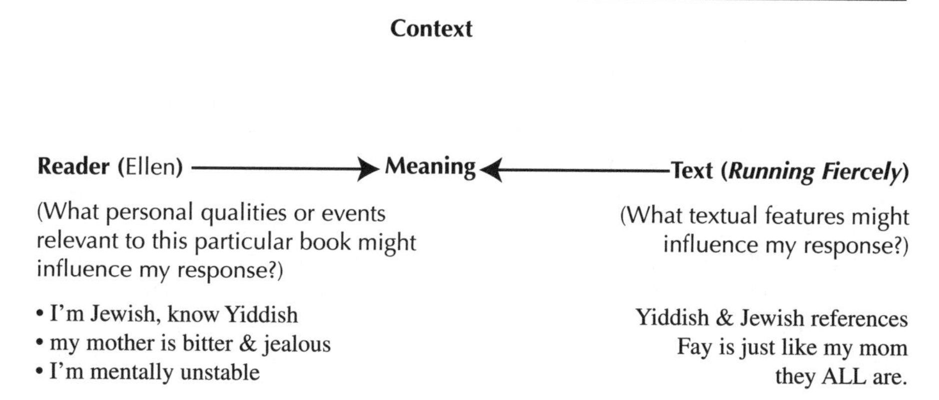

Context

Meaning statement: I don't know that there is a good meaning for this book. I think Judith Katz wrote this as therapy. I could tell it was based strongly on her life. She wanted to pull out everything that pissed her off and write about it—the stereotype lesbians, the good girls, and the crazy ones. Some people shouldn't have kids, just because they can get pregnant. Having kids doesn't void you of jealousy. Books don't have to have redeeming, happy endings because a lot of lives don't. Not all mothers are good. Almost any nutcase can get pregnant. A smart person would give that some thought.

instead concluded, "I don't think there is a good meaning for this book," a response remarkably similar to Mark's. It may, in fact, have been the first thing they had in common.

The contrast of these two students helps make two points about the use of reader-centered pedagogy in the classroom. I am not suggesting that Rosenblatt argued that students would map their own personal qualities onto the text and the better the match the greater the response would be. For the record, she never claimed anything like that. Our individual qualities, she asserted, would inform our responses to a text but would not necessarily dictate what they were. In practice, though, we have tended to select texts that in provocative ways provide matches of our students' worlds and the worlds of the characters. While in many ways it may be fruitful to do this, it may also be dangerous, as this contrast points out.

First, we may misinterpret how experiences and characteristics that a student shares with the characters may affect his or her response. In some ways, as Ellen's case illustrates, the closer the students' own experiences are to the text the more likely those students may be to reject the text. For example, adolescents dealing with suicide attempts of friends or family members might find *Ordinary People* too excruciatingly close to home to read. Second, we may be inadvertently giving students a dangerous message: If you can't "relate" to the book, you may not be able to find meaning in it, or as Mark so succinctly claimed: "I found little meaning in this book; it doesn't apply to me."

In *Authorizing Readers*, Michael Smith (Rabinowitz & Smith, 1998) addresses some of the issues that arise in what he calls "the pedagogy of personal experience" (p. 119). He claims that an emphasis on the personality of the reader, which is at the heart of many reader-centered theories and pedagogies, may cause students to ignore the differences and respect for those differences that is, ironically, one of the goals that is central to our attempt to diversify the curriculum.

We also trivialize some of the profound and perhaps irreconcilable differences between us. As Smith points out, we may be able to appreciate a character's situation, but we never will be able to fully understand it; and we reduce the power of literature and the representations of those experiences by pretending that we have such understanding. Smith claims that the pedagogy of personal response can make it difficult for students to realize that one doesn't necessarily have to be able to relate to a character to respond to a literary text. He believes that it is unrealistic to expect the paths of our lives to map meaningfully onto the lives of characters. Our pedagogy of personal response, he claims, limits students' ability to derive meaning out of texts that describe worlds and experiences far different from their own, a reason, again ironically, why many of us began to love literature in the first place.

Smith quotes a student who feels she cannot respond to Toni Morrison's *Beloved*: "I felt alienated by how their family interacted. I had no basis on which to relate or empathize" (p. 124). Smith feels that perhaps Toni Morrison is counting on exactly this to make her point—that you can never understand, and that's exactly a part of what you need to understand. This point is especially important in the next section, where we consider the responses of a different literature class to Richard Wright's *Native Son*.

READER RESPONSE AND *NATIVE SON*

Unlike Carolyn's classroom, Martha's 12th-grade English class is located in a suburb, filled with white-collar families and three-car garages. As part of her AP curriculum, Martha has introduced her students to critical theory. They have read a variety of works, both canonical and nontraditional, including *Beowulf*, *Much Ado About Nothing*, *The Things They Carried*, *Hamlet*, *Frankenstein*, and *Snow Falling on Cedars*.

Martha's students are familiar with the term *reader response*. In fact, they have completed Activity 8 (see Appendix) on the poem "Mushrooms" and discussed some of the factors that influence their responses to particular texts. They also seem to understand that there are several approaches to a literary text, of which reader response is just one. On the other hand, they do have a tendency to oversimplify the concept of reader response as simply personal meaning: What does this book mean *to me*? That is, they conflate the concepts of personal meaning with the identification of personal characteristics that may affect their responses. They need to clarify their understanding.

Martha has decided to teach Richard Wright's *Native Son* and wants to approach the novel through a variety of critical lenses—social class (a natural for this novel), gender, and reader response. Martha also hopes that the distance between her mostly White, mostly middle-class students and the novel's African American and sometimes violent protagonist, Bigger Thomas, will help her students see that literary responses are not dependent on one's similarity to a character. She believes, as Smith argued, that in fact the differences are sometimes precisely the point.

Martha and her students spend about 2 weeks discussing various aspects of the novel. Then she divides the class into four groups and has them complete an activity called Theory Relay (see Appendix, Activity 32), in which they visit a reader response station, a historical/biographical station, a gender station, and a social-class station. The students are asked to describe how each of the four theoretical perspectives informs their understanding of *Native Son*. Each station includes some supporting documents such as biographical information on Richard Wright, explications of social-class and gender literary theory (see Chapters 4 and 5), and some quotations from the text that are particularly relevant to each theoretical perspective. Students move around the room from station to station as they listen to the blues.

When students arrive at the reader response station, there is a description of reader response and a reader response diagram tailored for *Native Son* (see Appendix, Activity 11). As did Carolyn's class, the students first listed the relevant reader characteristics that came into play as they read the text. They then listed the textual characteristics that influenced their responses to the text. Finally, they listed the meaning statements that they derived from their reading transaction. In what follows we can see how Martha's students characterized those transactions with *Native Son* from the perspective of reader response.

READER CHARACTERISTICS

My religious background tells me that killing is wrong.

I think the death penalty should be applied in some circumstances.

I have strong views on justice and on taking responsibility for your actions.

I don't believe in the death penalty.

The fact that only women are murdered would have an effect as well. I seem to be very sympathetic to remorseful criminals.

I know that it is wrong, but sometimes I am racist and sometimes others are racist against me. I was picked on by a group of Black girls when I was in sixth grade.

I am Black in America.

I'm reading the book in a class full of White students with a White teacher.

TEXT CHARACTERISTICS

The way the book is set up from the beginning of White versus Black.

How gory Mary and Bessie's deaths were.

The descriptive nature in which the author describes the murders and the racist treatment of the Black people; the detailed arguments of the lawyer, who tries to give reasons for why things are the way they are also influences my response.

Reading the closing statements from the prosecutor and just that whole side of the case is really appalling, especially when Bigger is referred to as a beast and other things, which flat out classify him as not being human simply because he is Black—not even because he killed two women—I was quite shocked.

MEANING STATEMENTS

Even with oppression, free will can exist.

There will always be the resistant or rebellious element in human beings as long as they are oppressed.

Because I am a White female, Mary Dalton's case is just as tragic as Bigger's, if not more so, because of her brutal death without any responsibility. Because I am educated, Bigger Thomas owes much of his demise to his lack of education and could have done something, if only a bit, about this. Prejudice: Bigger Thomas was under tremendous emotional stress because he was targeted on the basis of his race alone and we should all sympathize with him.

I feel Bigger Thomas was made into who he is by his society.

Racism used to be much worse in society than it is now. Segregation is no longer legal, but people still segregate themselves.

Being female I understand the discrimination Bigger faced every day and sympathize with his feelings of rage and helplessness.

DISCUSSION

The reader response diagrams helped Martha's students isolate the features of the text as well as the personal characteristics that influenced their responses to *Native Son*. As we might expect, many of those responses clustered around issues of race, gender, and class. Students thought about not only their own race but also their own feelings about race relations. They also confronted the intersection between race and gender. White females in particular felt torn between their sympathy for Bigger as an oppressed person and their disgust for his violence. Violence also affected students' responses in terms of their feelings about the death penalty as well as in terms of their visceral reaction to the violence in the story. The reader diagrams forced students to think explicitly about the mechanics of their responses and to map those factors in relation to what belonged to them and what belonged to the text. They made their transactions explicit to themselves, to their teacher, and to their classmates.

Sometimes, completing the diagram forced students to confront the degree to which they were unable or unwilling to have an emotional reaction to the book. For example, one student wrote: "My response as a whole has been quite unemotional. I read Wright's work with interest, see his points, and it raises interesting questions, but I am quite uninvolved, probably largely as a result of my boredom with my life, especially school, and a number of distractions in my mind." Under "reader characteristics" she wrote: "As a young White, middle-class female, I feel I am perhaps better furnished to sympathize with Mary than with Bigger. It is difficult to truly understand the factors in a life leading to such an end, as such pressures and oppression have happily been completely absent from my life." Under "text characteristics" she wrote: "The brutalities Bigger commits are atrocious and while Wright succeeds in explaining Bigger's condition, it does not justify Bigger's actions. Wright intentionally makes his book confusing and therefore disturbing, raising questions about the collective versus the individual in racial issues."

The reader response station helped to make the mechanics of the reader response explicit and helped students locate the sources of the factors that contributed to their responses. Many students were able to empathize with Bigger Thomas despite the profound differences they named between their situations and Bigger's. Others, like Mark in Carolyn's class and the student Michael Smith quotes as she reads *Beloved*, were unable to construct meaning, because the text bore no relevance (or so they thought) to their protected and privileged suburban, middle-class lives. Hence, the frequency of meaning statements such as "This book was not relevant to us," "One's White, middle-class background makes it hard to relate to the text," and "This is obviously very difficult for me to personally relate to."

This dismissal because of difference is often where a reader-centered discussion ends: The text was not relevant to me; therefore, I found no meaning in it. As Smith points out, this is the inherent irony and limitation in a pedagogy of personal experience, especially when we read multicultural literature or other texts that portray worlds far different from our students'. Martha's students could not simply come up empty-handed because of an unsatisfying personal transaction with the text. Because their reader response exercise was situated within a multiple perspective approach, they were invited to find meaning in other ways.

In addition, the fact that reader response was part of a multiple-theory relay allowed students to critique the relative usefulness of the reader response lens. Martha asked her students to compare and evaluate the four theoretical approaches. She then asked which lens seemed to be most consistent with the intention of the novel, which lens was the most difficult to apply, and which lens was the most informative. Not surprisingly, most students found the social-class lens among the easiest to apply or the lens that seemed most consistent with the intention of the novel. Most students found it to be particularly difficult to apply the gender lens.

While there was some general agreement about the relative usefulness of these two lenses in terms of *Native Son*, they seemed much more divided about the usefulness of the reader response lens, with some students reporting that it was the hardest lens to apply and others reporting that it was the most applicable.

DIFFICULTIES STUDENTS REPORTED AS THEY APPLIED THE READER RESPONSE LENS TO NATIVE SON

> I'm so used to having to write great statements of theme that when I was presented with an opportunity to simply state my opinions on meaning, I had great difficulty.
>
> The lens that was most difficult to apply for me was the reader response lens because I questioned what exactly I brought to the text.
>
> One lens I found surprisingly hard to relate to was reader response. I feel like I haven't had enough experiences with oppression or racism to relate

> at all to this book. I can't relate to Bigger's feelings because I live in a world that has never limited my options. . . . Also, the feelings of hate the Whites have for Bigger is incomprehensible for me.

SUCCESSES STUDENTS REPORTED AS THEY APPLIED THE READER RESPONSE LENS TO NATIVE SON

> The reader response lens seemed to be the most attractive to the text. I liked it because it was open-ended and I can use it to interpret *Native Son* as I wanted to.

> The reader response lens seems to be the most consistent with the intention of the novel. Richard Wright is a Black man who writes about Blacks' points of view for White people. The Blacks already know what he is trying to say; it is the White people he is trying to make an impact on. He wants his White audience to think about their own lives and do the best they can to try to relate to the Blacks.

> It seems that with the novel, as with any work of art, the artist (author) is most interested in the individual effect each reader experiences. Hence, it seems logical that the lens most consistent with Wright's intention would be reader response, gauging what one has personally gained from reading the novel.

TOWARD A SOLUTION: MULTIPLE VISIONS AND THE NAMING OF PARTS

The reader response movement was a friendly antidote to the tyranny of the text that characterized some of our earlier approaches to the teaching of literature. It provided students with a way to engage personally with literature, opened up the possibility of multiple interpretations of individual texts, and made our students the meaning-makers of texts. In fact, to some, the reader actually became more important than the author. But when reader response becomes not just *a* way, but *the* way, of reading texts, it is an ideology, regardless of how appealing it might be. We need to challenge the overly simplistic notion of the individual that has characterized our "pedagogy of personal experience." As I have argued in this chapter, we can do this by directly teaching the elements of reader response.

Martha's and Carolyn's classes demonstrated the value of making our reader response teaching more explicit. In addition, we've seen that by recontextualizing reader response within a multiple-theoretical framework, we can create a critical and comparative context that can help us use what is best about the lens of reader response and, at the same time, guard against its excesses by not having it be the only way we encourage students to respond to texts.

Martha's students did indeed consider their reading of *Native Son* from a reader response perspective, but they did so as they concurrently considered three other theoretical perspectives—Marxist/social-class, feminist/gender, and biographical/historical criticism. The students considered the viability of those other perspectives as well as their relative effectiveness in helping them make sense of the text. This multiple-theoretical or comparative perspective can help keep our practice from veering into dogma. The next two chapters deal with the social-class and gender lenses and how they can contribute to the larger systems that are at play as we read texts and learn to interpret our world through critical encounters.

CHAPTER 4

What's Class Got to Do with It? Reading Literature Through the Lens of Privilege and Social Class

It is *not* that we shouldn't care about individual students and texts. We should, and I do. We also recognize, however, that students and texts are embedded in huge, living, sometimes contradictory networks, and if we want students to understand the workings of textuality, then we have to think about those larger systems.

—Bruce Pirie, *Reshaping High School English*

There is, in fact, no need to drag politics into literary theory; as with South African sport, it has been there from the beginning. I mean by the political no more than the way we organize our social life together and the power relations which this involves.

—Terry Eagleton, *Literary Theory*

The Philosophers have only interpreted the world in various ways; the point is to change it.

—Karl Marx

A THEORY BY ANY OTHER NAME?

In the past few years, many teachers who are eager to invite students to consider the ideological underpinnings of class in both texts and their lives have been reluctant to introduce the Marxist lens, so named. Some schools may confuse the introduction of Marxist literary theory with the practice or indoctrination of Communism, and teachers may receive negative reactions from parents, community members, administrators, and other teachers. Indeed, discussing the differences between Marxism and Marxist literary theory is a difficult but necessary element to introducing students to this critical lens. Those discussions may indeed help diffuse some community resistance. On the other hand, that very resistance may be the strongest proof that we need the vision the Marxist lens provides to read our ideologies and to teach our students of literature to do the same, regardless of what we call it. While one might be tempted to suggest that it is precisely that kind of timidity that teaching with theory is designed to combat, it would be cavalier and unfair to underestimate the political pressure that is brought to bear on teachers, or the degree to which certain terminology can imperil an innovative curriculum.

So, after conferring with dozens of teachers across the country, I will refer to *the Marxist lens* as *the social-class* lens for the rest of the book. Given the broad range of critics and scholars who do this work, I think it is a fair expansion and hope that theoretical purists will forgive this generalizing move. As one 10th grader put it, "you could call it the who's-got-the-cheese lens and we think we'd know what you mean." In places within the chapter, especially when quoting the works of others or quoting student-teacher interactions in the past, the term *Marxist literary theory* will appear as well.

WHY DO WE NEED SOCIAL-CLASS LENSES?

While the study of literature in the secondary schools has shuttled somewhat uneasily between text-centered and reader-centered approaches (Applebee, 1993), cultural studies and political approaches to the teaching of literature have moved through our profession like a brush fire. At many colleges and universities, the inclusion of social-class and gender lenses (see Chapter 5) has become the rule rather than the exception. In fact, some have been left to wonder whether the subject of English as we have known it is actually dead and whether we shouldn't rename our enterprise something like *cultural studies* (Boomer, 1988; Pirie, 1997).

Critical theory in college-level literary studies has become something of a lightning rod, a conduit of contention about our goals, purposes, and methods of teaching literature (Graff, 1992, 1995; Slevin & Young, 1996). For some, critical theory has energized a once staid and quaint field on the verge of becoming anachronistic. For others, cultural criticism and postmodern theories have drawn us away from what they believe should be at the center of our study—great books—and into a morass of subjectivity, relativity, and political correctness.

While most high school classrooms are clearly far removed from this frenzied state of affairs, more and more secondary teachers have begun to consider using social-class and gender lenses with the texts they teach. Slowly, yet palpably, more secondary teachers have recognized the potential richness and utility of introducing cultural criticism to their students and encouraging them to view literature through political prisms. Several new secondary literature textbooks have begun to include chapters on cultural criticism. For example, both Harper and Row and Prentice Hall have published anthologies that include chapters on criticism and literary theory (Guerin, Labor, Morgan, & Willingham, 1992; Guth & Rico, 1996). The 12th-grade level of the College Board's *Springboard* has an entire section on multiple perspectives. Holt, Reinhart and Winston's 2009 *Elements of*

Literature, Grades 6–12 includes a grade-appropriate strand of literary perspectives, including the "political" perspective. Further, high school teachers have begun with increasing frequency to adapt critical materials, such as *The Bedford Reader*, that are prepared for college students. This series provides commentary on such well-known works as *Heart of Darkness*, *Hamlet*, *The Tempest*, *Gulliver's Travels*, *The Secret Sharer*, and *Frankenstein* from a variety of critical perspectives, including psychological criticism, gender and social-class lenses, and reader response. It appears that the time may be right to encourage secondary teachers to integrate political literary theory into their literature instruction.

In some respects, there is a great deal of similarity between the social-class lens and the gender lens. Both are political, both interrogate textual features with considerations of power and oppression, and both invite us to consider the kinds of prevailing ideologies that construct the social realities in which we participate, sometimes unwittingly. However, the kinds of questions that are relevant to those lenses—as well as the texts, activities, and student responses to the lenses—differ significantly enough that I explore them in two separate chapters, this one and Chapter 5.

WHY TEACH THE SOCIAL-CLASS LENS NOW?

This is a particularly appropriate moment in the time line of literacy education to introduce the lens of social class into our classrooms. There are numerous reasons why this is so, among them our increasingly diverse literary canon as well as the changing nature of our students.

Our evolving canon has caused us to consider the cultural and historical factors inherent in looking at a work of literature. Teachers feel compelled to teach background knowledge, including cultural and historical aspects, especially when dealing with multicultural literature. Faced with new literary and cultural territory, teachers find themselves rethinking their approaches to literary texts (Desai, 1997). For example, they may find themselves considering particular aspects of the political content of the text, the author, and the historical and sociocultural context of the work. They may also find themselves thinking about how their students as readers are situated culturally, politically, and personally in relation to the content of the text (Willis, 1997).

Of course, as new historical critics might assert, one could argue that these careful contextual considerations are relevant for all works of literature. Yet when teaching multicultural literature, teachers seem to have a more acute need to fill in their own knowledge and provide the context for their students. Many teachers express discomfort or a kind of insecurity that springs from their unfamiliarity with the cultural background of the author, the issues that underlie the text, or even the structure of the narrative itself in cases such as Morrison's *Beloved* or

Silko's *Ceremony*. This quest for additional knowledge helps set the stage for cultural criticism or for political/social-class and gender lenses.

Besides our evolving and more inclusive literary canon, the increasing diversity of our students, even in primarily White suburban school districts, underscores our need to integrate cultural criticism into our literary study. In classrooms across the country, teachers have been called upon to heed the different cultural backgrounds of their students and to anticipate how those differences may come to bear on the reading of the literary texts they choose to teach, be they canonical or multicultural. As we acknowledge the diverse backgrounds and perspectives of the students who will read and discuss literary texts together, we might also acknowledge the need to consider particular issues of race and class deliberately and thoughtfully (Hines, 1997). In *Loose Canons: Notes on the Culture Wars*, Henry Louis Gates Jr. (1992) argues that race *is* a meaningful category in literary studies and the shaping of critical theory. He writes:

> Ours is a late twentieth-century world profoundly fissured by nationality, ethnicity, race, class, and gender. And the only way to transcend those divisions—to forge, for once, a civic culture that respects both differences and commonalities—is through education that seeks to comprehend the diversity of human culture. (p. xv)

For Gates, of course, that education is both a literary and a theoretical one that challenges the centrality of what he calls "our master's pieces" and urges us to consider "the politics of interpretation" as we encounter literature with our students.

This new knowledge is requisite not only for the reading and interpretation of literary texts but also for the development of a kind of classroom community in which students begin to understand each other and their perspectives (Hines, 1997). This kind of knowledge extends beyond the personal and anecdotal; it extends beyond the individual into the community. For students to be able to understand themselves and each other, they need to be able to contextualize their knowledge in terms larger than themselves; in other words, they need to be able to place their own particular situations and the texts they read into a larger system or set of beliefs. It is for precisely this reason that the particular lens of social class can be useful.

WHAT THE SOCIAL-CLASS LENS HELPS US SEE

The social-class lens offers several approaches for literature instruction. One approach is to consider the political context of the texts themselves. Gerry Graff presents the issue of the political content of texts in *Professing Literature* (1987) as well as in *Beyond the Culture Wars* (1992). He quotes George Orwell: "No book is genuinely free from political bias. The opinion that art should have nothing to do with politics is itself a political attitude" (Graff, 1992, p. 144). Graff and others argue that politics has always been inextricably woven into our literary tradition; like all art, it provides both a representation of ideology and a way to resist it.

Theory, then, helps us pose those political questions, thus reframing what it is we do when we read literature. Bonnycastle (1996), for example, advocates the use of Marxist literary theory because "it places the study of literature in the context of important social questions" (p. 199). This rationale has long been one aspect of what Applebee (1993, p. 3) calls our "competing traditions" in the teaching of literature. Engagement in important ideas or social issues has clearly been a goal that has shaped our canon, curriculum, and classroom practice. Political lenses such as social class and gender ask us to interrogate rather than simply acknowledge the texts that are part of our cultural heritage.

Using this perspective, students can consider the issues presented in the text through the lens of the prevailing ideologies of the author's political and historical context. For example, in reading *Of Mice and Men* or *The Grapes of Wrath*, students might consider the plight of migrant workers, the motives of John Steinbeck as muckraker, and even Tom Joad as an emblem of the pursuit of freedom (Greene, 1988, p. 49). The lens of social class may make possible such readings as the following:

- "The depiction of the sterility of European bourgeois capitalism in the early twentieth century in T. S. Eliot's 'The Wasteland'" (Bonnycastle, 1996, p. 202)
- The axis (centrality) of class in the worlds portrayed in the novels of Jane Austen or the Brontës
- The plight of African Americans as seen through the eyes of Bigger Thomas in Richard Wright's *Native Son*, and Wright's eventual indictment of American society as racist.

In addition to examining the political content of texts, the lens of social class also encourages students to consider the ways in which literary texts and the reading audiences for those texts—including themselves, their classmates, and their teachers—are socially constructed. As McCormick (1995) argues, using culturally situated theories such as the lens of social class is important

> so students can see that they, as readers, are socially constructed subjects, that texts are also constructed in particular social contexts—which may be quite different from their own and which they may need to study—and that different ways of telling stories have consequences. (p. 307)

Pirie (1997) also underscores the importance of students' awareness of audience construction and the role that theories such as those concerning social class and gender can play in facilitating that awareness:

> For any text we can ask students what kind of ideal audience is being constructed. Who does this story think its readers are? Who would it like them to be? What does it assume about the reader's attitudes, values, and prejudices and about the best ways of trying to change those attitudes? Or is it trying to change the reader at all? We can then compare our responses as actual audiences: Do we willingly allow the text to construct us in the shape of its ideal reader, or do we find ourselves resisting at some points? Should we? Marxist/social class and feminist/gender critics have for some time enacted the possibility of audience resistance by constructing readings that expose and critique the ideologies of canonical works, but this form of reading is still uncommon in high school literature classes. (p. 30)

Mary Beth Hines (1997, p. 129) quotes a college teacher who uses social class and other forms of cultural criticism to promote his pedagogical priorities of social justice: "I want to stress that the text is a social construction, and if it's a social construction, then who constructed it, what's it doing, and what are the mechanisms that are at work here." This notion of construction is a central element of students' ability to learn to read and interpret literature, to read both resonantly and resistantly (Wolf, 1988).

It is not only the political content of the texts themselves or the ways in which audiences are constructed by those texts that can be read through the lens of social class; these theories make visible the idea that literature itself is a part of ideology. Bonnycastle (1996) writes, "A further role of Marxist [social class] criticism is that of pointing out and documenting the way in which literature and 'the literary' function as a part of ideology" (p. 203). He claims, "Theory is subversive because it puts authority in question. . . . It means that no authority can impose a 'truth' on you in a dogmatic way—and if some authority does try, you can challenge that truth in a powerful way, by asking what ideology it is based on" (p. 34).

Selden (1989) explains Terry Eagleton's assertion of the relationship between literature and ideology this way:

> The text may appear to be free in its relation to reality (it can invent characters and situations at will), but it is not free in its use of ideology. Ideology here refers not only to conscious political doctrines but to all those systems of representation which shape the individual's mental picture of lived experience. The meanings and perceptions produced in the text are a reworking of ideology's own working of reality. (p. 42)

In response to William Bennett, Henry Louis Gates Jr. (1992, p. 35) writes, "the teaching of literature *is* the teaching of values; not inherently, no, but contingently, yes; it is—it has become—the teaching of an aesthetic and political order in which no women or people of color were ever able to discover the reflection or representation of their images, or hear the resonances of their cultural voices."

Secondary teachers can use the lens of social class to help bring into greater visibility the issues of power, class, ideology, and resistance that are embedded in the texts they read with their students. When paired with canonical texts, the lens of social class can be especially useful in revitalizing texts that seem tired or anachronistic. This is in part what Graff (1992) refers to in his now famous argument on "How to Save Dover Beach": "I concluded in my *Harper*'s essay that the best way to rescue poems like 'Dover Beach' was not to try to protect them from the critical controversies about their value, but to use those controversies to give them new life" (Graff in Slevin and Young, 1996, p. 133). The lens of social class can help shape that debate, whether it centers on the literary merit of the text itself, on reading the text politically, or on recognizing the text as a cultural construction or part of our overarching ideology.

In the following section a secondary teacher uses the lens of social class with *Hamlet* to encourage students to consider ideology and social power they read literary texts.

READING *HAMLET* THROUGH THE LENS OF SOCIAL CLASS; OR, WHY DO THE GRAVEDIGGERS SEEM TO KNOW MORE ABOUT LIFE THAN ANYONE?

In a suburban classroom, where the student parking lot is filled with cars far nicer than those their teachers are driving, an AP English class is studying *Hamlet*. With few exceptions, the students in this class have lives that are privileged and full of possibilities. Nearly all these students, sons and daughters of white-collar professionals, will go to college. They think nothing of dropping hundreds of dollars on prom night. They are the envy of the rest of the students in the school: the beautiful people—smart, popular, and affluent. They're basically good kids, motivated learners, and engaged students, but they hardly ever think beyond the boundaries of their own comfortable world.

Michael, their teacher, has ambitious goals. He wants to engage his students in great literature. He wants to teach a college prep English course rigorous enough to help his students sail through the year-end AP test. He wants to help his students create some provocative links between Hamlet's world and their own, links that extend beyond the connections of personal response, as powerful as those responses might sometimes be. Somewhat hesitantly Michael explains, "I've always worked on getting kids to respond to whatever we read on a personal level, to relate to the characters and their situations by thinking of similar situations of their own, to find a way into the text through their own personal experience. But lately I've been thinking, I don't know, more politically. I want my students to think about the worlds these texts both represent and invoke. I want them to think about what set of beliefs drive these characters and, in some cases, help seal their fate. I want them to think about the author's relationship to those sets of beliefs. I think I sometimes forget to help them see the big picture. And lately, I've been doing all this reading on contemporary criticism and I found myself thinking that these suburban kids never talk about class or privilege, even though, or maybe because, they're surrounded by it. So, I thought I'd try the social-class/Marxist lens with *Hamlet* this time and see what happens."

On a drab winter morning colored only by the bright blue classroom carpeting and a bulletin board full of senior class pictures, Michael begins class by asking his students to consider the role of power in *Hamlet*. "What kinds of power do you see operating in the play?" asks Michael. There is a cacophony of response.

"Power about who rules."

"Power about who's king."

"Power about property."

"Power over other people's lives, like Rosencrantz and Guildenstern."

"Power over whether certain countries go to war and who gets to fight them."

"Personal power. Like Hamlet over Ophelia."

"Okay. Let's think about power in a particular way today," says Michael, "who's got it, who doesn't, and why. And let's think about where power comes from, both now and in Shakespeare's time. I understand that some of you took Russian history with Mr. Murphy last semester. What can you guys tell me about Karl Marx?"

"Father of Communism?"

"Power to the proletariat!"

"What's the proletariat?"

"Power to the people!"

"Same thing!"

Michael distributes a handout titled "Key Ideas of Marx" (see Appendix, Activity 12) and quickly reviews it with the students. In addition to Marx's beliefs about the stages of history and dialectical materialism, the class discusses capitalism, class struggle, working-class misery, and class consciousness. Then Michael says, "In addition to the Marxism we've been talking about, there is also something called Marxist literary theory. Marxist literary theory is a kind of political lens through which we can read works of literature. Marxist literary theory asks us to consider the social structures that are portrayed in a particular work and how power is allocated among different social groups. Many Marxist critics believe that we cannot understand individual people or literary characters or even authors without understanding their social positions and the larger systems in which those social positions operate. Marxist literary theory also asks us to notice in the texts we read what is revealed as the dominant view of the world, a prevailing set of beliefs, or ideologies. What are some ideologies or sets of beliefs that you've come across?"

"Freedom of speech."

"Equality."

"Democracy."

"How the world was created. I think there are a bunch of ideologies about that!"

"Anyone can succeed if they try hard enough."

"That's crap."

Michael smiles and says, "Hmmm. We'll be getting to that later. Now what seems to be the prevailing ideology or ideologies that operate in the world of *Hamlet*?"

"The divine right of kings."

"That women are powerless."

"Yeah, they couldn't even play themselves."

"We are born into our lot in life."

"Royalty are better than other people and have the right to rule other people."

"Gravediggers have a much different view of the world from the bottom than Claudius does from the top."

"Great, Alex. You bring me to my next question. Aren't we in some way thinking about society as a social ladder, kinda like we do with things here at this school? Take a look at this." Michael then distributes a handout titled "Reading *Hamlet* Through the Marxist/Social-Class Lens" (see Appendix, Activity 13). He directs them to a drawing of a "social ladder." Then, after a spirited discussion about the social ladder of their particularly cliquish school, the students consider the social ladder of the play. Michael designed a vertical diagram to demonstrate graphically the existence of hierarchy—something that is important not only in the discussion of Marxism/social class but also in laying a conceptual foundation for a discussion of patriarchy, which will come during a discussion of gender that Michael has already begun to think about (see Appendix, Activity 13).

Michael next asks his students to consider pairs of characters in terms of who has power and who does not. He asks students to indicate which of the sets of power struggles they listed might be considered class conflicts. Michael wants his suburban students to be able to read the text with a heightened awareness of class and privilege—their own and the characters'. He encourages his students to examine the agency of social class in the play as well as in their reading of it. In fact, when they are asked to consider where they would situate themselves relative to issues of power, their responses are telling. Michael asks students to place a mark on a concentric-circle graph that indicates where they are in relation to the center of money and power. There are five concentric rings: Number 1 is the closest to the center of power and money, and 5 is the most distant (see Appendix, Activity 13).

More than 75% of the students place themselves in the second or third circle closest to the center of money and power. One student places himself in the fourth circle and one places herself in the fifth circle, the one farthest from the center of power. By contrast, one student actually places himself right in the center!

Even though Michael carefully constructed this part of the activity so that students would reflect privately on their own economic status, his usually compliant students seem a bit uncomfortable with this exercise; in fact, some are overtly hostile. "What does our social status have to do with reading *Hamlet*?" asks Tim, an Ayn Rand fan. "Social status isn't that important. People make too much of it. And besides, Marx wasn't born until after Shakespeare died, I mean, like, way after? Marxism wasn't around then. So, how can we use it to read the play?"

Michael isn't quite prepared for this resistance. He finds himself challenged and feels even more strongly about the importance of pursuing this line of inquiry. He asks his students to try to consider how issues of class might have affected their reading of *Hamlet*. He also asks them, "What characters in *Hamlet* do you feel most closely represent where you are socially?"

The student responses are varied. They struggle desperately to discover a Shakespearean middle or upper-middle class, one that would mirror their own location. Many students think that characters such as Laertes, Polonius, Horatio, and Ophelia somehow make up that middle class:

> I am an average middle-class person. Closest to Ophelia.

> Polonius and his family. I guess they were right in the middle.

For the students, the middle class represents people with some resources and power but also with a reasonable perspective that neither royalty nor the lower class seems to possess. These middle-class characters, according to the students, allow them to understand both groups—those who are more and those who are less fortunate than they. It is clear that students feel that this is a perspective they have, not only on the characters in the play but also on their own lives:

> I think being in the middle of things, I can be pretty open-minded about the class structure on the whole.

> Being in between having the power and having no power, I am able to sympathize with all groups.

Many students express affinity for Horatio—neither rich nor poor; not quite a commoner, not quite royalty—a sort of Everyman with class:

> I'm like Horatio. Being in the middle, it's easier to be unbiased. I can see both ends of the spectrum—those with money and power and those without.

> Horatio seems most like me. He's in the middle of the ladder but sort of near the top.

> I identify with Horatio a great deal. He is involved with the upper class but not because he's vying for a place in circle number 1. He focuses on his friends, not on their social and economic worth.

This "Horatio affinity" characterizes the responses of most of the class, both in character identification as well as in economic identification. Students seem comfortable marking themselves as being close to power through either money or friends, like Horatio, but not totally within the epicenter of the prevailing power structure, like Hamlet.

While most of this suburban AP class is solidly middle to upper-middle class, there are a few students whose social status is quite different from that of their more wealthy classmates. These students marked the fourth and fifth circle out from the center of power and seemed eager to claim affinity for a different set of characters as well as to announce their less fortunate economic status:

> I have more in common with the lower social characters; I root for the underdog.

> Probably the lower-class servants. They have to work pretty hard and can't advance right now anyway because of circumstances. I live with my mom because my parents were recently divorced and there is no child support coming.

Interestingly, many female students felt they related most closely to Ophelia. For them, issues of gender seem to be more salient than issues of class. A few noted the conflation of gender and class. Here are a few illustrative comments:

> I feel closest to Ophelia because although she is high class (because of family, like me), she is a woman and doesn't get much consideration for her own well-being.

> I probably feel I am most closely represented by Ophelia. Ophelia is one of the few females in the book and she does not have a lot of power, money; but she's not near the bottom of the social scale.

And, of course, several students unabashedly related most to Hamlet. These students (all male) self-identified in either the second or the first circle of power and privilege:

> It may sound egotistical, but it is hard not to identify, at least a little bit, with Hamlet.

> Hamlet is the character that I most identify with, since his positions and responsibility force him to distance himself socially.
>
> I *am* Hamlet. I am not going to be king, but how Hamlet thinks and acts I can definitely relate to.

Many students reported that they had never seriously considered issues of class before and didn't feel that issues of power and class affected their reading of *Hamlet*. These students seemed almost offended by or apologetic about the suggestion that considerations of power and privilege might have affected their reading:

> If my social status affected my interpretation of *Hamlet* in any way, I honestly was not aware of it.
>
> I really did not feel like it affected anything.
>
> When I read *Hamlet*, I did not feel the class struggle applied to me in my life.

In summary, most students reported that issues of power and class clearly affected their response to the play, though they might not have been aware of it as they read. These students crossed all divisions of class—some saying that it affected their reading because they had power, some saying that considerations of status affected their reading precisely because they did not have power, and some who were in that middle "Horatio" position.

THE BIG QUESTIONS

> Marxist literary theory [the social-class lens] encourages us to look at big questions, and it has developed impressive tools for doing that. The main use of Marxism in literary studies rests in adapting those methods, especially those dealing with ideology, to help us talk about and resolve the smaller problems, which occupy most of us most of the time.
>
> —Stephen Bonnycastle, *In Search of Authority*

For the most part, Michael felt he had accomplished a good deal by having his students try on the Marxist/social-class lens, in however simplistic a version. He and the students had discussed the concept of ideology and read the text for evidence of it. They had discussed power and class structure in terms of how it affected the characters and the play and considered the characters not simply as individuals but as players in a large social and economic system. Michael also felt that students had, for perhaps the first time, considered their own social status and had explored the possibility that their own position in the prevailing social structure may have influenced their reading of the text as well as the level of affinity they felt for any particular character. Finally, Michael felt that reading *Hamlet* through the Marxist/social-class lens had enabled students to do precisely what Bonnycastle claims Marxism is particularly good at doing—encouraging us to ask both the big and the small questions. On the last question of the Marxist/social-class lens handout (see Appendix, Activity 13), Michael asked his students to think of such large and small questions grounded in the Marxist/social-class lens. He encouraged them to think of some questions that were concerned with the world of the text and questions that concerned them on a more personal level. Michael was gratified by the range and depth of questions and by the evidence that they had actually been peering at *Hamlet*, and at themselves, through the Marxist/social-class lens. Here are some of their questions:

ABOUT THE TEXT

- Is having so much power good for human nature?
- If Ophelia was so high up, why was her only point in the story to go crazy?
- Do women really have any power—even in the highest classes?
- Why does Hamlet feel he can dismiss the lives of Rosencrantz and Guildenstern?
- Why is it that the gravediggers seem to know more about life than anyone?

ABOUT THEMSELVES

- Why can the middle class be fooled so easily by the upper class? Does the upper class have the right to use the underclass like they do? Does social position justify treating someone as if they are inferior?
- Does power mean you can do anything, even if it's illegal?
- Are all people created equal? Darwinian evolution suggests they are not. By resisting class differences does one destroy human nature?
- Why should society be based on rank? Are you a better person because you have power or money?

As he and his students discussed these questions, Michael knew that the social-class lens enriched and complicated their reading of *Hamlet* and highlighted some details that might not have otherwise been heeded. He was glad that, in addition to the personal-response strategies and the textual and new critical strategies they brought into the class with them, they now had social-class literary theory as part of their interpretive repertoire, or tool kit.

CHALLENGES IN TEACHING THE SOCIAL-CLASS LENS

Teaching social-class literary theory in secondary schools is a complicated enterprise. Some students may be resistant to the whole notion of the social-class lens. As one student wrote in response to the Marxist handout, "I found this question to be offensive and pointless. My perception allows me to imagine myself at any point in the circle." Another said, "The social ladder is an arbitrary construct and I don't choose to think of myself in those terms. Therefore, the question is meaningless." One student wrote, "Thinking about the Marxist ideology makes me realize how Marxism undermines morality. Morality consists in making choices that respect the rights of others. By focusing on class conflict, Marxism obliterates the idea of personal responsibility and implies that any action is justified to help one win the class conflict, and thus no morality is possible." As Bonnycastle (1996) points out:

> There is an unconscious hostility to some Marxist ideas in most students, especially if they are consciously trying to "improve themselves." One way to measure how you are improving is to see how you are rising on the social scale; and if you feel you have moved yourself up to a new level, that is a clear indication of success. But this measuring stick entails a class system, with many of the unattractive features inherent in such a system, such as competition and the victory of the winner paid for by the suffering of the loser. (p. 200)

It is difficult for all of us, and especially for students, to critique and resist the prevailing ideology as we participate in it. Many of the students in Michael's suburban AP class found this perspective to be alienating and uncomfortable. And yet it was this very discomfort and students' obliviousness of their location in educational and economic privilege that contributed to Michael's desire to introduce them to the social-class lens.

In addition to applying it in this lesson on *Hamlet*, we used the lens of social class with *The Great Gatsby* (see Appendix, Activity 14) and with the powerful Sharon Olds poem "On the Subway" (see Chapter 8 and Appendix, Activity 24). In each case, students found that the direct consideration of class and power significantly enhanced their interpretation of the texts. In each case the prism of social class seemed to invite students into the central issues raised by each text. And in each case students were also encouraged to view the text from other perspectives, thus decreasing the likelihood that teachers would be perceived to be privileging one particular political perspective or reading over another.

Now let us turn to another political prism, the gender lens. It too encourages us, as Bonnycastle (1996, p. 205) said, to name and resist ideology, and to "look at the big questions," which in this case, are the "questions" of gender as they relate to the reading and interpretation of literary texts.

CHAPTER 5

The Social Construction of Gender: A Lens of One's Own

> The study of gender, within literature, is of general importance to everyone.
>
> —Judith Spector

> We don't know what women's vision is. What do women's eyes see? How do they carve, invent, decipher the world? I don't know. I know my own vision, the vision of one woman, but the world seen through the eyes of others? I only know what men's eyes see.
>
> —Viviane Forrester, *New French Feminisms*

> I have a male mind with male experiences. Therefore I see things through the perception of a man. I couldn't relate to some of Virginia Woolf's views and I despised the way she pushed her viewpoint on the reader. This was brought on by my masculinity, I feel.
>
> —Bill, Grade 12, after reading *A Room of One's Own*

> Being a feminist is not a gender-specific role.
>
> —Erin, Grade 11

Martha's 2nd-hour 11th-grade literature class is reading *Death of a Salesman.* In previous classes they've discussed the contemporary literary tool called the feminist lens, and frankly, they're a bit wary. The boys generally groan, steeling themselves for what they assume is another session of male-bashing. The girls seem astonishingly anachronistic in their positions toward feminism. Many of them make disparaging comments about militant females who hate men. They seem to reflexively equate feminism with unfemininity. Their attitudes sometimes provide a roadblock to productive conversations about literature. Still, Martha views their collective reluctance to discuss the feminist lens as all the more reason for them to do so. She realizes that her students evoke socially sanctioned and reified constructions of gender, constructions that can hold them hostage, in adolescence and beyond, to limiting social expectations of behavior.

"I'm tired of this feminist lens backlash," Martha says to me. "I wonder what would happen if we focused on the issue of gender." "Feminism does focus on the issue of gender," I reply in a slightly exasperated tone. "I know," Martha says conspiratorially, "but let's see what happens if we call it gender." "Okay," I say, remembering all the times teachers have made this very suggestion to me. "Let's give it a try," I agree.

We begin by offering the following explanation to our students: "Our ability to assign gender to words or constructs has to do with what some people call the social construction of gender. Using the feminist lens is one way to examine gender construction, but the notion of the social construction of gender broadens the lens to more fully consider how both men and women are affected by this social construction." We give the students a handout beginning with a series of words (see Appendix, Activity 18): *fashion, football, breadwinner, pilot, strength, flower, ambitious, perseverance, compassionate, bossy, helpless, thoughtful, soft, brassy, dangerous, perpetrator, victim, attractive, opinionated, hostile, emotional.*

We then tell the students, "Using your first instinct and without overthinking, write each word in the table column that seems most appropriate." The students work on their table:

Male	Female	Both	Neither

They scribble furiously, sometimes bursting out in giggles. The results of this simple and seemingly benign exercise were astonishing (see Figure 5.1). While there was some bleeding between categories with words such as *attractive*, there were other examples of gendered constructions. For example, not a single student categorized the words *emotional*, *victim*, or *thoughtful* as male. Not a single student categorized the words *pilot*, *football*, or *perpetrator* as female.

"Whoa, this was too easy," Scott says. "I agree," echoes Leah. "I didn't realize these categories were so fixed in my mind."

Indeed!

WHY TEACH GENDER/FEMINIST THEORY NOW?

Viviane Forrester's (1980) acknowledgment of the dominance of men's vision, or "what men's eyes' see," provides an explicit rationale for teaching contemporary feminist/gender literary theory to adolescents. Throughout this chapter, I will

Figure 5.1. Students' Assessment of Gender Traits

Death of a Salesman **and the Social Construction of Gender**

Word Options	*Male*	*Female*	*Both*	*Neither*
Fashion	0	33	4	0
Football	38	0	0	0
Breadwinner	10	2	20	3
Pilot	24	0	12	0
Strength	27	1	11	0
Flower	0	36	0	2
Ambitious	3	1	31	3
Perseverance	2	2	31	5
Compassionate	1	23	12	1
Bossy	5	12	18	2
Helpless	1	11	3	21
Thoughtful	0	10	22	4
Soft	1	25	4	8
Brassy	12	4	1	17
Dangerous	19	0	9	9
Perpetrator	15	0	4	13
Victim	0	17	13	6
Attractive	2	18	18	0
Opinionated	3	11	24	0
Hostile	10	2	11	13
Emotional	0	27	8	0

be using the terms *gender* and *feminist theory* interchangeably. While theoretical purists may rightfully object to the renaming, the change seems consistent with the calls of feminist theorists in the past 15 years to make certain that feminist theory is not limited to only women writers or women's experiences. As Nelly Furman (1988) writes,

> Since, for the textual reader, literature is not a representation of experience but something that is experienced, from a feminist viewpoint the question is not whether a literary work has been written by a woman and reflects her experience of life, or

> how it compares to other works by women, but rather how it lends itself to be read from a feminist position. (p. 69)

Gender theory provides us with a way of recognizing and naming other visions while promoting our own ways of seeing. It helps us recognize the essential quality of other visions: how they shape and inform the way we read texts, how we respond to others, how we live our lives. Theory makes the invisible visible, the unsaid said.

Theory asks us to treat the text and our responses to it as cultural objects. Rather than removing us farther from the world, feminist/gender theory asks us to invoke our world as we read, interpret, and evaluate texts. As Eagleton (1983) remarks,

> Literature, we are told, is vitally engaged with the living situations of men and women; it is concrete rather than abstract, displays life in all its rich variousness, and rejects barren conceptual enquiry for the feel and taste of what it is to be alive. (p. 196)

Feminist/gender literary theory invites us to consider a wide variety of issues of gender, of "the living situations" of men and women as we read. Feminist/gender literary theory asks us to attend to the cultural imprint of patriarchy as we read. We do this by heeding features of language, of canon formation and transformation, of the nuanced voices of female and male writers, and of the portrayal of masculine and feminine experience. As noted critic Sydney Kaplan (2000) explains:

> I desperately needed a method of study that might help me shape my life and extricate it from the patriarchal forces I confronted both at home and in the university. I quickly discovered that I could explore the issues that many of my contemporaries were approaching through consciousness-raising by transferring the formalist methods I was learning in class to texts that had personal meaning for me—texts by women writers. Yet, I should emphasize that this early work, contrary to some of the myths about the evolution of feminist criticism, neither focused on a critique of male writing nor was part of the "images of women" genre. It was *already* concerned with the intersections of literary form and the structure of gender relations—with how literary conventions embodied societal values and unconscious levels of ideology; in other words, it was, from the outset, a cultural critique. (pp. 1167–1170)

As Kaplan points out, theory attempts to capture the complexities of human existence as it is portrayed in literary texts. In Bruce Pirie's (1997, p. 97) recent plea to shift our notion of literary studies to a broader vision of cultural studies, he calls for a high school literature program that would "treat texts as constructions within intertextual webs, sponsored by institutions and interacting with audiences and would also encourage a study of our own situation as readers." Political literary theories such as those of gender and social class require readers to ask questions about the construction of culture, of texts, and of meaning as they seek to construct their own interpretations.

There are, of course, as many "feminisms" as there are "Marxisms," and it is easy for both teachers and students to become confused about feminist/gender theory, or even feminism, for that matter. As Elaine Showalter writes, "Not even feminist critics seem to agree what it is they mean to profess and defend" (Showalter, 1989, p. 169). Two of the classroom activities in the Appendix (Activities 15, 17) reflect a working definition of feminism. In true feminist tradition, the definition continues to evolve.

As with Marxist (social class) criticism, the point of reading with feminist (gender) theory, of course, isn't to transform unsuspecting and largely apolitical high school students into feminists (or Marxists); the point is to help adolescent readers read texts and worlds more carefully as they become aware of the ideologies within which both are inscribed. Bonnycastle (1996, p. 194) writes, "Feminist literary criticism has a political and moral dimension. It doesn't need to be revolutionary, but, like Marxism, it does aim at changing the world and the consciousness of people in the world."

Like the Marxist theories we discussed in Chapter 4, feminist/gender theory provides a lens through which students can interpret literature and life. As students read and interpret literary texts, feminist theory can help them to notice salient issues of gender—the portrayal of women in the world of the novel, the gender of the author and what relevance it may bear on how the work is both written and received, the ways in which the text embraces or confronts prevailing ideologies of how men and women are situated in the "real world," and the ways in which our own interpretations as individual readers are gendered.

WHAT STUDENTS CAN SEE WITH FEMINIST/GENDER THEORY

There are at least four dimensions in which using feminist theory can transform students' reading—how students view female characters and appraise the author's stance toward those characters; how students evaluate the significance of the gender of the author in terms of its influence on a particular literary work; how students interpret whole texts within a feminist framework; and finally, and perhaps most important, how students read the gendered patterns in the world. To explore how feminist theory can inform the literary experience of adolescents, I developed some activities to use with a variety of texts. Working with teachers in both urban and suburban classrooms, I introduced students to the feminist/gender lens and chronicled their attempts to adopt gendered considerations of texts, of authors, of characters, of themselves as readers, and of the world around them. Four of these literary transactions follow.

1. What Color Are Your Walls? Changing the Way We View Female Characters

One way the feminist/gender lens can inform how students make meaning of texts is by refocusing their reading of female characters. As some feminist critics assert

(Showalter, 1985), readers should learn to recognize what happens to female characters under the "male gaze" of authors. How does the fictional portrayal of female characters reflect the reality of women's lives? How does the creation of female characters reinforce or resist certain social attitudes toward women? And finally, how are we as readers implicated in what is essentially a gendered act as we read and interpret the lives of women who people the pages of the works of literature we read?

In previous work (Appleman, 1993), I illustrated how students' interpretive vision adapted easily to the lens of feminism as they considered characters from *Of Mice and Men*, *Ordinary People*, and *The Great Gatsby*. We asked students to make traditional descriptions of these female characters and then to make a different sort of statement in light of our discussion of feminist theory. Here are some of the resulting examples:

CURLEY'S WIFE

Traditional Statement: She was a bad girl, a tease, and a flirt.

Feminist Statement: She's just been treated poorly by her horrible, selfish, chauvinistic husband. She is not bad.

BETH

Traditional Statement: She's the great American bitch.

Feminist Statement: She's a repressed woman who is trapped by society's expectations of what a wife and mother should be.

DAISY

Traditional Statement: She was a "beautiful little fool" who depended on her husband to take care of her.

Feminist Statement: Her husband took control of her and wouldn't let her think for herself. She was doing her best within the limits of women's role in society.

I decided to explore feminist theory with Martha Hargrove's students, who had just finished reading *Hamlet*. (We met Martha in Chapter 3 as she introduced her 12th-grade students to multiple critical approaches to *Native Son*. We'll spend yet more time with her in Chapter 7.)

As part of our introduction to the feminist lens and as part of our larger purpose of demonstrating that different classical or canonical texts can be viewed from more than one theoretical perspective, we asked students to read Gertrude and Ophelia through a feminist lens. Note that these students had already considered *Hamlet* from a Marxist/social-class perspective (see Chapter 4). In addition to encouraging multiple perspectives, we wanted to emphasize the intertextual nature of interpretation. That is, a critical lens is not an artifact of interpretation suitable to only a particular text but rather is a flexible tool that can be used with a variety of texts.

After a brief explication of the feminist lens (see Appendix, Activity 16), we asked students to consider Gertrude and Ophelia from the perspective of the feminist lens and to contrast that with statements using a "traditional" perspective, one that didn't consciously incorporate any considerations of gender into its interpretation. Here are some of the resulting descriptions:

GERTRUDE

Traditional Statements:

She is an adequate woman of the times, and she plays her role of loyalty and servitude toward the men in her family.
Gertrude is the queen who lost her husband and immediately married another.
Wife of two kings.
She is a queen who lives how she wants to live.

Feminist Statements:

She is more of a plot device than of thematic importance herself.
She's defined by her husbands and her son.
Despite the illusion of power, she is actually powerless. She is not allowed to advise on matters of importance but must be advised in all she does. She is not really trusted to take care of herself.

OPHELIA

Traditional Statements:

Sheltered and devoted to those who love her; always tries to please her family while following her heart.
Emotional, young, innocent, weak, fragile; she needs protection.
Ophelia was a girl of reasonable status in the kingdom which implanted a daring notion that she may someday marry the prince, Hamlet.

Feminist Statements:

Her feelings and identity have been repressed by the male figures in her life. When her father is killed, she is separated from that control and goes crazy with the release of her pent-up identity.

Trapped in her traditional role, she's always being told what to do by a man—her father, her brother, Hamlet.

Any woman of sound body and mind like Ophelia had, at least to begin with, should have the power and right to pursue life as she pleases without the restraint of society's rules and arranged marriages.

She is forced into insanity by the forces of the men in her life. All of her emotions depend on Hamlet's actions.

This exercise enabled students to cast two characters they already knew well in the light of a feminist interpretation. They seemed to be able do so with ease. The contrast of the traditional perspective with the feminist perspective helped underscore some of the more salient features of a feminist interpretation. In addition, it helped students exercise a kind of mental flexibility, one of the goals of the multiple-theoretical approach to literature advocated in this book. That is, rather than viewing things from a perspective that is rigid (or dualistic, as cognitive psychologist William Perry, 1970, might characterize it), students have the opportunity to develop a kind of theoretical pluralism from which they can consider characters from more than one point of view. Here is an incident from one of Martha's classes that reveals the students' ability to view female characters from the feminist perspective:

We are discussing Virginia Woolf's *A Room of One's Own* during first period. Ever since we began discussing the feminist lens and *A Room of One's Own*, there's been a kind of edge in the air, especially with the male students, who are outnumbered by the female students by almost two to one. Adam and Tom look even more bored and contemptuous of the day's activities than usual. Kevin, an outspoken member of the alternative-theater crowd, is sporting a new hair color (bright yellow) and seems particularly feisty.

"I'm, like, so over this Virginia Woolf," he says. "I think she goes way overboard; she overgeneralizes. She takes her argument too far, plus, she nitpicks."

Belinda asks, "What do you mean 'nitpicks' and 'overgeneralizes'? How can she be doing those two things at the same time?"

Kevin looks a bit taken aback. "She just takes things a bit too far."

"Like what?" Belinda persists. "Can you think of anything from the text?" (This kid has been well trained!)

"Like that part about Shakespeare," Kevin finally answers.

"What about it? Be specific." Belinda now seems to be doing a full-out imitation of her teacher.

"Well, you know. She says that Shakespeare writes for men and writes all these strong roles only for men. But in my opinion, when it comes right down to it, there are a lot of good women in Shakespeare. I mean, take Beatrice in *Much Ado About Nothing*, for example. I mean, need I say more? I mean, who could be a stronger role model than Beatrice? Didn't you just *admire* her? I mean, I did, and I'm a guy. Just think about Beatrice and you'll see. Virginia Woolf is wack," Kevin concludes with a flourish.

"Yeah, Beatrice *is* something," Belinda concedes. "You've got a point there."

This classroom episode is illustrative of the lively and engaged discourse that was fostered by the introduction of the feminist lens. In addition to being notable for the students' evocation of the lens, this episode is remarkable for the intertextual nature of the argument. That is, Kevin uses Shakespeare to support his point about Virginia Woolf. These students seem to be thoroughly in charge of their own interpretations. They use the feminist lens to cajole each other into reconsidering a character from another perspective. How encouraging to think that they may be able to view their peers, teachers, and families from other perspectives as well!

2. Changing the Way We View Texts, "Feminist" and Otherwise

Analyzing female characters is only one way the feminist lens can inform students' reading; the sociocultural context of texts can also be viewed through the feminist lens. This holistic view can illuminate classic texts, as it did in our reading of *Hamlet*, or more contemporary texts, as it did in our reading of *Native Son*. While the feminist lens can be fruitfully applied to any work of fiction, it may have different purposes when applied to texts that are authored by men and those that are by women. As Elaine Showalter (1989) points out:

> Feminist criticism can be divided into two distinct varieties. The first type is concerned with woman as reader—with woman as the consumer of male-produced literature and with the way in which the hypothesis of a female reader changes our apprehension of a given text, awakening us to the significance of its sexual codes. Its subjects include the images and stereotypes of women in literature, the omissions and misconceptions about women in criticism, and the fissures in male-constructed literary history. . . . The second type of feminist criticism is concerned with woman as writer—with woman as the producer of textual meaning, with the history, themes, genres, and structures of literature by women. (p. 170)

While the feminist lens can be used profitably with a number of texts, as I demonstrated with the re-rereading of *Hamlet*, *Native Son*, *The Great Gatsby*, and *Ordinary People*, among others, many feminist critics point to some seminal (excuse the expression) literary texts that serve as flashpoints for feminist scholarship and virtually demand a feminist reading. These include *The Awakening*, *A Room of One's Own*, "The Yellow Wallpaper," and "A Jury of Her Peers." (See Selected Literary Texts for a complete list of texts and authors.)

Whether to use these "feminist" texts or traditional texts in the teaching of the feminist/gender lens is an interesting question for teachers. Texts that, for the purpose of this discussion at least, I have labeled "feminist" help make the case to doubters or skeptics and broaden the discussion to larger considerations of women writers, women's ideology, and even whether there is such a thing as a "feminist text." On the other hand, the "eureka moments" of unexpectedly altered vision through the power of critical lenses can sometimes occur more dramatically with texts that don't seem "loaded" or predisposed to a feminist treatment. In this case, as in many others, I promote the notion of "both and" rather than "either or" and try to include several different kinds of texts as I help students peer through the feminist lens.

Two classic texts that deal directly with feminist issues are "The Yellow Wallpaper," by Charlotte Perkins Gilman, and *A Room of One's Own*, by Virginia Woolf. I have used both to introduce the feminist lens to high school students and offer both strategies and examples of student responses in the following section. While the previous lesson focused on student responses to female characters using the feminist lens, the following activity is a consideration of an entire text from the feminist perspective.

I introduce the idea of a whole-text interpretation by presenting a concrete poem (see Figure 5.2). This lesson gives students the opportunity to create an interpretation of an entire work with a contained and literally concrete text. It gives them an opportunity to interpret a text as a cultural object. In addition, students are asked to consider a text about which they have not been able to form any investment, defensiveness, or prior expectations. The students in small groups note some of the physical features of the poem, for example, the serpentlike *S* that makes *he* into *she*, the *h* for *Homo sapiens* and the *e* for *Eve*.

They then try to regard the lens from a feminist perspective in light of the basic tenets of the definition that they were given (see Appendix, Activities 15–18). In other words, they attend to features of gender, to what statements this poem might make about the relationship between the sexes, about the prominence of the letter *S* and the cultural encodings of the relationship between men and women. Here are some samples of the students' readings of this concrete poem:

> She is better than he because the *S* creates a more developed, more aesthetically pleasing he.
>
> She is encompassing he.

Figure 5.2. From "Epithalamium—II"

> Women are strong and bold but still bound by the central power of men. He is ever present inside a woman controlling all of her actions and thoughts. He is the center of she.

It's useful for students to see that they can disagree on the implications of a feminist reading of this poem—that is, for some it represents a feminist victory over male dominance; for others, it's just the opposite. Both interpretations rely on a feminist lens to provide meaning. Reading with theory doesn't necessarily lead one to particular conclusion about texts; it is not a prescription for dogma. Rather, it suggests a framework in which a variety of interpretations can be articulated. There is no one single feminist reading of a particular text, and this exercise seems to illustrate that plurality of possibility fairly well.

After students discuss this initial foray into "reading feminist" with the concrete poem, we move to a consideration of "The Yellow Wallpaper," which, for various reasons, is an important starting point for our exploration of the feminist lens. Annette Kolondy, for example, remarks on the significance of Charlotte Perkins Gilman's short story for feminist literary scholarship. First, "The Yellow Wallpaper" is an example of "previously lost or otherwise ignored works by women writers" (Kolondy in Showalter, 1989, p. 144) that have returned to circulation as a result of feminist literary scholarship. Originally published in 1892, Gilman's story was reprinted in 1973; in the ensuing years it has become something of a feminist sensation, widely anthologized and taught.

Kolondy remarks on the difficulty that Gilman faced in publishing her piece initially as well as on the resistance it met from readers after it finally saw print. Readers, as Kolondy points out, could easily have found resonances of Edgar Allen Poe's work in Gilman's. Yet they did not display the same willingness to follow the interior tour of the disturbed mind of Gilman's trapped protagonist as they apparently had Poe's counterparts. Kolondy views "The Yellow Wallpaper" as a kind of metacommentary on the sexual politics of literary reading and production. Kolondy points to the significance of the female protagonist, whose imagination is limited by her proscribed activities and confinement and whose experience as described in the text cannot be accurately read or interpreted by her male audience.

"The Yellow Wallpaper," then, presents multilayered aspects of feminist meaning. It seems, therefore, to be a natural place for students to use the feminist lens. As a follow-up to the reading of the concrete poem, I asked students to apply the feminist lens to write a brief analysis of the narrator in "The Yellow Wallpaper," her situation, and perhaps Gilman's intent in writing the piece. In addition, they were to consider Gilman's audience and, finally, what meaning(s) they derived from the text. Here are some of their resulting analyses:

> It shows the effects of the repression of woman's will by what men saw as care and protection. John won't allow her to write or care for her child,

> two important expressions of who she is, because he doesn't want her to get tired. She is the toy that can't be played with because it will decrease in value, that has no personal value because it can't be put to its use.
>
> Charlotte Perkins, it seemed, was writing for her own struggle. The woman was trapped within the wallpaper while maybe Perkins was trapped in her words, thoughts, and positions. The woman was trapped, and the expression in her writing presents the struggles with her husband as a "Nora" (from *A Doll's House*). They don't know her exact sickness or ailment but she is to stay in bed, cooped up to be better. But she needed to get out.
>
> This woman is treated as if she were no more important than the wallpaper. Her husband has no regard for her well-being because, as she states early in the journals, she hated the wallpaper. By her husband forcing her into that room, telling her she is okay, he metaphorically pushed her into the wallpaper, a nonexistence. I believe Perkins wrote this story to help the women see their helplessness and inability to control their own destiny, although most probably, though, Perkins was crazy.
>
> I would like to look at this through a mixture of lenses. In order to do this story justice, I must mix historical and feminist lenses. The feminist lens may show an idea of oppression, but the addition of the historical lens shows triumphant behavior. Around the time when this was written and many years after, women were controlled by their "male figures." These figures could be fathers, brothers, husbands, or even sons. By showing how she is able to make a small step toward her own decisions, this woman has made a statement to the community of women readers.

These are complex and perceptive responses to a fairly difficult text. Perhaps some of these themes of entrapment, manipulation, helplessness, and the psychological war between the sexes (at least as represented by the narrator and her husband) might have emerged from students' readings if the feminist lens had not been a part of their interpretive repertoires. But the students' ability to view the text as a cultural artifact, as a challenge to a prevailing ideology, to amplify the struggles of the narrator to include those of all women, including Gilman's struggle as a writer, to understand the dialectical role the piece plays—all these seem to demonstrate the influence the feminist lens had on their reading.

3. "Men Have Gender, Too!" *Death of a Salesman* and the Social Construction of Gender

As one can see from the previous examples, classic feminist texts such as "The Yellow Wallpaper" and *A Room of One's Own* can help adolescents to employ the gender lens. Many teachers have reported that studying the feminist lens in combination with the use of literary texts that can be read as "feminist tracts" made the reading experience too overtly feminist for comfort, especially for many male students. This is precisely why in this chapter I encourage the use of the more inclusive term *gender*. In addition, to help students see that issues of gender affect males and male characters as much as they do females and female characters, I developed a lesson on the gender lens with *Death of a Salesman*, a classic work widely used in secondary classrooms and one that clearly illustrates the entrapment of men in the gender regime of contemporary American society (see Appendix, Activity 18).

The lesson begins with an examination of the gender of particular words, the activity described at the opening of this chapter. Following that is a consideration of the notion of the social construction of gender, including a careful consideration of the fact that masculinity is socially constructed, just as is femininity. Next is an examination of representations of the characters in *Death of a Salesman* as they appear in a reader's guide as well as in a film adaptation of the play. Finally, students consider the ways in which the characters are "held hostage" to social expectations of gender. Here are some of their responses:

> Willy is expected to be the breadwinner of the family and provide more than he is physically able to. He is expected to be a respected salesman and not a carpenter. He is expected to raise his sons to be successful. He is expected to be confident and all-knowing. The combination of these are too harsh for Willy to handle—he becomes suicidal. This led me to see that Willy was confined by expectations—he couldn't be who he wanted to be.

> Linda is held captive not only to the restrictions accompanying being a stay-at-home mother but also to the need for success that binds Willy. Since Willy is the measurement of *her* success in society, she feels the need to keep his fragile world from breaking because it is hers as well. When Willy's world falls apart there is no hope for her—in the movie her hair is gray and her life feels meaningless. For this reason she fights against Biff and Happy when they try to accuse the man to whom her identity is bound.

> Willy struggles deeply with the gender expectations of males and how he is unable to meet some. He fails to be a wealthy and successful man, and psychologically that is really hard for him. Where he fell short, he pushes his sons harder to excel, such as in sports and with women. Because he never made an overwhelmingly good salesman, he increasingly became obsessed with it until it took over his mind and drove him to suicide. He also felt forced to not openly share his emotions, struggles, and shortcoming with the rest of the family. In the movie Willy was played as a man who was very distraught and almost frantic. He definitely lacked real stability.

> Biff Loman is constrained by both his father's expectations and society's expectations. His father's expectations stem from the societal expectations that a man must work in a respectable job with a solid salary after achieving athletic glory as a youth. The contrast between Biff's high school and adult experiences highlights the fact that Biff does not wish to conform, and his relationship with his family has been ruined as traditional male roles are forced upon him.

As these responses indicate, the students were able to use the gender lens to read the social construction of conceptions of both masculinity and femininity. Now, I wondered, could they transfer this awareness from the classroom to the world outside school? Could they apply this gendered way of reading the ideologies inscribed in texts to the ideologies that are inscribed in our world? After all, isn't real-world relevance central to reading with critical lenses?

4. Reading the World: From Text to Context

There is a quiet revolt that seems to be gathering steam in Martha's 5th-hour literature class. The students have just finished discussing Charlotte Perkins Gilman's "The Yellow Wallpaper" and are in the throes of their consideration of feminist literary theory. They are trying the feminist lens on literary characters whom they have previously met, such characters as Curley's wife from *Of Mice and Men* and Daisy Buchanan from *The Great Gatsby*. They apply the feminist lens to *Hamlet*'s Gertrude and Ophelia, and to a concrete poem (see Appendix, Activity 16).

David, seated near the front of the room, is absolutely bursting at the seams. For weeks he has fumed silently through the explanation of the feminist lens and through class activities that applied feminist theory to several literary texts, but now he seems unable to restrain himself.

"All this stuff is *construed*," he suddenly exclaims. "It's BS! Isn't there a *masculine* lens? This 'feminist lens' just isn't working for me."

"Of course it's not working for you!" Maria interjects from across the room. "You're a man. *You* can't see it, but *I* can see it because I live it." She continued firmly, "Besides, I was watching your face when we were reading about feminist literary theory. You were already shaking your head." (David shakes his head.)

"Yes, you were, David. You are so closed-minded."

A spirited discussion ensues between David and the other female students in the class, who come quickly to provide unnecessary but welcomed support for Maria. The other male students listen in stony silence, refusing to rescue their self-appointed spokesperson, who is besieged by his frustrated female classmates. David doesn't seem to mind.

"I just don't buy it," David goes on. "Just because a man writes a book doesn't mean he disses women."

"Oh, yeah?" says Robyn. "Let's take your favorite book—of course by Hemingway. What about Lady Brett Ashley? How does Hemingway portray her?"

"Yes, as a sex object, of course," David concedes.

"See?" says Robyn triumphantly.

"Wait a minute," replies David. Now he's angry. "You mean, women *never* do that to men? Women authors *never* portray men as sex objects? You mean, there's no such thing as reverse sexism?"

"David." Maria is almost pleading. "Don't you realize you can only see things one way? It's because you're a man!"

"Well, you can only see things one way because you're a woman."

"No, that's not true. I have to see things from the masculine perspective because that is the perspective that dominates our society. And I also have to see things from a feminist perspective because I'm a woman." (I can't help but think of W. E. B. Du Bois's concept of "double consciousness" as Maria speaks.)

David shakes his head and tightens his jaw.

"Just try the lenses on, David! You can always take them off if they don't work for you!"

"I know, I know. But I still think it's construed."

This exchange, difficult though it was in many ways, indicates that, for these students, feminist theory has begun to move from the pages of their assigned reading to the foundation of their world. This notion of reading the world and culture against the grain is, of course, one of the primary goals of introducing students to literary theory. While many students move from textual to personal on their own, others need encouragement and practice in reading culture against the grain, and resistantly, as feminist theory encourages us to do.

To help facilitate this movement from textual to personal, I created an activity to encourage students to read the world through feminist eyes (Appendix, Activity 15). First, students are asked to look at several cultural artifacts, such as Mount Rushmore; the Miss America pageant; reactions to vice presidential candidate Sarah Palin; Hillary Clinton's bid for the Democratic nomination for president; and the immense celebrity of such personalities as Paris Hilton, Lindsay Lohan, and Britney Spears. The students are then asked to write two sentences about those objects or situations that contrast a traditional perspective with the feminist perspective. Here are some of the responses:

MOUNT RUSHMORE

Speaks to the fact that we had founding fathers and not founding mothers. And why? Because at the time, women weren't allowed to participate in society as leaders.

Let's face it! History glorifies men and excludes women. Period.

These are all presidents. A woman should have been president by now.

Behind each of these men there is a woman who helped this country.

THE MISS AMERICA PAGEANT

Women walk around parading on heels and dressed up like dolls for the benefit of the male public.

It is a tribute to our obsession with the physical appearance of women.

It's a parade of women who starve themselves so that a bunch of ignorant men can drool at them.

HILLARY CLINTON'S BID FOR THE DEMOCRATIC PARTY NOMINATION FOR PRESIDENT IN 2008

Would she be where she is without her husband?

I notice that she always wears pants—is she trying to defeminize herself?

I can't believe how she was pounced on when she cried—they would never have done that to a man.

These responses are indicative of the students' ability to cast these cultural artifacts in the interpretive light of feminist literary theory. Yet the goal of teaching theory is not to produce discrete interpretations of individual artifacts; it is to help us interpret, understand, and respond to our lived experiences. To encourage students to expand their interpretive skills so they can move from texts to objects to actual events, the final section of this activity poses the question: "Can you think of anything that has happened to you or to a friend of yours in the past 2 weeks that could be better explained or understood through a feminist/gender lens?" Here are some of the resulting narratives:

GENDER TALES: READING THE TEXTS OF OUR LIVES

I am a waitress and the other night I received a very large tip from two men. When I told one of my male co-workers about it, he made a very obscene remark along the lines of "What did I have to do for it." It was a very dirty, nasty thing to say, and even though it was a joke, it was not right. Feminist lens: He disrespected me.

Yesterday in gym we were picking teams for handball. There are only two girls in the class and, as always, they were picked last. Everyone is okay with that because we all assume they are just bad at sports.

Being a cheerleader, I am subjected to stereotypes every time I step into uniform. People joke about us; they automatically assume we spend more time doing our hair than practicing. They do not consider us athletes and believe the only reason we are cheering is to be close to the boys. Through the feminist lens, cheerleaders would be a part of a male-dominant society, only there to cheer the males to victory.

Last week I tried to help a girl carry a set of lights that were obviously too heavy for one person to try to carry. She did not want any help and almost dropped all the lights. A feminist would applaud the girl for trying to show that women can do jobs usually assigned to males. Even if the lights might have broken, it was okay. Women have to take risks in order to gain complete equality. The way I approached it was completely colored by gender. I was easily offended and very defensive. I feel I always have to be defensive nowadays. I am a Man.

As Judith Fetterley (1978) starkly reminds us, reading and teaching literature is political:

> Feminist criticism is a political act whose aim is not simply to interpret the world but to change it, by changing the consciousness of those who read and their relation to what they read. (xxii)

Learning to read with feminist theory means learning to attend to the ideology of patriarchy, to the gendered nature of textual worlds, and to the significance of our responses as male and female readers. Gender theory provides a critical lens that can transform students' visions as they interpret individual characters, as they evaluate the cultural significance of particular texts, and as they read and respond to the gendered patterns in the world. Finally, they are also able to see how their own gender affects their response to literary texts.

When the students were asked how their gender affected their reading of *A Room of One's Own*, they offered such comments as the following (see Appendix, Activities 15 and 31):

I was not really affected by it despite my being male. The book itself seemed to be, for the most part, indifferent towards men; it dealt mostly with the women. (Justin)

> I think my gender did affect my reaction because I could directly relate to some of the things she complained about. I have run into people with the opinions that women can't be as smart as men. I have never believed that, but I have felt the shock of people when I do well in math and science, traditionally male fields. Things are nowhere near as extreme for me as they were back in 1928, but that occasional feeling of being an oddity is much easier to relate to as a woman than I think it would be for a man. I think men are pretty aware of the big issues but sometimes I think they might miss the importance of little things such as looks and tone of voice. As a woman I felt much more connected to what Virginia is talking about. (Shannon)

> My gender definitely did play a role in my reading of *A Room of One's Own.* It was difficult for me not to feel a bit defensive when it seemed that Virginia Woolf was attacking my fellow males and me. Still, after the initial impulse to defend myself and my gender, I was able to evaluate Woolf's ideas a bit more objectively. I believe that if I had been a woman, my reading would have been a bit different; I probably would have been a bit quicker to identify with Woolf. (Eric)

> Yes, I think being a female somewhat influenced my reaction to *A Room of One's Own.* In many ways, I can see Woolf's arguments and problems because I can see them for myself in everyday situations. She talks about how men had all the freedom and women had none. Although this is, I believe, taken to an extreme, it is easy to understand these things because of my experience as a female. Also, I think it is easier to side with Virginia Woolf because I am a female and she is too. It's sort of like rooting for your own team because you are a part of it. (Jenny)

> I think my gender affected my reading of *A Room of One's Own* slightly. I noticed myself paying attention more to the successes (or at least what Virginia Woolf saw as a success) of women. I read those passages and felt proud of the individual women and of women in general. When Woolf talked about the injustices against women, it didn't affect me as much because I haven't experienced it. I sort of looked at those with a sense of "look at what women have accomplished," but from a third-person sort of way. (Jessica)

Understanding the role that one's gender plays as one reads is a significant step toward understanding one's gender role in society at large. Through texts such as *Death of a Salesman*, *The Great Gatsby*, "The Yellow Wallpaper," and *A Room of One's Own*, adolescent readers become acutely aware of gender and how it is socially constructed. Gender/feminist literary theory provides a way for young men and women to make meaning of their reading, their schooling, and their gendered place in the world. The process of recognizing textual politics and taking a stand with or against authors and characters enables students to begin to articulate a more generalized sense of their places as women and men who create, out of necessity, gender readings not only of texts but also of lived experience.

Columbus Did What? Postcolonialism in the Literature Classroom

> Until lions have their own historians, tales of hunting will always glorify the hunter.
>
> —African proverb

In early March, Peter's 11th-grade world literature class is deep into its reading of Joseph Conrad's *Heart of Darkness*. A skilled and resourceful teacher, Peter is already planning to show Francis Ford Coppola's dark film *Apocalypse Now*, which follows the basic plot outline of *Heart of Darkness*. Peter has also provided opportunities for the students to find intertextual connections, with Chinua Achebe's *Things Fall Apart*, which the class read in the fall. Yet something seems to be missing from the discussion of this complex work. Discussion of characters center on obvious comparisons; no one mentions the hierarchy embedded in the text; and while Peter offers some brief historical and biographical background information, the discussion has remained largely apolitical.

The texts we read in literature classrooms can reflect our history. One potent example is literature that was "produced in the crucible of colonization and its aftermath of independence and postindependence movements and struggles" (Dimitriadis & McCarthy, 2001, p. 3). While the teaching of literature need not always be both historical and political, Peter's eager students seem to be circling around those very aspects of *Heart of Darkness*.

WHY POSTCOLONIALISM?

As school populations become more diverse, the task of helping students see themselves in the literature they read becomes more challenging for teachers. As more immigrants and refugees enter our classrooms, we must consider a broader range of literary texts in order that our students may see themselves and their circumstances in the works they read. In addition, we need to consider the perspectives and identities of populations that historically have not seen themselves as part of the American mainstream. If we can successfully demonstrate for students from such groups that alternative ideologies belong within the American imagination, we will reveal the emancipating power of literary interpretation. Direct attention to postcolonial literature provides an entry point into understanding our national imagination.

We should also think of the benefits that postcolonial perspectives provide for majority students. Colonialist worldviews underpin much of the ideology that pervades mainstream American culture. If we set as one of our goals the ability of our students to read the world in multiple ways—to see things through a variety of lenses—we will need to acquaint them with the lenses of colonialism and postcolonialism. Those of us raised in the United States have experienced an environment shaped by traditional Western values and beliefs. While many of these values serve us well, we have to distinguish those that drive us toward the highest ideals of democracy and equality from those that provide advantage to us and adversity to others. In her very helpful primer on critical theory, Lois Tyson (2006, p. 417) remarks that postcolonial criticism helps us see "connections among all the domains of our experience—the psychological, ideological, social, political, intellectual, and aesthetic—in ways that show us just how inseparable these categories are in our lived experiences of ourselves and our world." Postcolonial theory, in other words, makes better readers of us all.

Studies in postcolonialism often begin with the work of the literary critic and professor of English and comparative literature Edward Said. His memoir, *Out of Place* (1999), details the experience of leaving the Middle East to study in the United States. The title of this work might well name the feelings of many new Americans. His most well-known work, *Orientalism* (1978), describes what he thought to be incorrect assumptions about "the East," based on Western cultural presuppositions. This cultural worldview, as Said saw it, reduced the Arab world to a few stereotypes, ignoring the complexity, diversity, and humanity that its people represent.

An understanding of postcolonial viewpoints is crucial for students if we are to educate new generations of Americans who are willing to move beyond Western preconceptions and biases. It is also an essential component of literary study that moves beyond universal standards of judgment and allows diversity of opinion in criticism, especially a criticism that reflects the multiplicity of the United States today (Bonnycastle, 1996). Whatever ideologies postcolonial theory might challenge, its most important benefit is that it empowers students to reflect on their own cultural knowledge as they build interpretations of literature. It thus becomes an essential component of inclusive literary pedagogy.

Perhaps most important, postcolonial criticism provides an opportunity to level a playing field that has been tilted since the beginnings of Western identity. In her explanation of colonialist ideology, Lois Tyson (2006) summarizes the origin of the problem—the construction of a worldview that inherently privileges the perspectives of those who constructed it:

> The colonizers believed that only their own Anglo-European culture was civilized, sophisticated, or, as postcolonial critics put it, *metropolitan*. Therefore, native peoples were defined as savage, backward, and undeveloped. Because their technology was more highly advanced, the colonizers believed their whole culture was more highly advanced, and they ignored or swept aside the religions, customs, and codes of behavior of the peoples they subjugated. So the colonizers saw themselves at the center of the world; the colonized were at the margins. (p. 419)

This colonialist ideology constructs a world that imprisons both sides. It precludes any ability for Western peoples to learn from histories and cultures of the colonized and to incorporate ideas and values that have successfully sustained non-Western societies for centuries, often with less detrimental effects than those of Eurocentric cultural practices. Most important, it provides an opportunity for our students to employ their imaginations to the fullest extent.

LITERATURE AND COLONIALISM

For a very long time, authors, poets, critics, and scholars have made the case that literature reflects cultural heritage. Largely as a result of this understanding, literary study has traditionally been divided into literature of historical periods and national literatures. We established historical and cultural contexts for literary study to help provide a map of our cultural history, and for many decades this practice went unquestioned. We saw literature, then, as a celebration of human advancement, the apex of our linguistic achievement, and the most beautiful expression of our sentiments. Dominant societies created images of themselves by publicly recognizing what they thought to be the best representations of their arts and sciences. Featured among these representations were literary masterworks thought to capture the essence of who we were and what our societies stood for at various points and places in the past.

In time, however, it became clear that the images created within our national literatures provided a less than complete understanding of our history and heritage. Only those people who had historically participated in the construction of our cultural imagination found themselves fairly represented, and their voices were predominantly White, male, and of the upper social classes. Members of racial and ethnic groups who were not part of the mainstream found themselves and their cultures represented from the outside. They themselves became the creations of a cultural imagination that neither understood nor sympathized with them. The same was true for women. The source of this misrepresentation was a cultural predilection that reflected the products and processes of Western civilization. Foremost among these processes was colonization—an ostensibly benevolent expansion of our best cultural principles.

Among the cultural themes represented in Western literature are conflicts that pit Civilization against "savages," peoples generally defined by non-Christian and non-European values and practices. Within literary representations of these conflicts, Western supremacy in technology quickly translates into superior power, principally in navigation and weapons. As Conrad's *Heart of Darkness* shows us, industrial and economic superiority are culturally transfigured. They justify colonization, imperialism, and even genocide. Kurtz's closing exclamation in his treatise captures the worst sentiment of Western hegemony: "Exterminate all the brutes!" The colonialist worldview thus imposes on other landscapes and peoples its own images of the colonized as it wishes them to be. Competing worldviews are summarily dismissed.

THE ORIGINS OF POSTCOLONIAL READING

In the late twentieth century, with the ascendancy of the movement toward civil rights, equal rights for women, and an expanded understanding of cultural sovereignty, literary critics attempted to broaden the scope of cultural exploration. Thus they began their investigation into an expanded literary canon: a more varied list of works and authors representing diverse cultures. The underlying idea was that the colonized needed to have their stories heard. In many cases their stories had already been written, but they had not been included in the literary canon of their colonizers. They were not recognized as a part of the whole. The movement that we now call postcolonialism was both an invitation and a recognition. Those who had not yet told their stories had the opportunity to write themselves into the literary record. Those who had already written their stories could be included in the literary conversation.

Postcolonialism focuses on literary works from and about countries that formerly had been colonies of Western nations. It calls attention to propensities of the Western world: the privileging of science over custom, the imposition of economic structures onto societies that had developed their own, and an understanding of Western causes and effects that rendered Western institutions powerful and others powerless. Christianity frequently served as both a motivation for colonization and a means for defining the colonized. European commerce prompted a search for resources and riches that, in Western eyes, lay unclaimed among the uncivilized. In general, it was the perspective of more developed nations that their cultural, commercial, and religious superiority gave them license to take what they needed for their own advancement. The results were often violent.

From the 16th to the 20th century, the voices of colonized peoples were largely unrecognized. Political, economic, and military superiority provided a platform for European literary art, which carried forward the ideology of the colonizers. The literatures of the colonized, to the extent that they were allowed to exist, were dismissed. The hallmark of the postcolonial movement today, then, is its opposition to imperialist cultures and the identities they constructed for those they had colonized. Africa and East Asia, the primary geographic targets of European colonialism, are sites today for rich postcolonial literary expression. The Caribbean is another area of contested cultural identity in both literature and music.

QUESTIONS OF CULTURAL IDENTITY

A consistent outcome of colonialism is the inability of colonized people to determine their own cultural identity. Their religious practices are frequently replaced, most often by those of Christianity. Rituals that create unity and cultural continuity are discouraged. Languages are supplanted by the tongues of the conquerors. Colonized people are robbed of distinctions they hold dear—the traits and heritages that separate them from their neighbors—by a European worldview that sees no point in differentiating them one from another.

In European inscriptions of history and culture, colonized people lose not only their ability to construct their identities in the present but also the power to represent their cultural achievements of the past. Their histories are suppressed, their secrets are revealed (a grievous fault in traditional societies) to a world that has no context for understanding them, and their values are denigrated. Achebe's *Things Fall Apart* tells a story, set in Nigeria, about the impact of Christianity and of a European justice system that humiliates and imprisons those who resist its orders. Ngugi wa Thiong'o's *The River Between* sets up a conflict between Christian missionaries and traditional tribal practice in Kenya that is seemingly irreconcilable. Derek Walcott and V. S. Naipaul each won the Nobel Prize for Literature while investigating the ideologies that established European dominance in the Caribbean. By telling their stories to the world, they recapture a history that had been stolen from them, along with the dignity and identity that had long been reserved for the colonizers alone.

American Indian cultures—to the extent that they are preserved—are frequently misrepresented and idealized by a Western society that wishes to make peace with its own history but is unwilling to acknowledge its own exercise of ideological suppression. These themes of colonization also play out in American history: Christianization of native people, suppression of indigenous languages, and the imposition of economic practices such as farming through the Dawes Act. This act and other such laws were intended to "civilize" American Indians by forcing a Eurocentric culture on their well-established ways of life. The effect of the Dawes Act was to remove them from the lands that had supported and defined them. Since the late 1960s, a rich literary tradition has sprung up among American Indian writers who now have the opportunity to reclaim their history and identity by writing about them. Frequently, as in the case of Leslie Marmon Silko's *Ceremony*, this recovery takes the form of a return to tribal customs and beliefs. A common theme is the reclamation of cultural identity.

In the colonial mindset, the colonized come into existence when they are "discovered" by the colonizers. This explains, for example, the colonialist claim that "Columbus discovered America," a statement we will revisit later in Peter's classroom. It is as if prior to this "discovery," American Indians did not exist, or they existed in a state that had little meaning or significance for people from the "civilized" world. To the extent that American literature represents the discovery and conquest of the North American continent, its Western biases reflect the perspectives of the "civilized," even to the point of justifying colonization and westward expansion. A particular aim of postcolonial theory is to reclaim a history and cultural identity for American Indians.

WORKING AGAINST A "UNIVERSALIST" UNDERSTANDING OF LITERATURE

It has been common to suggest that the study of literature leads us to understand that which is universally shared within the human experience. As Peter Barry (2002, p. 192) points out, "If we claim that great literature has a timeless and universal significance, we thereby demote or disregard cultural, social, regional, and national differences in experience and outlook, preferring instead to judge all literatures by a single, supposedly 'universal' standard." This thinking necessarily privileges the standards and perspectives of the dominant culture. Postcolonialism, by contrast, recognizes the differences that give peoples their identities, their uniqueness, and their histories. Through this approach, English teachers create more inclusive classrooms. It validates the experiences and perspectives of readers from outside the mainstream.

Because the manner of our inquiry determines the ways in which we create meaning, we need to think clearly about the questions we ask about literary works. As Bonnycastle (1996, p. 208) suggests, this means questioning cultural supremacy and the literature that it favors. Reading literature with a postcolonial lens does just that.

Interpretations traditionally break down along the line that separates colonized from colonizers. By contrast, a postcolonial lens allows for the possibility of interpretations that cross this line, because it provides a basis of historical and cultural understanding. These will not be universalist interpretations, but rather interpretations based on new understandings of political and historical contexts and the cultural identities they acknowledge for the peoples they represent.

Another important point to keep in mind is that multicultural treatments of literature must not turn their subjects into objects. They must instead accurately represent the values, ideas, customs, and beliefs of the non-Western world as they would be seen through non-Western eyes. Edward Said (1978) characterizes the conflict this way:

> Consider how the Orient, and in particular the near Orient, became known in the West as its great complementary opposite since antiquity. There were the Bible and the rise of Christianity; there were travelers like Marco Polo who charted the trade routes and patterned the regulated system of commercial exchange . . . ; there were the redoubtable Eastern conquering movements, principally Islam, of course; there were the militant pilgrims, chiefly the Crusaders, although an internally structured archive is built up from the literature that belongs to these experiences. Out of this comes a restricted number of typical encapsulations: the journey, the history, the fable, the stereotype, the polemical confrontation. These are the lenses through which the Orient is experienced, and they shape the language, perception, and forms of encounter between East and West. . . . Something patently foreign and distant acquires, for one reason or other, a status more rather than less familiar. (p. 58)

The aim of postcolonial study, then, is to restore the history, dignity, validity, cultural contributions, and global significance of those whose experiences have been represented within a worldview that provided no way to include "the Other" except through direct contrast with itself. This type of binary construction—Western/non-Western, civilized/uncivilized, Christian/non-Christian, democratic/nondemocratic—necessarily reduces everything and everyone it encounters. It diminishes not only the complexity of the colonized world, but its legitimacy as well.

Including a non-Western perspective in American education provides a means for moving students outside their familiar patterns of thinking as they try to understand the larger world, and to successfully read the world they the must have this larger perspective. Gayatri Spivak (1988), who was born in India but has spent years teaching in American universities, relates this challenge that she put to a group of her honors students concerning their own ideological indoctrination:

> Suppose an outsider, observing the uniformity of the mores you have all sketched in your papers, were to say that you had been indoctrinated? That you could no longer conceive of public decision-making except in the quantified areas of your economics and business classes, where you learn all the rational expectations theories? You *know* that decisions in the public sphere, such as tax decisions, legal decisions, foreign policy decisions, fiscal decisions, affect your *private* lives deeply. Yet in a speculative field such as the interpretation of texts, you feel that there is something foolish and wrong and regimented about a public voice. Suppose someone were to say that

> this was a result of your indoctrination to keep moral speculation and decision-making apart, to render you incapable of thinking collectively in any but the most inhuman ways. (p. 99)

The point she makes is that her students seemed to want to undertake sociocultural analyses as unique individuals. To broaden their sphere of understanding in addressing social issues, they needed to think of themselves as public individuals as well. This need, she said, came from the fact that their "historical-institutional imperatives [were] proving stronger than [their] individual good will" (p. 98). As their teacher, she trusted their intelligence and their positive motivations, but she could not trust that they had a broad enough view to see the world that their own decisions as future leaders would bring into being.

TEACHING THE POSTCOLONIAL LENS: COLUMBUS DID WHAT?

Although he might not state it quite the same way, Peter, like Spivak, wants his students to be able to see the world broadly and interpret texts such as *Heart of Darkness* with both private and public awareness. Peter's 11th-grade world literature class is lens savvy and theory rich. The students have worked through reader response, the social class lens, and the lens of gender. As Peter anticipates teaching the next book in his curriculum, which will be *Heart of Darkness*, he decides that for his students to fully understand the novel, they need to add another tool to their interpretive tool kit, this tool being the postcolonial lens. Peter believes that, although both the social class and the gender lenses have helped students see how the dynamics of power and oppression are often inscribed in the texts we read, the dynamics of the colonized and the colonizer need to be underscored in a separate lesson.

Peter begins his lesson on postcolonialism with a few introductory explanations (see Appendix, Activity 19). After he explains the basic premises of the postcolonial lens, he asks students to rephrase, from a postcolonial perspective, the following sentence: "Christopher Columbus discovered America." At first, the students giggle nervously; the weight of a decade of historical misunderstanding seems to freeze their pens. Then they begin to write. Here are some of the resulting rephrasings:

> Columbus took control of land inhabited for centuries by native people, and in the process stripped them of their independence and unique culture.
>
> Columbus was an explorer who arrived at the North American continent[,] already populated by several different societies[,] and facilitated the destruction of these cultures for profit.

Christopher Columbus landed in America.

Christopher Columbus exploited the natives of America and dehumanized them of their right to own land. In saying that he discovered the country, it is indicating that the people living there were inconsequential.

Columbus stumbled upon land unclaimed by other European countries, starting an epoch of oppression of Native Americans.

The students seem to take to the idea quickly. This simple exercise helps Peter's students see how the postcolonial lens quickly shifts the focus from the colonizer to the colonized. Peter then moves to a literary text and hands out the following poem by Native American poet Diane Burns:

Sure You Can Ask Me a Personal Question

How do you do?
   No, I am not Chinese.
No, not Spanish.
   No, I am American Indi-uh, Native American.
No, not from India.
   No, not Apache.
No, not Navajo.
   No, not Sioux.
No, we are not extinct.
   Yes, Indian.
Oh?
   So, that's where you got those high cheekbones.
Your great-grandmother, huh?
   An Indian Princess, huh?
Hair down to there?
   Let me guess. Cherokee?
Oh, so you've had an Indian friend?
   That close?
Oh, so you've had an Indian lover?
   That tight?
Oh, so you've had an Indian servant?
   That much?
Yeah, it was awful what you guys did to us.
   It's real decent of you to apologize.

No, I don't know where you can get peyote.
  No, I don't know where you can get Navajo rugs real cheap.
No, I didn't make this. I bought it at Bloomingdales.
  Thank you. I like your hair too.
I don't know if anyone knows whether or not Cher is really Indian.
  No, I didn't make it rain tonight.
Yeah. Uh-huh. Spirituality.
  Uh-huh. Yeah. Spirituality. Uh-huh. Mother
Earth. Yeah. Uh-huh. Uh-huh. Spirituality.
  No, I didn't major in archery.
Yeah, a lot of us drink too much.
  Some of us can't drink enough.
This ain't no stoic look.
  This is my face.

—Diane Burns

Peter asks the students to begin by writing down two or three sentences in a personal response to the poem, as well as any questions or points of confusion. Then in groups of four or five, the students discuss their personal responses and their questions. Peter wryly comments that before he considered using literary theory, his lesson about the poem might have ended there. He then asks the students to consider the basic tenets of postcolonial theory from the handout. He instructs each group to construct a postcolonial reading in groups of three or four. Here are some of the group's postcolonial readings of "Sure You Can Ask Me a Personal Question":

> The author feels like no one understands Native American culture, only the stereotypes surrounding it. She does not apologize or attempt to explain, only answers the question.
>
> Instead of being proud of her Indian culture, the speaker seems to be offended at how the world sees her differently. She doesn't like that the world makes stereotypes about who she is. Through a postcolonial reading, one might say that the rest of society in fact destroyed her culture because things that they found beautiful are now looked at as ordinary.
>
> The most striking idea in this poem is the binary approach taken in this discussion; there is clearly a colonizer (the questioner) and an "other" (the Native American). It appears that the questioner has no malicious intent, however, from the questions one can see that the speaker in the poem is

> nevertheless offended. By grouping all Indians together with cheap Navajo rugs, liquor, and a past servant, the questioner inadvertently calls into play a number of derogatory stereotypes.
>
> The conversation is between the oppressor and the oppressed. It shows the way White civilization destroyed the lives of the natives and uses their history, livelihood. The oppressed speaker had an indignant and retaliatory attitude [which] highlights [reaction to] the postcolonial attitude.

In these responses, Peter's students demonstrate that they are clearly seeing the poem from a postcolonial perspective. Peter is convinced that the themes of oppression and marginalization that the students uncovered are rendered much more visible through this lens. Peter concludes that his students are now ready to read *Heart of Darkness*.

The following day, after the students have read several chapters of *Heart of Darkness*, Peter asks them to list characters as colonized, colonizers, or both. He then asks students to write some questions that have emerged from their postcolonial reading of this text, questions that will shape their future discussions of the novel. Here are a few of their questions:

- Would you consider Marlow a true colonizer? Or does he just follow along with what the company does?
- Who in this book is isolated and who does the isolating?
- What shapes the image of colonization in the West?
- How does Marlow's sympathy with the colonized alter his stance as either the colonizer or the colonized?
- What motivation is more detrimental in colonization: an economic motivation or a civilizing motivation?
- Why does Marlow describe the natives as animals?
- Who was more of a factor in Marlow's changed view: Kurtz or the cannibals?
- How can an "uncivilized" person resist colonization?

Peter is pleased with these questions. He sees that his students understand the pervasiveness of colonist ideology in the novel and the degree to which it translates into a kind of colonial psychology in the characters. He also knows that colonialist ideology has far from disappeared from American society. As Tyson (2006) writes:

> White supremacist backlash, for example, as witnessed in the proliferation of racist hate groups; the persistence of covert racial discrimination . . . in housing, employment, and education; the othering of the homeless, indeed their virtual erasure from

> American consciousness and conscience; and all the forms of othering that still flourish in this country today make it clear that America's neocolonialist enterprises around the globe will be accompanied by versions thereof at home for a long time to come. For colonialist psychology and the discriminatory ideologies it supports are a part of our historical and cultural legacy. . . . And this is a reality that will have to be confronted anew by each generation of Americans. (p. 445)

Peter believes that by using the postcolonial lens in his literature classroom he has given his students an important interpretive tool. In doing so he has also introduced this generation of Americans to the insidious nature of the psychological heritage of colonialism.

CHAPTER 7

Deconstruction: Postmodern Theory and the Postmodern High School Student

Between the unspeakable world and the text that will never shut up, where are we?

—Robert Scholes

Deconstruction is dumb. It's people who want to feel important trying to destroy meaning.

—Tim, Grade 12

The words fall over themselves, trying to assemble into a meaning that even the author doesn't believe in.

—Annie, Grade 11, on reading *The Things They Carried*

There is a music video that is relevant to the consideration of postmodern theory in the secondary classroom. The singer is Natalie Umbruglia, and the video is for the song "Torn," which was on the top 10 list for several weeks a few years ago. In the MTV video, as in many music videos these days, the singer acts out a tortured and doomed relationship with a handsome male model pretending to be her boyfriend. They pace around a set designed to look like a 20- or 30-something's apartment right out of a TV sitcom.

The premise for the video is a familiar one—two young people trying to figure out what happened to their once passionate relationship. Familiar, too, are the sunken eyes, flat bellies (heroin chic), khaki pants, and melodic lament. But something is very different about this particular video.

As the singer proceeds with her song, construction workers arrive and begin to disassemble the set, take it apart, *deconstruct* the "apartment" piece by piece, revealing it to be nothing more than a bare sound stage. The viewer then recognizes the pretense of the assumptions on which the video is based. Similarly, the singer and the actor playing her boyfriend step out of their respective roles, revealing themselves to be two disconnected and unrelated people pretending to care about each other for the purposes of selling a CD. In a remarkably self-reflexive move, the video portrays the dissembling of the set, and then the layers of pretense and the artifice of the music business are stripped away.

The willing suspension of disbelief in which readers and viewers willingly engage as we enter the constructed world of a cultural artifact—be it a poem, short story, novel, magazine article, film, or music video—is revealed, interrogated by the structure of the video itself. This re-examination of the constructs of the music video can serve as an interesting starting point for adolescents in exploring deconstruction. After all, deconstruction invites us to "unravel" the constructs that surround us and to re-examine the relationships between appearance and reality.

DEFINING DECONSTRUCTION: AN EXERCISE IN FUTILITY?

Even those literature teachers who may be well versed in some of the other critical lenses we've discussed to this point may shudder at the notion of teaching deconstruction. Because it challenges the very iconic nature of the high school curriculum and the fixed meanings that have been assigned to canonical texts, it is a lens that most secondary language arts teachers have avoided. Another impediment, as Lois Tyson points out, is that major proponents of deconstruction, such as Jacques Derrida, as well as their "translators" often attempt to explain the basic principles of the theory in language that is alienating and difficult. Finally, deconstruction has frequently been misunderstood as a destructive methodology, one that ruins our love and appreciation of literature through a superficial and trivial attack that amounts to nothing more than academic wordplay (Tyson, 2006).

What *is* deconstruction and why does it inspire both fear and loathing? Here is one deconstructionist's hypothesis:

> Perhaps deconstruction has fired fear in people because it is difficult to define, and what cannot be defined cannot be pinned down and labeled; yet here lies the productive energy of deconstruction. In the very difficulty of naming and defining deconstruction, in the slipperiness of language that refuses to be pinned easily, deconstruction demonstrates and represents an understanding of language as vibrant and creative, opening up possibilities for meaning making. (Leggo, 1998, p. 186)

Despite his claim that it is difficult to define deconstruction, Leggo proceeds to offer a clear and lucid explication:

> Deconstruction is a practice of reading that begins with the assumption that meaning is a textual construction. Perhaps even more useful than the noun "construction" is the verb "constructing" because deconstruction is a continuous process of interacting with texts. According to deconstruction, a text is not a window a reader can look through in order to see either the author's intention or an essential truth, nor is the text a mirror that turns back a vivid image of the reader's experiences, emotions,

> and insights. Instead, deconstruction is a practice of reading that aims to make meaning from a text by focusing on how the text works rhetorically, and how a text is connected to other texts as well as the historical, cultural, social, and political contexts in which texts are written, read, published, reviewed, rewarded, and distributed. (p. 187)

Deconstruction seeks to show that a literary work is usually self-contradictory. As J. Hillis Miller explains, "Deconstruction is not a dismantling of the structure of a text, but a demonstration that it has already dismantled itself. Its apparently solid ground is no rock but thin air" (Miller in Murfin, 1989, p. 199).

In other words, a reader does not destroy or "dismantle" a text. She or he uses the interpretive strategies of deconstruction to reveal how a text unravels in self-contradiction. The source of those contradictions lies in the instability of language, the "undecidability" of meaning, and the ideologies that are often unconsciously revealed in the text. Appignanesi and Garratt (1999) emphasize this aspect of unintended meaning:

> Deconstruction is a strategy for revealing the underlayers of meaning in a text that were suppressed or assumed in order for it to take its actual form. . . . Texts are never simply unitary but include resources that run counter to their assertions and/or their authors' intentions. (p. 80)

As Barnet (1996) puts it, deconstructionists "interrogate a text and they reveal what the authors were unaware of or thought they had kept safely out of sight." Barnet also offers a definition of deconstruction that is accessible to high school students:

> [Deconstruction is] a critical approach that assumes that language is unstable and ambiguous and is therefore inherently contradictory. Because authors cannot control their language, texts reveal more than their authors are aware of. For instance, texts (like some institutions as the law, the churches, and the schools) are likely, when closely scrutinized, to reveal connections to society's economic system, even though the authors may have believed they were outside of the system. (p. 368)

Here is another good explanation of deconstruction (see Appendix, Activity 21), which forms the heart of the lesson described in this chapter:

> Deconstructionist critics probe beneath the finished surface of a story. Having been written by a human being with unresolved conflicts and contradictory emotions, a story may disguise rather than reveal the underlying anxieties or perplexities of the author. Below the surface, unresolved tensions or contradictions may account for the true dynamics of the story. The story may have one message for the ordinary unsophisticated reader and another for the reader who responds to its subtext, its subsurface ironies. Readers who deconstruct a text will be "resistant" readers. They

> will not be taken in by what a story says on the surface but will try to penetrate the disguises of the text. . . . They may engage in radical rereading of familiar classics. (Guth & Rico, 1996, p. 366)

"Radical rereadings of familiar classics" and resistance to what a story says on the surface are consistent with the original aims of deconstruction. For example, Johnson and Ciancio (in Soter, Faust, & Rogers, 2008) offer a lesson on how to deconstruct the power relationships in *Othello*. Yet it is easy to jump to an oversimplified conclusion that deconstruction means nothing more than to "take apart" or "analyze." The term is now stripped of its once radical sheen. *Deconstruction* seems to be used and overused by pundits and commentators and CNN reporters, as in "Let's deconstruct what happened during Hurricane Katrina," or "Let's deconstruct this film." But these commentators don't unbuild or systematically examine the underlying constructs of, say, a political system or a leader or the ideology of a country or the motifs and conventions (binary or otherwise) that are presented in a film. They simply analyze their subject for its "deeper meaning," a move the deconstructionists abandoned. Deconstruction is a particular kind of unbuilding, one that takes into account the very nature, weight, and composition of the constructs it dismantles.

As Moore (1997) points out, many have confused *deconstruction* with *destruction*, a confusion that could be amplified by a careless use of the video that opened this chapter. Deconstruction is not a mindless dismantling; it is a mindful one. It is not destruction; it is de*construction*. It is not, as Barbara Johnson (1981, p. xiv) has pointed out, "a kind of textual vandalism." While deconstructionists discount particular sources of meaning, such as the binary oppositions of the structuralist or the notion that a text can have a single, fixed meaning, it does not assert that literature, or the study of literature, for that matter, is meaningless. Rather, it posits that a text will yield multiple meanings, depending on the ways in which an individual reader may attempt to resolve the ambiguities and inconsistencies in the text.

Murfin (1989) points out that despite its difficulty, there is something almost irresistible about deconstruction:

> Deconstruction has a reputation for being the most complex and forbidding of contemporary critical approaches to literature, but in fact almost all of us have, at one time, either deconstructed a text or badly wanted to deconstruct one. Sometimes, when we hear a lecturer effectively marshal evidence to show that a book means primarily one thing, we long to interrupt and ask what he or she would make of other, conveniently overlooked passages that seem to contradict the lecturer's thesis. Sometimes, after reading a provocative critical article that almost convinces us that a familiar work means the opposite of what we assumed it meant, we may wish to make an equally convincing case for our old way of reading the text. It isn't that we think that the poem or novel in question better supports our interpretation; it's that we think the text can be

> used to support both readings. And sometimes we simply want to make that point that texts can be used to support seemingly irreconcilable positions. (p. 199)

WHY ADOLESCENTS NEED DECONSTRUCTION

Despite the natural appeal of deconstruction that Murfin describes, the utility of deconstruction is fiercely debated even within literary circles. Even those who are firmly convinced of the usefulness of other kinds of literary theory readily dismiss deconstruction as both frivolous and difficult. Like a theoretical house of cards, deconstruction is easily dismantled. It is often accompanied by or practiced with a cynical, dismissive, and even contemptuous tone. Barnet (1996) complains:

> The problem with deconstruction . . . is that too often it is reductive, telling the same story about every text—that here, yet again, and again, we see how a text is incoherent and heterogeneous. There is, too, an irritating arrogance in some deconstructive criticism: "The author could not see how his/her text is fundamentally unstable and self-contradictory, but *I* can and will issue my report." (p. 123)

Others view deconstruction as passé—no longer the relevant or startling literary and theoretical enterprise it was when it crashed on the scene in the late 1960s and really took hold in the academy in the 1970s. In fact, in *A Teacher's Introduction to Deconstruction*, Sharon Crowley (1989, p. 24) quotes a newspaper clipping declaring that deconstruction is in fact "dead."

So why should something so peripherally relevant even within the esoteric world of literary criticism be seen as something important for today's adolescents?

As argued in Chapter 1, contemporary adolescents are faced with a bewildering and confusing world, one that presents them with a dizzying array of social and psychological constructs, some as benign perhaps as the "Torn" video, with which this chapter began, others more potentially destructive. Some have argued, in fact, that adolescence itself is a complicated and often cruel construct of our postindustrial society. As Moore (1989) points out in an argument for the relevance of semiotics to adolescents:

> In adolescence students read the world that is represented to them, but they also socially construct a world in which they want to live, one that creates the identity they desire in the difficult landscape between childhood and adulthood. (p. 211)

Moore quotes T. McLaughlin, who emphasizes the necessity of theory in the classroom. It is "equipment for post-modern living" (p. 212), and he contends that students are ready for it. They are adept at reading the artifacts of their culture, a culture "[which] values image over reality, which has replaced product with information" (p. 218).

Reading this postmodern culture requires that we reconsider which artifacts or elements of culture actually can and should be read. In other words, we must redefine "texts" to include a variety of forms, both print and nonprint, literary and nonliterary. While the expansion of the concept of text can clearly accompany any of the previous lenses we discussed and is indeed a requisite part of these critical encounters, it seems especially useful to redefine the concept through the lens of deconstruction. The interrogation of the meaning of *text* is a requisite part of deconstruction:

For many deconstructionists, the traditional conception of literature is merely an elitist "construct." All "texts" or "discourse" (novels, scientific papers, a Kewpie doll on the mantle, watching TV, suing in court, walking the dog, and all other signs that human beings make) are of a piece—all are unstable systems of "signifying," all are fictions, all are "literature" (Barnet, 1996, p. 124).

In his invitation to English teachers to rethink the school subject "high school English," Bruce Pirie (1997) points out that English teachers must learn to redefine texts and refocus the objects of study in our classroom to include the artifacts of popular culture and to learn to read them as texts. As Garth Boomer (1988) argues, "if the profession of English studies and English [instruction] is to survive and have any relevance for our students at all, we need to expand our idea of texts to include the multivariate multimedia stimuli that surround them." Pirie quotes Boomer:

> Once "text" is conceived of as a cultural artifact, any text, past or present, classic or popular, fiction or non-fiction, written, oral or filmic, can be admitted to the English classroom for legitimate and regarding scrutiny, from the standpoint of "Who made this? In what context? With what values? In whose interest? To what effect?" (Boomer, 1988, in Pirie, 1997, p. 17)

It is not only for the survival of our profession but for the survival of adolescents as well that our students, now perhaps more than ever, need critical tools to read the increasingly bewildering and text-filled world that surrounds them. Those texts can range from the literary to a galaxy of artifacts in the external world. As the students in Martha's class recently pointed out—we met Martha in Chapter 3 as we were studying reader response—texts can include the following: videos, TV commercials, billboards, newspapers, magazines, and facial expressions.

Adolescents are often, as noted by psychologist William Perry (1970), excessively dualistic in their thinking, which prevents them from being able to imagine, let alone sustain, multiplicity of thought. The dismantling of binaries, a requisite part of the deconstructive move, helps adolescents see the limits of binary thinking. According to Terry Eagleton (1983),

> Deconstruction . . . has grasped the point that the binary oppositions with which classical structuralism tends to work represent a way of seeing typical of ideologies.

> Ideologies like to draw rigid boundaries between what is acceptable and what is not, between self and non-self, truth and falsity, sense and nonsense, reason and madness, central and marginal, surface and depth. Such metaphysical thinking, as I have said, cannot simply be eluded: we cannot catapult ourselves beyond this binary habit of thought into an ultra-metaphysical realm. But by a certain way of operating upon texts—whether "literary" or "philosophical"—we may begin to unravel these oppositions a little, demonstrate how one term of an anti-thesis secretly inheres within the other. Structuralism was generally satisfied if it could carve up a text into binary oppositions and expose the logic of their working. Deconstruction tries to show how such oppositions, in order to hold themselves in place, are sometimes betrayed into inverting or collapsing themselves or the need to banish to the text's margins certain niggling details which can be made to return and plague them. (p. 133)

The unraveling of the binary oppositions also helps unravel the ideology that set those polarities into motion and supported their production. For Jacques Derrida (1989), it is through the dismantling of false binaries that we see the limitations of the ideology they were constructed to support. Deconstruction is often viewed as ultimately antiauthoritarian, a stance needed by those oppressed, as Roland Barthes (1981) noted, by the overbearing and oppressive systems around them. Bonnycastle explains (1996, p. 112): "Deconstruction is often talked about as though it were primarily a critical method, but it is best understood as a way of resisting the authority of someone or something that has power over you."

This antiauthoritarian aspect of deconstruction has natural appeal for adolescents. But rather than simply stoking their rebellious fires, deconstruction provides adolescents with interpretive tools for critiquing the ideology that surrounds them. It teaches them to examine the very structure of the systems that oppress them and thereby to intellectually dismantle them, thus making them rebels *with* a cause.

The interpretive openness and flexibility of deconstruction is appealing to adolescents. In the sense of multiplicity, the appeal is similar in some ways to that of deconstruction's sloppier cousin, reader response:

> What is especially commendable about deconstruction as an approach for responding to poetry is that readers, especially young readers in classrooms, do not have to be unnerved by self-deprecating fears that their responses to a poem are wrong. Instead of right and wrong answers, deconstruction encourages plural responses. Instead of a hidden meaning that must be revealed, the poetic text is a site where the reader's imagination, experience, understanding, and emotions come into play in unique performances. (Leggo, 1998, pp. 187–188)

Finally, Tyson (2006, p. 240) explains what deconstruction offers readers: "It can improve our ability to think critically and to see more readily the ways in which our experience is determined by ideologies of which we are unaware because they are built into our language."

INTRODUCING DECONSTRUCTION TO ADOLESCENTS

In addition to the music video that begins this chapter, I have found other ways to introduce deconstruction to secondary students. Sometimes I begin by projecting or passing around a picture of the pop singer Michael Jackson. After the inevitable snickers of discomfort, I ask students to consider why it is that Michael Jackson is so hard to . . . comprehend. He seems to vacillate within several different pairs of constructs: He seems both male and female (I once saw him on TV and thought he was Latoya!); he seems both childlike and adult; and he seems, following a series of plastic surgeries and skin lightening, both Black and White. Michael Jackson is difficult to understand because he straddles the binaries that deconstructionists claim we have created precisely so that we *can* see things. Michael Jackson is a walking example of deconstruction!

I've also used the animated film *Shrek* to introduce deconstruction. As with much postmodern fiction, *Shrek* is a text that does some deconstructive work for us. Besides troubling the archetypal categories of hero/villain, protagonist/antagonist, prince/monster, and princess/heroine, the film deconstructs contemporary notions of beauty and femininity. It strategically calls the viewer's story grammar (Applebee, 1978) by beginning with an evocative leather-bound text and ending with a page that calligraphically proclaims, "They lived *ugly* ever after." These images act as bookends that present the film as a fairy tale, but one that questions our usual assumptions about both character and narrative structure. Students can apply several critical lenses to *Shrek*, including that of deconstruction (see Appendix, Activity 20).

DECONSTRUCTION IN THE LITERATURE CLASSROOM: ONE APPROACH

Once students are introduced to the concept of deconstruction, we are ready to apply it to literature. Many of the definitions offered in the previous section seem understandable to adolescents. I incorporated these definitions into Activity 21 (see Appendix). Many teachers and I have found that when students are allowed to absorb, discuss, and then paraphrase the definitions, they are well on their way to a fairly solid understanding of this difficult concept.

The lesson itself is designed as a kind of heuristic device, first taking students through an explanation of deconstruction, then proceeding to deconstruct some common metaphors and John Donne's poem "Death Be Not Proud," a widely anthologized work that many students may have encountered previously. Finally, either working alone or in small groups, students deconstruct a text of their own. This particular exercise focuses on the aspect of deconstruction that invites us to consider the fact that language is slippery and imperfect—as one teacher I know describes it, "Words wiggle."

To underscore the idea of language as slippery, we considered the following metaphors:

- Love is a rose.
- You are the sunshine of my life.
- The test was a bear.

If, as the deconstructionists argue, language reflects our own imperfection and the fact that words do wiggle, then metaphors may not have the effect the poet intended. Therefore, I asked students to "unpack" the metaphors and describe both their intended and unintended meanings. This exercise serves as a warm-up for the next section, which asks students to deconstruct "Death Be Not Proud."

The value of having students deconstruct a familiar and frequently taught poem is described succinctly by Guth and Rico (1996) in their introduction to a deconstructive reading of William Wordsworth's "A Slumber Did my Spirit Seal":

> The . . . deconstructionist reading . . . clears away much of the apparent surface meaning of the poem. The critic then discovers a new and different dimension of meaning as the language used by the poet dances out its own significance. (p. 863)

As with the deconstructive reading of the Wordsworth classic, the intent of this part of the deconstruction exercise is to help students see how the commonly understood reading of a widely anthologized poem can unravel through the tools of deconstructive analysis. The analysis we used did not employ the deconstruction of the false binaries that Derrida originally offered. Rather, it focused on Barthes' notions of the "shifting meanings in the weave of the written text" (Moore, 1997, p. 77). Other critics have referred to the shifting and unstable nature of the meaning of a literature text as "undecidability." As Tyson (2006, p. 252) explains, "To reveal a text's undecidability is to show that the "meaning" of the text is really an indefinite, undecidable, plural, conflicting array of possible meanings, and that the text, therefore, has no meaning, in the traditional sense of the word, at all."

In Activity 21, I ask students to contrast the author's intended meaning and the tools of traditional literary analysis with the consideration of how the poem might break down and work against the poet's intentions. They are also invited to consider places where the text falls apart, where the threads of meaning begin to unravel. The students attended to inherent contradictions in the poem and noted some of its internal inconsistencies. Here are some of their observations:

> The poem breaks down when he offers that the only way to never have to face death is to die.

The poem is very contradictory. Donne attempts to dissect death and make it smaller, but the contradictions in the poem thwart the attempt and death ends up staying powerful and frightening.

He is trying to console himself, not the reader, in this poem. I don't think he successfully manages to console either.

Although the poet is trying to convey that we must fight off death, that we are stronger than death, we, and he, cannot deny our fate.

The last line is completely indefensible. The punctuation also seems to add to confusion and may result in some unintended meaning.

The students then worked in pairs and reconsidered a reading on their own, using the heuristic device of the exercise with "Death Be Not Proud." The texts they chose to deconstruct were wide ranging and included some of those listed in Figure 7.1. For each text the students described their understanding of the author's purpose, and then gave specific examples of how the text broke apart. Figure 7.2 shows an example of how a student read against her own original reading to reveal possible conflicts in interpretation:

Finally, the students offered some reflective comments on deconstruction:

Deconstruction is cynical.

Deconstruction is very hard to do. When I look at poems they do seem solid, with one main idea and no contradictions. It's extremely interesting, though. I'm going to keep trying, trying to see the contradictions.

Does deconstruction show flaws on the part of the writer or on the part of the reader?

I think that Tim O'Brien has written a story [*The Things They Carried*] that is at war with itself. In some passages he describes war's beauty and seems to love war, yet in other passages he claims to hate it. This is a war of themes. He hasn't decided for himself what he feels, so he puts his feeling on paper, using his emotions as truth and lying for evidence. He admits he can't decide how he feels many times, so I guess my main response is: If he can't decide, how can I, even? Who am I to say whether it is a love or war story?

Deconstruction reveals more than meets the eye. When viewed through the deconstructive literary technique, the main ideas, values, and beliefs of

Figure 7.1. Texts for Use with the Deconstruction Exercise

Books	Poems
1984, George Orwell	"Bright Star, Were I Steadfast as Thou Art," John Keats
A Doll's House, Henrik Ibsen	"Do Not Go Gentle into That Good Night," Dylan Thomas
A Room of One's Own, Virginia Woolf	"I Saw a Chapel," William Blake
Brave New World, George Orwell	"I Wandered Lonely as a Cloud," William Wordsworth
Catcher in the Rye, J. D. Salinger	"Kubla Khan," Samuel Taylor Coleridge
Heart of Darkness, Joseph Conrad	"My Papa's Waltz," Theodore Roethke
Native Son, Richard Wright	"Ode to My Socks," Pablo Naruda
Of Mice and Men, John Steinbeck	"Shall I Compare Thee to a Summer's Day," William Shakespeare
Romeo and Juliet, William Shakespeare	"Sonnet 18," William Shakespeare
Sister Carrie, Theodore Dreiser	"The Executive's Death," Robert Bly
Snow Falling on Cedars, Dave Guterson	"The Road Not Taken," Robert Frost
The Age of Innocence, Edith Wharton	"The Universe," May Swenson
The Awakening, Kate Chopin	"The Unknown Citizen," W. H. Auden
The Things They Carried, Tim O'Brien	"Traveling Through the Dark," William Stafford
The Trial, Franz Kafka	

the author are revealed to be neither monstrous nor heroic. This view helps [us] to understand hidden meaning not otherwise apparent.

On the whole, the lens of deconstruction works well with high school students. It seems especially compatible with their adolescent sensibilities, which are often characterized by a burgeoning iconoclasm. The students I worked with, for the most part, took readily to this lens. Yet there is a serious downside to using deconstruction. While all the other lenses we've discussed—reader response, gender, social class—meet with their share of resistance from individual students for particular reasons, the resistance to deconstruction seems especially poignant and potentially harmful. In considering the use of deconstruction, teachers should consider the following incident, which occurred when I introduced deconstruction in Martha Hargrove's class. After reading about the incident, teachers may want to proceed with caution.

Figure 7.2. One Student's Deconstruction Worksheet

Text: *The Awakening*, by Kate Chopin

When I *deconstruct* this text, here's what happens. I think the main idea the author/poet was trying to construct was:

This society's oppression of women is tragic, preventing their development and fulfillment in life.

But this construct really doesn't work. The idea falls apart. The language and construction of the text isn't able to convey what the author meant to convey. There are places in the text where it just doesn't work. For example:

In the opening island scene with the wives talking, Chopin wants to show how bored the women are (because they have nothing to do), but they end up seeming flighty and dull. Edna's suicide is supposed to be driven by society's oppression only, but her own weakness is very apparent as well.

So in the end, even though the author meant the work to say

Edna was essentially the victim of an oppressive society,

it really said:

Edna ended up killing herself; she had the option of living but just gave up.

(Optional) I'd also like to say that:

Kate Chopin probably had personal doubts that were involved in this book. Perhaps she saw herself in Edna and was attempting to justify her own failures through her.

THE DANGER OF DECONSTRUCTION: RACHEL AND HER PLEA

The school year is drawing to a close and the students in Martha's senior English classes have been introduced to numerous types of critical lenses. It's a dream class—the students are lively, bright, engaged, and a bit feisty. They've taken the class content seriously and have frequently challenged the usefulness and relevance of each theoretical perspective. But today will present a different kind of challenge. It is time to discuss deconstruction, one of the most difficult lenses of all.

The class thinks through the deconstruction handout. We read together the definitions of *deconstruction*. I try to keep the tone light—to keep us all from feeling overwhelmed. We're "playing with deconstruction," I say. We practice with metaphors (Appendix, Activity 21) and discuss intended and unintended meanings. We then consider Donne's "Death Be Not Proud" and attempt to deconstruct it together. The previous week, these students had completed the AP test. This is probably important; we are not only deconstructing a traditional reading of the poem, we are also in effect deconstructing the entire AP test and a particular way of interpreting literature.

The deconstruction exercise works well. Perhaps too well.

After we go through the entire lesson, including a deconstruction of a reading of their choice (see previous section, "Deconstruction in the Literature Classroom"), the students seem both comfortable with their understanding of deconstruction and, at the same time, unsettled by that understanding. They get it and they can apply it—but they hate it. They seem uncomfortable, as if they managed to chew something unpleasant without choking but now the aftertaste is killing them.

Jessica is the first to speak. She has always struck me as a remarkably self-possessed young woman, confident and self-assured. Her high school education will be over in 2 weeks; in the fall she is off to the University of Michigan. Jessica is pragmatic. She takes a no-nonsense approach to many things, including literary interpretation. She seems mostly reality bound—firmly located in the here and now. She is also quite bright and has been able to engage enthusiastically in the varieties of literary discourse we've explored.

Jessica has never been shy about speaking her mind. She's one of the "beautiful people," the kind of girl other girls love to hate; she is part of the "in" crowd. She has gravitas, the weight of popularity surrounding her. She is from a fairly well-to-do family and seemed somewhat resistant to the social-class lens when we studied it (see Chapter 4). She appears to be having a relatively successful adolescence and somehow doesn't seem particularly vulnerable to the vagaries of deconstruction.

Today, however, she is positively wailing. "Why did you teach us this? I'm so sorry I know about this. How could you have told us about this? What are you trying to do—destroy us? How am I supposed to live with this knowledge? You've just demonstrated that everything we've learned up to this point has been a sham. Now what? Here I am at the end of my high school education, and now it seems as if everything I was trying to do is worth absolutely nothing. Nothing means anything. Is that what I'm supposed to believe? I feel as if all of my illusions have been torn down. And here we are left with nothing. What am supposed to replace it with? It's not just what we've studied and how we've studied it—it's everything. Now I feel like everything I've done in school has been a big lie."

Martha and I are absolutely shocked and disturbed by this outburst. The class undertakes a metaphysical debate the likes of which I can't remember ever being a part of before. Sarah says that deconstruction should be taught at home, since "we were going to find out all this stuff anyway, right? Better sooner than later."

The class erupts into a debate about whether deconstruction is indeed harmful to kids. No one, oddly enough, is debating whether it is true or not—only whether kids should learn about it. It strikes Martha and me as odd that the very students who generally make a very strong case for their being full-fledged adults and for the rights that go with such status are asking to have something be kept from them. It is not only during the class discussion that students' discomfort with deconstruction is evidenced. Although Jessica and Sarah bravely announced their issues with deconstruction in class, other students waited to confess their confusion in their journals. Kevin echoes Jessica's discontent in this entry from his reading journal:

> Earlier this year, I wrote a paper on the literary lens of deconstruction and thought that I had a fairly complete understanding of the concept. I found out today that my understanding was not complete. I love it when I learn something new! I find literary deconstruction to be very thought-provoking but have unresolved conflict within me. I understand the concept of literary deconstruction, but isn't it destructive?
>
> The meaning of any work is questionable, but if some meaning isn't assumed, will we ever get anywhere? I have always believed that assumption is the worst thing any human can do, but educated assumption is necessary for humans to survive. We must assume that the sun will appear every morning and disappear every evening. We must also assume that we won't spontaneously combust.
>
> Assumption is necessary given human emotion. Assumption allows humans to feel comfort which helps them lead a contented life. If we didn't assume that the sun would rise in the morning, many would lead horrible lives. Many would constantly worry and suffer about the future. Yes, assumption is not 100% safe, but nothing in this world is. One can safely assume many things if one takes the time to research things. Those who fear assumption are those who will end up on Prozac and Valium. Mental stability thrives in comfort. Uncertainty does not create comfort.

Are Jessica and Kevin right? Is deconstruction too potentially destructive for adolescents? The challenge doesn't arise as a result of the students' inability to understand such a difficult and complex concept. Oh, they get it all right. The challenges arises because understanding the implications of this particular lens is extremely frightening to them.

Perhaps for Jessica the fragile and artificial constructs on which she's based her entire high school career have come crashing down on her. Perhaps the lens of deconstruction has helped her see that her own adolescence and the constructs she uses to define it may be as artificial and impermanent as the set of the "Torn" video.

Others have addressed this by-product, as it were, of deconstruction:

> As we have seen, deconstruction asserts that our experience of ourselves and our world is produced by the language we speak, and because all language is an unstable,

> ambiguous force-field of competing ideologies, we are, ourselves, unstable, ambiguous force-fields of competing ideologies. The self-image of a stable identity that many of us have is really just a comforting self-delusion, which we produce in collusion with our culture, for culture, too, wants to see itself as stable and coherent when in reality it is highly unstable and fragmented. We don't really have an identity because the word identity implies that we consist of one, singular self when in fact we are multiple and fragmented, consisting at any moment of conflicting beliefs, desires, fears, anxieties and intentions. (Tyson, 2006, pp. 250–251)

> In my undergraduate English studies I was trained to look for meaning, like a beagle on the trail of a rabbit. The rabbit might twist and turn and hide, but if I persisted I could outwit the rabbit. Deconstruction reminds me that there is no plump rabbit seeking to avoid my capture and consumption. (Leggo, 1998, p. 187)

The reaction of Jessica and her classmates to deconstruction serves as a caveat to teachers considering using this lens with high school students. While the privileging of "the personal" in reader response and the anti-ideology stances of gender and social class theory seem to be developmentally appropriate for adolescents, deconstruction is intellectually more challenging and psychologically more frightening for students at this age.

In my experience, students have seemed uncomfortable with deconstruction. For the students described in this chapter, at least, deconstruction ultimately proved a somewhat dangerous tool for literary analysis, one that called into question the foundations of their personal identities and core beliefs. As Erik Erikson, James Marcia, Carol Gilligan, and other theorists have noted, adolescents follow a developmental imperative to construct an identity. The fragility and instability of identity construction during adolescence apparently makes the nihilistic nature of deconstruction too painful for adolescents to integrate. The students' ability to understand the theory was not in question. Rather, they just seemed too vulnerable to have their shaky foundations torn from under them. As Bonnycastle (1996) reminds us,

> If you go to deconstruction to find a set of values or a philosophy of life, you enter a world that is anachronistic and solipsistic—a world in which each person is essentially alone and cannot communicate with others, and social groups fall apart because they have no coherence. This, I think, is an almost impossible world to live in, but it is an interesting one to know about. (p. 115)

To be sure, high school students do, as Bonnycastle suggests, find the elements of deconstruction "interesting." And despite its potentially nihilistic side effects, it seems to be worth teaching. Perhaps more than any other literary lens, that of deconstruction can inspire a particular kind of intellectual suppleness (M. Rose, personal communication, August 18, 1999). Like gender and social class theories, it requires the reader to read ideology. Deconstruction helps students question the certainty of meaning without relying exclusively on the personal lens of reader response. Like reader response, it requires the reader to be an active meaning-maker, but unlike reader response, with its sometimes sloppy overgeneralization and overapplication, deconstruction requires the rigor of a close reading.

Like the political prisms of social class and gender literary theory, deconstruction teaches students to resist surface meaning and to read ideology—two critical skills students need to become autonomous and powerful adults. It is what they need to make meaning in the world and to evaluate cultural norms and expectations so that they do not merely succumb to them. This is not only important for the interpretation of literary texts, it is essential to the skills of critical interpretation of the media that surround adolescents through print, video, and other new media. Lynn (2008) points out that "a deconstructive stance not only may help us anticipate some of the ways that even simple texts can be misread, it may also help us see what is being excluded or suppressed in a text" (p. 94). Deconstructing an ad for a "Hemingway cap" that plays on constructs of masculinity, Lynn points out that adopting a deconstructive stance encourages an acute alertness to rhetorical strategies and even the assumptions these strategies depend upon (pp. 94–95). This acute alertness contributes to helping young people become vigilant witnesses (hooks, 1994) as they learn to read and resist they ideologies inscribed in the texts that surround them.

In *Textual Power*, Robert Scholes (1985, p. 21) creates a metaphor for education. Students, he says, operate in an endless web of growth and change and interaction. As teachers, our task is "to introduce students to the web, to make it real and visible for them" and "to encourage them to cast their own strands of thought and text into this network so that they will feel its power and understand both how to use it and how to protect themselves from its abuses."

By introducing students to the power of deconstruction we may indeed put them at intellectual risk as they call everything into question. Yet with care and guidance, we may finally bestow upon them the "textual power" Scholes calls for by finally removing the artificial barrier between school knowledge and the knowledge that counts in the "real world." As Scholes states: "We must open the way between the literary and verbal text and the social text in which we live" (p. 24).

• C H A P T E R 8 •

Lenses and Learning Styles: Acknowledging Student Plurality with Theoretical Plurality

> A man with one theory is lost. He needs several of them, or lots! He should stuff them in his pockets like newspapers.
>
> —Bertold Brecht

Perhaps one of the biggest misconceptions about the use of literary theory with secondary students is that it is most appropriate for college-bound or AP students. Many teachers choose not to incorporate literary theory into their regular tracked classes, because they assume that literary theory is both irrelevant and too difficult for their "average" students. In fact, nothing could be further from the truth.

Literary theory is not just intellectual cake for adolescent cake eaters—those who are privileged by social status and other factors to have significant educational advantages. Because many of the theories deal with issues of power, students on the margin, for particular reasons—ethnicity, class, ability—are often more receptive to the basic ideological premises of these theories than are their more privileged peers, who sometimes view theories such as those of gender and class as mechanisms for using the master's tools to dismantle the master's house.

In fact, kids on the margins seem to be savvier about theory. Many of them have been reading the world and its inequities for a very long time. They've been reading patterns of privilege and inequity their whole lives; they naturally challenge hegemonic beliefs as well as the status quo. As Luis Moll (Gonzáles, Moll, & Amanti, 2005) remarks, these students have the "funds of knowledge" to apply their perceptions of the world to a literary text.

Lisa Eckert (2006, p. 9) believes that literary theory has a particular salience for reluctant learners. In *How Does It Mean*, she writes, "Learning how to effectively argue for a particular interpretation is ideally suited for adolescent learners, whose behavior is often oppositional, anyway." Eckert argues that literary theory requires readers to take an active role in their reading and to become more engaged and involved readers:

> Introducing different theoretical approaches into the literature classroom encourages students to consciously use everything they know to construct meaning from a text, and gain an understanding of what they are doing when they read and respond. They discover how they are constantly interpreting signals whenever they read, even though they may not be aware of doing so. (p. 8)

Similarly, Allen Carey-Webb (2001) claims that literary theory makes literature seem more rather than less relevant for our students by making robust connections between their lives and the literature they read. He continues,

> It is not so much that our students need to be entertained—though some have seen it this way—but that they need to understand the purpose and meaning of what we are doing if we are going to succeed in keeping them engaged. (p. 159)

Thus from both dispositional and motivational perspectives, literary theory is well suited to a wide range of adolescent readers.

This is true from a cognitive perspective as well. While there may still be those who cling to the misperception that literary theory remains the province of the erudite and intellectual elite, or in the case of secondary students, the definitively college-bound, that is simply not the case. Using multiple perspectives to read and interpret literature doesn't require that students be already operating at a certain level of intellectual flexibility; it is an instructional approach that actually helps increase that intellectual flexibility.

To be sure, readers need to be at least at the stage of "formal operational," from a Piagetian perspective. In other words, they probably need to be in at least sixth or seventh grade. Lev Vygotsky (1978) reminds us that learners, regardless of their ability or initial predisposition, can learn practically anything if teachers provide the appropriate scaffolding. This holds true for literary theory. With the appropriate guidance and prior knowledge, nearly all secondary students can read and interpret texts from multiple perspectives. In fact, most of the activities that accompany this book are constructed as a kind of scaffolding to allow students of all abilities to participate. Let's look at one of the activities as an example.

A SAMPLE "MAINSTREAM" LESSON IN MULTIPLE PERSPECTIVES

Activity 26 (see Appendix) asks students to read a Gary Soto poem from three different perspectives. I have worked with teachers who have used both "Oranges" and "Ode to Family Photographs" for this lesson. First, teachers use some of the introductory activities that are explained in Chapter 2. Then, teachers offer students the Literary Perspectives Tool Kit handout (see Appendix, Activity 4), which is specifically written to be accessible to students with a wide range of abilities.

Next, the teacher distributes a brief biographical sketch of Gary Soto. Finally, students read either "Oranges" or "Ode to Family Photographs," poems that are easily readable and comprehensible at the literal level yet are rich enough to yield multiple interpretations.

Ode to Family Photographs

This is the pond, and these are my feet.
This is the rooster, and this is more of my feet.

Mama was never good at pictures.

This is a statue of a famous general who lost an arm,
And this is me with my head cut off.

This is a trash can chained to a gate,
This is my father with his eyes half-closed.

This is a photograph of my sister
And a giraffe looking over her shoulder.

This is our car's front bumper.
This is a bird with a pretzel in its beak.
This is my brother Pedro standing on one leg on a rock,
With a smear of chocolate on his face.

Mama sneezed when she looked
Behind the camera: the snapshots are blurry,
The angles dizzy as a spin on a merry-go-round.

But we had fun when Mama picked up the camera.
How can I tell?
Each of us is laughing hard.
Can you see? I have candy in my mouth.

—Gary Soto

Oranges

The first time I walked
With a girl, I was twelve,
Cold, and weighted down
With two oranges in my jacket.

December. Frost cracking
Beneath my steps, my breath
Before me, then gone,
As I walked toward
Her house, the one whose
Porchlight burned yellow
Night and day, in any weather.
A dog barked at me, until
She came out pulling
At her gloves, face bright
With rouge. I smiled,
Touched her shoulder, and led
Her down the street, across
A used car lot and a line
Of newly planted trees,
Until we were breathing
Before a drug store. We
Entered, the tiny bell
Bringing a saleslady
Down a narrow aisle of goods.
I turned to the candies
Tiered like bleachers
And asked what she wanted—
Light in her eyes, a smile
Starting at the corners
Of her mouth. I fingered
A nickel in my pocket,
And when she lifted a chocolate
That cost a dime,
I didn't say anything.
I took the nickel from
My pocket, then an orange,
And set them quietly on
The counter. When I looked up,
The lady's eyes met mine,
And held them, knowing
Very well what it was all
About.

Outside,
A few cars hissing past.
Fog hanging like old

Coats between the trees.
I took my girl's hand
In mine for two blocks,
Then released it to let
Her unwrap the chocolate.
I peeled my orange
That was so bright against
The gray of December
That, from some distance,
Someone might have thought
I was making a fire in my hands.

—Gary Soto

The poems, the explanation of the lenses, and the biographical information are all written at a level that is accessible to most students. The skill of reading through multiple perspectives can be taught with students of a wide range of abilities; it is simply the choice of texts that needs to be modified. With students at a higher grade level or with more advanced reading or interpretive skills, one can teach a very similar lesson using a more complex text and more elaborated instructions and explications of the literary lenses. I have used an activity very similar to the one discussed above: but rather than using a fairly accessible, or as some might argue, elementary, poem, I have used Kate Chopin's "The Story of an Hour," with a set of somewhat more elaborate instructions.

In sum, critical lenses can and should be used with a wide spectrum of learners. The following cases, drawn from schools across the country with real students in diverse classrooms, will help illustrate the range of learners that literary theories can reach.

Marcos

Marcos is a 10th-grader in the English class of Yvonne Sanchez. Yvonne teaches a Puente class in a community a few miles outside Los Angeles. Puente is a program designed to encourage underrepresented students, especially Latino students, who hope to increase their college readiness. Nearly all the students in her class are native Spanish speakers. Yvonne readily admits to having had skepticism when she first learned about using literary theory with her specific student population at a Puente workshop. But, always adventurous, Yvonne decided to try.

She began by trying the lenses with one of the students' favorite poets, Gary Soto. Modifying the activity described earlier in this chapter, Yvonne had them read the poem "Oranges" from three different theoretical perspectives.

Marcos is a solid if not unusually engaged student; he generally receives B's and C's. English, he claims, is not his favorite subject. Marcos is reading exactly at grade level. He tends to read all the work that is assigned but is not a particularly avid reader and rarely reads on his own for recreation. He is a bit vague about his post–high school aspirations. "I'd like to go to college maybe. I'm just not sure it'll happen."

During Yvonne's lesson on using lenses with the poem "Oranges," Marcos, like many of his classmates, was easily able to move from the consideration of gender roles and Latino machismo to considerations of class to reader response associations of first loves. In the activity, Marcos seemed to move comfortably from one theoretical perspective to another. When he read the poem through a gender lens, he pointed out that the "boy was taking charge, showing off to buy his girl something he really couldn't afford. Like he's supposed to be the provider or something. Hey, it's what we're brought up to believe, you know, Latin men take charge. Hey, it's machismo!" Marcos then moved to a consideration of the poem from a social-class perspective, the perspective about which Yvonne, like many teachers, was the most dubious or wary (especially when it was labeled the "Marxist lens"). Marcos noted in class discussion that the boy in the poem "didn't even have enough money to pay for an orange. . . . He was probably poor or something. Actually I think they both were, because the poem takes place in a grocery store, not a store like Macy's or something. Like, who's gonna to go to the corner grocery to buy your girl something in the first place?"

Marcos then moved, somewhat reluctantly, to the reader response perspective. "Yeah, I mean, I can relate to wanting to give a girl something, though I wouldn't pick a dumb orange. That's for sure. And I guess I want my girl to think I can give her stuff. Um, I liked the ending, too, cause it seems [Marcos blushes] like, when you are with your girl, everything is, um, stronger, more intense, you know, like the sun was in the poem."

Encouraged by this initial success, Yvonne included theory-based activities throughout her yearlong class, with canonical works such as *Romeo and Juliet* and more contemporary texts such as *House on Mango Street*. Marcos also used literary lenses as he read adolescent novels such as *The Giver*, *Monster,* and *Bronx Masquerade.*

In his final exam, in "reading the world" (see Appendix, Activity 30) Marcos writes,

> Using multiple perspectives broadens my ability to see all sides of the story. It keeps me from feeling personally victimized. It also says a lot about where you grew up economically and socially as well as what type of household you grew up in. It makes you realize where your life is now and why you are there.

In a personal interview, Marcos concluded,

> At first I thought the lenses stuff that Ms. S was teaching us was going to be too hard, but then I tried it and it wasn't that hard. She says this the

way people read poems and stories in college. Hey, I even think about it when I listen to lyrics and stuff. I tell Ms. S she ruined me.

As an experienced teacher of non-native speakers of English, Yvonne believes that lenses are appropriate for her students: "My bilingual kids are actually more adept at switching perspectives than are my English speakers. After all, switching language codes is a survival tactic for them, and we all know that when you switch from one language to the next you also switch perspectives."

Ayanna

Ayanna often thinks of herself as "a stranger in a strange land." She is the only student of color in Greg's AP literature and composition class, which has 34 majority students. This demographic composition is reflective of the school as a whole, which enrolls fewer than 12% students of color. When Ayanna entered ninth grade, her family moved from their city neighborhood in Minneapolis to this suburb, well known throughout Minnesota for its high-quality school system, so that she could have a better education.

Although she is a successful athlete and generally well liked by her peers, Ayanna feels as though the social ice she skates on is very thin, and she could "fall through at any moment." At lunch, she is a social chameleon, moving from group to group to try to fit in. Indeed, the climate around her sometimes feels as chilly as a Minnesota winter.

Issues of race come up almost daily for Ayanna, no more so than in English class, both because of the literature the class reads and because of the themes that Greg likes to raise. For Ayanna, Greg's diverse curriculum is something of a mixed blessing. Novels such as *Invisible Man*, *Their Eyes Were Watching God*, *Sula*, *Beloved*, *Adventures of Huckleberry Finn*, *Heart of Darkness*, and *Waiting for the Barbarians* and plays such as *Othello* and *Fences* surely are more adventurous and diverse fare than one finds in most secondary classrooms (Applebee, 1993). At the same time, they offer the opportunity and necessity, perhaps, for many difficult discussions and uncomfortable moments.

Ayanna used to feel that a giant spotlight would shine on her whenever issues of race were raised in class discussions. And despite the atmosphere of politeness (referred to as "Minnesota nice") and the lack of overt racial comments, Ayanna often felt uncomfortable. Greg struggled, too. "I want us to be able to go beneath the surface of the texts," he confided, "but every time I see Ayanna's face in this sea of White faces, I can feel myself backing down. I don't want to put her on the spot or make her uncomfortable in any way. For everyone's sake, I wish our classroom were more diverse, but it isn't. And there are things we need to discuss, regardless of who is (and isn't) in the room."

Somehow, for both Ayanna and Greg, the literary lenses, especially those of social power and gender, provide a way to discuss the issues more comfortably.

The lenses not only move the focus away from her but also provide a way to help her classmates see what she has always seen. In a personal interview she explains:

> I guess, as a person of color, I've always had to "read" what's going on in terms of people's attitudes toward race and stuff. I used to think it was just a personal lens, but now [I] see that some of the, like, more political lenses . . . provide a way of thinking about what's going on in the world, not just what's going on with me. It gives us a way of talking about it that's, um, more, comfortable. (Personal communication with author, April 24, 2008)

Ayanna remembers when her class read *A Raisin in the Sun* and *Their Eyes Were Watching God.* By using the postcolonial and social class lenses, her classmates were able to see particular issues in ways that were depersonalized and general. It moved the discussion away from Ayanna. The lenses brought issues of power and equity into sharp relief but, says Ayanna, in a different context:

> The lenses make me feel less isolated. I finally feel as if, being a person of color, I am at an advantage rather than disadvantage. The lenses help my classmates see what I've seen my whole life. This is how I see the world.

Jenny

Jenny is a 10th-grader at Lincoln High School, a comprehensive school in an inner-ring suburb. At Jenny's school, the graduation rate is less than 70% and the school has had difficulty meeting the AYP (Annual Yearly Progress) level mandated by the No Child Left Behind Act. Less than 60% of the student body attends college or some other form of postsecondary education as compared with the well over 96% who do so at Ayanna's school. Seventy-two percent of the students are White, and 28% are students of color, with the largest percentage of the latter being African American, followed by Asian, Latino, and Native American.

When Michael, Jenny's 10th-grade American literature teacher, decided to infuse literary theory into his yearlong course, both his colleagues in the English department and his students were mystified. "Isn't this college prep, AP stuff?" one of his colleagues challenged. "Why teach literary theory to students who aren't going to college?" Why, indeed?

Influenced by the work of Bruce Pirie, bell hooks, Robert Scholes and others, Michael believes that his obligation as an English teacher is to help his students become what Scholes (2001) calls "crafty readers." He believes that teaching students to read and teaching them to become able interpreters of literary texts are inextricably intertwined. His approach is what Hephzibah Roskelly has dubbed "an unquiet pedagogy" (Kutz & Roskelly, 1991).

Like Yvonne, Michael teaches all the theoretical perspectives to his students, regardless of what level English course they happen to be enrolled in. He simply modifies the explanatory material using the Literary Perspectives Tool Kit (see Appendix, Activity 4) and, of course, considers his students' abilities and interests as he makes his text selections. Michael finds that with students such as Jenny, applying the lenses with shorter texts such as short stories or poems seems to be a bit more successful than using it with whole texts, at least initially. Michael also finds that Jenny seems much more interested in applying the lenses to real-world situations than she does to literary texts.

Jenny is in good company with this preference. Robert Scholes (1985) remarks, "The relationship between the text and the world is not simply a fascinating problem for textual theory. It is, above all others, the problem that makes textual theory necessary" (p. 31). bell hooks (1994) concurs: "Being an 'enlightened witness' means becoming critically vigilant about the world we live in" (p. 60). Bruce Pirie (1997) also invokes the larger textual world in which Michael finds that students such as Jenny can more easily engage:

> It is *not* that we shouldn't care about individual students and texts. We should, and I do. We also recognize, however, that students and texts are embedded in huge, living, sometimes contradictory networks, and if we want students to understand the workings of textuality, then we have to think about those larger systems. (p. 96)

Michael provides his students with several opportunities with which to apply the multiple perspectives that literary theory affords everyday events. For both the gender and social-class lenses, Michael invites students to consider real-world incidents that can be better understood or explained through a particular theoretical reading. For example, when she was asked to bring in a cultural artifact that needed to be "read" from a particular perspective, Jenny brought in a computer screen shot of a Victoria's Secret advertisement for swimsuits. The assignment asked students to "read" the cultural artifact as a text and to discuss its significance, using a particular lens. Jenny wrote:

> I found a picture on the Victoria's Secret website while browsing through the swimwear. As I was looking at the different swimsuits they have to offer, I noticed something about every girl/picture. On each picture there would be a girl in her swimsuit with oil on her body, looking sort of seductive. Each girl on the entire website was extremely skinny. Then I thought about the gender lens, about the portrayal of women in society, and here's what I came up with. In order to sell their swimwear, they got the skinniest and prettiest models. Nowhere on their website, not one place, is there a plus-sized or even an average-sized woman. This suggests the idea that if they were to have an average- or a plus-sized model their product would not sell. Victoria's Secret is not the only place in the world that supports the message "skinny sells."

In a final assignment, titled "From Reading Words to Reading the World: Critical Lenses in Literature and in Life" (see Appendix, Activity 30), Jenny was asked to consider a real-world event or issue and apply two lenses to it. She chose to write about fights in the school hallway and described them thus:

> The psychological lens helps me interpret these fights very well. It brings up questions like: Are they scared? Do they enjoy it? Why are they doing it? Do they know what will happen afterwards? This lens increases our understanding by asking why. The gender lens also helps us understand fights. In our society, guys are taught to be "tough" and not take anything from anyone. They often resort to violence and think violence actually solves something, which is absurd. Gender lenses show us that males are more prone to fighting and the sexes are raised in different ways.

The assignment also asked, "How do you think the multiple perspectives can help you understand some things about yourself and your life outside school?" Jenny responded:

> Being able to use these lenses and perspectives helps me be more open-minded about things. It helps me think about certain situations and events in more than one perspective. It allows me to learn more and think more in depth about issues that I haven't before. It's like taking a look at a picture and noticing something different.

The work of Jenny and her classmates demonstrates that literary theory is not an intellectual parlor game. Through her insights and engagement, Jenny shows that the reading and interpretive skills that theory facilitate are accessible to, and important for, the large majority of secondary students, students whose worlds may not include college, students who are ready and eager to read their world and are sometimes even better at it than their college-bound counterparts.

"ON THE SUBWAY": CONVERSATIONS ABOUT DIVERSITY

In addition to providing conceptual interpretive tools for a wide variety of students, literary theory can provide students (and their teachers) with ways to talk more easily and productively about issues of diversity, such as those of race, class, and gender. Molly teaches 11th-grade English in an inner-ring suburban school. Although technically in a suburb, Molly's district, like many in inner-ring suburbs in the United States, is diverse. Nearly 40% of her students are nonmajority. Twenty-nine percent of all students are on free or reduced-cost lunch.

Molly's classroom reflects the overall diversity of her community. In a building that is both overcrowded and sometimes full of social tension, Molly wants to create an environment where the students feel safe enough to confront difficult issues in class discussions. She is grateful for the diversity of her classroom, but she also feels, as do many teachers, that it is precisely that diversity that makes such discussions difficult. "I want to teach with honesty and teach edgy stuff that brings up issues of race, class, and gender, but I worry about my ability to lead discussions on touchy issues, or even to ask students to read texts they might find offensive. There is always someone who might be offended," Molly says ruefully.

On the suggestion of a colleague,* Molly decides to tackle the poem "On the Subway," by Sharon Olds.

On the Subway

The boy and I face each other.
His feet are huge, in black sneakers
laced with white in a complex pattern like a
set of intentional scars. We are stuck on
opposite sides of the car, a couple of
molecules stuck in a rod of light
rapidly moving through darkness. He has the
casual cold look of a mugger,
alert under hooded lids. He is wearing
red, like the inside of the body
exposed. I am wearing dark fur, the
whole skin of an animal taken and
used. I look at his raw face,
he looks at my fur coat, and I don't
know if I am in his power—
he could take my coat so easily, my
briefcase, my life—
or if he is in my power, the way I am
living off his life, eating the steak
he does not eat, as if I am taking
the food from his mouth. And he is black
and I am white, and without meaning or
trying to I must profit from his darkness,
the way he absorbs the murderous beams of the
nation's heart, as black cotton
absorbs the heat of the sun and holds it. There is

*Special thanks to Todd Huck for the poetry suggestion.

no way to know how easy this
white skin makes my life, this
life he could take so easily and
break across his knee like a stick the way
his own back is being broken, the
rod of his soul that at birth was dark and
fluid and rich as the heart of a seedling
ready to thrust up into any available light.

—Sharon Olds

Molly is afraid of this poem—afraid to teach it, afraid it might offend and enrage her students, both Black and White. Yet it is this very fear that makes her think she should teach it. Its power and directness cause her to both shudder and smile as she considers how to approach it. After all, she teaches literature precisely because it is the mirror of human experience, in all its beauty and ugliness, precisely because reading literature offers a way to address important issues with adolescents.

Using the gender, class, reader response, and formalist lenses, Molly divides the class into four, giving each group a separate handout, a separate way into the text (see Appendix, Activities 22–25). The lenses offer a way of triangulating the subject so that students can address the issues without completely personalizing them.

The students meet in their theory groups for about 20 minutes, reading the poem through their assigned lens. Molly then moves them into a "jigsaw" configuration, so that in each group there is one student from each of the previous groups. Thus in each new group, every lens is represented. Molly is pleased as she walks around the room, which fills quickly with voices from each group—high pitched, engaged, and exuberant. The small groups have allowed even the most reluctant of students to participate, and the lenses seem to offer a way to discuss the undiscussible without fear or embarrassment.

As a closing activity, Molly uses one of her favorite prompts, "What/So What?"; the prompt asks each student to respond to the following two questions:

"What?" (What was the poem literally about?)
"So what?" (What is the significance or meaning in what you read? Why does it matter?)

Here are three students' responses:

EMMA (WHITE FEMALE)

What? Sitting across from a Black man on the subway, Sharon Olds discusses the implications of race in society.

So What? In a society where race and racial tensions are regarded as "risky," we must challenge ourselves to challenge our assumptions. Encountering our fear is the only way to overcome it. Literature provides a way for us to step outside our protective bubble into situations that are foreign and scary, and through these encounters embrace and accept our uneasiness as a way to overcome it.

JOE (LATINO MALE)

What? Speaker differentiates himself from the Black man across from him. He leaves no room for gray . . . only black and white. He talks about his fear of him; the Black man's power is in violence. White power is in superior standing. He talks about class difference. He talks about how society promotes this. He talks about the persistence of the minority.

So What? The poem asks or presents the question: Are these thoughts and distinctions of race and gender present or latent in our minds? If so, are they supposed to be there? The "so what" of this poem is the importance of exploring whether or not it is morally wrong to make superficial distinctions. Are these distinctions even superficial? If we are thinking about them, should we keep them to ourselves or discuss them with others? In an age of political correctness, we have a booming responsibility to answer these questions.

ALICIA (AFRICAN AMERICAN FEMALE)

What? A wealthy White woman sits across from a poorer Black boy and contemplates what he could do to her—and what she is doing to him by being White and well off.

So What? It is somewhat of a paradox in race and class relations that the author addresses. The White woman and the Black man are both holding each other hostage in some way—the man through the violence and crime that makes up his life and the woman by her inherent ability to have money and power. It is a question as to which of these powers is greater—him taking her life by force or her gradually taking away his right to a prosperous life. The author doesn't give us any information that we don't already know about the tensions involved in race, class, and sex. But what this poem does is ask us what the next step is. It helps the reader decide whether it must always be like this (if society is stuck in a rut of prejudices and fear) or if there is room for balance and change. Instead of all new insights the author chooses to pose the questions of societal fate to her readers.

Molly is impressed with these responses. She knows there is a tendency to underestimate "average" students in "regular" classrooms, and she laughs off the skepticism of those who doubt her students' ability to read insightfully and through multiple lenses. Her literary gamble has paid off, and she is emboldened to continue to use the lenses to help pave the way for such discussions.

Far from being the singular province of "advanced" students, literary theory, as we have seen from these cases, can serve the needs of diverse learners in diverse classrooms. With the possible exception of deconstruction (see Chapter 7), literary theory is accessible to all different kinds of students at many ability levels.

As we saw in the cases of Marcos, Jenny, and Ayanna, literary theory is not only within the reach of diverse learners, it can actually serve their intellectual and psychological needs. By our modifying the difficulty of texts, and using some of the approaches suggested here, all students can enjoy the benefits of viewing both textual and actual worlds through the multiple perspectives that literary theory affords.

• C H A P T E R 9 •

Critical Encounters: Reading the World

To understand the craft of reading is to understand the world itself as a text and to be able to read it critically.

—Robert Scholes, *The Crafty Reader*

A better understanding of the world in which we live, it seems to me, automatically comes along for the ride when we study literature, and the study of critical theory makes that enterprise even more productive.

—Lois Tyson, *Critical Theory Today*

The world is like a huge novel that needs to be interpreted. It has a very broad and confusing plot with a variety of settings and many different cultures and themes.

—Jesse, Grade 11

Critical lenses are devices of interpretation. Just as they are used to interpret literature they can be used to interpret the world. A critical lens can be used to "read" the world because there is little, if any, difference between what is real and the literature it is customarily used for.

—Carmen, Grade 12

It's a warm May Friday afternoon in St. Paul, Minnesota. The 5th-hour bell has just rung at Groveland High School. The usual formation of rows in Martha's literature classroom has been abandoned in favor of clusters of desks that today are called "learning stations." Over each station is a hand-lettered sign. One station has the name "Gender" over it, another says "Social Power/Class," another says "Reader Response," while another is called "Historical/Biographical." Besides looking different today, the classroom sounds different: the blues of Robert Johnson, Miles Davis, Billie Holiday, and Bo Diddley competes with the afternoon announcements for the students' attention—and the blues wins.

In groups of four, the students scurry from one station to the next, one minute considering feminist readings of Bigger Thomas's violence toward women, the next reading biographical data on Richard Wright and considering its relevance to the themes of *Native Son* (see Appendix, Activity 32). As they progress from station to station, the students recall the critical theories they have discussed all year. They adroitly apply and critique each theory. Their minds seem to shift as quickly as their feet as they move between stations, creating multiple interpretations of an often taught classic of American literature, using contemporary literary theory to guide their way.

Later, in small groups, the students consider how these critical encounters enhanced their understanding of the text. They also evaluate the relative applicability of each lens to *Native Son*. This is no cookie-cutter exercise, no one-theory-fits-all approach. Martha knows that some students will assert that certain theories do not help their reading of this novel. She welcomes the dissonance because she also knows they will be able to explain why certain theories are more useful for particular texts than others. She welcomes the resistance because critical resistance has been something she wanted them to learn. She welcomes the multiple critical encounters her students had with *Native Son*. As she surveys her disorderly room, chairs askew and folders opened at each station, she is reminded of how messy and unpredictable critical encounters can be.

CRITICAL ENCOUNTERS WITH TEXTS

Critical encounters with literature, with the world, and with each other are at the heart of this "theory relay." These critical encounters also form the core of this book. Through the lenses of literary theory, the students and teachers who appear in these pages transformed their study of literature into theoretical odysseys marked by significant critical encounters. Rather than simply covering literature as cultural content or focusing exclusively on the skills of reading and writing, these students and teachers used the lenses of literary theories to construct multiple ways of reading texts. Together they constructed and enacted a different kind of knowing in the literature classroom. As Cochran-Smith and Lytle (1993) remind us,

> We begin with the assumption that through their interactions, teachers and students together construct classroom life and the learning opportunities that are available. Essentially, teacher and students negotiate what counts as knowledge in the classroom, who can have knowledge and how knowledge can be generated, challenged, and evaluated. (p. 45)

Critical encounters with theory help students and teachers reevaluate what counts as knowing in the literature classroom. Contemporary literary theory helps students reshape their knowledge of texts, of themselves, and of the worlds in which both reside. In a special issue of *Theory into Practice* dedicated to the teaching of literary theory in the high school classroom, Meredith Cherland and Jim Greenlaw (1998) remind teachers of the importance of teaching with theory:

> High school English teachers are under pressure to teach their students to read literature in ways that lead to more flexible formulations of meaning, in ways that are more relevant to their contemporary lives. . . . New forms of literary theory have useful applications in high school English classrooms and they support effective teaching practices in three different ways. First, literary theory has implications for *how people read.* Secondly, literary theory has implications for *what is read.* Thirdly, literary theory simulates the production of ideas and *discourages reductive thinking*. (p. 175)

In her introduction to *Critical Theory Today: A User-Friendly Guide,* Lois Tyson (2006) summarizes the importance of studying theory and how that study transforms what we mean by knowledge:

> For knowledge isn't just something we acquire; it's something we are or hope to become. Knowledge is what constitutes our relationship to ourselves and to our world, for it is the lens through which we view ourselves and our world. Change the lens and you change both the view and the viewer. This principle is what makes knowledge at once so frightening and so liberating, so painful and so utterly, utterly joyful. (p. 10)

Jack Thomson (1993) views contemporary literary theory as a way of helping students control texts, as a way of redistributing the interpretive power in the classroom:

> Too often our students see literary criticism as the practice of subordinating their human, ethical, and political reactions to some ideal of literary value. I think we have a responsibility to help them unravel and evaluate the themes and ideologies of texts they read rather than see them as some divine or secular authority. (p. 136)

Although many of the adolescents in the classes described in this book were initially skeptical and viewed the lenses as simply another kind of analytical tool for finding the often predetermined, singular "hidden meaning" in literature, they eventually integrated the theories into their own interpretive repertoire and offered appreciative insights about the impact of theory on their literary understanding. The excerpts below are from the reading journals and final exams of several students, representing a range of abilities, educational contexts and backgrounds, who confirm that they found that reading with theory created significant and meaningful critical encounters with texts. The students' own words demonstrate how theory became powerfully and positively integrated into their study of literature:

> Critical lenses give opportunity to view literature in ways never thought of before and broaden the reader a little more to open up and see things in a different light. The lenses make the reader think.

> Critical lenses allow us to look at something in different ways to understand what is taking place around us. If people look at things in different

> ways, it is possible to see the intent of other people and, in turn, [to] understand them.
>
> It is sometimes difficult to grasp the meaning of a work through one's own eyes. One's experiences in life greatly influence the way one views the world around [one]; this most likely limits one's understanding of a piece of literature. Literary theories or critical lenses are tools that will open up many windows in one's understanding. They make the reader take on a different personality, with different views of society and [oneself], thus leading to a better, wider, clearer understanding of a work.

THE IMPORTANCE OF MULTIPLE PERSPECTIVES

> Critical lenses are about looking into elements of the world in different ways, thinking about things from different perspectives. This will never be a bad thing, no matter what [they are] used to view. . . . Seeing many different sides of stories only benefits everyone.
>
> —Joelle, Grade 11

Multiplicity, or the ability to "see many different sides of stories," as Joelle puts it, is central to the idea of teaching literary theory to adolescents. Students' ability to read texts, the world, and their own lives is enhanced not only by the study of individual theories themselves but also by the notion of multiple perspectives. In his impressive argument for using literary theory to read adolescent novels, John Moore (1997) quotes Henry Louis Gates Jr.'s apt metaphor for theory as prism, one that changes the entire nature of what is viewed when we view it through a different angle of the prism:

> Literary theory functioned in my education as a prism, which I could turn to refract different spectral patterns of language use in a text, as one does daylight. Turn the prism this way, and one pattern emerges; turn it that way, and another pattern configures. (p. 187)

By viewing individual texts through the prisms of varied theories, students were able to construct multiple perspectives. Moore (1997) underscores the importance of literary theory in helping students learn to construct and sustain a plurality of perspectives:

> We can help our students understand what it means to read literature differently if we value multiple readings (or interpretations) over a single authoritative reading. Literary theory helps us understand that there are many ways to know texts, to read

> and interpret them, but many secondary school teachers are unfamiliar with the changes that have occurred in literary theory over the last four decades. (p. 4)

This volume not only provides teachers with the tools they need to become more familiar with contemporary literary theory, it also emphasizes the value of multiple perspectives of multiple readings of texts. As I argued in Chapter 2, the ultimate pedagogical goal of teaching with theory is to facilitate students' ability to understand different perspectives. To that end, I encourage teachers to use several different critical theories with individual literary texts. With high school teachers and their students, I have developed variations on the kind of "theory relay" that opened this chapter (for theory relays on *The Things They Carried* and *Frankenstein*, see Appendix, Activities 27 and 28). These relays help students consider different critical interpretations side by side. In doing so, they become flexible thinkers, skilled interpreters, and are able to see, as Bonnycastle (1996, p. 32) reminds us, that the problem of approaches to literature is really "a problem of ideologies."

READING WORLDS

Critical encounters with literary theory help students to read the world around them. Teachers hope that students will be able to integrate successful strategies for learning in school and to adapt those strategies to life. As argued in Chapter 1, students need to learn to read the world around them in order to function as literate participants in an increasingly complex society. Jack Thomson (1993, p. 130) has written, "All our regular institutional and social practices, including our social rituals and ceremonies, are texts to be read and interpreted."

In *The Crafty Reader*, Robert Scholes (2001, p. 78) reiterates this: "The human condition . . . is a textual one and has always been so." Learning to read the world as text is an important result of high school literature instruction that includes theory. In a culminating activity called "Critical Encounters: Reading the World" (see Appendix, Activity 29), I ask students to bring in both artifacts and examples of things they've observed to see if they can use the lenses of literary theory to shed light on these artifacts and experiences. Teachers have used this activity as an assessment tool, a kind of final exam on how well students are able to apply the critical tools they have learned in their literature class to real-life situations. Here are some items students brought in for cultural analysis:

- A variety of magazine ads, television commercials, and commercial Web pages, generally using beautiful, young, thin women to sell everything from toothpaste to milk
- A *People* magazine edition featuring "the 50 most beautiful people in the world"

- Body piercing and tattoos (in some cases, they offered up themselves)
- Credit card ads
- Military recruitment posters
- College view books
- Music videos

In addition to presenting these artifacts, students discussed particular individual experiences for cultural analysis, among them the following:

- Quitting a part-time job because of perceived sexual harassment
- A misunderstanding between two friends because one couldn't inhabit the other's perspective
- Overhearing two male friends discussing how women can't be sportscasters because they are not good at it
- Fighting with a sibling over the car
- Listening to gossip and wondering why we do it
- Attending the homecoming dance
- Moving to another school

In groups and as whole classes, the students described how they used particular literary theories to understand these artifacts and incidents. Students offered analyses that were frequently acutely influenced by theories of gender, social power, postcolonialism, and reader response. They noticed, for example, the dominance of pink and red in print advertisements for sugar substitutes and described how women were visually drawn into the page. They scanned the *New York Times* and noticed the juxtaposition of ads for Cartier watches and luxury cars with articles about the endless cycle of poverty in our cities and around the world. They discussed the power structure of high school, noting how power was enacted within their own relationships with peers.

Two teachers, in search of a concrete assessment of literary understanding in this standards-driven world, helped me create another culminating activity, mentioned earlier, "From Reading Words to Reading the World: Critical Lenses in Literature and in Life" (see Appendix, Activity 30). Here is a compilation of how some of these teachers' students, both urban and suburban, "regular" tracked and college bound, responded to the two final questions, as shown below,

> *Question*: Now think of something you've heard about or seen outside class that struck you as worth thinking about. Describe this event or issue and explain why it is important.

- I think the Virginia Tech shootings were an important event in America history.

- Whether wearing a headscarf indicates oppression and radical Islam or a simple act of being close to one's religion/culture.
- The only time my mom and I have time together is when we are at the grocery store.
- Watching the news this morning, there was a story about underage drinking and how more and more frequently bars are serving alcohol to underage people.
- My parents getting divorced and my dad moving to Cleveland, Ohio. This is important because it changed both my mom's life and mine forever.
- There is a new immigration bill that is an unusual mix between Republican and Democrat views regarding Mexico.
- The new school policy that limits the number of excused and unexcused absences a student can have before being failed or dropped from a class.
- Finding a summer job. This is important because I need to start saving money for college and other stuff.
- The continuing war in Iraq.
- The fights in the hallways at school.
- The response or lack of response to poor people during Hurricane Katrina.

Question: How do you think the multiple perspectives can help you understand some things about yourself and your life outside school?

- Multiple perspectives allow one to attack all aspects of a problem or situation, ultimately leading to an inevitably enhanced level of understanding of the predicament. In terms of myself, I can begin to develop my philosophical rationale, my set of beliefs, as I read literature and am exposed to others' thoughts. I also can apply my learning in this class to my life outside school so I can understand others' opinions, especially those with opinions that clash with my beliefs.
- I think the multiple perspectives can help me understand how to look at the world through the eyes of a person other than myself. I get sick of just seeing the world through my sheltered eyes; I would like to be able to see every event in many different, opposing ways.
- I think sometimes we only look at things from our perspective because especially as teenagers we don't have a lot of other experience and our main focus is ourselves. So sometimes we have to make a conscious effort to "put on" other lenses in order to see the different sides of a situation.
- Multiple perspectives allow me to pull away from the event, step back and just examine it before acting upon it. It's like thinking before you act. It can't really do much harm, it can only end up helping me to make better decisions in my life.

- We can use them in the world, and I think that's why we are taught that we've [been using some of] these lenses all along. We actually have a name for it now.

CONCLUSION

The final student comment in the preceding section reminds us that when we teach theory, we are, more than anything else perhaps, naming what it is that we naturally do. We all try to construct a framework or worldview to help us make sense of the seemingly disconnected events that confront us. Our place in the world is a theoried one. As Steven Lynn (2008, p. xiv) writes, "Whether we are aware of them or not, theories of some sort inevitably must guide our perceptions, our thinking, our behavior." W. Ross Winterowd (1989), in his introduction to Sharon Crowley's book on deconstruction for teachers, makes the case even more strongly:

> Every English teacher acts on the basis of theory. Unless teaching is a random series of lessons, drills, and readings, chosen willy-nilly, the English class is guided by theories of language, literature, and pedagogy. That is, insofar as teachers choose readings and plan instruction, they are *implementing* a theory. The question, of course, is whether or not teachers understand the theory that guides their instruction. If we do not understand the theoretical context in which we function, we are powerless. (p. xiii)

Both teachers and their students have less power over their environment if, as Winterowd said, they do not understand the theoretical context in which they function. We may not be able to name our theories, nor are we always aware of how our ideologies (for that is what they are) become internalized and may in fact prevent us from understanding worlds and perspectives different from our own. We also may not be able to recognize an oppressive ideology when we are confronted with it, whether it's in a textbook, a tracking system in a high school, or in the workplace. The critical encounters encouraged by the approaches in this book will help us name our theories and consider multiple perspectives as we find our place in the texts we read and the lives we lead.

APPENDIX

Classroom Activities

Note to teachers: Several of the activities use the original terms *feminist* and *Marxist*, rather than or in addition to *gender* and *social power/class*. Teachers should feel free to adapt the materials for their classrooms.

ACTIVITY 1

Little Miss Muffet

Russell Baker

One of the fascinating aspects of American English is its diversity, and one of the causes of this diversity is the specialized vocabularies of different occupations in America. Russell Baker's report of a conference dealing with Little Miss Muffet, taken from Poor Russell's Almanac, *illustrates several varieties of occupational jargon.*

Little Miss Muffet, as everyone knows, sat on a tuffet eating her curds and whey when along came a spider who sat down beside her and frightened Miss Muffet away. While everyone knows this, the significance of the event had never been analyzed until a conference of thinkers recently brought their special insights to bear upon it. Following are excerpts from the transcript of their discussion:

Sociologist: We are clearly dealing here with a prototypical illustration of a highly tensile social structure's tendency to dis- or perhaps even de-structure itself under the pressures created when optimum minimums do not obtain among the disadvantaged. Miss Muffet is nutritionally underprivileged, as evidenced by the subliminal diet of curds and whey upon which she is forced to subsist, while the spider's cultural disadvantage is evidenced by such phenomena as legs exceeding standard norms, odd mating habits, and so forth.

In this instance, spider expectations lead the culturally disadvantaged to assert demands to share the tuffet with the nutritionally underprivileged. Due to a communications failure, Miss Muffet assumes without evidence that the spider will not be satisfied to share her tuffet, but will also insist on eating her curds and perhaps even her whey. Thus, the failure to preestablish selectively optimum norm structures diverts potentially optimal minimums from the expectation levels assumed to . . .

Militarist: Second-strike capability, sir! That's what was lacking. If Miss Muffet had developed a second-strike capability instead of squandering her resources on curds and whey, no spider on earth would have dared launch a first strike capable of carrying him right to the heart of her tuffet. I am confident that Miss Muffet had adequate notice from experts that she could not afford both curds and whey and, at the same time, support an early-spider-warning system. Yet curds alone were not good enough for Miss Muffet. She had to have whey, too. Tuffet security must be the first responsibility of every diner. . . .

Book Reviewer: Written on several levels, this searing and sensitive exploration of the arachnid heart illuminates the agony and splendor of Jewish family life with a candor that is at once breathtaking in its simplicity and soul-shattering in its implied ambiguity. Some will doubtless be shocked to see such subjects as tuffets and whey discussed without flinching, but hereafter writers too timid to call a curd a curd will no longer . . .

Editorial Writer: Why has the government not seen fit to tell the public all it knows about the so-called curds-and-whey affair? It is not enough to suggest that this was merely a random incident involving a lonely spider and a young diner. In today's world, poised as it is on the knife edge of . . .

Psychiatrist: Little Miss Muffet is, of course, neither little or a miss. These are obviously the self she has created in her own fantasies to escape the reality that she is a gross divorcée whose superego makes it impossible for her to sustain a normal relationship with any man, symbolized by the spider, who, of course, has no existence outside her fantasies. Little Miss Muffet may, in fact, be a man with deeply repressed Oedipal impulses, who sees in the spider the father he would like to kill, and very well may some day unless he admits that what he believes to be a tuffet is, in fact, probably the dining room chandelier, and that what he thinks he is eating is, in fact, probably . . .

Student Demonstrator: Little Miss Muffet, tuffets, curds, whey, and spiders are what's wrong with education today. They're all irrelevant. Tuffets are irrelevant. Curds are irrelevant. Whey is irrelevant. Meaningful experience! How can you have relevance without meaningful experience? And how can there ever be meaningful experience without understanding? With understanding and meaningfulness and relevance, there can be love and good and deep seriousness and education today will be freed of slavery and Little Miss Muffet, and life will become meaningful and . . .

Child: This is about a little girl who gets scared by a spider.

(The child was sent home when the conference broke for lunch. It was agreed that he was too immature to subtract anything from the sum of human understanding.)

Now it's your turn to recast a familiar fairy tale or another Mother Goose rhyme from at least three perspectives. Work in groups of three or four, and use Mr. Baker's piece as a guide.

ACTIVITY 2

Group Exercise for "Separating," by John Updike

Read the story "Separating" on your own. Then, get into groups of three or four and work together on the following questions.

1. List all the characters that appear in the story.

2. From whose point of view is the story told?

3. Summarize the story from that character's point of view. That is, according to the character you named in question 2, what happens in this story?

4. Now, pick another character from those you listed in question 1. Summarize the story from the viewpoint of that character.

5. Reread the last two paragraphs of the story. Speculate together on what will happen next. Is there any reason to believe that Richard and Joan might not separate?

6. Extend the story. Write at least one page *from the point of view of the character you used in question 4.*

ACTIVITY 3

A Matter of Perspective

Let's explore the notion of perspective. Much contemporary fiction violates traditional narrative expectations by telling the story from the perspective of different characters, rather than from the perspective of a single protagonist.

1. Tell the story of "The Three Little Pigs."

2. Now look at the children's book *The True Story of the Three Little Pigs, as Told by A. Wolf.* What differences does that switch in perspective make?

3. Think of a family story, preferably one that is retold often and is a part of your family mythology. In a paragraph or so, tell that story from your own perspective. Write your version below.

4. Now think of another family member, and retell the story from his or her perspective. Write that version below.
   FAMILY MEMBER: ___________

5. In groups of no more than four, share those stories and discuss the difference that perspective makes. How can we know what the "true" version of the story is?

ACTIVITY 4

Literary Perspectives Tool Kit

Literary perspectives help us explain why people might interpret the same text in different ways. Perspectives help us understand what is important to individual readers, and they show us why those readers end up seeing what they see. One way to imagine a literary perspective is to think of it as a lens through which we can examine a text. No single lens gives us the clearest view, but it is sometimes fun to read a text with a particular perspective in mind because you often end up discovering something intriguing and unexpected. While readers typically apply more than one perspective at a time, the best way to understand these perspectives is to employ them one at a time. What follows is a summary of some of the best-known literary perspectives. These descriptions are extremely brief, and none fully explains everything you might want to know about the perspective in question, but there is enough here for you to get an idea about how readers use them.

The Reader Response Perspective: This type of perspective focuses on the activity of reading a work of literature. Reader response critics turn away from the traditional idea that a literary work is an artifact that has meaning built within it; they turn their attention instead to the responses of individual readers. Through this shift of perspective, a literary work is converted into an activity that goes on in a reader's mind. It is through this interaction that meaning is made. The features of the work itself—narrator, plot, characters, style, and structure—are less important than the interplay between a reader's experience and the text. Advocates of this perspective believe that literature has no inherent or intrinsic meaning that is waiting to be discovered. Instead, meaning is constructed by readers as they bring their own thoughts, moods, and experiences to whatever text they are reading. In turn, what readers get out of a text depends on their own expectations and ideas. For example, if you read "Sonny's Blues," by James Baldwin, and you have your own troubled younger brother or sister, the story will have meaning for you that it wouldn't have for, say, an only child.

The Archetypal Perspective: In literary criticism, the word *archetype* signifies a recognizable pattern or model. It can be used to describe story designs, character types, or images that can be found in a wide variety of works of literature. It can also be applied to myths, dreams, and social rituals. The archetypal similarities between texts and behaviors are thought to reflect a set of universal, even primitive, ways of seeing the world. When we find them in literary works. they evoke strong responses from readers. Archetypal themes include the heroic journey and the search for a father figure. Archetypal images include the opposition of heaven and hell, the river as a sign of life and movement, and mountains or other high places as sources of enlightenment. Characters can be archetypal as well; some examples are the rebel-hero, the scapegoat, the villain, and the goddess.

The Formalist Perspective: The word *formal* has two related meanings, both of which apply within this perspective. The first relates to its root word, *form*, a structure's shape that we can recognize and use to make associations. The second relates to a set of conventions or accepted practices. Formal poetry, for example, has meter, rhyme, stanzas, and other predictable features that it shares with poems of the same type. The formalist perspective, then, pays particular attention to these issues of form and convention. Instead of looking at the world in which a poem exists, for example, the formalist perspective says that a poem should be treated as an independent and self-sufficient object. The methods used in this perspective are those pertaining to close reading, that is, detailed and subtle analysis of the formal components that make up the literary work, such as the meanings and interactions of words, figures of speech, and symbols.

The Character Perspective: Some literary critics call this the "psychological" perspective because its purpose is to examine the internal motivations of literary characters. When we hear actors say that they are searching for their character's motivation, they are using something like this perspective. As a form of criticism, this perspective deals with works of literature as expressions of the personality, state of mind, feelings, and desires of the author or of a character within the literary work. As readers, we investigate the psychology of a character or an author to figure out the meaning of a text (although sometimes an examination of the author's psychology is considered biographical criticism, depending on your point of view).

The Biographical Perspective: Because authors typically write about things they care deeply about and know well, the events and circumstances of their lives are often reflected in the literary works they create. For this reason, some readers use biographical information about an author to gain insight into that author's works. This lens, called *biographical criticism*, can be both helpful and dangerous. It can provide insight into themes, historical references, social oppositions or movements, and the creation of fictional characters. At the same time, it is not safe to assume that biographical details from the author's life can be transferred to a story or character that the author has created. For example,

Ernest Hemingway and John Dos Passos were both ambulance drivers during World War I and both wrote novels about the war. Their experiences gave them firsthand knowledge and created strong personal feelings about the war, but their stories are still works of fiction. Some biographical details, in fact, may be completely irrelevant to the interpretation of that writer's work.

The Historical Perspective: When applying this perspective, you view a literary text within its historical context. Specific historical information will be of key interest: information about the time during which an author wrote, about the time in which the text is set, about the ways in which people of the period saw and thought about the world in which they lived. *History*, in this case, refers to the social, political, economic, cultural, and intellectual climate of the time. For example, the literary works of William Faulkner frequently reflect the history of the American South, the Civil War and its aftermath, and the birth and death of a nation known as the Confederate States of America.

The Social-Class Perspective. Some critics believe that human history and institutions, even our ways of thinking, are determined by the ways in which our societies are organized. Two primary factors shape our schemes of organization: economic power and social-class membership. First, the class to which we belong determines our degree of economic, political, and social advantage, and thus social classes invariably find themselves in conflict with each other. Second, our membership in a social class has a profound impact on our beliefs, values, perceptions, and ways of thinking and feeling. For these reasons, the social-power perspective helps us understand how people from different social classes understand the same circumstances in very different ways. When we see members of different social classes thrown together in the same story, we are likely to think in terms of power and advantage as we attempt to explain what happens and why.

The Gender Perspective: Because gender is a way of viewing the world, people of different genders see things differently. For example, a feminist critic might see cultural and economic disparities as the products of a "patriarchal" society, shaped and dominated by men, who tend to decide things by various means of competition. In addition, societies often tend to see the male perspective as the default, that is, the one we choose automatically. As a result, women are identified as the "Other," the deviation or the contrasting type. When we use the gender lens, we examine patterns of thought, behavior, value, and power in interactions between the sexes.

Deconstruction. Deconstruction is, at first, a difficult critical method to understand because it asks us to set aside ways of thinking that are quite natural and comfortable. For example, we frequently see the world as a set of opposing categories: male/female, rational/irrational, powerful/powerless. It also looks at the ways in which we assign value to one thing over another, such as life over death, presence over absence, and writing over speech. At its heart, deconstruction is a mode of analysis that asks us to question the very assumptions that we bring to that analysis. Gender, for example, is a "construct," a set of beliefs and assumptions that we have built, or constructed, over time and experience. But if we "de-construct" gender, looking at it while holding aside our internalized beliefs and expectations, new understandings become possible. To practice this perspective, then, we must constantly ask ourselves why we believe what we do about the makeup of our world and the ways in which we have come to understand the world. Then we must try to explain that world in the absence of our old beliefs.

 ACTIVITY 5 

Literary Theories: A Sampling of Critical Lenses

Literary theories were developed as a means to understand the various ways in which people read texts. The proponents of each theory believe that their theory is *the* theory, but most of us interpret texts according to the "rules" of several different theories at one time. All literary theories are lenses through which we can see texts. There is no reason to say that one is better than another or that you should read according to any of them, but it is sometimes fun to "decide" to read a text with one in mind because you often end up with a whole new perspective on your reading. What follows is a summary of some of the most common schools of literary theory. These descriptions are extremely cursory, and none of them fully explains what the theory is all about. But it is enough to get the general idea.

Archetypal Criticism. In criticism *archetype* signifies narrative designs, character types, or images, which are said to be identifiable in a wide variety of works of literature, as well as in myths, dreams, and even ritualized modes of social behavior. The archetypal similarities within these diverse phenomena are held to reflect a set of universal, primitive, and elemental patterns, whose effective embodiment in a literary work evokes a profound response from the reader. The death-rebirth theme is often said to be the archetype of archetypes. Other archetypal themes are the journey underground, the heavenly ascent, the search for the father, the heaven/hell image, the Promethean rebel-hero, the scapegoat, the earth goddess, and the femme fatale.

Gender/Feminist Criticism. A feminist critic sees cultural and economic disabilities in a "patriarchal" society that have hindered or prevented women from realizing their creative possibilities, including woman's cultural identification as merely a passive object, or "Other," and man is the defining and dominating subject. There are several assumptions and concepts held in common by most feminist critics:

- Our civilization is pervasively patriarchal.
- The concepts of "gender" are largely, if not entirely, cultural constructs, effected by the omnipresent patriarchal biases of our civilization.
- This patriarchal ideology pervades those writings that have been considered great literature. Such works lack autonomous female role models, are implicitly addressed to male readers, and shut out the woman reader as an alien outsider or solicit her to identify against

herself by assuming male values and ways of perceiving, feeling, and acting.

This type of criticism is somewhat like Marxist criticism, but instead of focusing on the relationships between the classes it focuses on the relationships between the genders. Under this theory you would examine the patterns of thought, behavior, values, enfranchisement, and power in relations between the sexes. For example, "Where Are You Going, Where Have You Been" can be seen as the story of the malicious dominance men have over women both physically and psychologically. Connie is the female victim of the role in society that she perceives herself playing—the coy young lass whose life depends on her looks.

Social-Class/Marxist Criticism. A Marxist critic grounds his or her theory and practice on the economic and cultural theory of Karl Marx and Friedrich Engles, especially on the following claims:

1. The evolving history of humanity, its institutions, and its ways of thinking are determined by the changing mode of its "material production"—that is, of its basic economic organization.
2. Historical changes in the fundamental mode of production effect essential changes both in the constitution and power relations of social classes, which carry on a conflict for economic, political, and social advantage.
3. Human consciousness in any era is constituted by an ideology—that is, a set of concepts, beliefs, values, and ways of thinking and feeling through which human beings perceive, and by which they explain what they take to be reality. A Marxist critic typically undertakes to "explain" the literature of any era by revealing the economic, class, and ideological determinants of the way an author writes. A Marxist critic examines the relation of the text to the social reality of that time and place.

This school of critical theory focuses on power and money in works of literature. Who has the power/money? Who does not? What happens as a result? For example, it could be said that "The Legend of Sleepy Hollow" is about the upper class attempting to maintain its power and influence over the lower class by chasing Ichabod, a lower-class citizen with aspirations toward the upper class, out of town. This would explain some of the story's descriptions of land, wealth, and hearty living that are seen through Ichabod's eyes.

New Criticism is directed against the prevailing concern of critics with the lives and psychology of authors, with social background, and with literary history. There are several points of view and procedures that are held in common by most New Critics:

1. A poem should be treated as primarily poetry and should be regarded as an independent and self-sufficient object.
2. The distinctive procedure of the New Critic is explication, or close reading: the detailed and subtle analysis of the complex interrelations and ambiguities of the components within a work.
3. The principles of New Criticism are fundamentally verbal. That is, literature is conceived to be a special kind of language whose attributes are defined by systematic opposition to the language of science and of practical and logical discourse. The key concepts of this criticism deal with the meanings and interactions of words, figures of speech, and symbols.
4. The distinction between literary genres is not essential.

Psychological and Psychoanalytic Criticism. Psychological criticism deals with a work of literature primarily as an expression, in fictional form, of the personality, state of mind, feelings, and desires of its author. The assumption of psychoanalytic critics is that a work of literature is correlated with its author's mental traits:

1. Reference to the author's personality is used to explain and interpret a literary work.
2. Reference to literary works is made in order to establish, biographically, the personality of the author.
3. The mode of reading a literary work itself is a way of experiencing the distinctive subjectivity or consciousness of its author.

This theory requires that we investigate the psychology of a character or an author to figure out the meaning of a text (although to apply an author's psychology to a text can also be considered biographical criticism, depending on your point of view). For example, alcohol allows the latent thoughts and desires of the narrator of "The Black Cat" to surface in such a way that he ends up shirking the self-control imposed by social mores and standards and becomes the man his psyche has repressed his whole life.

Reader Response Criticism. This type of criticism focuses on the activity of reading a work of literature. Reader response critics turn from the traditional conception of a work as an achieved structure of meanings to the responses of readers to the text. By this shift of perspective a literary work is converted into an activity that goes on in a reader's mind, and what had been features of the work itself—narrator, plot, characters, style, and structure—is less important than the connection between a reader's experience and the text. It is through this interaction that meaning is made. Students seem most comfortable with this school of criticism. Proponents believe that literature has no objective meaning or existence. People bring their own thoughts, moods, and experiences to whatever text they are reading and get out of it whatever they happen to, based on their own expectations and ideas. For example, when I read "Sonny's Blues" I am reminded of my younger sister who loves music. The story really gets to me because sometimes I worry about her and my relationship with her. I want to support her and am reminded of this as I see that Sonny's brother does not support Sonny.

Other theories we'll be discussing in class include the following:

Deconstructionist Criticism. Deconstruction is by far the most difficult critical theory for people to understand. It was developed by some very unconventional thinkers, who declared that literature means nothing because language means nothing. In other words, we cannot say that we know what the "meaning" of a story is because there is no way of knowing. For example, in some stories (such as Joyce Carol Oates's "Where Are You Going, Where Have You Been?") that do not have tidy endings, you cannot assume you know what happened.

Historical Criticism. Using this theory requires that you apply to a text specific historical information about the time during which an author wrote. *Historical*, in this case, refers to the social, political, economic, cultural, and intellectual climate of the time. For example, William Faulkner wrote many of his novels and stories during and after World War II, a fact that helps to explain the feelings of darkness, defeat, and struggle that pervade much of his work.

ACTIVITY 6

Literary Theory Cards

Gender Criticism

Assumptions

1. The work doesn't have an objective status, an autonomy; instead, any reading of it is influenced by the reader's own status, which includes gender, or attitudes toward gender.
2. In the production of literature and within stories themselves, men and women have not had equal access.
3. Men and women are different: They write differently, read differently, and write about their reading differently. These differences should be valued.

Strategies

1. Consider the gender of the author or the characters: What role does gender or sexuality play in this work?
2. Specifically, observe how sexual stereotypes might be reinforced or undermined. Try to see how the work reflects or distorts the place of women (and men) in society.
3. Look at the effects of power drawn from gender within the plot or form.

Social Power/Marxist Criticism

Assumptions

1. Karl Marx argued that the way people think and behave in any society is determined by basic economic factors.
2. In his view, those groups of people who owned and controlled major industries could exploit the rest of the population, through conditions of employment and by forcing their own values and beliefs onto other social groups.
3. Marxist criticism applies these arguments to the study of literary texts.

Strategies

1. Explore the way different groups of people are represented in texts. Evaluate the level of social realism in the text and how society is portrayed.
2. Consider how the text itself is a commodity that reproduces certain social beliefs and practices. Analyze the social effect of the literary work.
3. Look at the effects of power drawn from economic or social class.

(*continued overleaf*)

Assumption cards
1. Language meaning
↳ 3 → what + strat.
2. plot meaning
3. character dev.

Biographical Criticism

Assumptions

1. Because authors typically write about things they care deeply about and know well, the events and circumstances of their lives are often reflected in the literary works they create.
2. The context for a literary work includes information about the author, his or her historical moment, and the systems of meaning available at the time of writing.
3. Interpretation of the work should be based on an understanding of its context. That context can provide insight into themes, historical references, social oppositions or movements, and the creation of fictional characters.

Strategies

1. Research the author's life, and relate that information to the work.
2. Research the author's time (the political history, intellectual history, economic history, and so on), and relate that information to the work.
3. Research the systems of meaning available to the author, and relate those systems to the work.

Archetypal Criticism

Assumptions

1. Meaning cannot exist solely on the page of a work, nor can that work be treated as an independent entity.
2. Humankind has a "collective unconscious," a kind of universal psyche, which is manifested in dreams and myths and which harbors themes and images that are hard-wired in all of us.
3. These recurring myths, symbols, and character types appear and reappear in literary works.

Strategies

1. Consider the genre of the work (e.g., comedy, romance, tragedy, irony) and how it affects the meaning.
2. Look for story patterns and symbolic associations, such as black hats, springtime settings, evil stepmothers, and so forth, from other texts you've read.
3. Consider your associations with these symbols as you construct meaning from the text.

Reader Response Criticism

Assumptions

1. An author's intentions are not reliably available to readers; all they have is the text.
2. Out of the text, readers actively and personally make meaning.
3. Responding to a text is a process, and descriptions of that process are valuable.

Strategies

1. Move through the text in super-slow motion, describing the response of an informed reader at various points.
2. Or describe your own response when moving through the text.
3. React to the text as a whole, embracing and expressing the subjective and personal response it engenders.

Formalist Criticism

Assumptions

1. The critic's interest ultimately should be focused on the work itself (not on the author's intention or the reader's response).
2. The formalist perspective pays particular attention to issues of form and convention.
3. The formalist perspective says that a literary work should be treated as an independent and self-sufficient object.

Strategies

1. Read closely. You can assume that every aspect is carefully calculated to contribute to the work's unity—figures of speech, point of view, diction, recurrent ideas or events, everything.
2. The methods used in this perspective are those of close reading: detailed and subtle analysis of the formal components that make up the literary work, such as the meanings and interactions of words, figures of speech, and symbols.
3. Say how the work is unified: how the various elements work to unify it.

Historical Criticism

Assumptions

1. When reading a text, you have to place it within its historical context.
2. *Historical* refers to the social, political, economic, cultural, and intellectual climate of the time.
3. Specific historical information will be of key interest: information about the time during which an author wrote, about the time in which the text is set, about the ways in which people of the period saw and thought about the world in which they lived.

Strategies

1. Research the fundamental historical events of the period in which the author wrote.
2. Consider the fundamental historical events of the period in which the literary work is set if it is different from the period in which the author wrote.
3. View the text as part of a larger context of historical movements, and consider how it both contributes to and reflects certain fundamental aspects of human history.

Postcolonial Criticism

Assumptions

1. Colonialism is a powerful, often destructive historical force that shapes not only the political futures of the countries involved but also the identities of colonized and colonizing people.
2. Successful colonialism depends on a process of "Othering" the people colonized. That is, the colonized people are seen as dramatically different from and lesser than the colonizers.
3. Because of this, literature written in colonizing cultures often distorts the experiences and realities of colonized people. Literature written by colonized people often includes attempts to articulate more empowered identities and reclaim cultures in the face of colonization.

Strategies

1. Search the text for references to colonization or to currently and formerly colonized people. In these references, how are the colonized people portrayed? How is the process of colonization portrayed?
2. Consider what images of "Others" or processes of "Othering" are present in the text. How are these "Others" portrayed?
3. Analyze how the text deals with cultural conflicts between the colonizing culture and the colonized or traditional culture.

Structuralist Criticism

Assumptions

1. Draws on linguistic theory.
2. There are structural relationships between concepts that are revealed in language.
3. Linguistic *signs* are composed of two parts—the *signifier* (sound patterns) and the *signified* (the concept or meaning of the word).
4. Through these relationships, meaning is produced, which frames and motivates the actions of individuals and groups.

Strategies

1. Focus on the text alone, not on external information.
2. Examine the underlying *system*, or patterns of language. By examining the pattern of linguistic signs, we can establish the paradigm that will reveal meaning.
3. Identify and analyze contrasting elements, (binary oppositions) to determine the important elements in the text.
4. Look at structural elements, such as words, stanzas, chapters, or parts, and at characters, narrators, or speakers to see how they can reveal important contrasts and differences.
5. What system of relationships governs the work as a whole or links this work to others?

Deconstructionist Criticism

Assumptions

1. Meaning is made by binary oppositions, but one item is unavoidably favored (or "privileged") over the other.
2. This hierarchy is probably arbitrary and can be exposed and reversed.
3. The text's oppositions and hierarchy can be called into question because texts contain within themselves unavoidable contradictions, gaps, spaces, and absences that defeat closure and determinate meaning. All reading is misreading.

Strategies

1. Identify the oppositions in the text. Determine which member appears to be favored, and look for evidence that contradicts that favoring.
2. Identify what appears central to the text and what appears to be marginal and excluded.
3. Expose the text's indeterminacy. Whereas formalism assumes that you should read a literary work closely as if it made sense, deconstruction assumes the opposite: that if you read closely enough, the text will fail to make sense—or at least will contradict itself.

Psychological Criticism

Assumptions

1. Creative writing (like dreaming) represents the (disguised) fulfillment of a (repressed) wish or fear.
2. Everyone's formative history is different in its particulars, but there are basic recurrent patterns of development for most people. These particulars and patterns have lasting effects.
3. In reading literature, we can make educated guesses about what has been repressed and transformed.

Strategies

1. Attempt to apply a developmental concept to the work, or to the author or characters (e.g., the Oedipus complex, anal retentiveness, castration anxiety, gender confusion).
2. Relate the work to psychologically significant events in the author's or a character's life.
3. Consider how repressed material may be expressed in the work's pattern of imagery or symbols.

Adapted from theory descriptions on inside front cover of Texts and Contexts: Writing About Literature with Critical Theory, *5th ed., by Steven Lynn;*

ACTIVITY 7

Theory Wars: Looking at *Star Wars* Through Critical Lenses

In your groups, discuss the questions below. You will be asked to share the fruits of your discussion with the whole class in your symposium.

1. Try to recall the first time you saw this film. In what ways was the class viewing different from your first viewing? What were some things you noticed that you didn't notice before? What seemed to be important this time that didn't come through in a previous viewing?

2. Think back to our discussions of archetypes from last year. Describe how characters, plot, conflict, or theme in *Star Wars* could be viewed in archetypal terms. For example, is this a classic story of good versus evil? Is Princess Leah the typical heroine?

3. Read through the handout on literary theory. Select the two theories that you think might be most helpful in illuminating the film. Write down the theories below.
   1. __________
   2. __________

4. Now come up with some statements about the film for each of the theories you named in question 3. For example, if you selected feminist criticism you might discuss the lack of female characters and evaluate the role of Princess Leah from a feminist perspective. If you chose reader response theory you might describe how the film reminded each of you of a personal experience in your struggle with good and evil. (Use loose-leaf paper—journal potential.)

5. After you discuss these interpretations, decide how to present them to the whole class. Your presentation should be no more than about 10 minutes of your symposium.

ACTIVITY 8

Literary Theory: Prisms of Possibilities

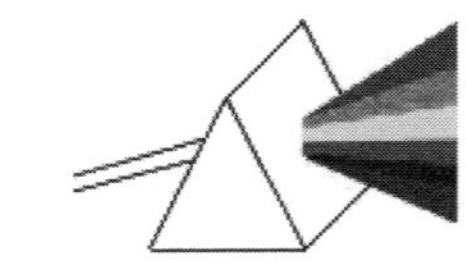

Read the Sylvia Plath poem and discuss it in your group, using the assigned lens. We will consider each lens when we reconvene as a large group.

	Reader Response	Biographical	Feminist/Gender	Marxist/Social Class
What aspects of the poem lend themselves to this particular lens?				
Cite specific textual passage(s) that support this reading.				
If you look through this lens, what themes or patterns are brought into sharp relief?				
If you look through this lens, what questions emerge?				
Do you believe in this reading? Why or why not?				

ACTIVITY 9

Upon Seeing an Orange

Gender theory asks:	What possibilities are available to a woman who eats this orange? to a man?
Formalism asks:	What shape and diameter is the orange?
Social class theory asks:	Who owns the orange? Who gets to eat it?
Postcolonialism asks:	Who doesn't own the orange? Who took the orange away?
Reader response theory asks:	What does the orange taste like? What does the orange remind us of?
Structuralism asks:	How are the orange peel and the flesh differentiated into composite parts of the orange?
Deconstruction asks:	If the orange peel and the flesh are both part of an "orange," are they not in fact one and the same thing?

ACTIVITY 10

Reader Response and *Running Fiercely Toward a High Thin Sound*

Context

(What factors surrounding my reading of the text are influencing my response?)

Reader (   ) ——→ **Meaning** ←—— **Text** (***Running Fiercely***)

YOUR NAME

(What personal qualities or events relevant to this particular book might influence my response?)

(What textual features might influence my response?)

Context

ACTIVITY 11

Reader Response and *Native Son*

Context

(What factors surrounding my reading of the text are influencing my response?)

Reader (   )————➤**Meaning**⮜————**Text (*Native Son*)**

YOUR NAME

(What personal qualities or events relevant to this particular book might influence my response?)

(What textual features might influence my response?)

Context

ACTIVITY 12

Key Ideas of Karl Marx

Stages of History

Marx believed that history moved in stages: from feudalism to capitalism, socialism, and ultimately communism.

Materialism

Each stage was mainly shaped by the economic system. The key to understanding the systems was to focus on the "mode of production." (For example, most production under feudalism was agricultural, while most production under capitalism was industrial.) It also was necessary to focus on who owned the "means of production." (Under capitalism a small class—the bourgeoisie—owned the factories. Under socialism, the factories would be owned by the workers.)

Class Struggle

"The history of all hitherto existing society is the history of class struggles." Each system, up to and including capitalism, was characterized by the exploitation of one class by another.

The Dialectic

Marx argued that great historical changes followed a three-step pattern called thesis-antithesis-synthesis (he adopted this idea and terminology from an earlier German philosopher, Georg Wilhelm Friedrich Hegel). Any idea or condition (thesis) brings into being its opposite (antithesis). The two opposites then conflict until they produced a new, higher stage (synthesis). For example, in the Marxist dialectic, the existence of the ruling bourgeoisie under capitalism made necessary the existence of its opposite, the proletariat, and the synthesis of their struggle would be a utopian classless society.

Internal Contradictions

Each class system therefore contained the seeds of its own destruction, which Marx sometimes called "internal contradictions." Capitalism, he believed, was plagued by such contradictions, which would get worse and worse until they destroyed it.

Capitalism

Marx saw capitalism as the cruelest, most efficient system yet evolved for the exploitation of the working majority by a small class of owners. It was the nature of capitalism, Marx believed, for wealth and ownership to be concentrated in an ever-shrinking mega-rich class. This was one of many internal contradictions of capitalism that would inevitably destroy it.

Working Class Misery

It was the nature of capitalist production methods to become more and more technologically efficient, requiring fewer and fewer workers to produce more and more goods. Therefore capitalism would be plagued by bouts of high unemployment. As machines made workers' skills less important, wages would be pushed ever downward. As each worker became simply an appendage of a machine, his job would be less satisfying, and he would become more alienated.

Class Consciousness

Such total exploitation of so many by so few could not last forever. The workers would inevitably develop "class consciousness," that is, an awareness of their predicament. When that occurred, it would be fairly simple for them to take over the factories and the state.

The End of History

Since class conflict was the engine that drove history, and since under communism there would be no class distinctions, history would come to its final resting place in a system free of exploitation.

ACTIVITY 13

Reading *Hamlet* Through the Marxist/Social-Class Lens

Act 1. Warm-Up Discussion

First things first. This stuff can be pretty cool, but it takes a bit of practice. It can be hard, but I've heard you're pretty smart readers. So here goes. Have you considered Marxist/social-class literary theory in your reading before? With what texts? How did that consideration affect your reading of the text as a whole?

The article you read, "Marxist Criticism" by Stephen Bonnycastle, states that in order to understand *Hamlet* from a Marxist perspective, you need to know something about Shakespeare's times and the class struggle present then. What *do* you know about that?

An **ideology** is a view of the world, a prevailing set of beliefs. What are some examples of ideologies you have come across?

What is the prevailing ideology that is represented in *Hamlet?* Are there other, differing views of the world that fight with one another within the text? Explain.

Act 2. In Three, and Then as a Class

Marxist/social-class criticism pays a lot of attention to the social structures that allocate power to different groups in society. List some of the social groups that are represented in *Hamlet*.

We've all heard the term *social ladder*. Try plotting some of the *Hamlet* characters on the social ladder diagram below.

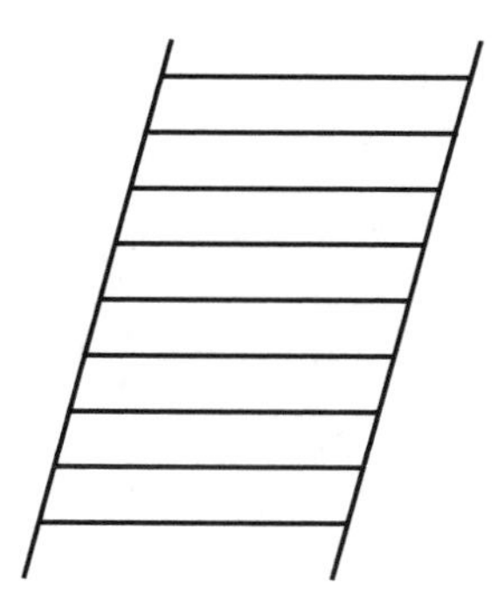

Name some of the primary power struggles that the play portrays. Who has the power, and who doesn't?

Conflict between

Has Power	Has No Power

Put a * next to the power struggles that could be considered class conflicts.

Act 3. On Your Own

The following questions should be done on your own. You don't have to share your responses to the first one, but we may discuss your responses to the second and third questions in class tomorrow.

Marxist literary theory asserts the importance of paying attention to class conflicts, power struggles, and how we place ourselves within the particular social structure in which we find ourselves. Draw a picture or diagram of the existing power or class structure in which you live. You can have it look like the social ladder we used above; you can draw concentric circles or use the ones below; you can map or web—anything is fine. Where are you, relative to where power and money is located?

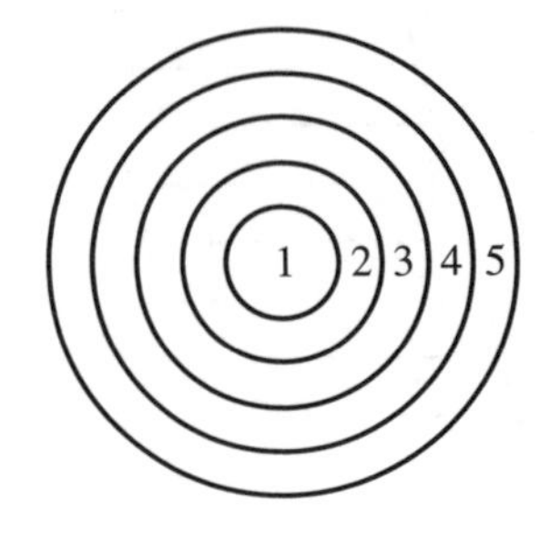

To what degree do you think this location may have affected your reading of *Hamlet*? Which characters in *Hamlet* do you feel most closely represent where you are socially.

Marxist literary theory encourages us to look at the big political questions that surround our more personal concerns. List below some of the big questions that emerge for you as a result of reading *Hamlet* through a Marxist lens.

Now think of one or two smaller, more personal, and perhaps more important questions that emerge for you as you think about issues of class conflict, ideologies or beliefs, and struggle. List them below.

ACTIVITY 14

Looking at *The Great Gatsby* Through Critical Lenses

Literary theories were developed as a means for understanding the various ways in which people read texts. The proponents of each theory believe that their theory is *the* theory, but most of us interpret texts according to the "rules" of several different theories at a time. All literary theories are lenses through which we can see texts. There is nothing to say that one is better than another or that you should read according to any of them, but it is sometimes fun to read a text with one in mind because you often end up with a whole new perspective on your reading. We are going to apply two lenses to *The Great Gatsby*, the Marxist/social-class lens and the gender lens.

Definitions

Social-class criticism grounds its theory and practice on the economic and cultural theory of Karl Marx and Friedrich Engels, especially on the following claims:

1. The evolving history of humanity, its institutions and its ways of thinking, are determined by the changing mode of its "material production"—that is, of its basic economic organization.
2. Historical changes in the fundamental mode of production effect essential changes in both the constitution of and power relations between social classes, which carry on a conflict for economic, political, and social advantage.
3. Human consciousness in any era is constituted by an ideology—a set of concepts, beliefs, values, and ways of thinking and feeling through which human beings perceive and by which they explain what they take to be reality. A social-class critic typically undertakes to "explain" the literature in any era by revealing the economic, class, and ideological determinants that inform the way an author writes, and by examining the relationship of the text to the social reality of the time and place in which it is set.

This school of critical theory focuses on power and money in works of literature. Who has the power/money? Who does not? What happens as a result?

Strategies for applying the social class lens include the following:

1. Explore the ways in which different groups of people are represented in texts. Evaluate the level of social realism in the text—how is the society portrayed?

2. Determine the ideological stance of the text—what worldview does the text represent?
3. Consider how the text itself is a commodity that reproduces certain social beliefs and practices. Analyze the social effect of the literary work.

Gender criticism is somewhat like social-class criticism, but instead of focusing on the relationships between social classes it focuses on the relationships between the genders. In using this theory, you would examine the patterns of thought, behavior, values, enfranchisement, and power in relations between the sexes. There are many different kinds of gendered literary theory. Some theorists examine the language and symbols that are used to see how language and use of symbols is gendered. Others remind us that men and women write differently and analyze how the gender of the author affects how literature is written. Many gender theory critics look at how the characters, especially the female characters, are portrayed and ask us to consider how the portrayal of female characters reinforces or undermines sexual stereotypes. Gender literary theory also suggests that the gender of the reader affects his or her response to a text. For example, gender critics may claim that certain male writers address their readers as if they were all men and exclude the female reader.

Much gender theory reminds us that the relationship between men and women in society is often unequal and reflects a particular patriarchal ideology. Those unequal relationships may appear in various ways in the production of literature and within literary texts. Gender theory invites us to pay particular attention to the patterns of thought, behavior, values, and power in those relationships.

Gender critics remind us that literary values, conventions, and even the production of literature have themselves been historically shaped by men. They invite us to consider writings by women, both new and forgotten, and also ask us to consider viewing familiar literature through a gendered perspective.

Strategies for applying the gender lens include the following:

1. Consider the gender of the author and of the characters. What role does gender or sexuality play in this work?
2. Specifically, observe how sexual stereotypes might be reinforced or undermined. Try to see how the work reflects or distorts the place of women (and men) in society.
3. Think about how gender affects and informs relationships between the characters.
4. Consider the comments the author seems to be making about society as a whole.

You can now use both these lenses to interpret characters, passages, and themes in The Great Gatsby.

The Question of Power

Name some of the primary power struggles that the novel portrays. Who has the power and who doesn't?

From the Perspective of Gender

Has Power	Has No Power

From the Perspective of Class

Has Power	Has No Power

Passages

Using the social-class lens, what is the significance of this passage?

> Every Friday five crates of oranges and lemons arrived from a fruiterer in New York—every Monday these same oranges and lemons left his back door in a pyramid of pulpless halves. There was a machine in the kitchen which could extract the juice of two hundred oranges in half an hour if a little button was pressed two hundred times by a butler's thumb. (p. 40)

Using the gender lens, what is the significance of this passage?

> Well, she was less than an hour old and Tom was God knows where. I woke up out of the ether with an utterly abandoned feeling, and asked the nurse right away if it was a boy or a girl. She told me it was a girl, and so I turned my head away and wept. "All right," I said, "I'm glad it's a girl, and I hope she'll be a fool—that's the best thing a girl can be in this world, a beautiful little fool." (p. 17)

Themes

Finish these sentences:

From the social-class perspective, *The Great Gatsby* is a novel about . . .

From a gender perspective, *The Great Gatsby* is a novel about . . .

Further Questions

Social-class and gender literary theory encourage us to look at the big political questions that surround our more personal concerns. List below some of the big questions that emerge for you as a result of reading *The Great Gatsby* through social-class and gender lenses.

Social-Class Questions:

Gender Questions:

Now think of one or two smaller and more personal questions that emerge for you as you think about issues of class conflict, ideologies or beliefs, gender, and power. List them below.

ACTIVITY 15

Through Rose-Colored Glasses: The Feminist/Gender Lens

1. What is the feminist/gender lens?

Feminist literary criticism helps us look at literature in a different light. It applies the philosophies and perspectives of feminism to the literature we read. There are many different kinds of feminist literary theory. Some theorists examine the language and symbols that are used and how that language and use of symbols is "gendered." Others remind us that men and women write differently and analyze how the gender of the author affects how literature is written. For example, feminist critics may claim that certain male writers address their readers as if they were all men and exclude the female reader. Many feminist critics look at how the characters, especially the female characters, are portrayed and ask us to consider how the portrayal of female characters reinforces or undermines sexual stereotypes. Feminist literary theory also suggests that the gender of the reader often affects his or her response to a text.

Like feminism itself, feminist literary theory asks us to consider the relationships between men and women and their relative roles in society. Much feminist literary theory reminds us that the relationship between men and women in society is often unequal and reflects a particular patriarchal ideology. Those unequal relationships may appear in various ways in the production of literature and within literary texts. Feminist theorists invite us to pay particular attention to the patterns of thought, behavior, values, and power in those relationships.

Feminist literary critics remind us that literary values, conventions, and even the production of literature have themselves been historically shaped by men. They invite us to consider writings by women, both new and forgotten, and also ask us to consider viewing familiar literature through a feminist perspective.

2. How do we apply the feminist/gender lens?

We apply it by closely examining the portrayal of the characters, both female and male; the language of the text; the attitude of the author; and the relationship between the characters. We also consider the comments the author seems to be making about society as a whole.

3. Application: Looking through the feminist/gender lens

Select two female characters from novels with which you are very familiar. They could be from works we have read together or from texts you have read in previous English classes. For example, you might choose Daisy from *The Great Gatsby*, Hester Pryne from *The Scarlet Letter*, or Sonya from *Crime and Punishment*.

Name each character and write two descriptive statements for each—one from a traditional masculine perspective and the second from a feminist perspective.

CHARACTER 1

Traditional statement:

Feminist/gender statement:

CHARACTER 2

Traditional statement:

Feminist/gender statement:

4. Try to interpret this concrete poem in two ways, from a traditional perspective and from a feminist/gender perspective:

5. Can the feminist lens be useful in everyday life? Please write two sentences about each of the following objects or situations, first using a traditional perspective, and then applying the feminist lens:

- Mount Rushmore
- The Miss America pageant
- Hillary Clinton's bid for the Democratic nomination for President

- The popularity and ups and downs of Britney Spears, Paris Hilton, and Lindsay Lohan

- The hooplah surrounding Sarah Palin as vice presidential candidate

- Ugly Betty

6. Can you think of anything that has happened to you or to a friend of yours in the past 2 weeks that could be better explained or understood through a feminist/gender lens? Pick a partner and share stories.

ACTIVITY 16

What Color Are Your Walls? The Feminist/Gender Lens

1. What is the feminist/gender lens?

Feminist literary criticism helps us look at literature in a different light. It applies the philosophies and perspectives of feminism to the literature we read. There are many different kinds of feminist literary theory. Some theorists examine the language and symbols that are used and how that language and use of symbols is "gendered." Others remind us that men and women write differently and analyze how the gender of the author affects how literature is written. For example, feminist critics may claim that certain male writers address their readers as if they were all men and exclude the female reader. Many feminist critics look at how the characters, especially the female characters, are portrayed and ask us to consider how the portrayal of female characters reinforces or undermines sexual stereotypes. Feminist literary theory also suggests that the gender of the reader often affects his or her response to a text.

Like feminism itself, feminist literary theory asks us to consider the relationships between men and women and their relative roles in society. Much feminist literary theory reminds us that the relationship between men and women in society is often unequal and reflects a particular patriarchal ideology. Those unequal relationships may appear in various ways in the production of literature and within literary texts. Feminist theorists invite us to pay particular attention to the patterns of thought, behavior, values, and power in those relationships.

Feminist literary critics remind us that literary values, conventions, and even the production of literature have themselves been historically shaped by men. They invite us to consider writings by women, both new and forgotten, and also ask us to consider viewing familiar literature through a feminist perspective.

2. Consider Gertrude and Ophelia from *Hamlet*. For each character, write two descriptive statements—one from a "traditional" masculine perspective and the second from a feminist perspective.

GERTRUDE:

Traditional statement:

Feminist statement:

OPHELIA:

Traditional statement:

Feminist statement:

3. How do we apply the feminist lens?

We apply it by closely examining the portrayal of the characters, both female and male; the language of the text; the attitude of the author; and the relationship between the characters. We also consider the comments the author seems to be making about society as a whole. Let's try to interpret the following concrete poem in two ways, from a traditional perspective and from a feminist perspective:

—Pedro Xisto

4. Now think about "The Yellow Wallpaper." Using the feminist lens, write a brief analysis of the narrator, her situation, and perhaps Gilman's intent in writing the piece. Consider Gilman's audience as well. Finally, what meaning(s) did you derive from the text as you applied the feminist lens? (Note: This is very similar to the kind of analysis you may be asked to do in a college English class.)

ACTIVITY 17

A Lens of One's Own: Using Feminist/Gender Literary Theory

1. What is the feminist/gender lens?

Feminist literary criticism helps us look at literature in a different light. It applies the philosophies and perspectives of feminism to the literature we read. There are many different kinds of feminist literary theory. Some theorists examine the language and symbols that are used and how that language and use of symbols is "gendered." Others remind us that men and women write differently and analyze how the gender of the author affects how literature is written. For example, feminist critics may claim that certain male writers address their readers as if they were all men and exclude the female reader. Many feminist critics look at how the characters, especially the female characters, are portrayed and ask us to consider how the portrayal of female characters reinforces or undermines sexual stereotypes. Feminist literary theory also suggests that the gender of the reader often affects his or her response to a text.

Like feminism itself, feminist literary theory asks us to consider the relationships between men and women and their relative roles in society. Much feminist literary theory reminds us that the relationship between men and women in society is often unequal and reflects a particular patriarchal ideology. Those unequal relationships may appear in various ways in the production of literature and within literary texts. Feminist theorists invite us to pay particular attention to the patterns of thought, behavior, values, and power in those relationships.

Feminist literary critics remind us that literary values, conventions, and even the production of literature have themselves been historically shaped by men. They invite us to consider writings by women, both new and forgotten, and also ask us to consider viewing familiar literature through a feminist perspective.

2. How do we apply the feminist/gender lens?

We apply it by closely examining the portrayal of the characters, both female and male; the language of the text; the attitude of the author; and the relationship between the characters. We also consider the comments the author seems to be making about society as a whole.

3. Is Virginia Woolf a feminist?

In groups of two or three, state whether the feminist literary lens would meet with Virginia Woolf's approval. Does she agree that our readings are "gendered"?

Does she believe that women characters and writers are marginalized? Be prepared to defend your statement with at least two quotations from *A Room of One's Own.*

Our position is :

Quotation 1:

Quotation 2:

4. Application: Looking through the feminist lens

Select two female characters from novels with which you are very familiar. They could be from works we have read together or from texts you have read in previous English classes. For example, you might choose Daisy from *The Great Gatsby*, Hester Pryne from *The Scarlet Letter*, or Sonya from *Crime and Punishment.*

Name each character and write two descriptive statements for each—one from a traditional masculine perspective and the second from a feminist perspective.

CHARACTER 1

Traditional statement:

Feminist/gender statement:

CHARACTER 2

Traditional statement:

Feminist/gender statement:

ACTIVITY 18

Death of a Salesman and the Social Construction of Gender

1. Consider the following words:

fashion, football, breadwinner, pilot, strength, flower, ambitious, perseverance, compassionate, bossy, helpless, thoughtful, soft, brassy, dangerous, perpetrator, victim, attractive, opinionated, hostile, emotional

Using your first instinct and without overthinking, write each word in the column that seems most appropriate:

Male	Female	Both	Neither

2. Consider the theory.

Our ability to assign gender to words or constructs has to do with what some people call "the social construction of gender." Using the feminist lens is one way to examine gender construction, but the notion of the social construction of gender broadens the lens to more fully consider how both men and women are affected by this social construction.

Read through the following explanations of the social construction of gender:

The Construction of Gender

This theory acknowledges that men and women are actively involved in constructing their own gendered identities. We adopt different masculinity and femininity practices depending on our situations and beliefs. Our understandings of gender are dynamic, changing over time with maturity, experience, and reflection. Thus, we are active in constructing our own gender identities. The options available to us are not unlimited, however. We are influenced by the collective practices of institutions such as school, church, media and family, which construct and reinforce particular forms of masculinity and femininity.

These widely accepted, dominant notions of gender often construct masculinity and femininity as opposites, ignoring a vast array of shared human characteristics, and traditionally valuing masculinity as more powerful. Such ideas may be accepted, challenged, modified, or rejected as individuals develop and shape their gender identities. Students need the critical skills to understand and assess narrow messages about the way they can live their lives.

Adapted from Understanding Gender *(retrieved February 9, 2009, from http://education.qld.gov.au/students/advocacy/equity/gender-sch/issues/gender-under.html)*

The Social Construction of Gender

The power of the ideology of gender lies in the way it encompasses fundamental cultural and social values pertaining to the relations between men and women. The ideology of gender determines:

- What is expected of us
- What is allowed of us
- What is valued in us

The manifestation of gender difference can be found in the construction of:

- Roles (what women and men do)
- Relations (how women and men relate to each other)
- Identity (how women and men perceive themselves)

The ideology of gender thus contains norms and rules regarding appropriate behavior and determines attributes; it also reproduces a range of beliefs and customs to support these norms and social rules.

Adapted from The Social Construction of Gender *(retrieved February 9, 2009, from www.hku.hk/ccpl/events/training/2003/27032003/4.doc)*

Briefly jot down your response to these explanations and any questions they raise for you:

3. Focus on one of the four members of the Loman family.

Select one of the four Lomans. Describe the ways in which this character may be held hostage to social expectations of gender, and say how those expectations affect the character's actions within the play. Now, as you think about the film version of the play, how did the social construction of gender affect the actor's portrayal of the character?

ACTIVITY 19

Getting to the Heart of the "Other": The Postcolonial Lens and *Heart of Darkness*

THE WHAT

Let's first review Steven Lynn's formulation of the basic tenets of post-colonial theory:

Assumptions

1. Colonialism is a powerful, usually destructive historical force that shapes not only the political futures of the countries involved but also the identities of colonized and colonizing people.
2. Successful colonialism depends on a process of "Othering" the people colonized. That is, the colonized people are seen as dramatically different from and lesser than the colonizers.
3. Because of this, literature written in colonizing cultures often distorts the experiences and realities of colonized people. Literature written by colonized people often includes attempts to articulate more empowered identities and reclaim cultures in the face of colonization.

Strategies

1. Search the text for references to colonization or to currently and formerly colonized people. In these references, how are the colonized people portrayed? How is the process of colonization portrayed?
2. Consider what images of "Others" or processes of "Othering" are present in the text. How are these "Others" portrayed?
3. Analyze how the text deals with cultural conflicts between the colonizing culture and the colonized or traditional culture.

Here's another definition of postcolonial theory:

Postcolonial literary theory attempts to isolate perspectives in literature that grow out of colonial rule and the mindset it creates. On one hand, it can examine the ways in which a colonizing society imposes its worldview on the peoples it subjugates, making them "objects" of observation and denying them the power to define themselves. The colonizers are the "subjects," those who take action and create realities out of the beliefs they hold to be important. On the other hand, it can focus on the experiences of colonized peoples and the disconnection they feel from their own identities. Postcolonialism also focuses on attempts of formerly colonized societies to reassert the identities they wish to claim for themselves, including national identities and cultural identities. When this lens is used to examine the products of colonization, it focuses on reclamation of self-identity.

One thing that postcolonial theory shares with deconstruction is the attempt to isolate "false binaries," categories that function by including dominant perspectives and excluding the rest, relegating outsiders to the status of "Other." Colonized people are always seen as existing outside the prevailing system of beliefs or values. As the dominant ideology asserts itself, it creates a sense of normalcy around the ideas of the colonizers and a sense of the exotic, the inexplicable, and the strange around the customs and ideas of the "Other."

In your own words, what is postcolonial literary theory?

THE WHY

Here's how one teacher explains why she teaches the postcolonial lens:

In other words, I am fully convinced that students can come to a clear understanding of the poststructuralist and gendered notions of socially-constructed subjectivity, and of postcolonial perspectives that reveal the presence of "the self" in "the other" (the master in the slave; the slave in the master), if they can find personal and cultural connections to those peoples they would otherwise perceive as antithetical to them. (Few of my mainstream American students can imagine there is any commonality, any common humanity, between themselves and "Communists" or "Arabs" or "lesbians" or "gays" or any of those groups demonized so often in our national consciousness. The task that I face in my classrooms most often is to allow students to see a hint of that common humanity, to deconstruct their preconceptions as a way to see that others, no matter how putatively different, might in circumstances and ideological convictions other than those we presently inhabit and uphold, be our colleagues, our comrades, our friends.)

From "A Pedagogy of Postcolonial Literature," by Lindsy Penteolfe Aegerter (College Literature, *1997; retrieved February 19, 2009, from http://www.articlearchives.com/society-social-assistance-lifestyle/ethnicity-race-racism/1045811-1.html*)

Respond to this quotation in a short paragraph.

THE HOW

1. Rephrase from a postcolonial perspective the following sentence: Christopher Columbus discovered America.

2. Read the poem "Sure You Can Ask Me a Personal Question." In groups of three or four, construct a postcolonial reading and explain it below.

THE TEXT

Using the table below, list all the characters you have met in *Heart of Darkness* in terms of their stance as the colonized or the colonizers.

The Colonizers	The Colonized

If it is true that the master is in the slave and the slave is in the master, select one character from each column and explain how each embodies both categories. Work with one other person on this question.

THE QUESTIONS

Using the postcolonial lens, what kind of questions emerge from your reading of this text? Write at least four questions below.

ACTIVITY 20

Contemporary Literary Theory and *Shrek*

First, consider the opening and closing minutes of the film. In what ways are we invited to read this film as a story? What are some of the assumptions about stories that you have internalized? (Some theorists call this a "story grammar.") How do you know that the film will resist the traditional story line?

Next, let's review the basic assumptions of the five lenses below. Fill in each square as we discuss the lenses.

	Gender Lens	Social Class Lens	Deconstruction Lens	Archetypal Lens	Reader Response Lens
What are the basic assumptions of this lens?					
List at least two episodes, moments, or incidents that seem to exemplify this perspective.					
Given this perspective, what is the film trying to say?					

View the film. Write down on a separate piece of paper particular moments that strike you. Then fit those moments under the appropriate lens if it works.

Now, with a partner, think about the messages that *Shrek* may be trying to convey. Together, discover the significance of *Shrek* from the perspective of each lens.

ACTIVITY 21

Deconstruction

Deconstruction is by far the most difficult critical lens for people to understand. It is an intellectually sophisticated theory that confuses many very smart people, but we think so much of you that we know you can understand it. It is a postmodern theory, and like most postmodernism, it questions many of the basic assumptions that have guided us in the past. In the traditional study of literature, those basic assumptions include the following:

- Language is stable and has meaning we can all agree on.
- The author is in control of the text she or he writes.
- Works of literature are internally consistent.
- Works of literature have external relevance.
- You can take the author's or poet's word for what he or she writes.
- There is a set of interpretive tools that you can reliably use to interpret a literary text.

Deconstruction calls all of these assumptions into question. It asks you to read resistantly—to not take a work of literature at its face value and to question the assumptions, both literary and philosophical, that the work or the author asks you to make. It is this kind of resistance that you folks are so good at. And it is that resistance, that ability to look beyond what seems to be intended, that will be a useful skill in the "real world." It helps us to become careful and skeptical consumers of culture, not passive recipients of "great works."

Deconstructionist critics ask us to probe beyond the surface, or recognizable constructs, of a finished story or text. By *construct*, we mean something that has been constructed by mental synthesis. That is, constructs are created when we combine things we know through our senses or from our experiences. They do not exist naturally; they are products of our manipulation of the order of the universe. When we reexamine and challenge the constructs employed by the literary writer, we "deconstruct." The term does *not* simply mean to take it apart. It means we need to look thoughtfully beyond the surface of the text—to peel away like an onion the layers of constructed meanings. It doesn't mean the same thing as analyzing. In the traditional sense, when we *analyze* a piece, we put it back the way it was and appreciate it more. When we *deconstruct* a piece of literature, we realize that there is something wrong or incomplete or dishonest or unintended with how it was put together in the first place.

Here is one good explanation of deconstruction:

> Having been written by a human being with unresolved conflicts and contradictory emotions, a story may disguise rather than reveal the underlying anxieties or perplexities of the author. Below the surface, unresolved tensions or contradictions may account for the true dynamics of the story. The story may have one message for the ordinary unsophisticated reader and another for the reader who responds to its subtext, its subsurface ironies. Readers who deconstruct a text will be "resistant" readers. They will not be taken in by what a story says on the surface but will try to penetrate the disguises of the text. . . . They may engage in radical rereading of familiar classics.
>
> *H. Guth and G. Rico,* Discovering Literature *(Prentice Hall, 1996), p. 366*

Here is another useful definition:

> Deconstruction is a strategy for revealing the underlayers of meaning in a text that were suppressed or assumed in order for it to take its actual form. . . . Texts are never simply unitary but include resources that run counter to their assertions and/or their authors' intentions.
>
> *A. Appignanesi and C. Garratt (Totem Books, 1995), p. 80*

We're going to play with deconstruction today in three steps: first with some common metaphors, then with a traditional poem, and then with some texts you've read for this class.

1. Unpacking metaphors:

Let's take some metaphors and see if there is anything false or unintended about their meaning. Under each, please write the obvious surface meaning, and an unintended meaning that may lie beneath the surface.

Love is a rose.

Intended

Unintended

You are the sunshine of my life.

Intended

Unintended

The test was a bear.

Intended

Unintended

2. Deconstructing a text:

Let's read the following poem, one that's often subject to traditional analysis:

Death Be Not Proud

Death be not proud, though some have called thee
Mighty and dreadful, for thou art not so,
For those whom thou think'st thou dost overthrow
Die not, poor death, nor yet canst thou kill me.
From rest and sleep, which but thy picture be,
Much pleasure, then from thee much more should flow,
And soonest our best men with thee do go,
Rest of their bones, and soul's delivery.
Thou art slave to fate, chance, kings, and desperate men,
And dost with poison, war, and sickness dwell,
And poppy, or charms can make us sleep as well,
And better than thy stroke. Why swell'st thou then?
One short sleep passed, we wake eternally,
And death shall be no more; death, thou shalt die.

—John Donne

What is the poem supposed to say? How would you approach it for, say, the AP exam? What traditional tools of analysis might you employ to unpack the meaning of the text?

Where does the poem break down? How might it work against the author's intentions? Write down some specific places where the text falls apart.

3. Reconsidering a reading:

Now, think of a poem, short story, or novel you've read that cannot be taken at face value, that may reveal, because of internal inconsistencies or unintended conflict and the failure of language to really communicate what we mean (even in the hands of gifted writers), a mixed message or an unintended meaning. On your own, or with a partner, please complete the following sentences about the text. We will ask you to detach this page from the handout and turn it in.

Name(s):

Text:

When I deconstruct this text, here's what happens. I think the main idea the author/ poet was trying to construct was:

But this construct really doesn't work. The idea falls apart. The language and construction of the text isn't able to convey what the author meant to convey. There are places in the text where it just doesn't work. For example:

So in the end, even though the author meant the work to say:

it really said:

(Optional) I'd also like to say that:

ACTIVITY 22

"On the Subway," by Sharon Olds: The Gender Lens

1. Read the poem aloud in your group.
2. Using the theory cards, glossaries, and any other information that you have, summarize what you think it means to apply a gender lens to a text.
3. As a group, underline lines that are particularly relevant to a gendered reading.
4. As a group, complete this sentence (more than one meaning statement might result):

   Using the gender lens, we think the poem means

   because
5. What larger questions about society does this reading raise for you?
6. Pick a reporter to summarize your group's findings.

ACTIVITY 23

"On the Subway," by Sharon Olds: The Formalist/New Critical Lens

1. Read the poem aloud in your group.

2. Using the theory cards, glossaries, and any other information that you have, summarize what you think it means to apply a formalist lens to a text.

3. As a group, list some of the important poetic devices that Olds employs to convey her meaning.

4. Underline lines that contain those poetic devices.

5. As a group, complete this sentence (more than one meaning statement might result):

   Based on a formalist analysis we think the poem means

   because

6. What larger questions about society does this reading raise for you?

7. Pick a reporter to summarize your group's findings.

ACTIVITY 24

"On the Subway," by Sharon Olds: The Social-Class Lens

1. Read the poem aloud in your group.

2. Using the theory cards, glossaries, and any other information that you have, summarize what you think it means to apply a social class lens to a text.

3. As a group, underline lines that are particularly relevant to a social class reading.

4. As a group, complete this sentence (more than one meaning statement might result):

   Based on a social class reading, we think the poem means

   because

5. What larger questions about society does this reading raise for you?

6. Pick a reporter to summarize your group's findings.

ACTIVITY 25

"On the Subway," by Sharon Olds: The Reader Response Lens

1. Read the poem aloud in your group.
2. Using the theory cards, glossaries, and any other information that you have, summarize what you think it means to apply a reader response lens to a text.
3. Have each person list the personal qualities, personal experiences, or both, that are relevant to the poem.
4. Have each person underline lines that are particularly relevant to those personal experiences.
5. Have each person in the group complete the following sentence:

   Based on my own reading, I think the poem means

   because
6. Pick a reporter to summarize your group's findings.

ACTIVITY 26

"Ode to Family Photographs," by Gary Soto: Three Perspectives

The Reader Response Perspective

Reread the poem with these questions in mind, and then discuss them with three classmates:

- What family photos of your own come to mind as you read the poem?
- Who is your usual family photographer? Why?
- What might people be able to tell about your family from the photographs?

The Formalist Perspective

Reread the poem with these questions in mind, and then discuss them with three classmates:

- What are some of the images that are conjured up as you read the poem?
- In what ways is this poem different from most poems you've read?
- How would you describe the tone of the poem? Support your response with specific lines or phrases from the poem.

The Biographical Perspective

Read the brief biography of Gary Soto that we provided; then reread the poem with these questions in mind, and discuss them with three classmates:

- What images or specific references do the two pieces share?
- What else do the pieces seem to have in common?
- In what ways does the information in the biography affect your reading of the poem?

ACTIVITY 27

Literary Theory: Among the Things We Carry

Please consider the stories from Tim O'Brien's *The Things They Carried* from the perspective of the four theories listed below. Each group will consider a particular lens and then we will discuss this together as a whole class. Note, too, that your paper assignment is also related to this exercise. Here is a list of the stories: "The Things They Carried," "Love," "Spin," "On the Rainy River," "Enemies," "Friends," "How to Tell a True War Story," "The Dentist," "Sweetheart of the Song Tra Bong," "Stockings," "Church," "The Man I Killed," "Ambush," "Style," "Speaking of Courage," "Notes," "In the Field," "Good Form," "Field Trip," "The Ghost Soldiers," "Night Life," "The Lives of the Dead."

	Reader Response	**Historical**	**Feminist/Gender**	**Marxist/Social Class**
Which stories lend themselves to this particular lens?				
Cite specific textual passage(s) that support this kind of reading.				
Interpret at least one character through this lens.				
If you look through this lens, what questions emerge?				
If these stories are to be considered as a coherent whole, what is the nature of the "glue" that holds them together?				
Do you believe in this reading? Why or why not?				

ACTIVITY 28

Literary Theory: A Frankenstein Monster

Please consider Mary Shelley's *Frankenstein* in light of the following theories. Fill out as much of the chart as you can. We'll be discussing it together as a whole class.

	Reader Response	**Psychoanalytic**	**Feminist/Gender**	**Marxist/Social Class**	**Other?**
Citation of a specific textual passage that supports this kind of reading.					
List at least two incidents that support this kind of reading.					
Interpret at least one character through this lens.					
If you look through this lens, what themes/issues emerge?					
What symbols do you see?					
Do you believe in this reading? Why or why not?					

ACTIVITY 29

Critical Encounters: Reading the World

> Literary theory raises those issues which are often left submerged beneath the mass of information contained in the course, and it also asks questions about how the institution of great literature works. What makes a "great work" great? Who makes the decisions about what will be taught? Why are authors grouped into certain historical periods? The answers to fundamental questions like these are often unarticulated assumptions on the part of both the professor (teacher) and the students. . . . Socrates said that the unexamined life is not worth living. . . . Literary theory is at its best when it helps us realize what we are really doing when we study literature.
>
> —Stephen Bonnycastle

1. On the basis of our reading and class discussions, briefly describe, in your own words, the following literary theories. Spend no more than a few minutes on this part of the exercise.

   psychological criticism

   feminist/gender literary theory

   Marxist/social-class theory

   reader response theory

   other (Choose one as a group)

2. In groups of three or four, select a literary work with which you are all familiar. It could be a poem, a short story, a play, or a novel. Or focus on the novel you are currently using for your reader's choice. Then think of two theories that would be fruitful to use to explore that text. In the spaces

below, briefly describe how each of those two theories might be used to illuminate the text.

Theory 1:

Theory 2:

3. Now think of something you've read, heard, or seen outside class that particularly struck you as worth thinking about. It could be an interaction between two people, a MTV video, a song, a film or scene from a film, a magazine article, or an ad. Briefly explain it below.

4. What lens might you use to help you understand this event or artifact? How would that lens affect or increase your understanding?

5. Can we use critical lenses to "read" the world? Explain.

6. What, if anything, do you find difficult about reading literature with critical lenses?

ACTIVITY 30

From Reading Words to Reading the World: Critical Lenses in Literature and in Life

We've spent a lot of time this year focusing on critical lenses. For a culminating activity, we would like you to reflect on the ways in which you personally have made sense of the lenses as a tool for reading texts and the world.

1. Reflect on our reading and discussion over this past year. Which lenses did you find particularly useful, interesting, or thought provoking? Which lenses seemed to offer the most explanatory power for your reading of literary texts? Rate the following lenses on a scale of 1 to 5, where 1 is the lowest rating and 5 is the highest:

__________ reader response theory
__________ formalist theory (New Criticism)
__________ archetypal theory
__________ postcolonial theory
__________ historical theory
__________ psychological theory
__________ gender theory
__________ social-class theory

In one or two paragraphs, explain why you have ranked the lenses as you did.

2. Now think of something you've heard about or seen outside class that struck you as worth thinking about. Describe this event or issue, and explain why it is important.

It could be related to school:

- An interaction between two people at school
- A school policy
- A social group at school
- Academics
- Athletics

Or it could be something outside school

- A state, national, or world event or situation
- A political situation or event
- A family situation

Consider this event or issue through at least two of the lenses we've been working with. What do you notice or what questions emerge for you as you apply these critical perspectives? How do these lenses affect or increase your understanding of the event or issue?

3. How do you think the multiple perspectives can help you understand some things about yourself and your life outside school?

ACTIVITY 31

Waking Up to *The Awakening*; or, What's Gender Got to Do with It?

Divide into gender-specific groups. Then respond to the following questions.

1. What kinds of relationships between men and women are portrayed in the novel? On the basis of those portraits, what kinds of generalizations can we make about the relationships between men and women that we see, especially about marriage?

2. Write a few sentences about how Robert is portrayed. Think about his physical description, his behavior, and his power or lack of it. What kinds of words are used to describe him? Be specific.

3. Write a few sentences about how Edna is portrayed. Think about her physical description, her behavior, and her power or lack of it. What kinds of words are used to describe her? Be specific.

4. In a sentence or two, summarize your current understanding of what it means to read a novel with a feminist lens.

5. From what you've read so far in *The Awakening* select a passage where reading with a feminist/gender lens proved useful or natural.

   Page(s) on which the passage appears:

6. How does being a female or male affect your reading of the novel? How might the opposite sex approach this novel differently?

WARNING!!!
IF YOU'VE ALREADY FINISHED THE NOVEL OR KNOW HOW IT ENDS, PLEASE EXCUSE YOURSELF FROM THE DISCUSSION NOW. WE MEAN IT!

7. Predict how the novel will end. Support your hypothesis with a reasonable argument and textual evidence.

We'll now reconvene as a whole class and compare our answers.

ACTIVITY 32

Theory Relay: Perspectives on *Native Son*

For the next hour, in groups of three or four, consider *Native Son* from a variety of theoretical perspectives: historical and biographical, reader response, Marxist/social class, and feminist/gender. We'll be doing this as a kind of relay. There are four theory stations around the room. Spend approximately 10 minutes at each station. Each person should turn in one of these sheets to his or her teacher on Monday. Make certain you've completed the journal entry at the end of the sheet.

Name:

Group Members:

Reader Response Station

Reread the explanation of reader response and study your reader response diagram. In the space below, write at least three meaning statements that are the result of your personal interaction with the text.

1.

2.

3.

Historical and Biographical Station

Skim together "How Bigger Was Born" (in your copy of *Native Son*), and skim the biographical articles that you find at this station. How does what you've learned, as well as any additional experience of reading you've had with other works of Richard Wright, affect and inform your understanding of *Native Son*?

Feminist/Gender Station

Consider the quotation you find at the feminist/gender station. As a group, construct an interpretation of the quotation that is informed by your collective understanding of feminist literary theory. When you consider *Native Son* from a feminist perspective, which characters, incidents, or themes are brought into greater relief? Write your response below.

Marxist/Social-Class Station

Consider the quotation you find at the Marxist/social-class station. As a group, construct an interpretation of the quotation that is informed by your understanding of Marxist literary theory. When you consider *Native Son* from a Marxist perspective, what characters, incidents, or themes are brought into greater relief? Write your response below.

Journal Entry

Reflect on your group's efforts to read *Native Son* through a variety of critical lenses. Which lens seemed to be most consistent with the intention of the novel? Which lens was the most difficult to apply? Which was the most informative? This entry should be at least two full paragraphs. Write it on a separate piece of paper, and attach it to this sheet.

ACTIVITY 33

Reader Response and (*Text*)

Context

(What factors surrounding my reading of the text are influencing my response?)

Reader (   )——➤**Meaning**◄——————**Text**

YOUR NAME

(What personal qualities or events relevant to this particular book might influence my response?)

(What textual features might influence my response?)

Context

ACTIVITY 34

Looking Through Lenses: Our First Look

Group Members:

Summer Reading Text:

1. In three or four sentences please summarize the plot of the book.

2. What were some of the most important things you noticed about the text before we read our discussion of lenses?

3. Which two lenses do you think might be most useful to apply to this text?

4. Which lenses do you think might not be particularly useful? Why?

5. Now try applying the two lenses that you selected in #3.

Lens 1

When we viewed this book through the _______________ lens, we looked at:

The lens helps us see the following things that we didn't notice before:

Therefore, we see that this might be a book about:

Lens 2

When we viewed this book through the ______________ lens, we looked at:

The lens helps us see the following things that we didn't notice before:

Therefore we see that this might be a book about:

* * * **Journal Entry** * * * **Journal Entry** * * * **Journal Entry** * * *

Reflecting on the above, write an entry in your journal summarizing what you discovered from this activity. What worked, what went "clunk"?

What were the most and least useful elements of this first application of critical lenses?

References

Appignanesi, R., & Garratt, C. (1995). *Introducing postmodernism.* New York: Totem Books.

Applebee, A. (1978). *The child's concept of story: Ages two to seventeen.* Chicago: University of Chicago Press.

Applebee, A. (1993). *Literature in the secondary school: Studies of curriculum and instruction in the United States.* Urbana, IL: National Council of Teachers of English.

Appleman, D. (1992). I understood the grief: Reader-response and *ordinary people.* In N. Karolides (Ed.), *Generating reader's responses to literature.* New York: Longman.

Appleman, D. (1993). Looking through critical lenses: Teaching literary theory to secondary students. In S. Straw & D. Bogdan (Eds.), *Constructive reading: Teaching beyond communication* (pp. 155–171). Portsmouth: Boynton/Cook.

Appleman, D. (2000). *Critical encounters in high school English: Teaching literary theory to adolescents.* New York: Teachers College Press & Urbana, IL: National Council of Teachers of English.

Baldwin, J. (1985). *The price of the ticket.* New York: St. Martins.

Barnet, S. (1996). *A short guide to writing about literature* (7th ed.). New York: HarperCollins.

Barry, P. (2002). *Beginning theory.* Manchester: Manchester University Press.

Barthes, R. (1981). Theory of the text (I. McLeod, Trans.). In R. Young (Ed.), *Untying the text: A post-structuralist reader* (pp. 31–47). London: Routledge.

Beach, R. (1993). *A teacher's introduction to reader-response theories.* Urbana, IL: National Council of Teachers of English.

Beach, R., Appleman, D., Hynds, S., & Wilhelm, J. (2006). *Teaching literature to adolescents.* Mahwah, NJ: Erlbaum.

Bonnycastle, S. (1996). *In search of authority: An introductory guide to literary theory* (2nd ed.). Peterborough, Ontario, Canada: Broadview Press.

Boomer, G. (1988). *Metaphors and meaning: Essays on English teaching* (B. Green, Ed.). Norwood: Australian Association for the Teaching of English.

Carey-Webb, A. (2001). *Literature and lives: A response based, cultural studies approach to teaching English.* Urbana, IL: National Council of Teachers of English.

Cherland, M., & Greenlaw, J. (Eds.). (1998). *Literary theory in the high school English classroom: Theory into practice, 37*(3), 175.

Cochran-Smith, M., &. Lytle, S. L. (Eds.). (1993). *Inside/outside: Teacher research and knowledge.* New York: Teachers College Press.

Crews, F. C. (1965). *The Pooh perplex.* New York: Dutton.

Crowley, S. (1989). *A teacher's introduction to deconstruction.* Urbana, IL: National Council of Teachers of English.

Derrida, J. (1989). Structure, sign, and play in the discourse of the human sciences. In P. Rice & P. Waugh (Eds.), *Modern literary theory: A reader* (pp. 149–165). London: Edward Arnold.

Desai, L. (1997). Reflections on cultural diversity in literature and in the classroom. In T. Rogers & A. Soter (Eds.), *Reading across cultures: Teaching literature in a diverse society* (pp. 161–177). New York: Teachers College Press.

Dimitriadis, G., & McCarthy, C. (2001). *Reading and teaching the postcolonial: From Baldwin to Basquait and beyond.* New York: Teachers College Press.

Eagleton, T. (1983). *Literary theory: An introduction.* Minneapolis: University of Minnesota Press.

Eckert, L. S. (2006). *How does it mean: Engaging reluctant readers through literary theory.* Portsmouth, NH: Heinneman.

Elkind, D. (1986). *All grown up and no place to go: Teenagers in crisis.* Reading, MA: Addison-Wesley.

Emig, J. (1990). Our missing theory. In C. Moran & E. F. Penfield (Eds.), *Conversations: Contemporary critical theory and the teaching of literature* (pp. 87–96). Urbana, IL: National Council of Teachers of English.

Fairclough, N. (1989). *Language and power.* London: Longman.

Fetterley, J. (1978). *The resisting reader: A feminist approach to American fiction.* Bloomington: Indiana University Press.

Fitzgerald, F. S. (1964). *The crack-up.* New York: New Directions.

Forrester, V. (1980). What women's eyes see (I. de Courtivron, Trans.). In E. Marks & I. de Courtivron (Eds.), *New French feminisms* (pp. 181–182). Amherst: University of Massachusetts Press.

Freire, P., & Macedo, D. P. (1987). *Literacy: Reading the word and the world.* Westport, CT: Praeger/Greenwood.

Furman, N. (1988). The politics of language: Beyond the gender principle? In G. Green & C. Kahn (Eds.), *Making a difference: Feminist literary criticism.* New York: Routledge.

Galda, L. (1983). Research in response to literature. *Journal of Research and Development in Education, 16*(3), 1–6.

Gates, H. L., Jr. (1992). *Loose canons: Notes on the culture wars.* New York: Oxford University Press.

Gonzáles, N., Moll, L., & Amanti, C. (2005). *Funds of knowledge.* Mahwah, NJ: Lawrence Erlbaum.

Graff, G. (1987). *Professing literature: An institutional history.* Chicago: University of Chicago Press.

Graff, G. (1992). *Beyond the culture wars: How teaching the conflicts can revitalize American education.* New York: Norton.

Graff, G. (1995). Organizing the conflicts in the curriculum. In J. F. Slevin & A. Young, (Eds.), *Critical theory and the teaching of literature: Politics, curriculm, pedagogy.* Urbana, IL: National Council of Teachers of English.

Greene, M. (1988). *The dialectic of freedom.* New York: Teachers College Press.

Greene, M. (1993). The passions of pluralism: Multiculturalism and the expanding community. In T. Perry & J. Fraser (Eds.), *Freedom's plow* (pp. 185–186). New York: Routledge.

Griffith, P. (1987). *Literary theory and English teaching.* Philadelphia: Open University Press.

Guerin, W. L., Labor, E. G., Morgan, L., & Willingham, J. R. (1992). *A handbook of critical approaches to literature* (2nd ed.). New York: Oxford University Press.

Guth, H., & Rico, G. (1996). *Discovering literature.* Upper Saddle River, NJ: Prentice Hall.

Hines, M. B. (1997). Multiplicity and difference in literary inquiry. In T. Rogers & A. Soter (Eds.), *Reading across cultures: Teaching literature in a diverse society* (pp. 116–134). New York: Teachers College Press.

hooks, b. (1994). *Teaching to transgress: Education as the practice of freedom.* London: Routledge.

Hynds, S., & Appleman, D. (1997). Walking our talk: Between response and responsibility in the literature classroom. *English Education, 29*(4), 272–294.

Johnson, B. (1981). Translator's introduction. In J. Derrida, *Dissemination* (pp. xv–xvii). Chicago: University of Chicago Press.

Kaplan, S. J. (2000). On reaching the year 2000. *Signs, 25*(4), 1167–1170.

Kutz, E., & Roskelly, H. (1991). *An unquiet pedagogy: Transforming practice in the English classroom.* Portsmouth, NH: Boyton-Cook.

Leggo, C. (1998). Open(ing) texts: Deconstruction and responding to poetry. *Theory into practice, 37*(3), 186–192.

Lionni, L. (1974). *Fish is fish.* New York: Random House Children's Books.

Lynn, S. (1990). A passage into critical theory. *College English, 52*(3), 258–271.

Lynn, S. (2008). *Texts and contexts: Writing about literature with critical theory* (5th ed.). New York: Pearson Longman.

Marshall, J. (1991). Writing and reasoning about literature. In R. Beach & S. Hynds (Eds.), *Developing discourse practices in adolescence and adulthood* (pp. 161–180). Norwood, NJ: Ablex.

McCormick, K. (1995). Reading lessons and then some: Toward developing dialogues between critical theory and reading theory. In J. Slevin & A. Young (Eds.), *Critical theory and the teaching of literature: Politics, curriculum, pedagogy* (pp. 292–315). Urbana, IL: National Council of Teachers of English.

Moore, J. N. (1997). *Interpreting young adult literature: Literary theory in the secondary classroom.* Portsmouth, NH: Boynton/Cook.

Moore, J. N. (1998). Street signs: Semiotics, *Romeo and Juliet,* and young adult literature. *Theory into practice: Literary theory in the high school English classroom, 37*(3), 211–219.

Murfin, R. C. (Ed.). (1989). *"Heart of darkness": A case study in contemporary criticism.* New York: Bedford/St. Martins.

Nelms, B. (Ed). (1988). *Literature in the classroom: Readers, texts, and contexts.* Urbana, IL: National Council of Teachers of English.

Perry, W. G. (1970). *Forms of intellectual and ethical development in the college years: A scheme.* New York: Holt, Rinehart, & Winston.

Pirie, B. (1997). *Reshaping high school English.* Urbana, IL: National Council of Teachers of English.

Purves, A., Rogers, T., & Soter, A. O. (1990). *How porcupines make love: Notes on a response-centered curriculum* (2nd ed.). New York: Longman.

Rabinowitz, P. (1987). *Before reading: Narrative conventions and the politics of interpretation.* Ithaca: Cornell University Press.

Rabinowitz, P. J., & Smith, M. W. (1998). *Authorizing readers: Resistance and respect in the teaching of literature.* New York: Teachers College Press & Urbana, IL: National Council of Teachers of English.

Rogers, T., & Soter, A. O. (Eds). (1997). *Reading across cultures: Teaching literature in a diverse society.* New York: Teachers College Press.

Rosenblatt, L. (1976). *Literature as exploration* (2nd ed.). New York: Noble & Noble.

Ryan, M. (1998). *Literary theory: An introduction.* Oxford: Blackwell Press.

Said, E. (1978). *Orientalism.* New York: Random House.

Said, E. (1999). *Out of place: A memoir.* New York: Knopf.

Scholes, R. (1985). *Textual power: Literary theory and the teaching of English.* New Haven, CT: Yale University Press.

Scholes, R. (2001). *The crafty reader.* New Haven, CT: Yale University Press.

Scieszka, J. (1989). *The true story of the three little pigs by A. Wolf.* New York: Penguin Books.

Selden, R. (1989). *A reader's guide to contemporary literary theory.* Lexington: University Press of Kentucky.

Showalter, E. (Ed.). (1985). *The new feminist criticism: Essays on women, literature, and theory* (pp. 144–167). New York: Pantheon.

Showalter, E. (1989). Toward a feminist poetics. In R. Con Davis & R. Schliefer (Eds.), *Contemporary literary criticism* (pp. 457–478). New York: Longman.

Slevin, J. F., & Young, A. (Eds.). (1996). *Critical theory and the teaching of literature: Politics, curriculum, pedagogy.* Urbana, IL: National Council of Teachers of English.

Sontag, S. (1969). *Against interpretation and other essays.* New York: Dell.

Soter, A. O., Faust, M., & Rogers, T. (Eds.). (2008). *Interpretive play: Using critical perspectives to teach young adult literature.* Norwood, MA: Christopher Gordon.

Spivak, G. C. (1988). *Other worlds: Essays in cultural politics.* London: Methuen.

Staton, S. F. (1987). *Literary theories in praxis.* Philadelphia: University of Pennsylvania Press.

Thomson, J. (1993). Helping students control texts: Contemporary literary theory into classroom practice. In S. Straw & D. Bogdan (Eds.), *Constructive reading: Teaching beyond communication* (pp. 130–154). Portsmouth, NH: Boynton/Cook.

Tyson, L. (2006). *Critical theory today: A user-friendly guide.* New York: Routledge.

Vygotsky, L. (1978). *Mind in society: The development of higher psychological processes.* Cambridge, MA: Harvard University Press.

Willis, A. (1997). Exploring multicultural literature as cultural production. In T. Rogers & A. Soter (Eds.), *Reading across cultures: Teaching literature in a diverse society* (pp. 116–132). New York: Teachers College Press.

Winterowd, W. R. (1989). Introduction. In Crowley, S., *A teacher's introduction to deconstruction.* Urbana, IL: National Council of Teachers of English.

Wolf, D. P. (1988). *Reading reconsidered: Literature and literacy in high school.* New York: College Entrance Examination Board.

Selected Literary Texts

NOVELS, SHORT STORIES, AND PLAYS

Achebe, C. *Things fall apart*. Reprint, New York: Knopf, 1994.
Chopin, K. *The awakening*. New York: Simon & Schuster, 1899.
Chopin, K. The story of an hour. In *The awakening and selected short fiction*. New York: Barnes & Noble, 2005.
Coetzee, J. M. *Waiting for the barbarians*. New York: Penguin Group, 1982.
Conrad, J. *Heart of darkness*. Reprint, Peterborough, Ontario: Broadview Press, 1995.
Conrad, J. *The secret sharer*. In *Heart of darkness and The secret sharer*. Reprint, New York: Penguin Group, 2008.
Crews, F. *The Pooh perplex*. Chicago: University of Chicago Press, 1965.
Ellison, R. *Invisible man*. New York: Knopf, 1995.
Faulkner, W. *As I lay dying*. Reprint, New York: Knopf, 1991.
Fitzgerald, F. S. *The great Gatsby*. New York: Scribner, 1953.
Frank, A. *The diary of a young girl*. Reprint, New York: Bantam Books, 1993.
Gilman, C. P. The yellow wallpaper. In *The yellow wallpaper and other writings*. New York: Bantam Books, 1989.
Glaspell, S. *A jury of her peers*. Boston: Small, Maynard, 1920.
Guest, J. *Ordinary people*. New York: Viking Press, 1976.
Guterson, D. *Snow falling on cedars*. New York: Vintage Books, 1994.
Hansbery, L. *A raisin in the sun*. Reprint, New York: Random House, 1995.
Hawthorne, N. *The scarlet letter*. Reprint, New York: The Modern Library, 1962.
Hegi, U. *Stones from the river*. New York: Simon & Schuster, 1997.
Hurston, Z. N. *Their eyes were watching God*. Reprint, Urbana: University of Illinois Press, 1991.
Ibsen, H. *A doll's house*. Reprint, New York: S. French, 1972.
Katz, J. *Running fiercely toward a high thin sound: A novel*. Ithaca, NY: Firebrand Books, 1992.
Kleber, F. (Ed.). *Beowulf* (3rd ed.). Boston: Houghton Mifflin, 1936.
Knowles, J. *A separate peace*. Reprint, New York: Simon & Schuster Adult, 1996.
Lee, H. *To kill a mockingbird*. Reprint, New York: HarperCollins, 2006.
Lionni, L. *Fish is fish*. Reissue, New York: Random House Children's Books, 1974.
Miller, A. *Death of a salesman*. New York: Penguin Group, 1976.
Milne, A. A. *Winnie-the-pooh*. Reissue, New York: Penguin Young Readers Group, 1988.
Morrison, T. *Beloved*. New York: New American Library, 1987.

Morrison, T. *Sula*. New York: Random House, 1993.
Ngugi wa Thiong'o. *The river between*. New York: Longman, 1990.
O'Brien, T. *The things they carried: A work of fiction*. Boston: Houghton Mifflin, 1990.
Remarque, E. M. *All quiet on the western front*. London: Little, Brown, 1929.
Said, E. *Orientalism*. New York: Knopf, 1978.
Said, E. *Out of place: A memoir*. New York: Knopf, 1999.
Salinger, J. D. *The catcher in the rye*. London: Little, Brown, 1951.
Scieszka, J. *The true story of the three little pigs by A. Wolf*. Reprint, New York: Penguin Group, 1996.
Shakespeare, W. *Hamlet, prince of Denmark*. Reprint, Cambridge: Cambridge University Press, 1985.
Shakespeare, W. *Macbeth*. In *The complete works of William Shakespeare*. New York: Barnes & Noble, 1994.
Shakespeare, W. *Much ado about nothing*. In *The complete works of William Shakespeare*. New York: Barnes & Noble, 1994.
Shakespeare, W. *Othello*. In *The complete works of William Shakespeare*. New York: Barnes & Noble, 1994.
Shelley, M. *Frankenstein; or, the modern Prometheus*. Reprint, Berkeley: University of California Press, 1984.
Silko, L. M. *Ceremony*. Reprint, New York: Penguin Group, 1986.
Sophocles. *Oedipus rex*. In *The Theban plays: Oedipus rex, Oedipus at Colonus, and Antigone*. Reprint, Mineola, NY: Dover, 2006.
Steinbeck, J. *Of mice and men*. Reprint, New York: Viking Press, 1965.
Steinbeck, J. *The grapes of wrath*. Reprint, New York: Penguin Group, 2002.
Swift, J. *Gulliver's travels*. Reprint, New York: Barnes & Noble, 2004.
Tolkien, J. R. R. *The hobbit or there and back again*. Reprint, Boston: Houghton Mifflin, 1999.
Twain, M. *Adventures of Huckleberry Finn*. Reprint, New York: Barnes & Noble, 2008.
Updike, J. Separating. In *Problems and other stories*. New York: Knopf, 1929.
Wilson, A. *Fences*. New York: Penguin, 1986.
Woolf, V. *A room of one's own*. New York: Harcourt, Brace, 1929.
Wright, R. *Black boy: A record of childhood and youth*. New York: Harper & Row, 1945.
Wright, R. *Native son*. New York and London: Harper & Brothers, 1940.

POETRY

Arnold, M. "Dover Beach."
Burns, D. "Sure you can ask me a personal question."
Donne, J. "Death be not proud."
Frost, R. "The road not taken."
Olds, S. "On the subway."
Plath, S. "Mushrooms."
Roethke, T. "My papa's waltz."
Soto, G. "Ode to family photographs."

Soto, G. "Oranges."
Stevens, W. "Thirteen ways of looking at a blackbird."

MOTION PICTURES

Adamson, A., & Jenson, V. (Directors). *Shrek* [Animated motion picture]. United States: Dreamworks Animated Studio, 2001.

Coppola, F. F. (Director). *Apocalypse now* [Motion picture]. United States: Paramount Pictures, 1979.

Jeffs, C. (Director). *Sylvia* [Motion picture]. United States: Universal Studios, 2003.

Lucas, G. (Writer/Director). *Star Wars* [Motion picture]. United States: 20th Century Fox, 1977.

Index

About the Author

Deborah Appleman is Professor of educational studies and the director of the Summer Writing Program at Carleton College in Northfield, Minnesota. She has been a visiting professor at Syracuse University and at the University of California–Berkeley. Prior to earning her doctorate at the University of Minnesota in 1986, she was a high school English teacher for 9 years, working in both urban and suburban schools. She continues to work regularly in high school English classrooms with students and teachers across the country.

Professor Appleman's primary research interests include adolescent response to literature, multicultural literature, adolescent response to poetry, and the teaching of literary theory at the secondary level. She is the author of many articles and book chapters and, with an editorial board of classroom teachers, helped create the multicultural anthology *Braided Lives*. In addition to the first edition of *Critical Encounters*, her books include *Reading for Themselves: How to Transform Adolescents into Lifelong Readers Through Out-of-Class Book Clubs* and (with Richard Beach, Susan Hynds, and Jeffrey Wilhelm) *Teaching Literature to Adolescents*. She is an author in Holt-McDougal's Elements of Literature series for secondary students, Grades 6–12.

Professor Appleman is currently exploring literacy practices among the incarcerated and teaches literary theory and writing at a men's high-security prison in Minnesota.